NATURAL
OUTLAWS
AND
FRACTURED
SOVEREIGNTY

S.M. PEARCE

978-1-7753439-3-6

978-1-7753439-5-0

Book Cover by Miblart

1st edition 2023

THE DIVIDNG
OCEAN

OSTRAIT

JARDAE

THE S...
GRAV...

TRADERS' TIDES

KA'LAN

GANJEME

THE WAILING
WATERS

HAUTNL

PULE

THE SINGING
SEA

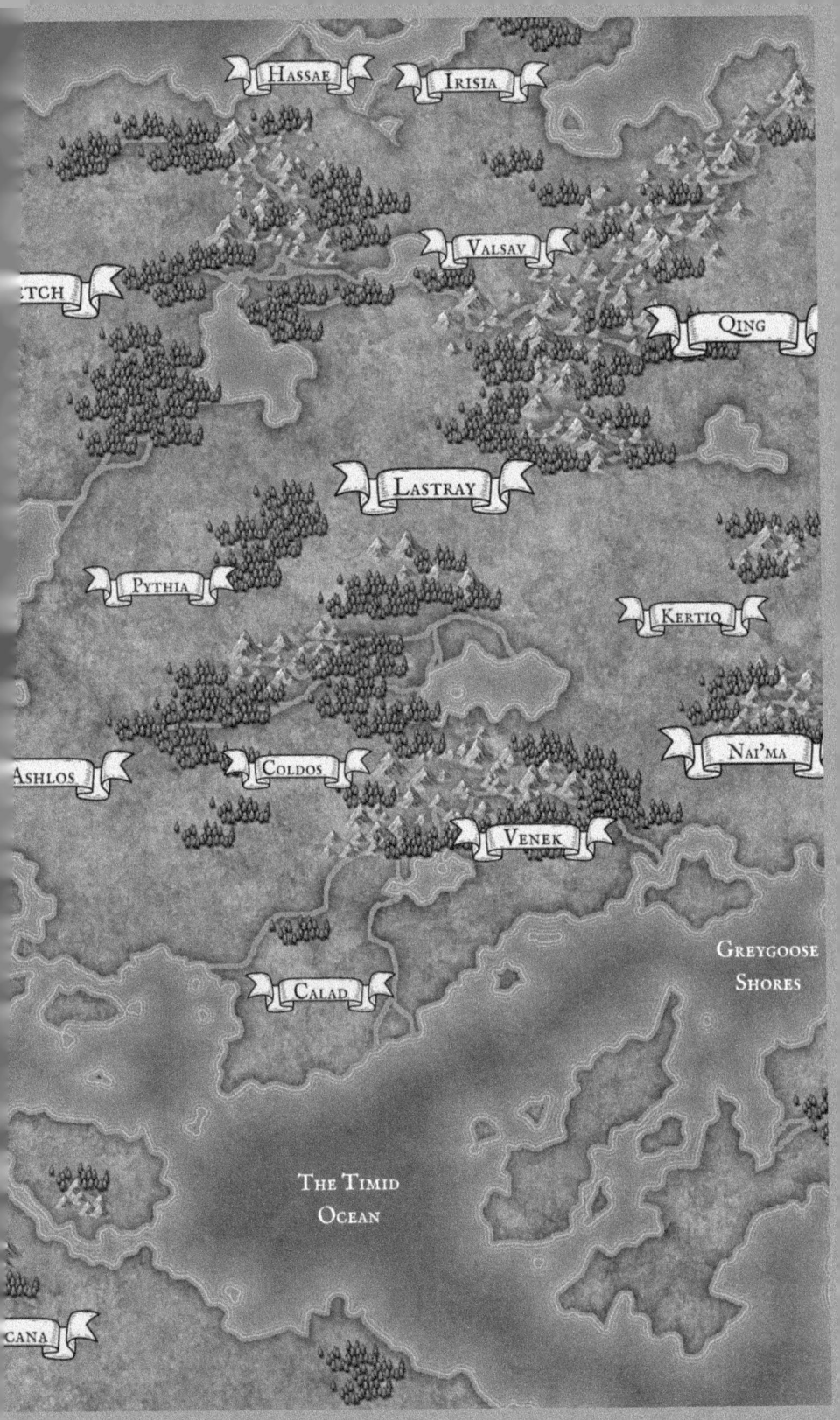

This book is dedicated to anyone who's ever been made to feel like the world doesn't have space for them. We'll make space.

Content Warnings:

Attempted suicide
Sexual assault/coercion
Mind control
Violent abuse
Drug/alcohol use
Queerphobia/fictional slurs
Classism
Colonialism (minor focus)
Death/grief
Mental health issues
Restrictive eating
Aquaphobia (fear of water)
Fantasy religious trauma

PROLOGUE

Sofnas 73, fra Hjemi bur. 51

S tanding on the edge of the roof, Kalen held his jacket closed against the chill of the wind. Hot tears stung his swollen eyes. He made the mistake of looking down.

He sucked in a shaky breath.

Nothing left. Absolutely fucking nothing.

He lifted a foot forward.

"Wait!" an unfamiliar voice cried out, breathless. Kalen turned their head, and someone across the roof tentatively walked forward. "Please don't do it."

"Do you fucking *mind*?" Could he not even manage to kill himself without someone telling him off?

Blurry as she was, Kalen knew he'd never seen her before—she wore a debtors' brown coat, and he wasn't allowed to keep that sort of company. So it really was none of her business.

"Please don't," she repeated.

The stranger only stood about a foot away from his ledge now. She put her hands out in front of her, as if to show she meant no harm, though harm was exactly what he needed to do and what she'd interrupted. And gods, that really *was* a fucking long way down. But what choice did they have?

Kalen's teeth chattered, and he could barely speak around the tightness in his throat. "What's it to you?"

Instead of answering his question, she asked, "Is it okay if I stand up here with you?"

He blinked, stammering out something as she crawled up onto the ledge. Now both his legs trembled. "What are you *doing*?"

Her eyes widened at the ground below. She hugged herself close.

"Look, I was kind of in the middle of something," he started, hating the relief that overwhelmed him. It shouldn't. This—whoever she was—she only made it harder.

"I know." She spoke so softly, it jarred them.

"So...get down."

She swallowed, averting her eyes as she struggled for balance. Kalen's heart pounded as she teetered forward with a gust of wind, and instinctively, he grasped her arm to steady her.

"Thanks." She smiled at them.

A foreign, gentle feeling warmed their chest. "I—I'm going to jump." Kalen looked back down at the moonlit cobblestones so far below him, desperately clawing at his mind for an ounce of conviction. "I'm gonna... You shouldn't be up here."

"I don't want to be up here. But I... Well, I'm going to stay until you come down with me." She took his cold hand firmly into hers. "Keep you company."

"Why in nine hells would you do something like that?" Kalen had several cracked ribs and a face bloodied to near-death. What kind of person would bother "keeping him company"? On the edge of a roof, no less.

Another burst of wind cut against their face.

Gooseflesh covered his skin, and his cheeks had grown comfortably numb. Gods, why couldn't he just get this over with? Why was he holding some stranger's hand?

How fucking pathetic was he that he couldn't even do this one last thing right? Real men wouldn't be up here in the first place, but they certainly wouldn't be afraid to jump if they were.

"I come up here to think sometimes," she said, "and I've thought about this before. Never got this far, though, 'cause Papa needs me. Still, I wonder about it. Do you think it will hurt?"

"You shouldn't find out," he muttered, turning his head away from her. Water poured shamefully down their face. "Go home."

It wouldn't hurt, would it?

"I can't just leave you here."

"Sure you can." Anybody else would.

But they couldn't force themself to drop her hand.

"Do you really want me to?"

"I..." Kalen squeezed his eyes painfully shut. "I can't go back. I can't go anywhere. He'd find me if I ran, and that would be..."

"Who would find you?"

The words started pouring out of Kalen. They told her everything. How medical training had been their last of last chances to become the respectable sort of man their family could tolerate, that they'd cracked under the pressure yet again, that Father was shipping him off to a military school that would only kill him slower and out of sight.

"Don't you get it?" Kalen's breaths hiccupped. "I have nothing. Nowhere to go. And nobody's gonna fucking miss me, anyway."

Calluses scraped their hand as she squeezed it, reassuring them that she was real. "You have somewhere to go."

⇁⇀⇝⁂⇜↼↽

"Here, just watch your step." The stranger—Blythe Caron, not a stranger anymore, he supposed—guided him over the remnants of a broken door.

The smell of stale piss and rot stunk the halls, but mint permeated the air as she pulled him deeper into her "apartment." Barely a room. An old man rose from his tiny cot, saying something Kalen couldn't hear past the ringing in his ears.

The floor swayed underneath their feet. Blythe said something to the man.

"Here, son."

Kalen suddenly sat on something resembling a chair, and a warm mug was placed in his hands.

"I'm sorry there's no lemon," the man said. "Just herbs around here."

Kalen took a disoriented sip.

"Have we got any bread left, Papa?"

Blythe stood behind them at a pantry with no legs or knobs. It was disturbingly bare, save for a small bag of some berries Kalen couldn't even name, a few handfuls of dried leaves and the like, and a piece of cheese fuzzed with green.

Was this all of their food? *Ludicrous.* But where else could they be hiding it?

"Siobann, next door," the man answered, and this seemingly made sense to Blythe.

Kalen watched dazedly as she grasped the bag of berries and set it in front of them. "Here, you can have some of these, at least. Sorry, there isn't more to go around."

He could only stare.

What was someone like her doing helping them? By the gods, she could have sold their coat for enough to fill her pantry with much more than moldy cheese and bird berries.

"Blythe, why don't you get the extra blanket, *myn caeure*?" the man asked, a rattle in his voice. "He looks like he could use some rest, I think."

And she didn't say "yes, sir."

"Good idea," she said instead. "Is that alright?" she asked Kalen, looking over as she put a beige blanket overtop the tiny cot. "Sorry, I don't think I got your name."

His hands shook as he set the cup on the floor. "Kalen."

"Is that alright, Kalen?"

Blood rushing through his head and black spots clouding his already-blurry vision, Kalen nodded.

Could I be alright?

Kalen woke in a cold sweat.

He jerked his head toward the gaping hole where a door should be. His breath came in short bursts. Father would burst in any moment to finish the job for him.

The apartment shrouded itself in darkness, but Kalen was horrified to make out the old man's figure lying on the floor across from the cot. Why in fifty hells had he given it up for Kalen? And wait, where was...

If Kalen hadn't already fixed his eyes on the door, he wouldn't have noticed her sneaking in. Almost didn't, somehow. She didn't make a noise, and their mind encouraged them to skip over her.

But as soon as her head lifted and she spotted him sitting up in the cot, she sighed and came back into clearer focus. "Sorry, I didn't mean to wake you." She placed two bags on the floor beside the pantry and began to unpack them.

"I...I don't want to take your father's bed." Kalen edged out of the cot. The older man didn't look well enough to be sleeping on a hard cot, never mind on the cold floor.

"He insisted."

Heart still pounding from the nightmare, Kalen counted backwards from ten in his mind. "What's all that?" they asked, gesturing to the bags.

"For you." She took out a bundle and placed it in his hands. "I have a friend who needs a roommate, but you'll draw too much attention in your clothes."

He'd never worn clothes as plain and dark as this. His family was wealthy enough to live in pastels, and their clothing featured delicate embroidery, much of it done by himself, to the dismay of his parents and mockery of his brothers.

"I don't understand why you're doing all this for me."

"You needed help." Blythe gave him a reassuring smile and placed an apple atop the bundle. The other bag bulged with a few food items inside. How had she managed to procure any of this? The shops were closed for the night.

She met his eyes, and shame crossed her face. Silence fell.

It was broken by a loud, watery cough that racked her father's body, and she quickly thrust a piece of paper into Kalen's hand. "My friend wrote her address on this. Will you be able to find it?"

She rushed to the old man's side, murmuring reassurances. "It's okay, I got your medicine."

Kalen's mind reeled. Terror stuck their feet to the floor, refusing to let them move an inch. "I can't." The words wouldn't form properly. "I... He'll find me. And I'll...I'm better off going back on the roof. I can't."

Blythe looked over, clearly torn between them and helping her father sit up. "You don't have to leave," she said, trying to hoist her father onto the cot but failing.

Kalen moved to grab his legs, and she accepted their help reluctantly for someone so eager to give her own.

"I can't stay here, either." He took a fistful of his hair, the reality of the situation crashing back onto him. Why had he let her drag him to this place? It changed nothing. Father would find him. No matter where Kalen went. He would find them eventually, and then Kalen would really wish they'd died first.

The two of them lay her father down on the cot, and the coughs subsided. "You're alright, Papa."

Blythe pulled a blanket over the man, and Kalen put his back against the cold, damp wall.

"Do you have a match?" they asked suddenly. It should have been obvious to them before. This was the only way.

"What?"

"A match," he repeated, hugging himself tighter. She wouldn't give them one—she'd already helped them too much, and winter approached. And then they'd have to go back up to that edge, and not be a coward this time.

"Oh, sure." She reached all the way into the back of the pantry, and then a match lay in his hands. "Sorry, I only have one."

"Just...like that?"

The world only existed for people like Father to torment him. But this stranger didn't seem to have a cruel bone in her body. She would give them this match without thinking, stand on the edge of a roof with them in the wind.

Something was very wrong with her.

But clutching the match in their hand also twisted a weird sort of feeling in Kalen's chest. It might have been hope.

And as he ran from the roaring fires of his father's mansion, he decided it was.

Blythe had saved their life. They intended to work hard to repay the favor.

Sofnas 78, fra Hjemi bur. 51

"Won't you say where we're going?" Blythe asked.

"We're almost there," Kalen promised. They both spoke in hushed tones and kept to the shadows—which he was quite bad at—as he led her through a rich district she shouldn't have been in.

Blythe wasn't sure how she found herself on the back steps of a mansion, pale with worry and stuck against the wall. They should not be here. *Why* were they here?

"Hold on." Kalen produced some sort of powder from his pocket, and the metal knob of the door fizzled as he sprinkled the powder over it.

Blythe's mouth hung open. "What are you *doing*?"

"Well, we've got to get in somehow," he said, throwing her a jarring grin.

She tried to tug him away. "We're going to get killed! And we can't just—just break in somewhere. It's such an invasion of—"

"They're gone for the winter, don't worry," he assured, as if that solved the issue.

Gods, what would Papa say? What price would there be? She couldn't do this. Something was obviously very wrong with him, and while she had a duty to help...

"You said you'd owe me a favor, right?" Kalen reminded.

"But—"

"Come on! You promised. It'll be fine." He pulled her along before she could protest again.

"What does this have to do with a favor?" He'd insisted on giving her reading lessons, and she'd naively accepted with the promise to owe him a favor. "I thought your house... Is there something of yours here, or...?"

"Did you know the men who live here have murdered twelve of their indentures? Not the official story, of course, because who's gonna call the guards? But we all knew. They made a lot of their money by owning half the grain stock in the province."

Bread only increased in price with each year. It cost almost a week of wall-building wages for a loaf, and stale at that. Flour wasn't much cheaper. The last time Blythe had managed to secure a bag on a steep bargain, she and Papa had paid for it with a severe Ergot fever.

"Why are you telling me that?" Blythe's eyes wandered from the large golden chandelier hanging from the ceiling to the shining marble underneath her tattered boots.

"So you feel less bad about raiding the place. Let's go!"

"What? I can't *steal*." Blythe backed toward the door. She stumbled against an enormous sculpture of some winged creature.

She never should have told him about the brand on her arm, which bosses checked too diligently for even her to secure men's work that *might* pay enough to survive on. She'd gotten by for years, but all the shit jobs she could find paid little more than indentures now, and the landlord had just doubled rent, again.

Kalen held his hands in front of him. "Okay. Okay, then at least we can have some fun, right? Have you *ever* taken a break to have some proper fun?"

He was out of his mind.

"What kind of...fun?"

⟫⟫⟫ ⟪⟪⟪

Blythe lay in a heap of silky clothes, eyes leaking from laughter. They were in the most enormous dressing room, with green carpets and yolk-yellow curtains. Kalen had on a bright, feathery scarf, a matching fuchsia dress, and a pair of snowshoes. Utterly ridiculous. A book in hand, he performed an extremely dramatic reading of a play that was supposed to be a tragedy.

Blythe couldn't stifle her scandalous laughter.

He collapsed beside her in the heap, unable to keep a straight face any longer. "I could be in the theatre, couldn't I? Proper rising star."

Gods, her face and stomach ached from the laughter. It was harmless, wasn't it? They would put everything back, and she owed him. She owed Kalen a favor, so she *had* to be here paying it. He needed to have some fun after being so distraught the first time she'd seen him.

But still... "We really should go." She'd been saying this since they arrived.

"You wouldn't deprive me of my final scene?" he asked with a pout.

And so they stayed a little longer. She almost forgot how absolutely fucked she was. Couldn't feel the rawness of her hands or the emptiness of her stomach. "Really though, I can't... It's wrong to stay here."

"Then take this." Kalen pressed a trinket into her hand, a shining red stone in the center. "And this." A pair of boots with buckles that would buy at least a dozen apples.

Her heart squeezed. She set the things on the floor and stood up from her pile. "Thank you, but I can't."

"Why not?"

What did he mean, why not? "It's stealing."

"Men like this, like my father, they steal everything from everyone. They stole everything from me, and from you. Why should you feel bad about getting a little payback?"

"The righteous don't seek revenge." Papa's voice urged her to flee. Get out of there and away from this clearly amoral or immoral influence. Even if it would save Papa's life. Even if it would mean they both survived a little longer. Even if the men who lived here were awful, awful people, she couldn't afford a fraction of their vices.

"You know, it was miserable," Kalen said. "They only care about their fortunes, status. That's why I was such a... You might be doing them a favor. The stuff certainly didn't make Father a cheerful man."

"I *can't*." Pressure built behind her eyes.

Because she wished she could. She wanted to take everything in this place and sell it, and pay off every debt, and get Papa his medicine, and help Paulette across the hall with hers, and— But wrong was wrong. And it always demanded consequences.

"Okay."

"Okay? You're just gonna let it go?"

"Sure, why don't you start heading down? There's something I wanted to check out first."

Blythe barely reached the door when something clattered overhead. She dashed back toward the stairs, and Kalen scampered down, a wild look in his eyes, his white hair—singed?

"We've got probably two minutes," he panted. "I hear fires move fast."

"What?" Blythe's breath left her. Her body went rigid.

"Place is gonna burn down anyway," he said and shot her the most outrageous smile. "What a terrible accident. Would be a worse shame to let all of those clothes and food and valuables go to waste, wouldn't it?"

"You—" Blythe could barely stammer out a response. "What the fuck!"

Black smoke snaked around the upstairs corridor.

Kalen opened the door. "I've gotta get out of sight before they see the fire. You're much better at the hiding thing."

Blythe stepped to follow them, but then her stomach growled and her eyes drifted to the kitchen.

It would go to waste, anyway.

All that food. Papa needed to eat for any hope of recovery. *She* needed to eat, or she couldn't keep up her work, and he would die.

She turned, but Kalen had already run out.

Blythe made a terrible choice. "I'm sorry," she said to nobody and dashed into the kitchen.

Kalen waited for her back in her cellar. He beamed when she appeared with a brown bag of groceries.

She bowed her head in shame. How much penance would she have to do for this?

He put a tentative hand on her arm. "I'm sorry for lying. You wouldn't let me help otherwise. And I've got a debt to pay you, for my life."

"You don't—"

"Yes, I do."

And despite how terrible it was, she whispered, "Thank you."

"I'm not done thanking you," Kalen said.

He...isn't? Blythe's mouth fell open.

"You know all these types have insurance? Victimless crime, really."

"By the gods, are you sure wolves didn't raise you?"

"Wolves in sheep's clothing, maybe." He nudged her arm amicably. The easy camaraderie was startling, as if they'd already known each other a long time. "What?" he asked. "Not regretting saving me already, are you?"

Was she? She pushed the question out of her mind and handed Kalen a plum. Nothing good could come of the answer.

I.

Aknas 31, fra Hjemi bur. 53

"For the last time, no." Blythe turned away, tending to the parsnip seedlings. "We shouldn't have started in the first place. And with the guards on alert for the 'invisible arsonists' now?"

A dense cluster of clouds blocked the sun and moistened the air. She and Kalen almost never needed to water and instead spent time adjusting little panes of glass that he'd suggested to amplify what light the plants could receive. They both came up here every morning they had a slice of free time, even if no real work could be done.

"But that's the best part: his men will be mostly out of town! It's our only shot, and after that, we'd be golden." Kalen leaned against her, looking up with wide doe eyes. "We'd never have to steal again," they sang.

"We shouldn't be stealing at all."

They had some variation of this conversation before every mission, but this time was different. They wanted to rob the *Governor's* mansion—too big, too greedy. She'd already become so appallingly accustomed to stealing that the smell of burning mansions had grown more familiar than that of her own apartment.

It was routine now. Kalen set the fires, and she clung to the idea that things would be ash anyway if she didn't take them. And only enough to keep afloat. She kept track, too. Her writing lacked competence, so sometimes just a little doodle, but she kept track on one cellar wall so she could pay it all back someday.

But what Kalen was suggesting went too far.

Not only because she would have to set the fire herself—they couldn't get close enough without being noticed, as some guards would remain. But they wanted to steal enough to pay every debt, buy a mansion of their own, feed the neighborhood twice over.

"It's good the beans are finally sprouting." Kalen came over to the box, peering closely at them. He was always curious about the mechanics when it came to their planting and foraging: how plants grew, what different species looked like.

"They're a different shade than last year," he mused as the two of them wiped their hands and headed out the half-rotted wooden door.

Blythe turned around to lock it, crouching with a metal pin in her hand. She'd first stumbled across this door a few years ago, and the lock had been so stiff with rust, it had taken days to crack open. Only she and Kalen had come up here in the past decade, it seemed, and she liked it that way. Not that she had earned it.

"Do you really think he deserves it all?" Kalen asked.

"You know that's not it." Blythe stood and started down the stairs. It wasn't about *deserving*. Revenge was not for the righteous, and retribution was for fate to dole out.

"Mmmkay," Kalen said, bounding down the stairs alongside her. "But as much as I love your papa, don't you think he's got more proverbs than sense sometimes? Think of the good you'd do with all that gold."

Blythe didn't have anything nice to say to that.

Kalen couldn't understand, because things were different for them. Blythe had known since childhood that her penance was greater than everyone else's, her moral debt higher, her risks more dire. When Mama died, Papa had known some god must be furious. Without knowing who they'd offended, he'd turned to *Deium Erium*, the god of charity, who could grant amnesty for those who did the penance of an ascetic, morally righteous life. Blythe's own belief in the gods manifested more vaguely; she'd never had any divine encounters herself, and the precise details of myths changed depending on the balladeer, so the gods were a more abstract force to her. But she *feared* all the same, and Papa's certainty had always guided her actions.

Not enough, lately.

And look where it had gotten her. She'd broken into one mansion two years ago, and now the "invisible arsonists" were considered the biggest enemy of the city. Any guard would get a handsome reward for her and Kalen's heads.

They reached the cellar just outside of the building, crawling down into their safe space where they could worry less about their volume.

"I said I was done with the last one. Someone almost got hurt."

And if she did this heist... She'd objected to Kalen's help, and their wasting time on her, but he'd always responded that they had a debt to pay for their life, and that she assisted them to pay it—that their soul wouldn't recover otherwise.

Once they were satisfied that supposed debt was paid, she'd have no excuse to indulge in their company. Her life drudged on as a miserable curse, but Kalen shone like a glimmer of joy that she couldn't drag down. They would sigh in relief and leave her behind, or else she would have to insist that he escape.

But why did that time have to come so soon?

The two of them sat with their backs against the concrete wall, and she stared ahead at the little table they'd crammed in there. All of Kalen's powders and potions and the old locks Blythe liked to play at picking cluttered it in a way that made her nostalgic.

What if they left anyway, once they realized she couldn't be helped?

"Fine," Kalen said, clearly dejected. "I'm dropping it."

"Here, I made this for you." She shifted to pull the cloth out from her bag, and they took it eagerly. Blythe drew with charcoal when the moon turned blue and she had leisure time, so she'd taken to sketching designs on fabric so that Kalen could embroider them.

He was always hungry for patterns and let out a soft gasp at this one. It depicted a cow in a meadow, framed by some abstract design bits. "It's beautiful."

"Nothing special." She shrugged, but her heart warmed. She let out a surprised laugh as they grasped her in an excited hug.

"It's perfect."

The two of them sat back, and she leaned her head against his shoulder. This was real, wasn't it? Even if Kalen paid his "debt" at the same time... Surely not every laugh they shared or every hour they passed served only as his own penance. Right? Blythe was never certain whether Kalen resented her company, only offering it because they'd sensed her loneliness—something to fix as part of their repayment. They could certainly act.

Kalen rifled through their own things. He took out the book, the one they'd been reading together for the past month, which they'd almost finished. Kalen read most of it because trying to get through more than a page proved tedious for her. He opened it up to where they'd left off last.

"I bet Claudius is going to find out this chapter," she said.

"Dunno, Hestia might murder him first."

Blythe let herself sink into the delusion of their friendship, for just a little while longer.

⟫⟫⟫ ⟪⟪⟪

"I'm home, Papa," Blythe called the next afternoon after a shift cleaning floors, which had followed a pre-dawn shift at the seamstress's place. "I'll be back for supper, I'm just going to bring some of the dried herbs down to Frida. Kalen won't make it, he's promised to help her crate up the ale she's made. I really do hope business grows enough for her with this new batch, that new tavern owner is—"

Blythe's breath caught in her throat.

She fell at his side in an instant, kneeling before the cot to check his pulse. A sickly sweat coated his face, and goose bumps coated his arms. *Alive.* Breathing, but there was something wrong with it. More wrong than usual.

"Papa?" She pressed a hand to his burning head.

"Hmm?" He stirred, barely.

Tears blurred her vision. She frantically rifled through the little stand beside his cot, a pit forming in her stomach as she clutched the brown bag of capsules in her hand. It was much too full—she had been expecting to need a refill soon. She'd been so wrapped up. Why hadn't she made sure he took them?

The water wouldn't boil fast enough.

She finally poured a glass and crushed three chalky capsules into it. More was better, wasn't it?

Blythe inclined her half-conscious Papa's head, urging him to drink. "Please. Please, just..."

It took an eternity for him to finish the glass, his eyes only half-open. She laid his head back down onto the pillow of the cot, straining to hear as he mumbled something barely intelligible.

"Too 'spensive, 's my fault, you shouldn't..."

"Papa, you *have* to take them." Blythe dug her nails into her palms, hard enough to break the skin.

He still trembled. The medicine had been a weak mitigation, and with the mold on the ceiling spreading, would he even get better like this?

Blythe did all she could, her efforts pitiful. The rage wouldn't stop rising and rising, burning her ears and eyes, even though she should have been blaming her own stupid selfishness. She ground her teeth together like a vise. The sight of Papa's frail, sleeping body—

She had to get out of here, or she would lose any sense she had left.

She ran out from the apartment into the freezing downpour, cloak forgotten. Her head throbbed. Why hadn't she done more?

Her sight blurred, and she dashed through the alleys, puddles drenching her thin shoes where the cobblestones broke apart.

Why did her papa sleep in a shitty, moldy apartment? Why hadn't she bought him a fucking mansion and his own staff of nurses? *He deserves better.*

She clung to the shadows as she passed a group of drunken men on a restaurant porch, escaping their notice as they hooted and hollered at some girls inside.

All her fault. Her crimes. Her selfish attempts at creating slivers of happiness. He would *die* because of her.

The tavern came into view.

He would die if she didn't do whatever it took to save him.

Blythe wrung her clothing out as she made her way up the steps, pausing to regulate her breath before she ducked inside the bustling tavern. The herbs for Frida remained in her pocket, and she made her way over to where her friend wiped down the bar counter.

"You stupid whore!" The new tavern owner's face was beet red, a vein larger than his eye pulsing from his forehead as he strode over to a nearby serving girl, who visibly shrank as he loomed closer. He swore about the spots she'd left on the previous tables, and the girl swam in tears long before he told her she could look for work somewhere else.

Blythe stumbled out of the way as the man barreled past her, out the door.

Frida met Blythe's gaze and offered a smile that was more of a grimace. "Third girl he's fired this week," she muttered.

Blythe rested an arm on the bar and fished the herbs from her pocket, unable to focus on offering a comforting expression as her mind continued swirling.

"But hey, there's always an upside, right?" Frida wiped a hand on her apron. "Rent isn't due for a few weeks yet, and costs could even go down soon."

Rent never went down. Anyone who defaulted could be coerced into an indenture, and their kids, too. So naturally, the government encouraged landlords to increase rates as high as they wished. "For the good of the economy." Her own rent increased almost every month, without warning.

Papa. He would die if they stayed in that apartment.

"What's wrong, *ninê*?" Frida asked, and Blythe's throat constricted.

He'sgoingtodie. He'sgoingtodie. He'sgoingtodie. "I don't want to drag you into this."

They'd never needed Frida on a mission before. There also had never been one this big. And she hadn't expressed interest in joining them until recently, when the tavern changed owners. Things had been stable when Frida'd found the job some years ago. The owner had liked her and given her an absurdly reasonable fixed lease for her apartment, so long as she worked overtime whenever he needed it. It had kept a roof over her and Kalen's heads, though now that might expire soon. Blythe couldn't stand the thought of putting her friend's life at risk. At least she was safer here than Kalen or Papa were.

He's dying. He's dying, and you're sitting here.

Blythe had already made her choice.

Frida screeched over a stool and sat down at the counter, lowering her voice. "Kalen already told me about the plan. I know I say you shouldn't be risking so much. But I don't know, now. I think we're gambling harder not doing anything."

Kalen appeared from around the corner where the kitchens were, casting a tentative look between the two of them.

He's going to die.

Blythe turned to Kalen as he wiped his hands on his smock. She swallowed. "Do you still want to do this?"

The three of them lingered in the woods bordering the mansion.

"Frida, you're *sure*?" Blythe had to ask one last time. Second thoughts had long progressed into third and fourth thoughts. She suppressed a shiver. "Because we won't be able to—"

"Trust me," Frida said, giving Blythe a reassuring pat on the shoulder, utter resolve on her face. "I need this."

Freezing air chilled Blythe to the bone, the feeling in her feet long since vanished. But the Governor would be back tomorrow, and they had no time to waste.

Kalen had fitted each of them with bombs—a skill he called "chemistry," and one of the few studies from *before* that he spoke of fondly. Frida's explosives hung from a thick belt, his were tucked within their coat, and Blythe's were attached to her sash of lockpicking tools. Having them strapped so close to her body sent flutters of anxiety through her chest. The matches were in her deepest pocket, hopefully not soaked. Or maybe it would be best if they were.

At least the trees concealed her in a comforting embrace of shadows. But that couldn't last.

"We'll count to one-eighty, yeah?" Frida fidgeted with her coat. She wouldn't admit to being nervous, but she must have been.

Even Kalen's share of the usual loot couldn't compensate for soaring rent and bread prices; they could only carry so much. Frida had insisted she couldn't pass up a chance for this kind of money, her only hope for a proper business beyond selling a few pints to regulars.

She and Kalen would move to opposing ends of the adjacent forest, setting off simultaneous explosions to draw out as many guards as they could. Plus, they would need to spread out to pawn whatever items Blythe grabbed as quickly as possible, before word got out about the fire and shopkeepers grew alert to suspicious sales.

"Good luck," they told each other.

As Frida charged deeper into the forest and Kalen turned to leave in the opposite direction, Blythe wanted to reach out and say something. But what?

So they left with an encouraging nod, and she scampered up the tree.

Tree by tree, nearly slipping from the wet bark countless times, she made it to the side of the Governor's house, feet teetering on a branch that connected to the roof. A window was embedded into the raised steeple. 173 seconds.

Blythe launched herself onto the roof, pulling herself up by a statuette. One explosion sounded to the south.

Then a second, to the west.

Guards shouted, footsteps shuffling within the building as many of them clamored to get outside. A good portion of them ran now, split into two directions as they'd hoped. She had to be quick. With all the stuff to carry, she couldn't make her exit through the same window and had to get out the back door in time.

Blythe rolled through to the first room as the attending man left, sticking herself behind a curtain for precaution. Her *bestowment* encouraged people to overlook her, but that only went so far. She could still draw attention. With these guards on high alert, it would be much harder to slip past their notice.

Gods, she was actually doing this.

"Everyone out!" a large man shouted from the hall, nearly drowned out by the thudding of boots. "Grab a bucket and don't let your rifles down. Move!"

Everyone?

They'd fallen harder for the distraction than she'd expected.

She made hasty work of one room and the next, stuffing items in her bag. She tried to keep them nondescript enough that they wouldn't raise brows in the marketplace: rings, candleholders, golden reliefs, rolls of tobacco. She didn't hold back this time—*couldn't*.

When she reached the back door, two bags weighed heavily on her shoulders.

She'd started several fires in the upper chambers, using some of Kalen's quieter concoctions. Any minute now, smoke would fill the air. The guards would be too busy trying to put them out to give real chase.

Blythe slipped out the door, ready to run.

Instead, she froze in her tracks.

"Evening."

She barely registered the countless rifles trained on her, gaping with horror at Kalen's and Frida's crumpled figures on the ground.

The Governor stood before her, a triumphant smile stretched across his face. "Quite the little thing, aren't you?"

Something hit her neck.

Her vision narrowed, her feet swaying beneath her. *Kalen and Frida. Kalen and Frida.*

Kalen...

2.

Aknas 33, fra Hjemi bur. 53

T he taste of metal pervaded Blythe's mouth, the pounding in her head relentless. Her vision swirled. She strained in an attempt to shift her body, but her limbs may as well have been unattached. Her heart raced, and her breathing grew erratic as she struggled to move a toe, a finger, *anything*.

Her head lolled down, and she could vaguely make out her legs through her bleary vision. Still attached, then.

I've been drugged. A new wave of panic washed through her. If she'd been drugged, then she wasn't alone. And she sat paralyzed.

"Oh, good, you've come to," said a low, masculine voice. "I was afraid our dear Viper might have put you in a coma. We expected you to be thugs, but we got a couple of *byjekam* instead." He laughed as if this were quite funny.

Blythe couldn't even lift her head to size the man up. But she didn't have to wait long to get a look.

He tipped up her chin with the barrel of a rifle. A pompous feather hat sat atop his head, several of his teeth gleaming with silver.

"Oh, don't worry, Blythe." The Governor spoke pleasantly.

Knots of terror tightened in her chest. Had she *really* thought the gods would allow her to succeed?

"It'll fade soon enough. We wouldn't have much use for a paralyzed thief."

Use? The gears in her head turned. They hadn't killed her yet. Did that mean Kalen and Frida were alive? Why? What could they possibly need them for?

Their crumpled bodies on the ground. *Please don't let them be dead because of me.*

"Kathebrntphh." She tried to force out sounds, but her tongue refused.

"Best give it a few minutes," the Governor suggested. "But I'm sure I can catch you up to speed while we wait."

He let her head snap back down, then tied it against the back of her chair so she could look forward at him. Black spots encircled her vision.

"You've caused a host of problems, you know. Those insurance payouts aren't cheap." He paced, footsteps tapping on the ground behind her. "But I'll admit, you've been clever at staying hidden. There were some rumors that the Baran kid was involved"—Kalen, that was Kalen's last name. Where was he?—" but nobody ever saw that byjeka in the markets. And the Ashlan? Worst we could find was unlicensed ale."

But how did he know *her* name? There were no gossiping strangers or witness statements to rely on.

They'd waited for the next attack, which meant they couldn't find her on their own. They'd acquired her name *after* the trap. Which either meant that one of her friends had given it to him, or...

"You and your accomplices could make it out of here alive and well, if you cooperate."

Alive. They were alive.

The Governor returned to face her again. "If not, we have some incentives."

Her vision beginning to clear, she made out several of the Governor's men standing behind him. A girl dressed in fine robes leaned casually against the wall, looking quite out of place. But something more important yanked the breath from her lungs.

Another figure lay bound across the room.

"*Papa?*"

〜≫≫ ≪≪〜

He didn't—couldn't—respond.

Her papa lay locked into a reclining chair, all sorts of tubes and clips and needles surrounding him. She choked on a sob. "What are you *doing* to him?"

The Governor's eyebrows shot up with a laugh. "Saving his life, you stupid git. For the moment, anyway."

Blythe's body went cold. The grisly room narrowed around her.

"Your landlord reported some strange things," the man continued, pulling up a stool to sit down in front of her, his ruffled breeches overflowing. "Too many people paying their rent on time, or trying to pay with more refined items: watches, stones. Turns out your building hasn't been supplying as many indentures or miners as it should be. Guards come for surprise collections and still people bail out. You can see how somebody such as myself, who cares deeply about our economy, would be concerned, no?"

She knew what he would say next.

She didn't want to hear the words.

"People weren't eager to talk, of course, but we have our methods."

The Governor rested his hands on his knees, regarding her with an unsettling, inquisitive expression. "It never occurred to us that you were anything more than a distributor, a forgivable oversight, considering. But this works better for our plans. And I knew any thieves worth their salt couldn't resist my leaving town. Could you?"

Blythe shrank in her chair, unable to disappear.

Her fault.

She'd stolen from the fires and tipped off the landlord. *She'd* made the guards crack down with harsher payments. *She'd* been stupid and selfish enough to think the solution to everything was the heinous idea of breaking into the Governor's mansion where, of *course*, he'd waited.

"My friends— Please, they... Please."

The man rolled his eyes, giving her a reprimanding tut. "See, this is why I was unsure of the whole thing. You byjekam and your bleeding hearts." He clicked his fingers in front of her face, turning serious. "Pay attention. You haven't even asked why I'm keeping you all alive yet."

He'd kept them all alive. She had to focus on that.

Plans. He'd said *plans*, hadn't he? Plans that required a thief he couldn't catch. "Why?"

"It's come to my attention you have a rather useful bestowment."

Not useful enough, apparently. Or else it wouldn't have caught his attention at all.

Blythe fought the tears brimming in her eyes. "What do you want from me?"

His smile was a wicked thing. "I want you to save this empire."

What did she have to do with anything of imperial importance? They menaced the city's elite, sure, but Ostrait was a very big nation. She was a thief, not a war general or agricultural administrator. He must have been toying with her, and she deserved it for all she'd done.

"Wouldn't you like that?" he asked. "A chance to finally do something right by your country instead of terrorizing it?"

Pinpricks stung her arms. Blythe managed to straighten her shoulders. "How?"

"Maintaining an empire is expensive." The Governor stood from his stool, gesturing vaguely to the green-clad guards for emphasis. He then looked at her with pointed derision. "And half of this country would rather starve than work honestly. Not to mention the shortsighted tribes and Ashlan pirates interfering with the Great Expansion."

Perhaps we should stop going to war with places. But she knew better than to speak aloud. The Governor's kind would never be satisfied with enough land or money.

Blythe sat completely exposed. Nowhere to run, nowhere to *hide.* The Governor's words whirled around in her unfocused mind. She flexed her fingers against the chair's arms.

"We are still winning, of course," the Governor added, somewhat hastily. "And once we have the Ka'lani in line, there's a plethora of wealth waiting there." The Governor crossed his arms over his lavender coat. "But there have been some troubling developments.

"Our trade agreement with Lastray has expired, and it appears they are now trading with the Fletch for some of their oil. This means they are no longer reliant on our alliance, and worse, they're making the Fletch even richer. That's not good," he said, "because we hate the Fletch and they hate us."

His patronizing tone made Blythe see red. Anyone above the age of five knew that.

Fletch and Ostrait had been at a precarious peace during Blythe's twenty-one years, but only because Ostrait waged war with too many other countries to afford a war with their biggest rival. Her papa had come from Jardae, a colony that had shifted hands from the Fletch to Ostrait in his childhood, after over a century of Fletch control. His Jardaen–Fletch accent hadn't made finding places to rent or work easier. Apparently, it had cost Ostrait a lot to claim the colony, and people resented it.

That was part of why Papa always said they had to rise above. *Keep the peace.*

But if Ostrait had the means to bite back against the Fletch, they would in a heartbeat. And if the Fletch had an incentive to go to war with Ostrait, it was inevitable.

And all too far above Blythe's head. "Wouldn't this..." How could she say this properly? "Wouldn't this be for the Finance Minister, or..."

An irritated look flickered across his face.

"It's beyond negotiations, isn't it?" she asked, afraid to speak above a whisper. She only wanted to retreat into the safety of the shadows. But she had to prove sensible enough to be worth keeping alive for whatever these plans were. "Fletch and Lastray are going to form an alliance, and then they'll go to war against us along with everyone else."

The Governor towered over her, blocking the rest of the room from sight. His jaw and fists clenched.

She braced herself for a strike.

"Ostrait does not *lose*," he spat. He inhaled sharply, then straightened and smoothed over his coat. "Of course, nothing could hinder our victory, but the gods work best for those that make assurances."

She stared up at him, heart racing.

"It would be in Ostrait's interest to stop the Fletch from allying with anyone, and to gain some extra gold in the process," he finally continued, walking over to a small window she hadn't noticed and could barely crane her neck to see. Light glistened on his oily white face as he thumbed the petal of a tulip.

"See, the new Fletch King is young and expects much ceremony before he'll consider an alliance. We've received word that he will be holding a competition of sorts between royal delegations, to determine who will reign beside him, and potentially to commit to a collective alliance between all countries present."

The Governor paused to let this sink in. He wiped his hands off on his pastel breeches, and leaned an elbow on the window ledge.

What he said couldn't be true. But then, why *wouldn't* all the other countries team up to take them on? The Fletch could almost have done it themselves, and with the incentive a marital alliance could offer...

War.

Young men rotting in trenches. Children burning in their homes. Civil bloodshed in Jardae. Villages starving to pay for bullets.

Once they wiped out Ostrait, what power would be enough to stop the Fletch from covering the whole world? Some may have thought any rule would be better than Ostrait's, but Blythe had heard tales that the Fletch were even more brutal. If a child's cry was not strong enough, they fed it to the wolves.

"Oh," was all she could say.

"Indeed," the Governor said with a nod. "However, as the gods know our cause to be just, they have provided us with a small opportunity. It so happens, the Fletch had the audacity to extend an invitation in secret to the nobles of Jardae. Just a couple of days ago, we intercepted their acceptance. It seems they were hoping for some sort of annexation."

Blythe clenched and unclenched her muscles. She could almost move her left leg now. Every instinct still screamed at her: *hide, hide, hide.*

Her nose and head both itched terribly.

The Governor continued on. "And so, it seems we have a need for someone with your uncanny ability to go unnoticed. Someone they won't question too hard, or notice sneaking around. Perhaps more luckily, you don't look unlike the Lady Esme, if you squinted and made her dirtier, at least."

Blythe stilled, a shiver creeping up her back. He could *not* be suggesting...

"We may yet see our way out of this financial dilemma and, by proxy, an untimely war."

All of the smoke fumes have finally made me delusional. Blythe stared blankly. "You want me," she said slowly, "to impersonate a noble lady, go with my crew to Fletch... And, what? Steal the royal treasury without anyone noticing?"

"The Crown Jewel would suffice."

"And how will this help to avoid a war?" Blythe asked. "Won't they just retaliate all the sooner?"

He sighed as if she were a very inept pupil. "Did you not hear the part about going unnoticed, byjeka?" The man stepped closer, and Blythe retreated as far back in her chair as she could.

She wished with all her being that he would just leave her alone.

"If you do the job right, they won't notice it missing until far too late. And what's better, you're going to cast their suspicion on other delegations. Cowards that they are, if the Fletch get even a whiff of disloyalty from their potential allies, they'll back right out. We will have the time and money to make our army immense, and then we'll sabotage the collective so that it cannot threaten us. By the time they realize it's our doing and try to form another alliance, we should already have Barcana and Ashlos at their knees. Nobody will stand a chance against us."

A tremor of fear rattled through Blythe, but with it, the shock of hope. "And you..." She looked down at the cement floor. There was a metal drain a few feet away, the reddish-brown not of copper, but of dried blood. Blythe lifted her gaze back up to the Governor and the bleak, ashen walls behind him. "You would spare my friends? My father?"

"Should you succeed, of course," he said, distastefully. "You and your associates would be forgiven for your crimes as payment."

He wanted her crew to pull off an unthinkable heist, which would prevent Fletch dominance and give Ostrait an opening to claw itself back into relevance. She would most certainly fail and be killed in the process, but they'd all die in prison otherwise. This could be a chance, however slim and outrageous, to save the people she cared about. The people she'd put in danger.

Stealing had gotten them into this mess. Could she really do another "last" mission? Look where it had gotten her.

Still, what choice was there? Papa lay frail and grotesque strapped to that cot, all of the life drained from his face and tubes Blythe didn't understand poking out of his skin and down his throat. If they really *were* helping him, it was in a way Blythe never could on her own. Certainly not with rationed, expired pills and an apartment unfit for breathing.

She would do penance for the rest of her life if it meant Papa wouldn't die. She would burn in twenty hells. Better to disappoint him than murder him.

And if the gods *did* approve like the Governor claimed...

"Why us?"

"Because it was such a pain in the ass trying to catch you." He flashed a silver key, gesturing to her chains. "Now, do we have a deal?"

3.

Aknas 33, fra Hjemi bur. 53

K alen's head pounded. Cold cement stretched underneath them, steel bars floating into their vision as they peeled open their eyes. The last thing they remembered... Lighting that fire in the forest, and then the impact of something against their head.

He'd gotten too cocky.

Thought they'd get more money than they knew what to do with, definitely more money than Blythe knew what to do with. That their alchemical bestowment would stop calling them to keep burning everything down. Things would finally be good enough that they could relax.

But Kalen had done what he did best: made everything worse.

And fuck.

Kalen groaned as they inched into a sitting position, taking the cell in with wide eyes. He was going to die. All three of them would hang.

Frida was just coming to, and she would be pissed. They'd pushed for this stupid idea for weeks, and Blythe was right—they shouldn't have gotten her involved. Frida wasn't even a habitual criminal, unless one counted her lack of license for the ale. But "legitimate" storefronts cost more than the Eighty Years' War these days, so it didn't count.

"Where..."

"I'm sorry." Kalen turned to reach for Blythe, to apologize to her for everything, but she wasn't there. She wasn't anywhere in this cell, or the next one over.

Gods, had they already—

No.

No.

She couldn't be dead. He would know. Wouldn't he?

"Nice to meet you, Sorry," Frida grumbled out, leaning against the wall with elbows draped over her knees. She heaved out a sigh. "The *one* time I try and get a leg up."

"Are you hurt?" they asked, swaying to their feet. Terror made his breath short as he peered out of the cell, careful not to catch the eye of any guards. People moaning, begging for help, screaming at the guards, cursing at each other. They packed the cells like sardines in a tin.

"Eh." Frida shrugged, also hefting herself up. Kalen turned slightly, and her eyes grew wide. "Your head, it's..."

"Oh." They tentatively touched their fingers to their temple, drawing away red. Dread pooled in their stomach. This was really happening.

"Really small in here." Frida paced, looking out the cell as if the door might open by force of will. "We've gotta do something. Who knows how much time we've got?"

"*Do* something?" Did she not see where they were? Doing something had gotten them into this mess in the first place.

"What, you'd rather sit here?"

Their head spun. Frida was right. They couldn't just wait here to die, hoping it would be a quick death. And Blythe, wherever she was—certainly not dead because it was too unthinkable—needed their help.

⇢⇢⇢ ⇠⇠⇠

"Come on, you stupid rock." Kalen's fingers bled. But if they could get the rock ground down thin enough to fit the cell's lock, maybe they could pick it. Blythe often worked on old locks beside him in the cellar, and she'd tried her hand at teaching him, with minimal success. But it mattered now.

Frida grunted with the strain of trying to separate two steel bars. One of them was rusted, she said. Weaker.

If only they had even one of their powders, or anything to use against the steel. But even the ones in the inner lining of his jacket had been jaggedly torn out.

His shoulders sagged with defeat. Everything told him to lie down and die.

"I'm not giving up." Frida wiped the sweat off her furrowed brow, resting a hand on her back as she breathed for a moment. "Don't you worry. We're getting out of here. All of us."

"That's the spirit," a man's voice cooed, with a few patronizing claps. "Really, it's the kind of stupid determination we need."

The Governor appeared before the cell, and Kalen startled back against the wall, cursing himself. His breath caught in his lungs.

"Ah, cat got your tongue, byjeka? Haven't seen you since you were small. I'd ask how the family is doing, but, well... Patricide is quite the conversation stopper, no?"

"You disgraced me!" Kalen's father spat, grabbing him by the collar. The Governor had come to visit their home for the first time—a crucial business meeting.

It had not gone well. Half-men did not earn respect.

"Leave him alone," Frida snarled. She stood in front of him, shoulders squared.

Kalen opened his own mouth to speak, but no words came. Only memories he didn't want.

Kalen had grown to accept their status as a half-man. Even if full manhood wasn't beyond their reach—legally too, now, as criminals didn't have a right to it—they couldn't live happily within its limits. But the sight of the Governor struck him with the old humiliation of his failure.

"How cute." The man rolled his eyes, and anger flared behind Kalen's.

"What do you want?" Frida asked bluntly, jaw clenched. She crossed her arms. "Where's our friend? Did you just come to taunt us before we hang?"

She was usually the most personable of the three of them. Frida would chat with anybody, and even after quite a few pints didn't pick fights. Whenever Kalen ventured down onto the main floor of the tavern, he managed to say something accidentally instigating, and she was always right there, squaring back against whatever man grabbed him by the shirt. Usually a warm, protected feeling emerged in Kalen then, and he'd do his best to laugh off the incident, to thank Frida by talking her up to a cute girl or not cheating at darts.

This time, no laughter came. Only shame and fear.

He couldn't turn it off.

He should stand up, yell at the Governor, and go down fighting for their lives, their dignities.

"I don't waste my time on such trivial matters," the man said, nose in the air. His face wrinkled, as if he'd smelled something unpleasant. Kalen clutched his hand around the sharp rock, letting it dig into his skin. "As for your *friend*, we've come to an understanding. For your sake as well as hers, I hope you'll cooperate with the arrangement."

"Where *is* she?" Kalen choked out.

The notion of a life-debt had quickly transformed into an obvious pretense when they became friends, justifying the time they spent together to Blythe's gods. It covered for the despairing affection that actually drove Kalen to push reckless schemes like this, ignorant enough to think he might help her. She deserved so much more.

His lungs struggled for air.

The Governor waved over to the guards. "Get *them* to *their* feet."

Frida helped Kalen to stand before the guards reached the door, putting her arm in front of him. "Where are you taking us?"

"I'd like you all to meet an associate of mine."

The executioner, no doubt. *They won't make it quick.*

Kalen and Frida had barely crushed Blythe in a hug, he'd barely processed the relief of seeing her alive, when the guards ripped all three of them apart.

The men tied them to chairs, side by side, and held their rifles at the ready from across the room.

"Are you alright?" Frida asked, straining from her chair to see Blythe.

Blythe took a shuddering breath. "It's Papa. There's a deal."

What does Louis have to do with any of this?

The Governor cleared his throat, and all of their attention turned to him. "A deal, indeed," he said. An unfathomable explanation followed. The Governor spoke of this monumental heist as the most normal thing.

Monumental. But maybe not impossible? Could they actually stand a chance of surviving? Or was this some cruel joke meant to torment them a little more before execution day?

The Governor had always held a reputation for unusual methods, to put it mildly. Unleashing luminescent hogs here, sending plague-toddlers there. With the smallest pittance of a province to preside over, he scrambled for unconventional ideas that would impress the King. But one or two of them had worked. The province wasn't as tiny as it used to be.

Stretching their bound hands, Kalen locked his pinky finger with Blythe's, and she offered him a small comfort with her brief, uneasy smile.

"However, I have taken measures to ensure your cooperation doesn't falter," the Governor said, and a wink shook Kalen to the core. "I know how byjekam struggle to meet expectations. I'd like you to meet my assistant, the Viper."

As if on cue, a girl near Kalen's age walked out from the anteroom in elegant strides. She wore a ruffled rosy gown with wide skirts, and golden pins decorated her ginger hair. The makings of a gentlewoman. She stood beside the Governor with her head bowed, until he said, "Take a look at your charges, dear."

Her calculating gaze swept over the three of them.

"The Viper can kill a man in hundreds of ways, though she's quite bestowed with poisons in particular. She will be your supervisor, alongside a team of guards, ready to act should you stray from your assigned roles."

Kalen swallowed. *Hundreds?* He exchanged glances with Blythe and Frida, all of their eyes wide.

The Viper's expression yielded nothing. She might have been a statuette, or a porcelain doll, were it not for the subtle rise and fall of her chest.

"She's...coming with us?" Frida asked.

"What, did you think I'd send you off without insurance?" The Governor scoffed. "The old man isn't *nearly* sufficient collateral. It took months to convince Our Majesty you could be useful at all."

Kalen's heart clenched. They were keeping Louis *here*? Blythe's trembling jaw and tensed arms indicated that she knew. Her typically rose-beige face had lost all color, stripped as white as chalk.

Louis didn't deserve this. He hadn't even been involved. How many good people had Kalen dragged down with him? They liked Louis a lot. They'd shared meals together, and he called Kalen "son" in a way that never sounded threatening.

"The Viper's looks are deceiving, so to ensure you don't kill yourselves with disobedience..." He turned to the girl. "Give them enough to be memorable. An hour's worth should do."

"Yes, sir."

The Governor shut the door behind him.

"Wait," Kalen blurted out, terror gripping his restrained body as she took out a thin blow dart. "Please, you don't—"

The pain burst, instantaneous and all-consuming.

Screaming.

Every vein in their body tearing itself to shreds. The fire turned against them as it consumed their mind.

He was sure he begged for death.

She was not merciful.

Father's hands around his neck. Squeezing and squeezing.

Kalen couldn't see through the hot water that soaked his eyes.

A boot cracked into his ribs. Again. Again.

Nowhere to run.

"Make it stop."

Please. I'm sorry. Please.

At some point, he was hauled to his feet. Every step stabbed a knife through his entire body. They almost didn't recognize where they'd ended up.

But that sound. That terrible sound. Waves, splashing against— The docks. He was at the docks. No. *No*, he had to get out of here. He had to get out.

Kalen flailed in desperation, a feral sound tearing from his throat as he tried to rip away from the stronghold of guards. *Not the water, anything but the water.* "Just fucking shoot me!"

4.

Aknas 33, fra Hjemi bur. 53

*T*he man towered over him, snarling as he tripped backwards and fell
into the wall. His face was half-scorched, raw and bubbling, his teeth
oozing red.

"You're dead," Kalen stammered out.

Father loomed closer, towering over Kalen's feeble, shaking frame.

"No... You're—"

"You always were too big a coward to look me in the eye."

Kalen was drowning. Sinking farther and farther into the icy water,
screaming for help that didn't come. He couldn't breathe. Air. It hurt.

Father's voice slithered in his ear. "I'll never be fucking dead."

Kalen gasped for breath. Their eyes darted wildly around the unfamiliar room, their vision a disoriented flurry. The same cedar covered the
walls and floor. The floor that he lay on, swaddled in a blanket. A dining
table stretched across the back of the room, barrels stacked beside it, and
stools packed in at the front. Pushing the blankets to the side, Kalen sat
up, clutching his throbbing head.

Wrong. Something was wrong.

It hit them like a punch to the chest. *The ground is moving.*

He was on a boat. The guards had dragged them here and—gods, they were trapped. The threat of the ocean on all sides robbed Kalen of his breath once more, narrowing his vision to only the slight wobble of a bowl on the table.

"Kalen? Kalen," a voice called.

They hadn't even noticed Blythe sat on a stool to their right. She descended to kneel above them, tone rife with worry. "What's wrong?"

Kalen wanted to answer her, but the words failed. *I have to get out.*

"Kalen? Kalen, you're not breathing—"

He squeezed his eyes shut, holding his knees against his chest.

"Viper!" She cradled his face. "Try to breathe. Please, just in and out. Can you hear me? Kalen."

Creaking footsteps.

Her hands fell away. "Please, you have to fix it. You gave him too much."

"I gave him the exact right amount. It's already worn off." That was the Viper's voice.

Their lungs screamed for air, but every breath was crushed out of them.

"Please, he can't breathe. An antidote, *something.*"

"I told you, it's worn off. Stop wasting my time with this. He wouldn't be on the ship if he wasn't useful. But that could change if you don't get him under control."

Steps—she left up the steps.

Blythe was crying, calling for Frida now. Kalen found her hand and gripped it like a lifeline. "I'm scared," he managed, eyes burning.

She took him in her arms, leaning him back and enveloping him with a secure embrace as she mumbled reassurances. "You're going to be okay."

"I'm dying."

Her hand trembled in theirs. "The...the Viper says you're not. And despite—I think if she wanted you to be dying, she'd say so. So you have to be okay."

"S'not the poison." Kalen knew that much. This was different. It was the crashing of the waves against the ship's hull, the smell of salty sea air penetrating their senses. "I'm *drowning*."

Kalen opened his eyes, looking up at her in a desperate plea.

Realization crossed her expression, and she held them tighter. "It's the water? You've never wanted to go near the docks. You don't come over when it rains."

His head slammed under the water again, forced into the sand at the bottom of the pond. Air. He needed air.

"You're not dying, you just... I don't know what to do. I promise I won't let them bring you on deck. You're safe down here, I promise. I don't know how to help, I'm sorry. I'm sorry."

Black spots dotted their vision. They had to snap out of this. That was what she wasn't saying. It was all in his head.

How fucking pathetic.

Gods, what must Blythe think of him?

But it paralyzed him, the small chokes of air not nearly enough to keep him alive. The room distorted and caved in around him.

"Breathe with me, okay?" Her chest rose against his back as she inhaled deeply, and they tried to do the same.

She tried again, and he did, too.

"That's good. That's good. One more time, okay?"

Inhale. Exhale.

"One more time, okay?"

Inhale. Exhale.

"Better. Just one more time."

And Kalen breathed. Their heart pounded in their chest, but they could breathe. Their ears weren't ringing anymore, and they could hear the thump of Frida's steps as she hurried down the stairs.

"You're going to be okay."

⟫⟫ ⟪⟪

He wasn't okay.

But Blythe let slip that in a hidden storeroom she'd found laudanum, a substance recently illegal in both Ostrait and Fletch. It would calm them down.

"That stuff is illegal for a reason," she said. "You don't know what it would do to you."

"I've taken it before. Please, I can't. I can't do this alone."

"You're not..." She trailed off, clicking her knuckles together with a worried brow. "It's not safe."

Kalen could have screamed. Every time he shut his eyes too long, he drowned. Each rock of the ship sent him trembling. Tiny chills sent him underneath the water, struggling for air again.

"Why can't you do this *one* thing to help me?" Immediately, the words stung them, and Blythe stood up, drawing back toward the steps.

She looked away, hugging her own arms. "If you think it will help."

The second she vanished behind the door, he wanted to call her back. But they *needed* it.

When Frida brought down the tincture, it dripped liquid relief on their tongue. His muscles relaxed and his breathing slowed, the terror fading to a blurry background noise he could almost tolerate if he didn't look too close.

"Blythe figured you wanted some space." Frida hesitated to leave the tiny jar on the table.

Blythe was wrong—space was the last thing they wanted. But the shame swelled too great to ask, even with his tongue growing loose.

"You shouldn't have taken me in," they said, lying back on the floor and staring up at the ceiling. There were a lot of interesting knots in the wood, some darker, one of them kind of like a set of eyes, watching him. "I'm such an asshole."

"You're an asshole," she said with a shrug, "but I don't regret it."

Kalen snorted out a laugh. The room swayed, but they swayed with it. "Even now?"

It was their fault all of them were here, after all. Frida could have figured something out if they hadn't persuaded her with this stupid mission. And now she would absolutely die for it.

"You didn't kidnap me, you know." Arms folded over her chest. She had much stronger arms than his, and that didn't feel fair somehow. "I'm a grown woman. I *chose* to come because, frankly, I'm tired of making the same brews for the same five customers, and staying cooped up in the bar waiting tables the rest of my time in order to stay afloat."

Afloat. Aflooaaat.

That was what Kalen was doing.

"What, you robbed the Governor out of boredom, then?" He didn't blame her. He'd done many a stupid thing out of boredom.

"No, I wanted to rob the Governor so I could have enough money for an actual business and not grovel to Bossman every waking minute. It was a chance to meet people, and for once in my life, do what *I* liked. We wouldn't have to scramble to make rent if I owned something. And this? It's the type of adventure I didn't imagine having."

"Adventure?" Nothing about this was an adventure. Didn't Frida know they were going to die in a foreign court soon?

"I thought I would, once. On those Ashlan ships." It did strike a vague recollection. Kalen thought she might have been kicked out of Ashlos for some reason, in a way that no licensed ship had ever seemed keen on hiring her. She never wanted to explain, said it was better in the past.

"Alright." Kalen drummed his fingers where they rested on the wooden floor. "So you don't care I got us killed? I guess we'll go out with a bang."

A bug crawled along the ceiling, blue with green specks. "Hello, friend," Kalen murmured, transfixed by the little insect.

"Why are you so set on us dying?" Frida started toward the stairs. "The spirits are gonna have to fight harder to take *me*."

"Aw, he crawled in a hole."

"Just... Get some rest, *stupite*."

Frida shouldn't bother with him. Maybe *he* should just crawl in some hole and...stop.

Kalen panted from another nightmare, looking around in a scattered attempt to prove that Father wasn't there. The scars that marked Kalen's own arms, from the fire of that night, proved the man was long dead. *Coward.*

He stumbled to the table and grasped the bottle of laudanum. One drop on his tongue. It didn't work fast enough.

The waves roared in his ears, making his breathing ragged.

Another drop. He was going to die anyway, so why not down the entire bottle and make it quick?

But he couldn't do it.

Kalen had pushed this big heist. Blythe hadn't even wanted to do it. Forget that silly pretense of paying her back for their life, they'd now almost certainly doomed hers. The court would eat her fucking raw. And it was their fault. Completely, utterly.

He only wished to take it back. To go back up to their garden or finish that book or start embroidering that beautiful cow while she sorted her lock collection by color and size. It didn't matter that she could only love him as a good deed, that as a martyr she would never choose him over her gods. That his love had to remain unspoken, and hers only existed as charity. He would content himself with it, never taking it for granted again.

If Frida was right, and there was a chance...

Didn't he owe it to the both of them to at least suffer it to the end? No easy exit.

The relief started to flow through him again.

Kalen would have to find a way to survive. As their senses dulled, it began to seem possible again. But they needed more. A distraction.

They ripped into a barrel of peanut oil, tearing apart the room for materials to make tiny cylinders of peanut dynamite. They only needed a match, now. If Father walked through the door, these could protect him.

He just had to stay down here.

With busy hands and the creeping euphoria of their high, Kalen could survive.

5.

Aknas 37, fra Hjemi bur. 53

The sails pulled taut and mist sprayed Blythe's cheeks as she stood on deck.

It had been a few days, and she did everything she could to make their voyage run as smoothly as possible. Kalen had been right—she *had* to do more to help them. It was her fault they were here in the first place. She'd wrought her curse on both of her friends, and now Kalen tarried in a personal hell, from all appearances. They wouldn't want her around, and there was nothing she could offer him except her absence.

The Governor's Viper demanded rigorous work on the ship, anyway. They only had a certain window of time to coincide with the Jardaen ship and could not spare any delays, which the Viper made them perfectly aware of.

Though perhaps, if not for the assassin, they would still have enough hands on deck. Seven guards had accompanied them onto the ship. They were gone the second morning. Every one of them, just like that.

"They would only have gotten in the way," the Viper had said dismissively. As far as the Fletch would be concerned, they'd perished in a storm.

She'd moved on quickly to decree that they would all speak only in Fletch, then tossed Blythe *The Courtier's Handbook* to memorize.

At least she hadn't much remarked on Kalen's absence. Frida had told her, in a choppy mess of Fletch-adjacent words, that one person must remain below deck anyway, to watch for leaks, and the girl had by some grace accepted it. The ship's owner, Saidh, hadn't objected.

Blythe worked triple-time to make sure the Viper never questioned it.

She'd hardly sat down in the days since they'd set sail. It didn't matter that her arms screamed at her with every bucket of water she hoisted over the edge, or every nail she hammered, or every mast she climbed.

Sleep was a luxury she didn't deserve.

When she'd briefly blacked out while adjusting the ropes—she'd only fallen *a couple* feet, really—Frida had overreacted and insisted she take a break. Deium Eriuem wouldn't approve.

So instead, Blythe found herself tucked in the shadows of the bow, watching their captain. Saidh was a large man, with a precise cut to his barb, medium-brown skin, and curly black hair. He wore a respectable green coat, with silver buttons and a moderate amount of embroidery—typical enough for a merchant, though not if he smuggled expensive opium products.

He'd barely spoken a few words to them, but he didn't seem closely aligned with the Viper beyond whatever deal they'd brokered. Could he be a potential ally? If Blythe couldn't work on the ship, she at least needed to figure out if he was another threat.

She was mesmerized instead by watching him navigate, adjust ropes, consult the sextant. Surely she could do something more productive than stalk the man. But a mixture of admiration and jealousy stopped her from tearing her eyes away.

Blythe had been trying to ignore just how *right* it felt being on the water. The wind at her face, the sight of the open ocean in front of her, the soothing rock of the ship. Even when she'd been rushing to dump buckets of water during the heavy rain, even when she'd burned her hands on the ropes, it invigorated her with that odd sense of aliveness Kalen had introduced her to.

Memories from her near-ancient childhood swam to the surface. Waving to the boats with Mama. Reeling in a fish on the docks with Papa. Before everything.

I'm meant to be here.

This hunger gnawed at her as she watched Saidh charting their course at his wheel, when he or Frida instructed her about which rope to pull but not why.

Blythe tried to shake it off. Providing they succeeded in Fletch, she'd return home to take care of Papa. He couldn't survive on a ship, and even if not for Papa, there was Kalen. Sure, he would leave once he felt his "debt" was paid. Even if he *had* seen their time together as more than a duty. If they survived, Blythe would have to overcome her selfish, hubristic attachments to people she could only pull down into misery with her. Still, part of her couldn't bear the thought of taking off without them to sea, where she couldn't even make a sorry attempt at letter-writing.

But wouldn't it be useful to learn the basics of sailing? If anything happened to Saidh on the journey, they could all be stranded.

Really, learning would be proactive, a measure to ensure the mission didn't fail.

Nobody even had to know. She could linger in the shadows and watch him work. As long as he didn't actively look for her, her bestowment would keep her on the outskirts of his perception.

His hands rested on the wheel, and his back remained straight as he looked out to sea. What was he gazing at?

Some gold ornament hung from his neck. A locket, maybe? An amulet?

He had a straight nose and thick brows—probably Lastrian. He almost looked military, with the rigid way he stood, but then why would he be working as a shady merchant in Ostrait? The army wasn't the sort of thing you retired from. Exile, then?

Oh!

He moved his hands up and— He scratched his nose.

Blythe sighed. Maybe it would be fine to ask him about sailing. For the mission.

She gave up on diverting notice and made her way over to him as casually as possible.

She rested an elbow on the wheel's podium. "How's it going?" She clicked her knuckles together.

"Fine?" he said, tone put off. "Was there something you wanted?"

"Well." Blythe steeled herself and inhaled. Then she shrugged, to appear nonchalant. "I was thinking that, uh, maybe you could teach me how to sail. It could be helpful for the mission."

After the briefest of pauses, he answered flatly, "No."

"Oh." Her shoulders deflated. "Okay." She turned to walk away. *It was a stupid idea anyway.*

"Why do you want to learn?" Saidh asked tentatively, and Blythe stopped dead in her tracks, turning around with what she hoped wasn't an eager expression.

There was no nice way to say, "We'll all be screwed if you die in a storm."

And she didn't dare admit that she actually wanted to know.

"I just figured I could help," she said finally. "It can't be easy, running a ship on your own?"

She waited out this silence, trying not to fidget. He'd turned his gaze to examine something carved beside the wheel, and she inched herself closer.

"Did the Viper put you up to this?"

She hadn't expected that question, and she blinked. "What?"

"She asked you to learn, didn't she? So I'd be disposable." He muttered something under his breath, and Blythe caught the word "cabin."

Her eyebrows shot up, and she threw her hands in front of her, scrambling to explain. "No! I mean, she told us to work on the ship, but not this specifically. I just... I want to help us get there in one piece. That's all."

Saidh gave her a wary look. Then, almost grumbling at himself, he said, "I guess it wouldn't hurt to teach you the basic stuff. I *do* need to sleep sometimes."

Blythe restrained the urge to bounce on her heels. No excitement allowed. "I promise, I'll try to help however I can. The Viper doesn't have to know, if you don't want."

"I'm pretty sure she knows everything." He paused. "But alright."

He led her to a small wooden ledge a couple of feet away. A pane of glass pinned down a yellowed map of the oceans and coasts.

"That's the nautical chart," Saidh told her. "If we lose that or the sextant, we're lost." Blythe hung on to every word as he pointed out key areas on the chart, though long verbal descriptions were notoriously difficult for her.

When they moved back to the wheel, he started to demonstrate where to put her hands. "You're going to want to hold around nine and three."

The wooden handle pushed up part of his sleeve, revealing a mark. On his wrist, the triangle and the circle. Like she had on hers, a mark that branded girls who tried to steal work from men by disguising themselves. But thick scars nearly obscured his.

"Or, ten and two if you're uncomfortable..." His eyes widened as he noticed her gaze on his wrist, and he instantly pushed his sleeve up. "That's not what you think," he blurted.

Blythe pushed her own sleeve up and gave him a small, reassuring smile. "They love to tell us what to be, huh?"

"I guess they do."

A look of understanding passed between them.

"I was in the army, in Lastray," he said. "I left on poor terms. The Viper knows they have a bounty on me."

"Maybe you could be free of her, after this."

"Maybe." He put his hands back on the wheel, straightening his back. "So, as I was saying. Nine and three—"

"Wait, do you see that?"

"*Oh.*" He sighed. "We better tell the others."

"Kalen?" Blythe started down the stairs. "I'm not trying to bother you, but you should know, we found the Jardaen ship. We'll be..."

The stench of peanut butter struck her, her path entirely blockaded by little cylinders and pouches, with oil dripping around their edges and fuses made of the same fabric as the curtains.

"You made bombs? Out of *peanut butter*?"

They crowded the entire floor. Kalen lay on the cot at the side of the room, tying a string into knots.

"Oh, did I?" they said vaguely, only then noticing she stood there. They smiled. "How's things? And don't tell Louis. He already thinks I'm a bad influence."

"I... What?"

"He asked me to propose, you know. Said it was shameful I hadn't. Dunno *how* he was surprised that I only fancy men."

Blythe blinked. Concern sweltered around her heart like humid air. Kicking some of the bombs—gently—to the side, she made her way to him. "Are you feeling alright?"

"Good as honey," they said. Whatever that meant. And obviously a lie.

Kalen turned back to the string, not acknowledging her hand as it pressed to their burning forehead. Their eyes were dilated too, wider than could possibly mean anything good. He was barely even there with her.

"I really *do* fancy men, though," he babbled, "like that new captain of ours? All mysterious and handsome and *mysterious*."

"Kalen." She clasped her hand around the vial beside his cot, shocked at its emptiness. "How much of this did you take?"

Gods, she should have made sure nobody left it with them. Laudanum was too dangerous. They could sink into a coma, and she should have *made sure*.

They ignored her.

Just like they'd ignored the plate of food and cup of water on the table. Blythe hastily grabbed the cup and urged him to sit up and drink. They obliged with an eye roll.

"Kalen, this stuff could *kill* you."

"That's nice," they said, not even meeting her eyes.

"We can't... You can't keep taking this." That got his attention.

An instant, desperate look filled his eyes as he tried to snatch the bottle back from her. "Yes, I *can*."

She stood and moved out of reach. "I'm sorry, but it's for the best. I know you're scared—"

"You don't know *anything*," they muttered, but seemed too lethargic to move after her. "For *your* best, maybe. Tired of looking at me."

A lump formed in Blythe's throat. "That's not true. You're—you're not thinking straight." But they'd been dying in her arms from panic, sheer terror in their expression. How much better was that? Could they survive like that, either?

There was only one option left. "We'll hold on to the doses. And make sure you don't take too much." It would be best if Frida brought them down. Even now, Blythe struggled to refuse.

They huffed and turned onto their side, with his back to her. "You're being mean."

Blythe's hand shook as she closed the door behind her.

Forget the mission. At this rate, Kalen wouldn't make it to Fletch alive.

6.

Aknas 37, fra Hjemi bur. 53

Everyone crammed into the dining cabin to discuss strategy for overtaking the Jardaen ship. Kalen was, unfortunately, nearly half-sober, and he wrapped his arms around himself, trying not to hear the waves outside.

Frida wouldn't give them another dose today. Not until they were safely on the next ship, she said. Ship—no. *Think of something else,* be *somewhere else.*

"Taking over a military ship isn't what I'd call a sure thing," Saidh said. He had a remarkably stern brow, but not the gravelly voice Kalen expected. "We'll need to take stock of the canons, any weaponry—"

"No, we won't," the Viper interrupted, walking in. She sat on the tabletop, pink skirts puffed around her and completely spotless. Kalen envied the confidence that emanated from her every word. "I'm here to deal with those things, if you recall. We *do* need a means of getting everyone aboard."

Anxiety twisted in Kalen's chest with each rock of the ship, but the remaining laudanum managed to untangle it some. They were fine. Fine,

fine, *fine*. Water didn't swish around them, something else did. Giants, maybe, pushing against the hull.

"Please," he gasped, coughing and spluttering.

He tied another knot in his string. Another. He wasn't sure what he was making, maybe some kind of ugly bracelet.

"Corvus, maybe?" Frida asked Saidh.

"It would damage the ship too badly. Grappling hooks?"

"But how to get close enough?"

"We'll lure them in with a distress signal," the Viper said decisively. "I have a white flag prepared, we'll just need a few smoke bombs to simulate a fire."

"That's— It's bad form," Frida protested.

"Kalen's not in the condition for that sort of thing..." Blythe's voice trailed off, and Kalen glanced over at her, mildly aware that this should concern them.

"He'd better be," the Viper replied coolly, straightening her sleeves with an expression made of stone. "Or what use do I have for him?"

Kalen flinched at another wave. *Focus on the string. Keep busy.*

"Can't you have a little compassion?" Blythe demanded. But Blythe never *demanded* anything. "He's having a hard enough time, and it's not fair to expect him to swing across the water and make bombs when he's barely conscious. We can figure something else out. But you need *me* for this mission, and I won't let you use him—"

"You misunderstand your position, Caron." The Viper stood tall over Blythe, with a pointed look at the bruise on Blythe's neck where the last dart had landed. Kalen reached to his own neck, jarred by the memory of that terrible pain. They had to remember she wasn't just a girl. She was *venomous*.

She could torture him into complying if she wanted.

"Please, we could—"

"I can make the smoke bombs."

Several sets of eyes trained suddenly on them, and they turned their own gaze back to the string in their hands. "I'll need saltpeter. Sugar. Whatever kind we have should do. Some kind of colorful vegetable... Beets, maybe."

"One of you can fetch the ingredients," the Viper said, settling the matter. "Figure out a way to transfer him onto the ship." She stalked out of the room.

Good thing, too, they'd have a new task. They'd run out of string to occupy their hands with.

Making bombs and other alchemist tasks had this way of grounding him. Maybe because if he didn't concentrate, that meant he could blow himself up, so the distractions fell away while he worked.

Kalen definitely needed grounding right now.

Once the ingredients were gathered, the others set out to do their own work. Blythe helped Frida, making grappling hooks or something of the sort, maybe. Saidh probably stood at the wheel with the wind blowing his hair, a brooding expression on his face. Maybe not, but Kalen's imagination could conjure what they liked.

They sat down at the dining table—a beautiful oak one, at that, with intricate little carvings of navy sailors and sea creatures. But he couldn't dwell on that, so he began cutting fabric into small squares.

They lost track of time as they worked, filling pouch after pouch and setting them in a pile in front of them. Better to have too many than not enough.

Kalen had to be good for something.

꙳꙳꙳   ꙳꙳꙳

How they arrived on the next ship was unclear. Another merciful dose of laudanum had helped with that, thank the gods.

Maybe it *wasn't* even a ship.

Smoke still lingered in the air, and they half-thought maybe they'd fallen asleep during one of their robberies. That wouldn't be good, but he also couldn't bother caring.

Unhappy voices surrounded them.

"You didn't have to *kill* them all."

"What did you think was going to happen? I'd just drop them off on an island and hope they didn't tell the Fletch ambassadors?"

Blythe. She was spluttering, and when Kalen looked up, her expression was some contortion of guilt and sorrow. "I—I don't know! I don't know, we could have..."

Oh.

Kalen had forgotten they would have to kill the Jardaens.

They doubted Blythe had *really*. She didn't leave Kalen alone to light those fires, even if she spiraled about it. She never blamed him, either, funnily enough—just swore to six hells they'd find a better way next time. Once, she had gotten this wild look in her eyes, and he could have sworn she'd enjoyed herself.

"Whatever you thought doesn't matter. Just get on with disposing of the bodies."

"We can't just throw them overboard," Saidh protested, but Kalen focused on the tears forming in Blythe's eyes. Would she cry more when he died, or the same as she did for strangers?

The Viper tapped her foot. "This isn't a debate. Honestly, you can burn down buildings, but you're too squeamish to throw some corpses in the water?"

"I need some air." Frida made a hasty retreat with her arm over her mouth and nose. Peculiar, because she'd handled a couple over-drunk corpses at the tavern with decent composure before. The conversation rolled too fast to pay her much mind.

"It's not proper," Blythe insisted, her words thick. "We can't just... They were *people*."

"I have extra bombs," Kalen said. They didn't seem to hear him, or else they ignored him, which wouldn't be nice. "Real ones. They smell like peanuts, but they'll make a good fire."

Saidh pinched the bridge of his nose. "What are you on about?"

Blythe's eyes widened. "A burial at sea," she murmured.

The walls wouldn't stay still in this room. They should probably get that fixed before they got to...wherever.

"I suppose that would be acceptable," the Viper said. "It would certainly ensure that nobody recognizes the bodies and alerts the Fletch."

"Peanut bombs?" Saidh asked.

Kalen laughed.

Soon, he heard the familiar roar of a flame. And a voice he wished he could forget.

Coward.

7.

Aknas 40, fra Hjemi bur. 53

"Why do we need all this now?" Blythe asked. "We aren't there yet." The Viper tied yet another layer of pastel skirts at her waist. Blythe was almost sure that the girl tortured her in this ridiculous costume because of the sea burial.

She could still smell the burning hair.

At least they'd been able to give the people their last rites. People that had died because of her.

"You have to wear these like you've worn them all your life," the Viper said, looking her up and down. "Clothing is just as much a part of your character as your disguise."

The Viper didn't even seem bothered about the dead Jardaens.

How could I have let this happen?

Blythe clenched her jaw. She had to focus; it had to have been *for* something. But how did anyone manage not to fall over in these long, poufy garments that were surely filled with bricks?

If you hadn't been so fucking greedy, there would be no assassin looming over you.

"You'd think you'd be grateful for a chance to wear something this regal, even if it is the Jardaen style."

"*Grateful?*" Did the elites like this Viper imagine that everyone else sat around all day wishing to be royal ladies and gentlemen? Maybe some of them did. But it only turned Blythe's stomach.

Far from a fantasy, this costume made Blythe's blood boil. It itched and constrained her movement, and made her have too much hips and boobs—unlike in her preferred attire.

But it was more than that. How many yards of expensive cottons and silks made up these skirts alone? Enough to dress half the children on her street, probably.

What were all these little gold threads and jewels worth? Surely enough to pay off Papa's debt and that of every other peasant in the province. The Fletch likely wouldn't even *notice* what they took during the heist, a fact that should have assuaged her guilt but only formed a lump in her throat.

The Viper pulled on the laces at Blythe's back. "Well, it doesn't matter if you can appreciate art or not," she huffed. "You're wearing it for a mission that has kept you alive. You'd do well to remember that before complaining that it's not covered in mud."

Interesting. The Viper cared about this in some way. Blythe had assumed the Viper wore such feminine clothing to make people underestimate her, but that must have been wrong. Keeping herself spotless, her impeccable work on the sails, it was all done with tangible passion.

Blythe might not share any of these inclinations, but Kalen did. What might she say? Purely to make nice, of course.

"This sort of thing escapes me. And I've not worn even a 'peasant' dress in a few years," Blythe admitted. "Maybe you could do me a favor and wear one of the other gowns? Show me how it's done? Lady Esme probably gave clothes to her lady-in-waiting anyway, so it would only look proper once we get to Fletch."

"I don't do favors," the Viper said, pursing her lips as if offended. "And I fully intend on taking my share of the wardrobe."

Blythe withheld a sigh. So much for that effort.

Should she even bother to try swaying the Viper to their side? After all this assassin had done? It was wrong to resent someone, wrong to be angry. But those *people*. That pain they'd all been in. She acted like it didn't matter—a footnote in her daily agenda.

Blythe reluctantly slipped her arms into a pair of mauve sleeves. A picture of femininity stared back at her from the mirror. Unfortunate that looking the part did nothing for her apathy toward girlhood.

She'd enjoyed being a girl once, hadn't she? At some point, that had stopped. Maybe when it was no longer Mama tying the bows in her hair.

The lavish lady in the reflection stirred neither euphoria nor revulsion. The flounces were merely another role to play, no different from pretending to be a boy to find work. Clearly femininity would always be an expensive gown that fit a bit wrong.

An expensive gown stolen from a dead girl.

How old had Esme been? Close enough to Blythe's own age. *Does she have a papa waiting for her back home?*

"Sit down," the Viper ordered, gesturing to the small wooden chaise by Esme's vanity—*her* vanity. She had to start getting in character. She had no time to sink into the horrible pit of despair. "The hair and face are next."

The pit the Viper had put her into. *All those people.*

Blythe couldn't do this. She dug her nails into her palm.

Everything itched or weighed her down. Her stomach growled because she'd skipped another meal, and the sound of the Viper's demanding voice began to incite an irrational amount of rage.

At home, Blythe did whatever she could to hammer away the anger that grew far too abundantly within her. Sometimes she would shock herself with a blast of icy water, or climb a tree until her arms threatened to give out. But there would be a lot of sitting still from here on out, and she already struggled to tame the vices coiling inside her.

The thought of her face being touched, smeared with sticky creams she couldn't smudge, her lips coated with something waxy she couldn't avoid tasting, it sent flutters of anxiety oscillating in her chest.

Not to mention having her hair wrenched from the simple twin plaits that usually pinned it back, to be wrangled into an elaborate coiffe, with wispy curls tickling above her eyes and around her neck.

"No."

The Viper clicked open a wooden box filled with fine brushes. "I don't think I heard you correctly."

The resolve withered as quickly as it had come. Kalen and Frida needed her. Papa needed her to keep it together. Grit her teeth and bear it. Push it down as far as it would go.

"Sorry. Never mind."

Two days later, everyone donned their glimmering attire.

Well, Kalen's didn't glimmer, actually. They'd found the invitation on the Jardaen ship, and it said they had to bring a servant as a gesture of good faith. Blythe had stupidly hoped they would be by her side—only so she could make sure *they* were safe, of course.

She had forced her costume back on without the Viper's help today, a tedious endeavor that had taken her double the time. Gods knew why there were so many strings to tie behind one's own back.

She couldn't bring herself to touch the assemblage of pastes and powders that the Viper had been caking on her face, calling it a "maquillage" when Blythe wished to call it a personal hell for her senses. The wig had only lasted five minutes before she'd ripped it back off.

The Viper, mercifully, wasn't present to correct her. After finishing Frida's costume very late last night, she'd locked herself in her cabin. Presumably to sleep, though the Viper had claimed she had finishing touches on her own costume to make.

The rest of them sat in the dining cabin. Frida and Saidh were kind enough not to mention that they were there because Kalen couldn't come on deck.

They were also, almost certainly, pretending not to notice that he was high.

"You can't tell me you don't love it just a *little*." Kalen sat upside down in their chair, legs dangling over the back of it. They tossed an orange up and down. "Not *one* bit?"

"I'd trade with you if I could," Blythe said, fidgeting. Kalen was meant for regal things like this, and pity did clutch her that he was the only one not allowed to wear them. To her, these items were a punishment, though an insufficient one.

"That makes it so much worse."

Blythe lowered her voice, just a little. "I'll give it to you when we get back home."

They grinned back at her. "Guess we'll have to make it back, then."

A melancholy affection swarmed her. Some fantasy that they'd return together and he'd stick around long enough to drag her along while he tried on lavish hats and coats. But that was all it was: fantasy. She had to keep reminding herself that they would do better to get on with their own life, find some alluring man to marry and bed, and forget all the strife that came with being her friend. It would be selfish to dream otherwise.

It was selfish for her to dream, period.

"Well." Frida looked around the elaborate dining area, and the rest of them followed her gaze. A high polished oak ceiling held three golden chandeliers, bookcases towered with volumes in every size and color, several oil paintings of what Blythe assumed to be the Jardaen landscape hung beside them, and countless silver anchor baubles decorated the space. The table seating the four of them could easily have fit fifty.

"I think we have much working to do," Frida announced.

And how prepared were any of them? They certainly weren't ready to behave as the actual people who found this sort of ship normal. Blythe probably couldn't even draw Fletch on a map.

And she was going to be the center of attention.

"We don't have long," Saidh said, worrying his barb. "I never even thought. We have a lot of training to do."

The Viper came in through the dining cabin door, clearly having overheard. They all looked to her, not quite daring to accuse her of an oversight, but desperate for some sort of plan.

She straightened her back, opening her mouth and closing it again, before finally speaking in her usual drawl. "Well, *obviously* more time would have been optimal, but needing to catch up with the Jardaens wouldn't allow it. And in any case," she deflected, "you mean to tell me you weren't already working on your own?

"Did you not even read the manual I gave you?" she asked Blythe. "Aside from your atrocious accent, it should have had everything you need to know about the court rules. The Fletch court isn't that different from Ostrait's."

"I've never been in *any* court." Blythe had tried to read the manual—despite having marginal enough literacy in Ostraitian—but half of the words didn't even make sense to her. The manual was clearly aimed at people who already knew the ins and outs of their own country's elite life.

While Blythe thought her inexperience evident, the Viper blinked, as if momentarily caught off guard. "Well... Well, obviously I know that. But there would be no mission at all if we hadn't caught the Jardaen ship in time. Besides, it's not like I'll have to teach you how to walk."

⤜⤜ ⤛⤛

Turned out, Blythe didn't know how to walk.

It had come as a surprise to Blythe, who had been walking since about ten months of age.

"Viper, it's been three hours," she said, trying without avail to reason with the girl. Though she shouldn't complain. "Wouldn't it be better to pick back up later?"

"Exactly. It's been three hours, and you still can't walk right." Her tone was curt and she leaned against the wall, making an impatient wave with her hand. "Again."

They had only three weeks left on their journey to Fletch, and Blythe trained from dawn to dusk.

In the mornings, she worked with Saidh, who would act as "Esme's" guardian and Jardae's representative on her behalf in various meetings. He knew a surprising amount about Fletch history and geography.

"I worked in tourism for a while" was his only explanation. Prying any further would clearly have been unwelcome.

Saidh also worked to correct her accent when the Viper wasn't picking at it, to make it both more Fletch and more upper-class. Frida—who still barely spoke any Fletch beyond curse words, and had been slipping into Ostraitian when the Viper wasn't around—teased that Blythe sounded like "a drunk chewing gum." Blythe had only ever spoken Fletch with Papa, really, and she'd always liked her accent because it was the same as his.

But even though they posed as coming from Jardae, their delegation apparently wanted to impress the Fletch badly enough to imitate them.

"It's not m*ae*ym," Saidh reminded her when they spoke, "it's m*eh*m."

It sounded sort of flat to Blythe but wasn't hard to mimic. Remembering to do so remained the sticking point.

The others' accents were of less concern. Kalen and the Viper spoke typical "proper" Fletch, thanks to their robust educations. Cooks were often imported from Ashlos, so Frida could hopefully get by. Only Blythe's inferiority was a pressing issue.

But working with Saidh turned out to be the most pleasant part of her days. After that, she would have a brief break to eat and instruct Kalen about his role of servant. He washed dishes back home plenty often; Frida was a messy cook, and sometimes the tavern let him work under the table. Laundry, too, was one of the bits of piecework he had done. But Kalen had no idea about the ins and outs of actual servitude, especially not about the unfathomable rigor in the Fletch court. Blythe had never worked for anyone richer than a merchant, but she did her best to share her experience.

The two of them worked below deck, and Kalen's focus was fleeting, to say the least.

"Good. You're doing good." Anxiety gripped Blythe's stomach.

Kalen might be going through the motions here, but they barely remembered from one lesson to the next. Still, she couldn't bear asking them to avoid the laudanum, because it held the panic at bay. Things had been *horrible* the last day it rained.

"I'm sorry." He sank onto the floor beside her. "I think I'm just made to screw things up."

"You know that's not true, right?"

They leaned their head on her shoulder. "Your accent sounds a lot better. More Fletch, I mean. It's kinda weird that you sound like a princess."

"Thanks," Blythe said, choosing to let the subject change. "It's weird for me, too."

"Drink?" they offered, and she took the cup gratefully. She barely had time to sit there with them and catch a break before her training with Frida. Which she did not look forward to in the slightest.

When Blythe worked with Frida, her muscles screamed in protest. She just wanted to give up. It wasn't like princesses were supposed to fight anyway, right?

"Frida, are we sure this is worth it?" she asked, shoulders sagging as Frida put her hands up. "I don't think I'm going to have the chance to punch anyone."

"You need to be protecting yourself," Frida insisted in her slowly progressing Fletch, with a stern dip of her brow.

Blythe couldn't come to terms with the idea of *hitting* anyone. She couldn't bring herself to throw a punch at Frida, or trip her, or do anything she was supposed to. It just wasn't right. That was her *friend*.

"I'm not making of glass, you know," Frida said. Really, she'd been more than patient.

"I'm sorry, I just... I think I'm wasting your time."

After one attempt at a throw left the both of them tripping over each other, Frida finally relented. They slumped together on the deck, taking swigs of water from the barrel.

A moment of silence blanketed them.

"Are you going alright, after the...poison?" Frida asked tentatively, looking at Blythe with an unearned gentleness.

Blythe swallowed, turning her eyes back to her water. "I nearly forgot about it." Not *really* a lie. She hadn't been stopping from one activity to the next, which gave her minimal time to dwell on how terrible that pain had been. And it paled in comparison to holding Kalen in her arms and watching him suffocate. "Are you?"

"Oh, sure. Tough like an elephant, you are knowing this." A probable lie in exchange.

Their friendship rarely included deep, honest conversations now. Neither could tolerate being fussed over, but both were inclined to care. Blythe didn't want to endanger Frida again. This had created a certain distance that, without outright saying so, they'd mutually agreed couldn't be bridged. And so, the platitudes.

It did make Blythe a bit lonely, in a way. But she couldn't force Frida to cry on her shoulder. A sweaty shoulder, after all of these failures wrestling about. "Yeah," was all she said.

"Speaking Fletch, though." Frida shook her head with a—nervous?—laugh. "I never know how I'm saying."

That was something, at least. Lighthearted enough, though maybe it shouldn't have been. They had only a couple weeks left now to prepare, and even if Frida could get by without being fluent, it must have been terrifying going into this mission with so little time to grasp the language.

"You're picking it up fast, though."

"I'm learning what to say all the food and spices, at least," she said, the corners of her mouth quirking up. She shrugged and leaned back on her hands. "You have the most talking, anyway."

Blythe could speak Fletch, but talking to courtiers? That might as well be another foreign language. The Governor was the highest-ranking person she'd ever spoken to, and she'd been focused on not dying.

"Have you ever been?" Blythe asked, changing the subject. "To Fletch?" She sloshed around the water in her fancy copper cup.

Frida hesitated for a moment before replying in Ostraitian. "Round-about sorta way."

Blythe leaned on her elbows, savoring the bounce of the waves beneath her.

"Me and... I was in Fletch waters once, with an unmarked Ashlan ship. But merchants were usually easier to outgun on other coasts."

The Ashlan government notoriously turned a blind eye to "unofficial" vessels that caused trouble, so long as they paid their taxes. That was why it was such a wonder that Frida had managed to be kicked out—she never said what for.

"What's it like, do you think?" Blythe asked.

The navy dusk of the sky had bled into inky black, dotted with glowing stars and the soft crescent of the moon. Cool air brushed Blythe's skin, a peaceful sensation that threatened to lull her to sleep.

Frida yawned. "Can't imagine it's too different from Ostrait. There'll be workers, fighters, rich assholes. Like anywhere else."

Blythe's eyelids grew heavy, and she groaned, heaving up her arms and legs made of lead. "We shouldn't fall asleep out here." It would get too cold in the coming hours to be exposed. She offered a hand down, but Frida hoisted herself up on her own, sighing her agreement.

The promise of sleep alone moved Blythe's aching body toward the cabin. At least she could rely on the solace of lying down and passing out.

Except the Viper stood in front of her door.

"If you've come to murder me, I might welcome it," Blythe said, a heavy sigh sagging her shoulders.

"No time for rest," the girl said. She adjusted the frilled white cuffs of her sleeves. "The costumes are finally inconspicuous enough, but we've so little time for etiquette rehearsal that it might not matter."

⤜⋙ ⋘⤛

It was halfway to dawn by the time Blythe collapsed next to Kalen, sequestered in one of the only cabins below deck that lacked a window, lying on a floor mat just big enough for the two of them.

"She's trying to work me to death, I think," Blythe said. Her mind was a pile of mush at this point. She'd half-forgotten that it would be best to unburden Kalen of herself. Their face kept her focused on the stakes, reminded her that resigning wasn't an option.

"*That's* where you've been all night?" Kalen asked, turning onto their side and propping themself up with an elbow. They sounded a bit too cheerful. "I figured you went to bed hours ago."

"I swear, there's rules for how a lady should *breathe*." That reminded Blythe to yank loose the laces of her stays before flopping back down onto her back. She didn't bother with minding her accent. "You've been holding up alright?"

"Oh, yeah. Great. Fantastic."

"No trouble sleeping, then?" There was no reason Kalen had to stay up this late.

They hesitated. Then shot her a mischievous grin. "'Course not. Not at all."

A wave rocked the ship, and their hand tightened like iron around her arm. Their face contorted instantly into abject panic, and she scooped them into a cradling hug. "Hey, it's alright."

She didn't know what else to say. Didn't fully even understand where this terror came from, let alone how to fix it.

They pulled away, blinking up with watery eyes. "Gods, he'd just love to see me now."

There could only be one "he" that Kalen meant. "Well. He can't exactly see shit, can he?"

She managed to startle a laugh from him with that. "Guess not."

Kalen squeezed their eyes shut, hands clasping tighter around Blythe's as they drew in a shaky breath. Her heart plummeted. A violent anger rose in her, making her seethe at a long-dead man. She didn't care if it was wrong, she wanted him to be burning in whatever hell he'd found himself in, she wanted—

"Could we just... Could you talk about something? Anything?" Kalen whispered, a soft plea in Ostraitian.

She pushed everything else from her mind. "I'm apparently a lost cause for dining etiquette."

Kalen opened one eye, then the other, looking at her with some kind of grateful amusement. "It's not like you can eat sweets with a gravy spoon."

"One of my many 'atrocities,' as the Viper put it."

"I'm sure you'll get the hang of it," Kalen said eventually. But they couldn't even keep a straight face.

"I *am* so charming and sociable."

"Compared to the table, maybe," they teased, but she was glad of it.

The two of them chatted awhile longer, though Blythe spoke the most. Kalen seemed relieved to have a distraction. The small doses of laudanum—smaller now that they approached their destination and needed to ease him off of it—didn't seem to be quite enough.

"Do you remember that day at the Fittons' house?"

But his eyes had drifted closed, pieces of hair fallen over his ivory face. Their brow relaxed, without a trace of the nightmares that so often woke him.

Blythe allowed her own eyes to drift shut.

⟫⟫⟫ ⟪⟪⟪

Water splashed Blythe's face, startling her awake.

"A lady doesn't sleep on the ground with servant boys." The Viper stood with her hands on her hips, watching with irritation as Blythe sat up. "If you tumble with *anyone*, it will be the King."

Blythe flushed. It did look odd. Kalen still sprawled asleep underneath the blanket, and Blythe only wore her shift, stays half falling off, and breeches. She almost wished the two of them *wanted* to do things like that. Maybe if they fell in love, or even lust, she'd have something worth-

while to give him, and it would be less selfish stealing his company all this
time.

"It's not like that," she said, but the Viper was already walking away
with the apparent expectation that Blythe would scramble after her.
Which Blythe did, because she had to.

That day, they filed off all of her hand calluses and reviewed forms of
address until her throat dried out.

For the remaining week, Blythe continued to see barely a wink of sleep.
Adequate progress with Saidh's lessons served as her only saving grace.
Frida was losing hope, and Blythe suspected that the Viper might have
been poisoning her as punishment for ineptitude because her stomach
always ached lately.

At the end of one day, she blearily stumbled over to the edge of the
ship. Looking at the waves rolling calmed her some.

But what was that toward the horizon? Land?

Blythe sighed in dismissal. Not the first time she'd imagined an end to
this painful journey in her exhausted blur.

"Hold on." Frida had appeared behind her and gripped the lip of the
ship, peering outward. "Is that *shore*?"

"Wait, you see it too?" Before her friend could even answer, Blythe was
dashing down the stairs to the cabin where Kalen had hunkered down.

The news certainly hadn't come too soon.

Blythe found them slumped in a chair across the room, waving their
fingers past dilated eyes, emptied doses of laudanum discarded on the
table.

"Kalen." He looked up with the vaguest interest. Her chest tightened.
She knelt in front of them, grasping their hands in her own in a search
for recognition. "Kalen, it's shore, we spotted shore."

Something clicked. They tilted their head, then frowned. "I'm prolly dreaming."

"By Lox, how much of this have you been..." Blythe drifted off, shaking her head. That wasn't the point, as much as it might choke her with fear. "No, you're not dreaming. I promise. We'll be on land by day's end."

Kalen let out a disbelieving laugh, eyes crinkling with sudden euphoria. They stood abruptly, pulling her up with them to spin around in a little dance. "It's land! It's land!" He gave her a grin, and Blythe couldn't help as her face stretched in response. Kalen waved around his hat with glee. "Goodbye, you stupid boat!"

Soon, Frida and Saidh bounded down the stairs to meet them.

"I can't believe this," Saidh said. "The fog must have covered it."

"Just think." Frida leaned back in her seat, beaming. "We're gonna be—"

"If there's land, no time to waste," the Viper said from the stairway, and all of them jumped. Blythe wasn't used to being the one crept up on, and she didn't care for it at all. "Best costumes on, and start speaking in character at all times."

"Are you sure I can't be a lady-in-waiting, too?" Kalen pouted, staring wistfully at the Viper's jewel-adorned dress.

"And *you*," the girl said, fixing on Blythe. Her tone was less of a kind warning than a threat. "Sober him up quickly, or I'll have to."

8.

With a crew of Fletch guards on the ground waving them through, they docked the ship outside the palace walls.

Kalen's elation at finally reaching the shore contended with the shaking of his legs as the others brought him up on the deck. The Fletch palace loomed just ahead, an endless expanse of white and gold arches, bordered by low wooden docks that sloshed with water. Swarms of armed guards bustled around them.

It's fine. Don't think about the waves. Don't think. Just look normal. Just breathe.

The laudanum was starting to wear off. Their stomachful of bread could spill out at any moment. Sweat coated his back, and gooseflesh prickled his arms.

"Delegation?" a tall guard in a stark red uniform asked flatly of Saidh.

Kalen kept their head bowed, staring down at a loose floorboard. *Air. He needed air.*

"Jardae," Saidh replied coolly. "Representing Lady Esme of the House Albret."

Blythe and the Viper stood fanning themselves as if bored on the other side of Saidh, and Frida stood in Kalen's corner. Kalen wanted to look up at her for reassurance, but even with his mind swirling, he knew it was a bad idea.

Hands forced him under. The cold water hit his face like a wall.

"And where's the rest of the crew?" the guard asked, raising a thick eyebrow.

"This all Jardae can afford?" joked another, and a few of the guards laughed.

Saidh did a good job of bristling. "We lost much of the crew during a storm. Surely your navy was aware of it?"

"Of course, apologies."

"And forgive me, sir," the eyebrow-guard asked, "but you don't look Jardaen."

"My mother was Lastrian, but I was raised on the island with my father." Saidh didn't miss a beat. He produced a sealed envelope. "A letter from His Grace, Duke Henri of House Albret, with some information regarding the extenuating circumstances of our departure."

He referred to the well-known "fact" that Jardae was allegedly keeping this mission a secret from Ostrait, and the letter they had forged explained that many of their Jardaen officials were under strict watch by Ostraki spies.

Kalen waited with a storm of anxiety in his chest. *Get me out of here. Just get me out of here.*

An agonizing seven seconds passed. But the guard pocketed the letter and gave Saidh a stiff nod. "You will all be escorted to your rooms for the standard examinations," the guard said.

Kalen cast a nervous glance at Frida. *Examinations?*

"Of course," Saidh replied, as if they'd already all known about this.

Waves crashed against the side of the ship. Kalen flinched.

He couldn't stay here. He couldn't breathe.

"We will also examine your gift. Following this, all members of the delegation will remain in isolation until the first *certatia*. You're lucky you arrived today, or there wouldn't be enough time to process you."

Gift. Wait—him?

"Thank you for your hospitality, *protigii*," Blythe said in an airy tone that was unlike her, allowing a guard to guide her down the ramp by a gloved hand.

Kalen's guard did not delicately guide him by the hand. In fact, the man only uttered the gruff word "follow" without so much as meeting Kalen's eyes.

Inhaling sharply, he tried not to give in to the trembling of his knees or the sweating of his palms. He'd trailed behind Father like this so many times, it should be a stale routine by now.

Don't think of the water. Don't think of the water.

He couldn't move.

The guard yanked him forward, and his feet touched the ground—real ground—within seconds.

Kalen shuddered with relief. But the threat still wasn't far enough away.

The rest of their crew had vanished from sight. All that remained were the damp cobblestones underneath Kalen's feet and the enormous guard at his side.

The docks grew farther, and some of the air returned to their lungs.

Breathe. Just breathe.

The cobblestones changed to worn oak as the guard turned the two of them down a corridor. The servants' quarters would not be far—the more valuable members of the court kept themselves closer to the security of the interior. Noisy chatter and movement reached Kalen's ears, and several pairs of feet entered his peripheral vision.

"You will now undergo the examination," the guard informed him. The man steered Kalen—who was *dying* to look around and get his bearings—into some small nook barely wide enough for the guard's shoulders.

And *what* examination?

"Hands on your head," the man instructed impatiently. In their confusion, Kalen took a second longer to comply. His eyes widened with realization when the guard began to roughly pat him down. *Oh.*

This kind of examination.

But wait— *Fuck.*

One of the smoke bomb pouches. He'd tucked it into his inner pocket, just in case. He'd actually tried to be prepared for once!

The guard had already reached Kalen's waist. The pouch was on the interior. It wouldn't be noticed—surely, it was small enough. Wasn't it?

Kalen's pulse beat in his ears. His breath grew shakier, and he tried to contain it. *Act innocent. You've not been caught for anything.*

Bile rose in his throat.

The guard patted past the pocket level of Kalen's breeches without remark. They could barely restrain the sigh of relief when the man finished at their ankles.

Unfortunately, nothing could stop the vomit from erupting out of Kalen's mouth.

The guard jumped back as Kalen fell to his knees, retching. He made a disgusted noise. "Not *another* one."

Kalen's arm shook as he wiped his mouth. "I—I'm sorry, sir."

"Just clean yourself the fuck up." The guard rolled his eyes, muttering as he walked away, leaving Kalen there, shaking and completely disoriented. "All these fucking seasick serfs... Not paid enough for this shit..."

Kalen gripped the rag on the floor. The guard must have thrown it. He willed his aching muscles to move.

Clean, you idiot. Clean before it's all blown. Come on.

The room went dark.

⋙ ⋘

A blaring pain throbbed in their head. They gingerly touched their temples, trying to steady the spinning around them. Where was he?

The nook in the servants' quarters. Every edge of the tiny space was beige plaster and tile, bleeding together.

As quietly as possible, Kalen sat up. They took a moment to catch their breath, relieved to hear only a few other servants bustling around in the quarters. No loud, thumping footsteps; no guards. Still, as he stood and peered around the corner, Kalen hesitated. His stomach flipped anew.

The entire voyage here had blurred somewhat. He had no idea if he could do this. In fact, they were almost completely certain they couldn't. He couldn't even travel here without— Gods, he needed more laudanum. How could he keep it together for nearly a whole *month*?

Kalen needed to get out.

The impulse to run overwhelmed him, hairs standing straight on his damp neck.

One foot after another. They could escape through all the hubbub. The guards were just concerned with who came *in* right now.

Kalen could get away and change their name, start somewhere new.

But Blythe wouldn't be there. He could start a new garden, but only she ever managed to keep the peppers alive. She didn't even like them. She only grew them because they were his favorite.

And even *she* could never forgive Kalen for running, because they would send the crew home for the faulty servant, and her papa would die.

And Kalen did like the idea of all that money. "You can do it," they whispered to themself.

By Lox, they *really* wished they had more laudanum.

The others had been trying to wean him off. It was illegal here, not an ounce to be found in the entire palace, apparently. But their body screamed and pounded at them, demanding it.

He took a quivering breath of air, steeling himself. *Just survive today.*

Kalen scooped up his coat, came out from the nook, and took a tentative survey of the box-like room.

It mostly shone white, except for the tan pine floors. They furrowed their brows for a half-moment, searching for beds or floor mats at the least, but nothing lay on the floor, not even a blanket. And the room wasn't extremely wide, in any case. It stretched taller than anything.

Cupboards stretched the full breadth of one wall. Some were half ajar, revealing thin pillows and wool blankets, all perfectly made and unwrinkled. Some were closed. Some had small golden latches on the outside.

"Just pick one that's open," a boy said, appearing beside him.

Kalen jumped, jerking away.

"You're one of the delegate gifts?"

"Yeah." His voice cracked.

"Careful not to mess up the beds," the kid advised. "Superior is all about education for the serving class." A translation floated into his mind: *Superior thinks the poor are dirty rats that need to be whipped out of their disgusting nature.*

Kalen cleared his throat and extended a trembling hand. "Thank you," they said.

The boy shook their hand with a brief nod. "They've been throwing a lot of new rules at us," he said. "*I* get confused, and I'm from here."

Confusion was one way to put it. "I'm Kalen," he offered.

"Gilles."

The bells affixed to the entrance started ringing. They grimaced at the excruciating noise. All the servants began rushing out of the room at once. Kalen staggered along just behind Gilles, moving with the mass.

"What's going on?" they asked. Instantly, regret stung them. Should a servant know this already?

"It means that His Majesty is finished with his company for the night," Gilles said, seeming to think nothing odd of the question. The boy pushed some reddish-brown hair out of his round, youthful face. "Our quarter is on call for cleanup, and to answer any of his needs."

"Oh, everyone's running so quickly," Kalen said with a little laugh. They slowed down a little, but Gilles didn't. "I thought there was something urgent."

"There is," Gilles insisted, tugging him along by the arm. "Don't you know better than to make the King wait? Who did you serve before, anyhow?"

Kalen opened their mouth to make some kind of excuse.

"Never mind," Gilles cut Kalen off, mercifully. He whispered almost inaudibly now. "The chambers are down this hall."

Blythe's words echoed in Kalen's mind. *A good servant is neither seen nor heard.* She'd said that one often, hadn't she? Kalen nodded and shut his mouth.

They all shuffled toward a looming burgundy door with brass lion-head handles, which four servants took hold of. The men waved the rest of the staff through, and Kalen concentrated as hard as possible on stepping quietly.

Luckily, the King was nowhere in sight.

So why had they all rushed to get here? Though, the King might return in a rage. The new tavern owner had sometimes enjoyed bursting in when the employees thought he'd be away, to catch them shirking off and deliver his obscenities, and he was an ant compared to a king.

Kalen hadn't even properly analyzed the room yet. They had no clue where to start.

The walls glittered with gold, silver, and rubies, decorated with various reliefs and nude paintings. An enormous bed stood at the back of the room, covered with wrinkled red silks. A thick oak table in the center of the room stood surrounded by curved merlot couches draped in shining violet throws and bottles of liquor. One couch to the left was overturned. Pillows, glass bottles, pieces of clothing, and stray pastries all lay scattered around the chamber.

Oh, and the bodies.

At least a dozen unconscious bodies decorated the floors and furniture of the room. Most nude. Some bruised.

Gilles had meant the King's *company.*

Were they supposed to clean around the people? Wake them up? Kalen glanced anxiously around at what the others occupied themselves with.

To his shock, several of the heftier servants began throwing unconscious figures over their shoulders, or hauling them by the arms or legs.
This bastard just had a dozen people to fill a sex room, and then cleaned
them up with the carpet stains on the regular?

What a prick.

Sorry—Kalen corrected themself—*what a prick, His Royal Majesty.*

They shook their head to snap out of staring. *Never stand around,*
Blythe had said. *It's better to do something useless than relax.*

A pillow lay discarded on the floor near his feet. Kalen picked it up and
gingerly placed it on the nearest couch. Nobody scolded them for it, so
they moved on to the next fallen object. A few others did the same. Now
that most of the bodies had been hauled off to somewhere—hopefully
their own chambers—the bigger fellows righted furniture while others
scrubbed and tidied.

With so many servants working, it hardly took any time until the room
shone spotless. They all hurried out as quickly as they'd entered. Some
of the tension in Kalen's shoulders released. He hadn't totally screwed
this up, so maybe he could survive a little longer after all.

Unfortunately, the group turned in the direction opposite to their
quarters.

"Where are we going?" they whispered to Gilles.

The boy raised a quizzical brow. The corner of his mouth quirked into
an uneven smile. "It's the night before the first certatia. What, did you
think we'd stop for a nap?"

"No," Kalen stammered out, trying to recover. They should be used
to tough servant hours, so they should expect that they'd be working all
night before a certatia—what the Fletch called competitive events. But
hiding out in Frida's and his apartment doing piecework, even if he did

manage to secure the occasional dishwashing shift, had not accustomed him to such a schedule. "No, I just meant, like, where is it in the palace?"

"Oh." Gilles nodded with understanding, and Kalen wiped their sweaty palms on their scratchy breeches. The kid walked faster than should have been possible for his little legs. "It's the Grand Dining Hall near the center. 'Bout a half hour?"

⤜⟫⟫ ⟪⟪⤛

Every part of Kalen ached.

Their arms were filled with rocks, but they were forced to lift them again and again. Hoisting tables a few inches over, then wait, no, a few inches back. Stretching to hang flower baskets on a teetering ladder.

And scrubbing. So. Much. Scrubbing.

If only they had just a *little* laudanum to take the edge off. Everything *hurt*.

Kalen didn't even see the point. Why should they make the floors clean enough for His Royal Shitbrick to see his pompous face in them? People were just going to step everywhere and spill food. And then they'd all have to clean up again, anyway.

"Fuck you," he snarled at a particularly difficult smudge on the oak floors.

He caught a glimpse of the Superior walking past, a disapproving look on his square face. *A good servant acts as if their work is a pleasure.*

Kalen punched himself in the leg. Then he resumed scrubbing vigorously.

Eventually, even Superior didn't see how the room could be improved upon. "You may put your supplies away and return directly to the quarters."

Kalen could have kissed the man. Sharp pain struck their knees when they finally stood up, but they didn't care. He marched—albeit lopsidedly—with his scrubbing bucket. Just put this away, and they could be done.

That was when they heard it. An outcry of boisterous laughter.

All of the servants bristled, standing at attention. Heat swelled behind Kalen's eyes, and he wanted to slap them all. *Move, you assholes! Before Superior asks us to stay!*

"Pierre, glad you're still here!" cried a man's voice. He'd entered the room, while the laughter remained behind him.

Superior walked over, posture especially rigid. "Good evening, milord."

The man dressed in much frillier court attire than that of Superior, with a cascading silk cape and intricate paisley embroidery along the waistcoat. However, his dress wasn't as luxurious as that of an inner member of the royal court would have been. It mimicked what Kalen had seen in paintings of the King, but from a few years prior, not recently, and his coat was a medium violet rather than the King's traditional red.

He must have been the Cote: the minor noble who served closest to the King and waited on him. Superior's superior.

Dread washed over Kalen. That meant the man really could make them stay.

"Yes, and to you," the Cote replied briskly. He waved around to gesture loosely at the servants. "I'd like you to keep your servants around. His Majesty has decided to dine with some of his court here tonight."

"Of course, Your Lordship."

What? Why in fifty hells would the King want to dine here, *of all places*, the night before a certatia? Weren't there a million other dining halls?

A good servant doesn't ask questions about the whims of their betters.

Kalen bit down on their tongue. The blood rushed to their face, but they had to be calm. This was normal. This was what servants did.

He puked in his mouth again.

The Cote gave a fraction of a nod. He disappeared for a brief moment, then reappeared through the arched doorway across the hall. A roaring bunch of men travelled alongside him.

"And then *I* said, that's not the *princess's* hand!" They all burst out in another round of obnoxious laughter.

That was when Kalen caught a glimpse of *him*.

His brown hair flowed gracefully in curls down to his shoulders. A cape of snowy ermine furs covered the back of his crimson coat, and a sash of gold cloth adorned his chest, pinned with sterling medallions. His face had not been embellished in the paintings—it radiated more beautifully in person, such that Kalen couldn't tear their eyes away. A hard, commanding jaw, and strong, sharp nose. Rosy-pink cheeks and full lips.

Kalen should stop staring. Blythe hadn't had to tell him that a good servant didn't ogle, and the last thing he wanted to do was upset the man. They'd gotten themself into trouble that way before.

But the biceps. The gorgeous layers of velvet red and gold that highlighted his every attractive feature. The tight sculpting of fabric around his legs.

Kalen's heart squeezed more than it should have when he caught a glimpse of the royal smile.

Throat dry, mouth agape... Why was Kalen behaving like this? They surely hadn't held the King in high regard after all these hours of scrubbing and that gross cleanup in the "lounge." But looking at him almost dulled their pains.

The men sat down at seats around the long mahogany table. The King kicked up his feet, and dirt fell off his boots onto the floor.

But Kalen's anger dissipated before it properly appeared.

"You're a right good shot, Stephen." The King grinned, playfully punching one of his associates in the arm. The warm overhanging candlelight flickered. "I have to admit, I was surprised. All that time you've wasted cooped up in the library!"

Stephen flushed. "Thank you, Your Majesty."

Maybe the other dining halls were closed, Kalen found themself thinking. *Maybe he just wanted to ensure his friends ate after a hard day out. Isn't that nice?*

The cooks soon brought out several platters of meats and pastries. The King and his half-dozen men ate jovially, mostly recounting the highlights of their hunting trip.

"You," the King called, waving in Kalen's direction. They froze, then glanced to their side. Him? "Yes, you, boy," the King said impatiently, and Kalen scrambled over. He nearly tripped over his own feet.

His pulse pounded in his ears.

They *should* have been nervous because this man could execute them if something displeased him. But this weird, nagging worry that he wouldn't *like* Kalen tugged at his mind, not just the fear of punishment. Some part of them wanted to make the King happy.

"Yes, Your Majesty?" Kalen asked. Again, he rubbed his sweaty palms over his pants.

"The wine?" the King said, as if it were obvious. Oh, and it was. Of course he wanted a refill of wine—Kalen stood right next to the cart of bottles, for Lox's sake! Their entire face must have looked like a tomato.

"Of course, Your Majesty," Kalen said, quickly filling the glass. It didn't spill, thank the gods, because his hands sure shook. "My apologies."

The King let out a loud chuckle, looking up at Kalen with...bemusement?

His Majesty looked back at his friends, who snickered in turn. "Where did you learn to speak, boy?" the King asked. "See how astounding our Fletch education is? Even the servants speak like little court *bellae*."

Kalen's heart dropped.

The chorus of other men's laughter would not relent.

"Well, what say you, *traverae*?" a man with thick black curls asked, taking a large bite of a lamb shoulder. "Who in our court is giving servants oration classes?"

"I...I'm Jardaen," Kalen struggled to say, mouth completely dry. "I served under the House Albret."

He should have been fine—he was hardly new to being insulted like this—but something sharp stung. Perhaps that he already caused suspicion, merely by speaking well. Perhaps that the need for another dose of laudanum clawed at their mind. Perhaps that despite the clear bullying, the King seemed so... Kalen didn't know, but a knife hit his gut that he was merely another servant to the man.

"A Jardaen!" Stephen choked out a laugh, spitting out some of his wine. "Even richer!"

"Oh, how sweet," the King said with a faux pout, taking a rough pinch of Kalen's cheek. "Those hicks are so desperate to impress, they made their servant into a proper little choir boy."

Kalen shrank within himself. He glanced over to Gilles, hoping for some sort of rescue. But Gilles wouldn't meet his eyes. Of course, he couldn't.

Not in two years had Kalen felt so much like a child, patronized and humiliated by his father. Expected to take it and be *fucking grateful.*

"Well, go on," a gold-spangled man across the table called. "You must have had singing lessons, too, bellae."

Kalen tried to say something, anything, in protest. His mouth was a desert. "I...I..." Blythe hadn't prepared him for this.

"Go on, sing for us," the King commanded. His smile was deceptively charming, and all his friends waited with maliciously eager grins.

"I don't know how, Your Majesty," Kalen managed. And it was true. He was an awful singer. The tutors had given up on almost every musical instruction by the time he reached six—only the harp had any hope, but his father shut that down as too "delicate."

The King's smile vanished in an instant. He stood, towering over Kalen with his imposing frame.

It happened so quick. Kalen didn't even see the slap coming.

The back of the royal hand struck his face and sent him to the floor. Pain burst throughout Kalen's head. He hated himself for the whimper that escaped him.

He couldn't do this.

Not again.

Another rule floated into his head: *When you are struck, remain on the ground until instructed otherwise. Let them know how powerful they are.* Not one of Blythe's.

Water leaked from his eyes, and blood wetted his cheek. But Kalen remained a statue, not daring to budge a muscle.

"You dare refuse your King?"

Kalen's mind swirled. *Answer questions quickly. Don't keep them waiting.* "No... Sorry, Your Majesty."

The King loomed over him for an agonizing three seconds longer. "Get the fuck up and sing, then."

9.

62 Printes, Reg. Marii 6

B lythe reached her chambers with the Viper by her side. Saidh had been positioned in the rooms next door, close by, as her guardian and diplomatic representative should be.

"You must remain in these chambers until you are escorted to the First Event," the guards instructed at the door. They had not met her eyes the entire journey. In fact, they'd fixed decisively on the ground. "The King will determine who is fit to be seen by the court after the Introduction Ceremony."

"Thank you, protigii," Blythe said in her best Fletch accent. She kept her back straight and her nose an appropriate amount in the air. "I bid you good evening."

"Good evening, Your Ladyship," they each said with a bow.

She then realized they had no plans to leave.

"Come, Lisette," Blythe said to the Viper. She couldn't be seen shrinking to her lady-in-waiting. "Let us retire."

"Yes, Your Ladyship." The Viper tucked her head obediently and opened the large oak doors.

Blythe entered first, and then the doors thudded behind the Viper. The obedient demeanor vanished as quickly as it had appeared.

"How many times?" the Viper demanded. She rolled her eyes and fell gracefully onto a small velvet couch near the entrance. "Just because you're a noble doesn't mean you stop using contractions. '*Let's.*'"

"Sorry," Blythe mumbled. They'd barely arrived, and she'd already fucked up. She had to do better. Too much teetered on the line.

She blundered further into the enormous chambers.

This entryway alone expanded bigger than the apartment she'd shared with Papa. Pink carpet covered the floors, and more pastels and florals decorated the walls than she'd ever seen. Several oil paintings hung from walnut-brown frames, with imagery of forest nymphs painted in all of their nude detail. Blythe flushed and averted her eyes. The furniture wasn't any less busy: boldly colored chairs, couches, and footrests, along with wooden nightstands and a matching vanity plated with gold and silver ornamentation. The bed extended wide enough for several people and was filled to the brim with fluffy pillows and silk blankets.

A lump formed in her throat. This was only the main room.

The Viper had informed her on the ship that there would be an adjacent bathroom, eating area, and dressing room. Sure enough, there was a corner to be turned. But Blythe couldn't deal with the overwhelm of another loud room like this.

Hefting her heavy skirts up, she hoisted herself onto the wingback chair across from the Viper. It had only been about a forty-minute walk, but the cumbersome outfit still drained the life out of her. That, and she'd spent weeks drilling for this role, scarcely sleeping. Blythe anxiously clicked her knuckles together.

"We'll have to fit you for the palace style tonight," the Viper said and gestured down the corridor. "My chambers should have been equipped with the right materials."

The Viper's chambers lurked down that little hall? It did make sense to have her adjoined, as a lady-in-waiting was probably needed most hours of the day.

But still. It was unsettling.

"I don't see what's wrong with the costumes we made," Blythe said. They looked the same as all the other dresses she'd seen walking around. A meter wide at the skirt, the floor-length robe a silky combination of embroidered motifs and sewn-in jewels she couldn't count, fixed over several petticoats and a bow-decorated stomacher.

"I'm not going over this again."

"Fine," Blythe huffed. *Who am I to have an attitude?* The Viper knew much more about all of this, and it would be heinous to begrudge her help. They wouldn't be here at all if it weren't for Blythe's mistakes. A splash of ice water would do her some good. "Sorry, I just thought we'd save time. You're right."

"Just hold still for once. It's late."

They walked over to the Viper's chambers, similarly decorated, though one corner housed immense wardrobes, each filled with all shades of fabric and innumerable accessories. The Jardaens must have paid for it in advance, or perhaps it was a gift from the King to the delegates.

"I said *hold still*," the Viper ordered, after "accidentally" drawing blood with a pin.

Blythe tried so hard to grit her teeth and bear it. But every time she managed to stand still, something or another itched terribly.

She let her thoughts wander in the hopes of a distraction, staring down at the swirling marble floors of the wardrobe area. Sometimes she could do that, make her body feel further away.

All she could think of at this moment was Kalen and Frida. Had they settled in alright?

Frida could certainly make a spot for herself among the cooks—she was talented and made friends as easily as she made soup. When they'd first met working on the walls six or so years ago, Frida had only just come to Ostrait and spoke barely a lick of the language, yet she'd gotten every half-starved, exhausted worker humming along to the same jaunty rhyme within her first week. It had been Blythe's first real sense of camaraderie, even if things had changed once the job ended how it did. Frida could last here, and being under Esme's jurisdiction, she was safe from corporal punishments.

Blythe's heart ached most to talk to Kalen. What if their lessons weren't enough? Kalen always did his best, but... Gods, she wished she could have taken their place. They'd risked everything to help her, and she'd never even fully explained what a lost cause she was. He shouldn't be in this much danger for her, even if they claimed they wanted the payout. And the state they'd been in...

Knowing her had doomed them, but now she remained their only hope.

If only she could see him. At some point, they'd become inseparable, and Blythe suffered his distance like she would the loss of her right hand.

It hadn't occurred to her just how hard it would become to reach them, all the way across the palace. She couldn't even ensure their safety; "Esme" had transferred his indenture to the Fletch King as the required gift, and nobody had to report back to her on his status. Only if he divulged their origins would anyone likely concern her with them again. Kalen was on their own for survival.

But she didn't want them to be.

Wasn't there any way Blythe could help? They'd be sleeping on the floor somewhere while she rested in this ludicrously lush bedroom, not even doing anything useful.

But all she could do was make this mission worth it. Even if she had to stand still as a statue.

"Done," the Viper said after some hours, taking the last pins out of the last gown.

Blythe stepped down from the little dressing platform, briefly shaking out her stiff limbs. She turned around so that the girl could untie her from her skirts. It was ridiculous that half of these dresses could barely be taken off by one person.

"Thanks," Blythe said without thinking.

The Viper looked almost uncomfortable, shifting on her feet. "You can return to your chambers and sleep." Then, seemingly as an after-thought, she added, "Gods know you'll need all the help you can get tomorrow."

Blythe did return to her chambers, but she didn't plan on staying.

Despite the Viper's show of power, she had to be as human as the rest of them. So it stood to reason that she would also be incredibly exhausted. And since they couldn't do anything until the certatia, why would she bother to stay awake? Blythe just had to wait long enough for the girl to fall asleep, and then she would slink past.

The dishonesty made her hesitate, but Blythe hadn't *agreed* to go to sleep. And if she could get some information, that would help the Viper, too, in the long run, wouldn't it?

Maybe she should just get into bed.

Blythe let the remaining skirts fall to the floor and crawled into the high bed to— *Oh, gods*. Blythe actually moaned when she lay down.

What fucking god crafted this—this— It was so *soft*. Blythe's body sank into the bed, cool silks falling over her skin.

Papa is not this comfortable right now. Neither is Kalen.

If Blythe aimed to find the good choice, staying comfortably in this bed certainly wasn't it. She waited long enough for the Viper to fall asleep. The girl snored, surprisingly, which helped.

Creeping out of bed without a sound, Blythe glued herself to the edges of the walls. She made her way to the Viper's chambers and peered inside.

The girl sprawled on her own bed, asleep. She looked remarkably different, lying there like that. It was the most vulnerable that Blythe had ever seen her, though getting close would almost certainly mean getting stabbed. The girl's brows furrowed in her slumber, mouth dipped into a frown, as if she were a child having a nightmare.

Blythe forced herself to move on to the dressing area. Weaving silently through the different clothes, she found the cheapest, darkest-looking garments she could—just one simple pair of breeches and a thicker shift that could hopefully pass for a servant's shirt.

After throwing them on, she analyzed her appearance in the large mirror. It wasn't nearly perfect. Closer to someone playing dress-up as a servant boy. And there was still the matter of her hair. She needed something to tuck it away in.

A navy cap, flat and unassuming if she plucked out the feather, rested high on a wooden shelf. Blythe stretched to the top of her toes to reach it. Her fingers just barely skimmed it.

Come on. Just a little more. She stepped up on one of the bottom cubbies. Finally, the hat came free!

"Oh, fuck."

The shelf teetered forward.

All sorts of items flew free and crashed onto the floor, even as she struggled to push the shelf back up. No carpet softened the sounds, and the metal buckles and ornaments clacked onto the tile.

Blythe let out a shaky breath when the shelf stood still again. Swallowing, she looked behind her.

"Are you out of your *mind*?" The Viper grasped her by the shirt. "Did you really think you could sneak out in that ridiculous ensemble and not draw notice? We can't even have a *whiff* of suspicion, and you want to parade around like a theatre troupe?"

"My bestowment," Blythe tried to explain. She shrank away from the Viper's grip. "I've gotten away with worse disguises."

"What part of 'remain in your chambers' is hard to understand?"

Blythe tried to appeal to the Viper's concern for the mission. "I can get information about those in attendance, help us to get ahead."

The Viper rolled her eyes.

Blythe awoke back in her bed.

⟫⟫⟩ ⟨⟨⟨⟨

"Apologies for the inconvenience," the Viper said languidly, lounging on one of the velvet couches and taking a delicate bite of a powdered doughnut. "But you do realize you'd have died, right? I thought we gave you this deal for your brains."

Blythe hated to admit it, but the girl was right. She'd made the wrong choice.

Everyone in the palace would be on high alert, and combined with her truly shitty disguise... She had a talent for staying hidden, not godlike powers of invisibility. Her guilt about Kalen had clouded her judgment, and she unfortunately had the Viper to thank that the mission, the *deal*, wasn't blown.

"I don't think the dart was necessary." Blythe's legs prickled with semi-numbness, but it was her own fault. She shouldn't complain.

"Do I look like someone about to take chances on a flight risk?"

"How much time has passed?"

"Only a few minutes." The Viper tilted her head, amusement playing on her face. "It only should have made you drowsy, but then, apparently you were awake plotting ways to alert Fletch officials about us."

Anxiety twisted in her chest. "And I have to lie here for the next six hours?"

She tried not to let it show, but anticipation of the certatia crept up on her. How could she wade through this enormous palace and convince these people she was born as shiny as the rest of them?

"There are quite a few enjoyable activities one can partake in on their back."

Blythe's eyes bulged. "What?" she choked out.

The Viper actually laughed. "I just mean, you look stressed." The girl stood from her chair and started toward her own chambers. She turned back, raising an eyebrow. "It won't do for court. Maybe take some time to...get rid of that perpetual scrunch between your eyes."

Blythe could only blink as the Viper disappeared around the corner.

The door thudded shut behind her.

Blythe cast a furtive glance at those paintings. *Unacceptable. Licentious.*

Sleep, on the other hand, was a need she couldn't dismiss. Her body sank into the soft bed, and a fog overtook her mind the second her eyes fell closed.

⤜⤜⤜   ⤛⤛⤛

An eternity later, the Viper yanked Blythe's stays much tighter than normal. Probably out of spite for the escape attempt. But what might have been discomfort instead grounded her. The fabric squeezed her anxieties down, holding her together.

She focused on maintaining a less-transparent expression, un-scrunching her face. *It's just a couple hours*, she reminded herself. That was how she had to think of it. Not weeks of deception and trials. Only this one dinner. It could be compartmentalized, and she could tackle the next challenges when they arose.

She imagined Papa happily sitting with his feet in the water of his own cottage pond. He'd have round cheeks and a thicker coat than he needed. He'd take a breath of fresh air without wheezing and excitedly reel in his fifth fish of the day. With their debt cleared, she'd do all the penance in the world to ensure the gods allowed him comfort.

A loud knock rumbled the door.

But first, dinner with the Fletch King.

"Are you ready, Your Ladyship?" asked Saidh, extending an arm.

"Of course."

The journey to the dining hall blurred by as Blythe concentrated on maintaining a pleasant expression. That sort of thing easily slipped her notice, especially when her heart actively prepared to explode.

The Viper and Saidh had to abandon her at the doors.

"Your seat, Your Ladyship." A Fletch servant pulled out Blythe's chair and gestured for her to sit down at the table.

Royal chatter bustled around them, some of the other guests having already arrived from more countries than she could name. They formed a sea of rich colors. Complicated musical harmonies drifted all around her, with so many instruments and minstrels that she couldn't tell what was violin or harp or flute or clavichord, intense compared to the simple pipe or drum music from home. Acrobats casually performed from the ceiling at one end of the immense room, with ballet dancers kicking underneath them. White sunlight shone from a large window in the ceiling, mingling with the warm orange candles and torches, which glinted off the vast array of silverware set beside each plate.

"Thank you," Blythe said with a small smile, taking her seat.

The servant's eyes remained on the floor, but they widened in brief surprise. He blushed. "Such Jardaen generosity. It is a sincere honor, Your Ladyship."

Oh. Shit. How many times had she been told not to thank the staff? But Papa would have been disappointed if she didn't. "That will be all," Blythe said, aiming for the haughty tone that all these nobles carried.

The boy shuffled away, leaving Blythe to take in her surroundings. Nobody sat directly in front of or beside her, but toward the other end of the table, two groups of nobles exchanged pleasantries. Ashlans, marked by their oceanic aesthetic of straight buttoned coats overtop white shirts called doublets, and Barcans in vibrant robes of pinks and purples, with thick orange or gold sashes tied at the waist.

There were a few in each group. All the other countries were big enough and stable enough to have multiple candidates, or else they grouped together in a coalition like the Telu Confederacy, so right off the bat "Esme" stuck out as a loner.

It didn't help that the table was so giant, or that its ninety seats were half-empty. She caught glances from others. *Can they already see right through me?* Anything could give her away. Was her posture correct? Was she supposed to join them, even though the servant had told her to sit here? Had they gotten her hair wrong, and now she'd be called out as a fraud?

And where was Kalen? A million servants swarmed here, but without his tufts of sandy hair poking out in the crowd, she couldn't spot him.

Oh gods, there were five forks on her serviette. Which one to use? They'd had three on the ship.

Blythe bounced her leg anxiously, as subtly as she could.

An insane relief hit her when the rest of the guests shuffled in and the food started to be set out. Eventually all of the candidates filled their seats, and only the King's at the head of the table was empty.

Why did he have to create this ridiculous competition in the first place?

Still, Blythe wanted to ask when he would arrive, because the anticipation was torture. Based on this first certatia, the King would immediately eliminate any candidates he found too repulsive to consider. After that, the Eunic Council—which seemed to serve as the only real limit to the King's power, able to veto budgets and exercise individual authorities over the divine cults—would extend some influence. Saidh said the Eunics would want to keep a semblance of order to the competition, base it on actual certatian performances, for "diplomatic" reasons. Tonight, though...

She could be gone on a whim. If her green-brown eyes were too muddy, or if he didn't like the way she pronounced a word.

All the more reason she needed to blend in seamlessly. Be likeable.

But correctly starting a conversation with any of these people proved impossible. Maybe her imperfect Fletch accent would prove lucky—they might assume her mistakes were part of a cultural barrier.

Suddenly, the music picked up in intensity, and the chatter died.

Everyone faced the grand doorway as the King stepped through, clothed in deep red and adorned with a cape of shining silver furs. He strode in with a confidence that only a monarch could possess, a lax smile on his youthful face.

He couldn't have been more than twenty-five. He had an athletic frame and square jawline, with waves of light-brown hair rolling down to his shoulders. He was handsome. Like those monarchs from fantastical realms in storybooks. *Maybe this whole candidate thing won't be so bad.*

Blood rushed to Blythe's cheeks as he briefly made eye contact with her, and she immediately looked away. They had to rob this palace, and she couldn't forget that for a pretty face.

Trumpets sounded, and the rest of the music stopped. A voice boomed from near the King. "Announcing His Royal Majesty, King Marius of the Fletch Empire, the son of King Cleatus and Queen Tricia, heir to the throne and all its rightful lands..." The introduction went on for some time.

Blythe's ears perked up when they finally mentioned the candidates, and she straightened in her seat. "His Majesty will first dine with all candidates. Following the meal, he shall share brief introductions with each before the festivities begin."

What was she supposed to *do* during these introductions? The lack of information could lead her into fatal mistakes. But at least she could get closer to King Marius...

What was *wrong* with her? He directly threatened everything she cared about, and she couldn't afford to stray.

Come to think of it, everyone's eyes were fixed on him and his dazzling smile. She'd heard he was charming, so perhaps she shouldn't have been surprised. And all of these royals likely worshiped the ground he walked on as their King, or aspiring in-law. *And who knows, maybe he's not a total asshole.* Blythe swiftly corrected herself. *Maybe he has a good reason for sitting in jewels while common folk starve? Unlikely.*

Servants followed the King and seated him at the head of the table, overlooking all the candidates.

Blythe resisted the urge to shrink herself down. She forced her leg to stop bouncing.

Once they were meant to eat, she surreptitiously examined the others' movements. What forks they used for what. She was desperate to remember her lessons. *Position the knife and fork together when cutting...*

They didn't even have cutlery at home. Not since she was nine or ten. They'd pawned it to pay Mama's healing-debt, like everything else after she died.

How could these people eat a giant feast like this? How could *she*?

"Lady Esme," a voice beside her interrupted her thoughts. She turned to face the man, one of a few Fletch candidates by the looks of the red crest pinned to his robes. Humor laced his tone when he spoke. "Is the King's Feast not to your refined Jardaen tastes?"

It was a joke. He was making fun of her.

Because Jardae was a small coastal country where seafood was the staple across classes. The Viper had briefed her that the upper class in Fletch ate unhealthy amounts of luxury meats, cheeses, and confections. That she would *have* to partake.

Her ears burned. "My Lord," she responded without a smile, hoping she'd used the right title. She summoned all the Viper's airiness into her voice. "Should one's tastes ever be so...uncontrolled that we forget our thanks to the deities?"

Praising herself for the quick reply, Blythe took a bite of lamb.

"Perhaps we should all pray that the gods grant you some grace," he said, glancing pointedly at her fork before turning to some others and laughing.

Blythe cursed under her breath. Where exactly had she gone wrong?

⤞⤞⤞ ⤝⤝⤝

"The Fletch court may now present to His Majesty, King Marius," the announcer from earlier proclaimed, overlooking the assembly of candidates and their delegations.

Blythe watched intently.

Saidh now stood at her side, but he remained stiff and kept his eyes on the announcer, jotting down notes on a pad of parchment. He had "to present her and take notes for Jardae's records" was all he'd been able to say.

Clutching at her skirts, Blythe wished she had Kalen's hand to hold instead. The music continued to pound in her ears, like her heart in her throat.

The Fletch candidates lined up in a row, same as every delegation from the foreign countries, but now their escort spoke loudly, eyes on the King. "First presenting Her Ladyship, Eleanore of the Eastern Province."

Thankfully they didn't go on with so many titles this time around. It would be impossible to remember them all, anyway.

Eleanore walked gracefully toward the King's throne and made a deep curtsy in her rose-colored dress, head bowed. "It is my humblest honor, Your Highness," she said, her voice soft and delicate. Most girls back home waited until nineteen to marry, but she looked seventeen at the most, with dark-brown skin and eyes round with innocence.

"Rise." The King nodded to her. The girl straightened and hesitantly met his eyes. Blythe's stomach turned at the way the King analyzed Eleanore's figure, his eyes lingering at the small breasts that her stays pushed up. A few moments later, he said, "Accepted."

She went back to her line, chin again tucked down, hand shaking subtly on her skirts.

"Presenting His Lordship, Ernst of the Southern Province," the Fletch escort said, and a young man made his way to the King.

Again, the King's eyes raked over the candidate as if he were deciding whether a selection of meat was of good quality. "Dismissed."

Blythe could scarcely call these introductions. The creeping, scrutinizing gaze of this king already intimidated her as she stood uncomfortably in this huge floral dress, suddenly grateful that her neckerchief covered any cleavage.

And yet, she wondered, *What will he think?*

She gave a worried look to Saidh, but he could only offer a reassuring nod and a twitch of a smile.

He straightened up at their turn and spoke clearly. "Presenting Her Ladyship, Esme of Jardae."

Her cue. Blythe took a sharp breath and began her walk to the King, eyes trained on the ground like the others. Was her posture okay? Were her strides measured enough?

"Rise," the King said in his superior tone.

Fear shook her legs as she obeyed. Surely, he'd recognize her peasantry at any moment, and he'd have her killed.

His eyes shone with haughty amusement, and Blythe struggled not to squirm as he seemed to strip her naked in his mind. But playing the dutiful candidate that desperately needed the Fletch's alliance, what could she do?

And somehow the thought of offending him was unwelcome.

"Accepted."

Blythe nearly let out a sigh of relief as she returned to her position beside Saidh. His jaw was set, and he looked forward. The next candidate was called.

At least she hadn't gotten them expelled from court—yet.

⟶⟫ ⟪⟵

The "festivities" after the King had finished assessing everyone consisted of a new cacophony of music, heaps of food offered by the servants, and mingling between the candidates, many of whom simply attempted to edge their way into a conversation with the King.

Blythe was wholly lost. She definitely didn't intend to clamor after the King. Despite that nagging curiosity.

But squeezing her way into one of the circles of conversation presented an equally daunting task. Her feet ached, and she just longed to be home cooking a terrible cabbage soup for Papa. Or tinkering on the cement floor with some new type of lock while Kalen worked beside her on his embroidery. Even scooping horse manure out of some merchant's stables or washing soiled sheets at the inn for barely half a coin.

Anywhere but this nightmare.

"Evening, Lady Esme." A small voice appeared beside her, and she jumped slightly before recognizing Eleanore.

"How d'you do?"

"Oh— Uh, well, thank you." The girl looked over at the King, then back to Blythe. "You're also nervous to approach him?" she asked quietly.

Blythe shook her head before she thought better of it. Eleanore furrowed her brow and gave a confused head tilt.

"No, sorry, I just mean that..." Blythe fumbled for the right thing to say. "I have doubts that I'd be chosen at all, in competition with such...esteemed nobility."

Some strange bubble of insecurity had taken root in her. All the delegates here looked and sounded, well, *regal*. She looked like a kid in a patchwork costume. The King might still throw her out for being ugly.

"Oh, yes, I quite understand!" The girl nodded quickly and offered Blythe a sympathetic smile. "Even with my family in such good royal standing, I'm unsure how I'd be chosen against a strong ally nation, such as Lastray. And, of course, the Barcans have sent their most stunning delegates. And those, Ki'la are they called? Not exactly courtiers, but they're surely fascinating."

Ka'lani, Blythe withheld from correcting.

Truth be told, the chatter of the noble girl was welcome. It gave her some sort of purpose standing in the giant ballroom, allowing her to pick up on some cues she'd been unsure about. More than that, perhaps the girl would reveal some sort of information in her friendliness. She was Fletch, so perhaps she knew something more about the palace that could help them plan their heist.

Was it wrong to use her like that?

"And can you come to believe the boldness?" the girl whispered, gesturing vaguely to a group of Barcans and Ashlans. "To call a royal certatia such as this a waste? By the gods, it's only a month as it is, three weeks if you don't count the wedding celebrations. Surely the war won't have turned much for the worse by then."

Oh yes, the Barcans and Ashlans already warred with Ostrait. The fight had gotten too big for them, hence the need to marry King Marius and get some military aid. The Telu Confederacy was in a similar situation, defending from Ostrait's latest expansion.

"I'm sure their words will come to hurt them," Blythe assured.

Eleanore nodded, lips pursed. "I should hope so. A connection to one of those kingdoms would be a drain on our military, and likely the royal purse."

One of those *kingdoms?* Esme had snuck to this palace to get Jardae out from under Ostrait's thumb—albeit, to get back under the arm of the Fletch, though their rule would likely be less iron-fisted.

The Jardaen rebels only made the Ostraitian government crack down harder on the rest of their people. Papa used to say that the "Annexers" sought trouble and that Ostrait would never cede such a vital territory. They'd won it fair and square in the last war. *Look at me now, Papa. On the precipice of starting another war.*

It was way too loud in here.

"Not Jardae, of course," Eleanore continued in a rushed, apologetic tone.

Blythe tried to fix her face, which had probably soured.

"You've so much beautiful land, and what would we do without our silver fox pelts?"

Blythe indulged the girl's nervous laugh, smiling along. Eleanore was clumsy but relatively harmless, and it didn't hurt to have an ally.

"Gods, aren't they *divine*?" Blythe replied, mustering up as much enthusiasm as she could.

Eleanore resumed her excitable talk. Blythe struggled to listen with music, the other groups' chatter, clinking glasses, and every other noise ringing in her ears.

Her costume, which she'd finally nearly forgotten about, suddenly became cruelly uncomfortable again. Blythe dug her nails into her palms, trying not to fidget with the fabric that wouldn't rest properly on her skin. Was she sweating? The makeup, piled inches thick, was sticky with the mild heat of the ballroom.

"That sounds lovely," she murmured back to Eleanore, absent-mindedly.

"Doesn't it?" the girl squealed.

A long night ahead.

A mild punishment to bear for her sins. She would survive it.

But would Kalen?

10.

B lythe's mind ached. Half past one, and the evening was only starting to wrap up. The King had left with some noble delegates.
Those who remained were largely tipsy, some speaking loud goodbyes
while others continued to mingle.

"And then this mongoose runs straight into the royal baths!" A surge
of obnoxious laughter erupted from a nearby circle of nobles, and Blythe
couldn't help but grimace.

Her eyes searched the room for the Viper. She just wanted to be
alone, in her own space, wearing a comfortable pair of breeches, with
strawberries harvested from her little garden. It would rot away now.

Surely it had been long enough she could at least sequester in her new
chambers?

Stop thinking about yourself. She shouldn't be wanting anything.
Wanting was a vice, and she couldn't add any more to the growing list.

"Is something troubling you, my good Lady Esme?" slurred Arash, a
Lastrian in the small circle she'd managed to squirm into. They drained

their goblet of wine and replaced it with another off a servant's round tray.

"Come now." A Fletch noble chuckled, clapping Arash on the back, then doing the same to Blythe. "Of course you're troubled! The blasted help hasn't given you so much as a glass!"

"Oh no, I couldn't," she stammered out with a polite smile. Her eyes darted quickly around again, in search of an escape. "Really, I'm fine. Actually, I'm quite tired from the journey still, I should probably be going—"

"Nonsense! You must... Here." The nobleman swiped a flute of some sparkling pink liquid off a servant's tray and thrust it into her hands. "It's a cultural delicacy, you know."

"Ah, thank you, really." She had to keep her head, but she couldn't offend the man either. "But I'm afraid it is a Jardaen holy month of, er, abstinence." She handed him back the flute with an apologetic smile and finally found the Viper across the room. The irony of that relief didn't escape her. "Oh, there is my lady-in-waiting. I must away for some important...business with her. Please, do enjoy it on my behalf."

"Do Jardaens even have their own holy months?" Arash mumbled behind her.

Blythe let out a sigh when she reached her lady-in-waiting and pulled her aside, tearing her from quite the amicable conversation with a group of ladies, by the looks of it. "Oh, Lisette, dear, I hate to cut our night short, but I'm afraid I feel a spell of faint."

They turned the first corner, out of earshot of the partying drunks.

The Viper rolled her eyes. She lowered her bitter voice to Blythe's ear. "You're gonna have to survive more than one night, you know."

Blythe whispered back, "We need to start figuring out where the vault is, don't we?" It was a solid excuse, even if not the truth.

"Well, when you put it in those terms..." The girl shrugged and discarded her glass beside a statuette. She spoke at a normal volume again. "As you wish. Let's retire, Your Ladyship."

"That doesn't look like the same dress you were wearing," Blythe noted as they walked out the doors. Far more lace and decorations were visible on this gown. Even the hat appeared to have gained a few flowers. When had the Viper found time to change it? Blythe had seen her there throughout the festivities.

The Viper waved her off. "It didn't fit properly anyway."

They wandered down the halls, voices once again hushed. The Viper leaned in a little when they had to whisper, as if she couldn't quite catch everything. The girl recounted a few stray pieces of information she'd learned from gossiping nobles, and Blythe shared what little she'd gained from Eleanore.

It was an oddly relaxed exchange.

"I'm fairly sure he headed to his chambers down here," the Viper said. She'd wisely suggested they stalk King Marius in the hopes of gaining some information. They hadn't found his chambers yet, but she insisted they should be down this hall.

"Don't you think it's a little..." Blythe trailed off as they approached a door left ajar, the King's rowdy voice standing out among others. "Oh."

Flattened against the shadowed wall beside the door, the two listened in.

"The desperation of some of them!" the King exclaimed with a hearty laugh. Blythe peered through the crack between the door and the wall. "Though perhaps it means they will be eager to please in *other* ways, as well."

"I daresay, it's a wonder they've not already disrobed for the court!" More laughing. Several men, all Fletch by the looks of it and presumably the highest of nobles, were sprawled across the U-shaped velvet couch with *His Majesty* so casually. A fireplace crackled with flame behind them, built with the same dark-brown wood as the walls and decorated with gold and statuary just the same as well.

"Perhaps you'll let some stay as *royal pleasures*, Your Majesty?" a noble asked, rather hopefully.

The King took a large sip of his wine, seeming to consider. "There are some lovely faces I'd hate to see go." The man grinned. Nervous-looking servants replenished the trays of fancy hors d'oeuvres and confections. "And it's not as if the lesser kingdoms are in much position to refuse."

Lesser Kingdoms? Likely a whole host of nations, from Jardae to Nai'ma to the Ka'lani. Blythe's breath hitched. The King's gaze on her while *clothed* felt violating enough, as if it had robbed her of something. She couldn't bear for him to see her exposed. They wouldn't start demanding things until after he had chosen, right? They wouldn't invite people to become consorts until then? By that time, her crew would have enacted the heist and would be getting out of there.

She would bear whatever price she had to for her misdeeds, anything to get Papa, Frida, and Kalen safe. But seduction wasn't something she was capable of. And she couldn't anger the gods further with discarded chastity.

But there she went again. Thinking of herself.

The crowd of nobles surrounding King Marius didn't look nauseated at all. Rather, they stared, captivated. Charmed.

"Of course, they'd probably rejoice," another nobleman supplied. He took a large bite of a jelly-filled pastry. "Escape from such squalor that they've got to rely on foreign servants."

Rude. Those were Esme's foreign servants they jibed at. If Jardae was their lost colony, shouldn't they bother with a *little* sympathy?

"And who wouldn't be begging for his royal cock?" Another man jostled beside Marius, who punched his arm as the nobles all roared with laughter.

"Ai, you'd know all about that, wouldn't you, Quinte?"

"Oh, fuck off, Remy."

"We all serve Your Royal Majesty," said another man. Then he made a crude gesture, while the rest spit out wine, howling.

King Marius beamed, taking a rough squeeze inside Quinte's legs. It boggled Blythe, because she'd never seen men—the masculine, high-status kind, like these—so much as *tolerate* being considered passive parties, let alone take near pride in it. There must be something different about addressing a king, recognizing his ultimate power.

"And you'll all get the best chance to show me that *loyalty*." King Marius took a large swig of wine and triumphantly smacked Quinte's thigh, earning another roar of audacious laughter. "The second certatia is sure to weed out some of the lesser kingdoms, anyhow." He gestured impatiently at a servant, who scuttled over to refill his glass.

Blythe pressed closer to the door.

They needed to know what this certatia was. Blythe had to prepare, or in all likelihood, she'd blow their cover. She suppressed the rising vomit, more than just bile now, with her stomach full enough to bloat for the first time in her life.

"Yes, a valiant choice of competition, Your Majesty!" one noble responded, nodding vigorously, his speech slurred. "It will certainly embarrass those deceitful whores—"

Voices echoed down the hall.

About to round the corner.

Cursing under her breath, Blythe tugged the Viper from the wall with a quick signal to warn her. With nowhere to hide on such short notice, Blythe and her lady-in-waiting smoothed out their skirts.

Feigning nonchalance, they ambled away from the door.

Ideally, they would have been out of sight by the time the Fletch guards turned into the corridor, but no such luck.

"You, there!"

Blythe and the Viper stopped. They turned around as if innocently surprised, while terror spiked the hairs on the back of Blythe's neck.

A brawny figure in a mix of crimson cloth and shining silver metal called out to them.

A taller and heftier man stood by his side.

"What are you doing in this wing?" the guard inquired, his voice gravelly. He muttered lowly to the other guard, "I thought all these foreign delegates were informed to stay away from the King's Quarters unless invited?"

The man shrugged his broad shoulders. "We sent out the memo."

"I'm so sorry," Blythe blurted, doing an excellent job of remaining inconspicuous. At the last minute, she twisted her tone into something she hoped was airy enough. "My lady and I are just looking for some fresh air, dear protigii. You do know how heated the ballroom can get. Perhaps you'd be able to, ehm, direct us?"

Sweat creased her brow in the eternal seconds that followed. *Come on. Just buy it. I'm just a stupid noble girl drunk from the party.*

"To the gardens, which are just outside the ballroom?" the guard asked in a flat tone, gesturing down the way Blythe and the Viper had originally come.

Blythe's heartbeat quickened. They'd catch her in the lie and have her whole crew investigated as spies. Of course, they'd be executed, then the

Fletch would declare war on Ostrait, and Papa would be killed for her failure.

"They are?" The Viper put on a false giggle. Blythe's eyes widened, but she refrained from looking over at the Viper, whose very demeanor had transformed. The girl moved her body loosely and touched the brawny guard on the arm. She leaned in as if letting the man in on a secret, batting her lashes. "To tell you the truth, we might be a *taaaad* tipsy."

Blythe realized the plan. She forcefully relaxed her face and posture, letting an easy and semi-bashful smile work its way onto her face. She hoped. "Really, we didn't mean any trouble. But that Fletch drink—what's it called, the pink one? It's like nothing I've ever tasted!"

The burly man glanced at the Viper's hand snaking up his arm and, blessedly, satisfied himself with the lie. "Perhaps some rest would do you good then, Lady Esme," the man suggested and nudged his partner in the side. "Why don't you accompany Lady Esme and ensure she arrives safely at her chambers." He scratched the back of his head. "I can escort your lady-in-waiting if she's no longer required?" Escort her where, the man didn't bother to specify.

Blythe glanced at the Viper, who nodded. The girl laughed again and put on a flirtatious tone, fawning over the man. "I really would appreciate the protection," she said, giving a little pout. "The castle seems ever so much bigger at night."

The guard straightened out his shoulders. "I would be honored to help you feel secure, milady," the man said, eyes flicking back over to Blythe. "That is, with your permission, Lady Esme?"

The Viper nodded at her again, discreetly.

Putting on the face of a tired, slightly tipsy, and over-pampered noble, Blythe waved her off with a gloved hand. "Yes, yes," she agreed. "I won't need her again until the morning."

Good, the Viper mouthed.

She had no doubt the girl could handle herself. She only hoped the guard could say the same.

Blythe walked, however reluctantly, beside the other guard, casting a fleeting look back at the doorway to the King's lounge. Time was ticking until the second certatia, and she didn't know if she'd catch him talking about it again.

If she couldn't prepare, was her failure all but guaranteed?

⤜⤛

"Fuck. *Off!*" Blythe whisper-screamed at the stupid knots at her back that would not come undone. She made a lashing attempt to rip them off, but the cords only burned her hands.

Alone in her chambers, the tears finally welled in her eyes.

"Please just come off," she whimpered, overstimulated beyond control and tugging uselessly at the knots. Hammers smashed in her aching head, and her skin crawled from the horrible, numerous fabrics that enshrouded her.

It hurt. A near panic swelled in her chest as she struggled with the garment. If she couldn't get these skirts off *now*, she would combust.

"Fuck!" She pounded her fist into the wall. Water poured from her eyes as she shook her hand. She just needed some help. She was overreacting like a stupid byjeka.

The overwhelming night crashed around her.

Every horrible thought and fear spun around in her mind.

When she couldn't take it anymore, she snatched a pair of scissors, not caring where she cut as she freed herself from all the fluffy, shiny garments that suffocated her.

Finally able to breathe, she collapsed onto her new bed in a naked heap.

~»»⫸ ⫷«««~

Streams of sunlight fell onto Blythe's immense puffy white bed. She groaned, pressing her eyes further shut. The back of her head squeezed into a tight ball of ouch.

Loud knocks on the door pierced her ears.

"Lady Esme?" a treble voice called from outside. "We've come to serve Your Ladyship breakfast and draw a mint bath, should you require?"

Oh, shit.

Blythe scrambled up from the bed, frantically searching for a dressing gown. Anything to cover her still-naked body that had been lying exposed on the bed.

"Just a minute!" she called back, throwing her shift back over her. Searching the racks of the wardrobe, she mercifully came across a powder-white dressing robe.

Catching a glimpse of herself in the mirror, Blythe recoiled. All of that smeared makeup and her disarrayed hair had her looking like a circus guiser. She wiped roughly at her face with a towel and made a pitiful attempt to smooth down her hair. Well, maybe they'd assume she was out partying late last night with the rest of them.

"Come in," she said, once seated properly on the gigantic bed.

Five servant girls rushed in, each with two trays in her arms. They placed the trays around her on the bed, and a sixth girl rolled in a metal cart with various platters atop it. *Holy shit...*

Blythe swallowed, trying not to look so astonished. "Than—" She stopped herself before being too polite this time. "You are dismissed," she said instead, cringing internally for it.

Five of the girls nodded, but the one in front spoke. "Do you not wish for a bath to be drawn, Your Ladyship?"

Blythe couldn't tell if they'd insulted her or not. She didn't think she smelled great, but they were too far away to tell.

Oh, but the female candidates *were* supposed to spend a lot of their time in between certatiae taking cool mint baths, to "calm their naturally hot humors and lustful impulses," which could be aggravated by too much stimulation. Her friends had decreed that a load of Fletch nonsense. Blythe was inclined to agree. But it did allow them all more downtime to scheme.

After a moment's hesitation, she said, "That would be lovely."

It slipped her memory, though it shouldn't have, that they would want to do the initial cleaning for her. Blythe's servant work had always been the house-cleaning sort more than the people-cleaning.

The servant girls whispered when she dismissed them again, insisting that she could handle the activity by herself. But it was outlandish to waste five people's time on such a task. And surely other nobles had made stranger requests before—it wasn't a servant's place to comment on something so benign, other than amongst themselves.

Blythe did her best to put the exchange aside.

After bathing, she sat atop the bed in long, floofy underpants and a simple cotton shirt, picking at the large breakfast of porridge, pastries, deli meats, and everything else the servants had brought her. It should have been a dream come true, all of this food.

Blythe sighed deeply. She stabbed her fork into a breakfast sausage but couldn't bring herself to eat. She would never pull this off. All this food—this second chance—was wasted on her. All she could see in it was Papa's heartbroken face. This feast could have fed the children in their building for a week.

Even proximity to all this decadence must enrage Deium Erium. She would have to satisfy him with double the time fasting when she returned home. Only sleep on the floor, with that old woolen blanket that gave her hives. She'd find a way to get Papa out of that apartment, but she would remain with the mold when she wasn't caring for him.

Her door creaked open, and Blythe's eyes darted up to see Frida sneaking in. With a bowl of fruit, no less, as if this room didn't have enough food in it. At least she was safe.

"Hey." Frida closed the door silently behind her. "I'm managing to get away for a bit now that breakfast has done. Aren't you gonna eat, *niné*?"

Frida grabbed the chair from the vanity and plopped it beside Blythe's bed.

Blythe shrugged. "Help yourself. I think I'm too nervous."

"It's gonna be fine," Frida said. She put down the bowl of fruit and grabbed a cheese scone. She took a bite, resting an ankle on her knee. The Ashlan clothing suited her. A light-blue garment like a long, open waistcoat came just to her thighs, with ruffles of white cotton fanning down at the chest and a thick black band tied around her waist, a leather belt secured overtop with small pouches at its side. Her black pants tucked into brown boots that nearly reached her knees.

"Maybe if anyone else was doing this." Blythe huffed, leaning back on her elbows. "I'm so sorry. Even the servants can tell I'm a fake."

"They will if you don't eat more."

"At least tell me you've heard something from Kalen?"

"He lives," Frida said, and Blythe's shoulders deflated with relief. "Was coming to the kitchens a few times with his quarter. A bit tired-looking. But alive."

Thank the gods. Of course he'd been tired; it just mattered that he was alive. Not badly hurt. If they were alright, Blythe's head could spin a little less wildly.

She took a small bite of bread to appease the worried wrinkle on Frida's forehead. She *did* have to eat enough to be coherent for the mission, while at the same time trying not to think about the sallow, starving faces on her street back home.

"And you?" Blythe asked, searching her friend for any injuries. She found only dark circles underneath her eyes and nails bitten down too far. Stress was expected for all of them, but that didn't make it less concerning. "You're holding up alright?"

Frida hesitated. Then she shot Blythe a grin. "Have I tell you the size of these kitchens, niné?" Frida's Fletch had come a long way in a short time, but Blythe still took a second to process past her accent. Frida grabbed another pastry off one of the platters. "They do huge cupboards of food and spices, though I'm not allowed to seasoning enough."

"Well, forget what we're doing. *That's* a crime." Maybe she shouldn't make light, but Frida's laugh was a worthy tradeoff. The long-past days of trading silly jokes floated around in Blythe's memory. "It's been good, though?"

"Same like the tavern, you know?" Frida brushed some crumbs off of her shirt. Her shoulders deflated a little. From fatigue? Or was there something she wasn't saying?

Frida didn't elaborate, but Blythe knew enough about why she hated the tavern to guess. Terrible boss? Being cooped up? Dreary routines that never changed?

"It won't be for long," Blythe tried to assure. "When we get out of here, your ale *will* take off. I know—"

Just then, Saidh slipped through the door.

Blythe had forgotten they'd all planned to meet before the first luncheon in a few hours. Kalen exempted, as they couldn't sneak away with a big feast coming. Frida had, but she might have claimed to be gathering some ingredients. And she hadn't been a gift to the castle like Kalen had. She had more room to do things for Esme's benefit.

"Any luck with the vault?" Blythe asked Saidh hopefully as he took a seat on the small couch across from her.

Who knew? Maybe the vault would be fairly easy to crack, and they wouldn't have to stay here the whole time. They could frame one of the delegations—oh, was that a cynical way to think?—and keep a war on Ostrait out of the picture and their deal intact.

Saidh shook his head. "I've got a decent map going," he said, pulling some folded papers from his pockets. "But this vault isn't anywhere obvious. And they've had me taking records for Jardae in all sorts of trade meetings. Nothing interesting unless you need more linens."

Saidh stood and set the papers on the vanity, presumably so they could look at them later. It *would* help if Blythe had at least some idea of how to navigate the palace, even if an early escape wasn't on the horizon yet.

His pockets must have been endless, because he also pulled out two small books and showed them to her. One was called *A History of Fletch Governance*, and the other was *Culture and Ambition: Manifesting Fletch Destiny*. "These might help, too, if you ever get time to read." He set them on the vanity beside the papers.

"Thanks." Anything Blythe could learn about this weird palace and country would help. She'd spend all night struggling through reading if she had to; failure wasn't something she could afford, no matter how abysmal the odds.

"Where's the snake-lady?" Frida asked, and they all giggled in a sort of conspiratorial way. "She's meant to being always with you, isn't she?"

Good question, actually. The Viper of all people wouldn't risk the mission, but she was supposed to be here in time to properly dress Blythe for the luncheon and give her better instructions about her table manners.

"I think she may have gotten carried away and distracted a guard," Blythe said. "We were close to finding out about the certatia last night, but we got interrupted. It's gonna be something the Fletch are good at, though, from the sounds of it."

"She should hurry up," Saidh said, leaning against the birch vanity. He plucked an eggroll off one of the many trays littering the room "You've only got a couple hours."

They talked a few minutes more before the door flew open. The Viper wore a wrinkled gown and a sly look on her face. Her ginger hair unkempt, cap nowhere to be seen, and pink lipstick smudged, the girl puffed down into a cushioned chair with an unusually contented sigh. Something about successfully reaching the palace might have stirred a change in her, but for better or worse, Blythe couldn't tell.

"Well, *I* had a great night." She began rifling through her vast dress pockets. "And seemed like a great morning too," she added, dumping some assorted jewels, coins, a couple vials of presumably dangerous liquids and herbs, and a small blade into her lap. She aggressively plucked a paper out from amidst them.

"Clearly," Frida said dryly.

"It might have been," the girl continued, "but I also managed to steal some troubling news."

Blythe tensed.

The Viper returned the jewels, coins, and vials to her pockets. She tucked the small blade in between her breasts and passed the paper over.

Blythe's face fell as the words came together.

"Did you get them to tell you where the vault is?" Saidh asked.

"Just the paper. You're welcome, by the way. Guard wasn't exactly conscious enough to chat."

Blythe furrowed her brow. "But you... Didn't you and the guard..."

"No," the Viper replied with a twitch of irritation. "I don't mix pleasure and business. I got some information, and the rest doesn't concern you or the Fletch army."

"Oh." Should she apologize? She'd known many good, honest people who worked from their beds, but still, many would view it as an insult. Had the Viper been offended? She couldn't tell. Well, it was always better to apologize when unnecessary than to not apologize when needed. "Sorry."

"Anyway," the Viper said without acknowledgement, tracing a finger along the paisley wall beside her, "judging by the memo, it seems they already have some fears about Ostraitian spies interfering with the competition."

"Well, that's good, isn't it?" Saidh asked. "If they're already in disarray, we can use that."

"No," the Viper said, as if it should be plainly obvious to him.

"If they think any interference is Ostraitian spies," Blythe began to string things together herself, "and if they already consider Jardae a puppet nation, Fletch will keep their other alliances as close-knit as possible.

The second anything suspicious happens, we'll be the first place they look, won't we?"

The group fell quiet. There was nothing good about this.

Blending in for three weeks challenged them enough. But when their delegation was already less trustworthy? Execution could arrive before they even *saw* the vault, and war would descend on her home. And if Blythe failed in the competition even *without* casting suspicion, they were all just as dead when they reached Ostrait empty-handed.

Finally, the Viper said, "It's time to get to work."

II.

63 Printes, Reg. Marii 6

Blood caked Kalen's knuckles and nail beds. Tufts of their hair stuck to their sweaty forehead and neck.

All night they had been scrubbing. Back and forth. Forth and back. They tried to wipe their eyes, but pain splintered in their arm when they raised it.

Superior clearly had it in for Kalen since last night. Lashes on his back. Lashes instead of execution, for disappointing the King. *Be fucking grateful you're not on the ropes.*

Laudanum. He needed it. He needed it. He *needed* it.

Only Kalen, to clean all the quarter's latrines. They hadn't really wished they were dead in a long time. After the roof, after Blythe, he was...healthier. Her company wrapped around him like a safety blanket, fending off the world's cold with the last match in the cupboard.

But now. They lifted their strained eyes to see several stalls still thick with filth. And a window at the end of the room.

Are we high up enough?

Back and forth. Forth and back.

Can't leave her out to dry.

Kalen finished when dawn nearly peeked through the window. A few hours, maybe, for sleep.

They stumbled across the halls in something of a stupor. Gait uneven, using the walls to stay upright. The quarters, the quarters, he just had to make it there.

Enclosing themself inside the strange cabinet bed, Kalen dizzily pulled the covers over their shoulders and blacked out.

Kalen ran for his life, the wind whipping against his face, a searing pain in his ribs. A blaze of smoke and fire stood before him, a poppy field roaring with heat. They didn't hesitate to dash under the cover of the flames, taking a deep inhale of the vapours.

The fire didn't hurt him.

Safe. They were safe here, they could hide here.

Some of the pain began to fade, their pulse slowed to a lull, and they almost forgot why they'd been running.

But the large man pushed his way through the heat. He towered, a monster made of coals. Embers flaked off his skin as he staggered toward Kalen.

Kalen froze.

His body wouldn't obey when he screamed at it. Run! Get out of here!

"Fire can't protect you anymore."

The man clenched his fist, and the earth rumbled underneath Kalen. Finally, he scrambled to his feet, forcing his legs to carry him further into the burning field, struggling for balance as the ground quaked.

"I always told you it was no use running." They couldn't even see the man anymore, but his snarling voice echoed throughout.

And then Kalen saw it.

This wasn't just a field, it was a shoreline. And the tide had pulled back.

He turned to run, but the man was there, laughing.

The wave crashed down.

Kalen was in the ocean. Drowning, drowning. He couldn't breathe.

"Please," he gasped, when his head finally breached the surface of the water. "Help me."

"You coward. Did you really think you'd escape?"

A loud horn jolted Kalen awake.

"Fuck me," they said, rubbing their head where they'd bashed it on the roof of the tiny cubby. Tears pooled in his eyes, and he hastily wiped them away.

If only he could just be numb again.

He scrambled out of the cupboard, stumbling onto his feet with the other servants. Some cast sideways glances at him, but he managed to lock the placard shut and face the front with everyone else, forming a perfect line of beige with their uniforms.

Silence loomed, anticipation heavy in the air.

Kalen couldn't handle it any longer.

"What's happening?" they whispered to Gilles, who stood perfectly straight beside them, arms flat against his sides.

Kalen flattened his unruly curls, trying to look somewhat more put together like the rest. A dizzy ache pulled at their mind.

"Shh," Gilles said, barely moving his mouth.

"But what—"

The thunderous boom of footsteps cut Kalen off. Superior emerged from the entryway across the narrow room. The man's shoulders pulled back and his chest prodded out as he cast a challenging stare onto them all.

Kalen lowered his eyes just too late.

The man got in his face an instant later, towering above as a lion over a mouse. "Are you eyeballing me?"

Kalen knew this situation well. It was a common question asked by his father. The problem was that it had rarely mattered how he'd answered.

"No, sir, my apologies." Kalen tried to shift his accent this time, but it wasn't easy to undo years of oration lessons. He should have left his room more at the tavern.

"And surely that untucked shirt was an honest mistake?" Superior asked, voice dripping with mockery. "Do you think I'll stand for disrespect, you wretch?"

Kalen's pulse thumped in his ears. "No, sir."

"Open your door."

Throat dry, Kalen bowed his head and complied.

"What a fucking disaster!" Kalen flinched as Superior turned to the other servants, face red. "Do you all see this terrible disloyalty to His Majesty?"

Kalen glanced inside the door, stricken with fear that he'd left a bomb hidden and forgotten about it. No, nothing like that.

His arms tensed. He'd forgotten to un-crinkle his scratchy, uselessly thin blanket when he'd stumbled out from that nightmare, and it lay wrinkled in the cupboard like a monument of defiance. Never mind that he didn't understand what a blanket had to do with loyalty. *How could I have fucked it up like this?*

"What do you think this is, you lout?"

Kalen's knees trembled, and he struggled for any acceptable response. "I... It's a blanket? Sir?"

Gilles sucked in a sharp breath.

Superior's mouth formed into a snarl.

The crack of a fist against his already purpled face. Kicks into his ribcage that made him curl. The spluttering of blood down his chin as he wheezed.

A vision of his father that wouldn't go away.

And then everyone had gone.

Just Kalen remained, curled inward and alone on the hard wooden floor. His head spun, and a moan escaped his lips. Hot water spilled from his eyes. *Why can't I do anything right?*

He couldn't even wake up without drawing painful attention. He would get himself and everybody else killed. Just ruin this last chance like they ruined everything.

And he couldn't take another blow.

Kalen's father's hands wrapped around his throat again.

A wet sob lurched out of him.

He was a small child again, cowering under the gaze of a man that saw him barely worthy of humanity.

Powerless. Useless. Good for fucking nothing.

Running might be futile. But what else could they do?

⟫⟫⟫ ⟪⟪⟪

"What are you doing here?" Saidh yanked Kalen into the room by the arm with an irritated whisper, quickly closing his door. "Do you *want* to get caught?"

"Please." Kalen's voice cracked. "I didn't know where else to go."

Only then did Saidh visibly register Kalen's fragile state. Broken. Face caked with blood and black bruises. Barely able to walk, they cradled their bad arm. Would it be wrecked for good, this time?

"Shit, man. Okay. Sit down."

Kalen allowed themself to be guided over to an armchair. One they probably ruined with all the bleeding. The fluttering white leaves that patterned the burgundy walls swam around in his vision, blotted by orange dots.

"What happened?"

"I just," Kalen spoke over swollen lips and cheeks. They swallowed, trying to find the words. Water pooled in his eyes, and there was no forcing it away for pride's sake. "I need to get out of here. Please. You must know a route."

"Is our cover blown?"

"No, but—"

"We should get you cleaned up, then, okay?"

Kalen's heart sank. "You don't understand. I can't... I can't do it. And I'm only going to screw it up for everyone."

Saidh sat beside them with a small bowl of water and a towel in hand. He spoke gruffly, but his hands dabbed tenderly at Kalen's face. "There's no turning back, so don't waste your energy trying. *That* will screw things up."

Kalen winced at the light touch to his cheek but didn't move. "Please, you have to know a way out. Nobody is going to care about a missing servant. I don't matter."

"That kind of thinking is what gets the hells beaten out of you," Saidh said, wringing out the stained towel. He softly wiped away the blood on Kalen's spinning head. "It makes you messy."

The gentle touches and damp cloth soon disappeared. At some point, when Kalen hadn't been paying attention, Saidh had produced bandages. "Your ribs, right?"

"Why are you helping me?"

Kalen lifted their shirt with their working arm. Heat flushed their face as Saidh's fingers skimmed their back, but it quickly vanished in a burst of pain as he yanked the bandages tight around their middle. Kalen fixed his vision on a painting of horses above the back wall's fireplace. *One horse, two, three... Fucking shit.* This wasn't helping at all.

"You die or do something stupid, we're done for." Saidh shrugged, knotting the fabric securely despite Kalen's hisses of pain. "And why shouldn't I?" Saidh moved with a militaristic precision. "Your shoulder next."

Kalen recoiled. It had dislocated again. "Surely servants commit suicide all the time. Couldn't we make it look as though I'd jumped from the window?"

"And how would we get into the vault?" Saidh asked, rolling his eyes. "Asking nicely?"

Kalen opened their mouth to respond. But they honestly hadn't thought of that. Did the crew actually *need* him for something more than appearances and the occasional stitch?

Speaking of stitches, Saidh had strangely good medical skills for a sketchy merchant.

"Why would a merchant know how to relocate my shoulder, anyway?"

"Why does an arsonist have surgical skills?"

Kalen laughed. Which was a bit deranged, considering they had just been beaten within an inch of their life. "Fair enough," they said. "But I asked first."

"Give me your arm," Saidh challenged. Not much of a bargain—answers in exchange for terrible pain.

Kalen swallowed. Everything already hurt so much.

They longed to crawl onto the wiry cot in their apartment, ducked under a blanket with the door and windows locked, Frida snoring soundly across the room. They'd never dreamed they'd miss that terrible cot or the rumble of snorts, but it had been solace in a way that life in Father's mansion never was. Security, ripped away from them now.

"I can't do this without the laudanum. The arm, all...all of it," Kalen pleaded, hating the sound of his own voice. "You're mapping every inch of the palace, right? And you were smuggling it. Please, you have to know where some is. Just a little. Just to wean off."

"Even if I knew where any was, I wouldn't give it to you."

"What did I ever do to you? You don't *understand*. I'm dying." Kalen startled at the sob that escaped his mouth.

"I've seen what it does to plenty of people," Saidh said with a heartbreaking resolve. He crossed his arms over his chest. "You're lucky there's none here, trust me. I'm sorry, but you just have to wait out the withdrawal. We already weaned you off the worst of it."

"I don't *care* what it does to me." Kalen wanted to attack the man. But he couldn't, could he, with his shoulder and all of this pain?

"Doesn't change the fact there is none."

Kalen groaned in frustration. But then Saidh said, "Maybe Frida would have some other painkillers, though. She's good with herbal remedies and things."

How well did Saidh know Frida? Perhaps they'd bonded at sea while Kalen had been half-conscious.

"Maybe." It would be enough. But it didn't help right now.

"What happened to your shoulder?" Saidh asked. "The first time? It's been hurt before."

A distraction. That was what they needed. Any distraction from this terrible, spiking pain.

"Used to pitch *kirne*-ball, if you can believe that. Was the only athletic-type thing I was ever good at. Even gave my parents a little hope, while it lasted. But my older brother Arne, he was always a jackass. And he liked to play jokes, so one day I was winding up to throw," Kalen babbled, trying to ignore the immense pressure behind his eyes.

A sudden agony caused them to bite down on their hand, suppressing a scream.

"Done," Saidh said.

Kalen looked through the blur as Saidh removed his hands from their shoulder.

"Sorry. It had to be done. Figured it would be easier."

It hurt.

Gods, it hurt like it would never stop hurting.

"Fair move," Kalen admitted, a shaky sort of laugh leaving him.

They tried to smooth out the bite marks on their palm with their other thumb. Anything to make the pain stop. Anything to take them away from this.

"Continue your story?"

With what might have been a nod, Kalen said, "Okay. Um, so. Arne comes along and sweeps my legs out. He always hated that I could pitch, you know, I mean he hated me in general, but he was the athletic one. It killed him that I beat him in that game, the little byjeka I was.

"So, I fell the wrong way," they continued, picking at a thread on the green velvet chair. Sweat stuck to his forehead. "Couldn't throw anymore, because the doctor said any more strain and I'd be crippled. And Father couldn't have that around the house. So I was meant to study instead."

Why was he even telling a near-stranger this? He flushed with embarrassment. "But anyway." Kalen did their best to push it off, but they squeezed their eyes shut at another stab of pain. *Deep breaths. Deep breaths.* Everyone would die if they couldn't survive this. Blythe. Frida. "I'd like some answers, too. Only fair."

Saidh shrugged, acquiescing. "I was in the military back home for a while." He took a sip from a flask and offered it to Kalen, who gladly accepted.

It was only *tea*. How absurd. But they were still grateful for the warmth.

Saidh leaned back in his own purple velvet chair. "Everyone gets medical training."

"And becoming a smuggling merchant in Ostrait was...a wise career choice?" Kalen asked, earning a rough bark of laughter.

They'd nearly drained the flask. But he was hurt, so it was acceptable.

"The army is pretty strict about some petty things," Saidh said. He extended his hand for the flask and scowled, in a good-natured way, when it proved empty. "We had our differences."

"Ah, a deserter then," Kalen said, and a smile crept onto his bruised face. "I can sympathize."

"Does it count as deserting if they chase you with guns?"

Kalen's eyes widened. "And you're *alive*?"

"The details aren't important." Saidh waved them off, shifting to rest a foot on his leg, but a hint of pride flickered over his features.

"Um, the details are everything." Kalen could almost trick themself into thinking the aches had dulled. They tried to pull all of their focus into the conversation and away from their injuries.

"Your turn," Saidh said, annoyingly. Natural, that somebody that handsome had a mysterious backstory. "Surgery to arson is quite the jump."

"Not really." Kalen adjusted themself delicately in their chair. The pain in his arm had dulled now, at least. "Always liked chemistry. Wasn't terrible at the natural sciences, either."

Kalen explained how they'd tried to whip him into a surgeon after discovering some of his embroidery projects, but it just couldn't mask all his other shameful failings. Military school had been presented as his best bet after that, even if he would only end up dying in the field as a medic or exploding while experimenting with artillery shells—it was less embarrassing than having him around.

The two of them continued to chat, providing a welcome diversion. Favorite Fletch foods, the last play they'd each read, what they thought of this and that.

When Saidh got to talking about certain subjects, like the Fourth Crimson War or the Irisian sail-making industry, any tough or secretive veneer vanished pretty quickly. The man couldn't shut up if he was explaining something. Only then did Kalen realize the beard had made him look much older. He might only be a couple years older than Kalen. Twenty-five? Twenty-six?

Kalen's posture bent with dismay when it grew too close to the next serving shift to stay any longer. Superior had left them on the floor but would expect them up and ready.

They didn't know if they'd make it halfway down the hall.

But maybe... Frida's kitchens, they were on the way, right? Kalen could stop, and maybe, like Saidh had said, maybe she could help. It wouldn't be enough. But it would have to be.

And any delay was comforting.

The thought of meeting Superior's gaze again constricted his breath.

"Bit of military advice?" Saidh offered.

"I don't think fighting them is really an option right now."

Saidh shook his head and leaned forward on his elbows. "Look, you've just gotta ride it out. Right now, they're training you like a stray mutt: negative reinforcement until complete obedience to Fletch. They need to be sure of you, because they're already unsure of Jardae."

"I'm not sure how knowing I'm a dog to them helps at all."

"Because you don't train a dog forever," Saidh said. "Once they believe you've had enough to be scared and loyal, they'll have better things to do so long as you don't act up."

"And if they never believe that?"

"Trust me. They won't waste their time," Saidh said. "You'll either pass, or... Just make sure they believe it."

"But how am I even supposed to know what they want me to do?" Kalen slumped back in the chaise, exasperated. "I got the shit kicked out of me because of a bed corner."

"You got the shit kicked out of you because you let nerves make you clumsy," Saidh said pointedly. "And you can't forget the bed corners. Fear is what they need to see, but you can't let it be too real. It ruins your focus, and we can't afford that."

"Thanks," Kalen said. It helped a little, maybe, knowing there might be a light at the end of the tunnel. *If* they could somehow manage this terrible pain and muster up some kind of short-term memory. "Seriously, for all of this."

But he didn't know how not to be afraid.

He'd thought he'd escaped his worst fears in that first fire, but he couldn't even leave his apartment when it rained—and that wasn't a rare occurrence in Ostrait.

"Hey, whether we like it or not, we're a team now."

And do you like it? Kalen might have asked. His heart wouldn't stop with the fluttering—from the injuries, no doubt.

They stopped at the door together, and an awkward pause blanketed the pair. Time to go.

Did they *have* to?

Couldn't he just stay there under the arm of someone out of his league, talking about anything other than the mission?

But the mission meant everything.

Blythe's father lay on the chopping block, and so did all of their freedom. And a chance for Kalen to repay Blythe—not for saving their life on the rooftop, like he always said, but for putting the air back in his lungs. For taking the time to know his favorite animals were cows, and for responding to his ramble about plant genetics with her own about lock tumblers, instead of rolling her eyes, and for letting him win at cards in the most endearingly obvious way possible.

Saidh took his arm off of Kalen, jolting them back to the present. He nodded to the golden, sunflower-patterned door. "You sure you can make it back?"

No. Keep me here and nurse me back to health. "Yeah," Kalen said, doing their best for a reassuring smile. It split their busted lip.

"Okay."

Another lull of dreadful quiet.

"Would you do me another favor?" Kalen asked. A rock of guilt weighed on him. They looked down at their shoes. "Could you not mention this to Blythe? I don't want her to worry."

Which was true. But they also couldn't bear her knowing they'd tried to abandon everything. She always thought him less selfish than he was, and it made him want to be.

⤞⤝

Kalen staggered back just a few minutes late for the cleanup shift. In a rare stroke of luck, Superior didn't notice him slip into line.

Frida had given them some concoction that numbed their aches a bit, faded the migraine to a gentle throb. It would help them heal better than laudanum would, she'd said, and they should come back whenever they could for more. It didn't taste great, but even the small amount of relief was monumental right now.

"Hurry, put this on," Gilles whispered, grabbing a smock from the cart he pushed. All the other servants wore them tonight. Kalen didn't want to know what that meant for the mess ahead.

"Thank you," Kalen mouthed. They kept carefully silent as they rounded the corner.

Gilles offered a sympathetic smile.

The two managed to make it through the night without further incident. The boy even managed to save Kalen once again when they were instructed to clean the windows, taking their place on the ladder. Shoulder still squeezing in pain at large movements, Kalen probably would have died trying to get up those rungs.

"Thank you for covering my ass," Kalen said, opening the door to their cupboard. He didn't want to rely on the kid, but the options were slim until he got the hang of things.

Gilles climbed into his own cubby with ease. "Somebody's got to." The boy laughed, and Kalen couldn't help joining in.

"The sad thing is," Kalen said, lowering their voice for dramatic effect, "I'm actually trying my best."

"That *is* sad." Within seconds of the kid's door closing, Kalen heard snores.

It took him a few minutes of struggle to get into his own cubby. Banged his damn arm on the bottom of it and whisper-screamed a whole host of curses.

Gilles's skill for falling asleep would have been handy. But the thought of slipping back into another nightmare kept Kalen's eyes open.

Somehow, when sleep finally did steal them away, no terrors awaited their mind. Instead, there was quite the pleasant dream of a certain rugged figure whisking them away from the luncheon on horseback. They woke up almost...calm.

He made it through the morning lineup and cleaning shifts without producing a disaster. And although the realities of serving the luncheon turned out to be much less romantic than his dream, at least they weren't a nightmare.

Hands shaking on the first platter, he placed it on the table.

Nobody shouted. So he walked away and got the next platter.

There was a chance they could survive the day.

12.

T he sun shone over the royal courtyard, the clouds overhead thin
and white, the sky a bright azure rather than pigeon gray. The
luncheon table stretched across an expanse of short, uniformly cut grass,
confusing both for the sheer volume of it and its unknown purpose.
Servants waited to the side with silver box-shaped carts and mountains of
food that only continued to astonish, with more approaching from the
bordering paths. Drinks had been served, with non-alcoholic fruit juices
as one of the options, thankfully.

"Do you have a *talent*?" Eleanore asked, taking a delicate sip from her
fluted glass. Blythe had been seated next to her, and while she normally
abhorred small talk, it was a relief that anyone thought she was normal
enough to speak to.

Still, the question made her bristle.

There was an unspoken rule, at least in Ostrait, not to ask someone
about their bestowment. Most could only claim a skill slightly above the
mundane as theirs, if they could claim any at all. Asking so tactlessly
risked putting someone on the defensive. It remained private until di-

vulged freely. Though Eleanore was young, and too nosy for her own good.

Blythe could make up a bestowment, but that couldn't possibly end well. And anyway, appearing modest didn't hurt. "The gods haven't blessed me yet," she said finally.

"Oh," Eleanore said, lips briefly quirking down. "Well, perhaps one of them will look fondly on you, yet."

Chatter surrounded them, combined with the metallic clangs of silver dishware, the clinking of fluted glasses, and the flurry of servants hefting ornate platters onto the long table. Far too much to take in. But Blythe threw her energy into it.

"Thank you. I should like to believe that."

Eleanore beamed. The girl sat straight in the tall sea-green chair, smoothing down her plum skirts. "Father believes I'm talented at the piano. He's sure my music would please even His Majesty's tastes. I do hope I'm able to play for His Majesty before he chooses. Do you think I'll have the chance?"

Blythe offered the poor girl a smile. "I'm sure you will."

Futile to try and convince the girl that she should find another life's purpose. Nor could Blythe say so without revealing her own plans. She would have to be especially patient and kind with Eleanore, at any rate.

The girl made a pleased sound.

Blythe restrained herself from offering her thanks to a servant as they placed her dish in front of her. Did Kalen hide somewhere in the bustle of servants? She couldn't see them, and worry twisted at her chest.

Eleanore adjusted a butterfly-shaped pin in her coiled black hair and pushed a few stray ringlets behind her ear. "Do you have any hopes for what the coming certatia will be?"

"Oh, I'm not sure," Blythe said. "Maybe some kind of art."

"You do watercolors? There must be lots of lovely natural subjects in Jardae."

The only nice thing anybody said about Jardae was that the landscapes were picturesque, especially the coast. And according to Blythe's training, watercolors were typical for young ladies to learn. "Yes, I really like florals," she lied.

In truth, she'd never painted with colors at all, even if she had created landscapes on floors and walls, using the charcoal sticks that Kalen made for her.

This table was so long, the servants so quick, that she still hadn't caught a glimpse of them. Maybe they weren't even serving at the luncheon like she'd believed.

They had to be alright. Surely nothing bad could have happened already.

As her eyes swept the table, she met a scrutinizing gaze.

It took Blythe a second to place the other candidate, now in Fletch clothing rather than the beautifully beaded Ka'lani dress she'd arrived in, though her hair remained in the same braids as those of the other delegates in their coalition. *Why* was Wapite staring at her?

Blythe swallowed nervously, adjusting her napkin. She offered a hesitant smile.

The servants all scuttled back, and a tiny bell rang.

"Let us eat well!" cheered the woman who'd appeared at the head of the table, clinking her fork against a glass of wine. It was Princess Lucretia's duty to lead the luncheon, and also certainly to report back to her older brother, the King.

Wapite tore her challenging stare away. She clinked her own glass, as did the rest of the nobles, beaming at the toast.

"This lamb roast is just divine," Eleanore murmured. The rest of the nobles sank into their meals as well.

Picking up the right fork with the utmost caution this time, Blythe forced herself to take a bite. Fletch cuisine was supposedly foremost in the world, but all the sauces coated it in a sickly sweet film. "Mmm, lovely," Blythe agreed to keep up appearances. Starving faces haunted her as she chewed.

She snuck another glance at Wapite. The picture of elegance, face poised for pleasantries with other candidates. There was no way to tell anything had been off just a minute ago.

But something *was* off.

Blythe had never even spoken to her. She hadn't done anything to draw attention to herself. In fact, she'd been counting on her bestowment to do just the opposite so long as she didn't screw up too badly.

So why had this random candidate, halfway across an enormous table, trained her eyes on Blythe? There was so much else going on, and Blythe hardly represented a politically important candidate, anyway. She wasn't used to being noticed for no reason, and her body stiffened.

Meanwhile Eleanore had asked yet another question, and Blythe had missed it in her web of thoughts. "Pardon?"

"I asked, is there much pheasant in Jardae?"

"There's enough," Blythe said. What was a pheasant? Perhaps similar to a turkey, which they did have in Ostrait. "Though we do tend to enjoy fish more than they do in Fletch."

"That's so quaint," said a candidate on her other side.

Eleanore wrinkled her nose. "I can't stand the smell of fish."

An Ashlan candidate laughed, taking a sip from his goblet. "You would not survive a day in Ashlos, then."

Blythe produced a pleasant laugh, grateful for the interjection. Why did Jardae interest these people? It was just a bunch of the same Fletch men controlling another piece of stolen land.

"Father discussed a marriage with Prince Manuel if I'm not chosen..." Eleanore confessed.

"I'm sure you will be," Blythe assured, patting the girl's gloved hand with her own. Though the thought of that girl being married to the King churned her stomach.

He seemed like such a charming man. Blythe shook away the idea. It took more effort to dislike the King than it should, but there was something about him. Maybe she'd misremembered their encounter, because something told her she was wrong to dislike him. *It's not his fault he was born a royal. He could be a good man.*

The gods chose kings for a reason, didn't they?

"But Lady Esme, what of your odds?" the Ashlan candidate inquired. He dabbed at his tan face with a serviette. "Surely you wouldn't give up his hand so easily?"

Blythe forced a polite smile. "Of course not, but... what is a competition without sportsmanship?"

A competition. The King had organized a whole competition for his hand as an ego boost. Only a horrible wretch of a man could do something so wasteful and degrading.

Maybe he just loves parties. Maybe he wanted to bring people together. And shouldn't any good ruler want to ensure he made the best alliance? Blythe shouldn't judge so harshly.

Something was wrong. And not only about Wapite.

Gods, Blythe wished she could talk to Kalen about all of this. Or Frida. She needed to see them both, to clutch them into hugs and know they were okay.

But it didn't matter what she needed. *It could be worse.* It didn't seem she'd been discovered yet, despite some suspicious looks. She just had to ride out the meal. That was what would help her friends.

So she did. From one boring topic to the next, nothing catastrophic happened. She didn't catch Wapite's eyes on her again.

Eventually, even the longest meal had to end.

Relief flooded Blythe's body when candidates began to shuffle out. Each paused to thank the Princess for hosting, and Blythe made sure she did the same.

"And on with grace," Lucretia said, receiving the deep curtsy.

Blythe waited until she turned out of sight before letting out a sigh. Saidh waited for her around the corner to escort her back to her chambers, and she took his arm gladly.

"Any word from Kalen?" she asked, voice low. "I only caught the barest glimpse of his face near the end, and I'm not even sure it was him."

"Haven't seen them," Saidh replied. "The luncheon went alright?"

Blythe hesitated, looking up at the man. "What are your thoughts on the King?" she asked once they'd entered the empty corridor that housed her chambers. Still, she kept her voice low in case it echoed off the stone walls.

"What do you mean?"

Blythe closed the door behind them in her chambers, ushering him over to the sitting area deeper in the room.

"Do you find him likeable?"

Saidh rolled his eyes. "Getting into character, are we? I'm sure he'll make a suitable husband."

Blythe scowled. A pillow was in the way as she sat down, and she threw it onto the bed. "Seriously. There's something—"

"Off about the King?" the Viper interjected, gliding in from her adjoined chambers, hair styled atop her head and powdered as pink as her robes. "I've noticed that, too."

"I tried prodding a bit," Blythe said, frowning. "But everyone seems to have a different idea about his bestowment. Some say strength, strategy, riding, archery, dance. There's no sense in it."

The Viper leaned against the wall, considering. "And did they seem to believe what they were saying?"

Blythe shrugged, crossing her legs underneath her and thumbing one of the pearls attached to her sleeve. "Well enough. It's almost as if they believe he's good at whatever they like best. The girls want to think he can dance, write poetry, ride them into the sunset. The masculine men want to think they've met their match in brawling, waging wars, leading."

"And what of the delegates who think this is stupid?"

"That's the thing." Blythe rubbed her hands over her eyes. "Even the ones who think the competition is ridiculous don't blame the King. It's like they've forgotten he made the whole thing. Most of them see him as an upside."

There are definitely worse people to be fake-competing for.

"I do." Saidh cleared his throat. "Find him likeable."

"As do I," the Viper said, wrinkling her nose. "Which means something is deeply wrong. He is a loathsome enemy. One person falling victim to an ill-suited fancy would be one matter, but this charm of his is more insidious."

"Charm," Blythe mused, leaning her head back in the chair. Chandeliers dangled from the ceiling, casting a tranquil glow over the space. "What a useful gift to have."

"It would explain why nobody's assassinated him for pulling an international stunt like this," Saidh added.

"And why he wants to meet so many world leaders," Blythe said. "Make every nation fall in love with him." Could he persuade them to give up grievances? Sign off on trade deals? Go to war?

If she were bold enough to question the gods—which she definitely wasn't because *all* of them were probably a step away from smiting her by now—she might wonder why they would bestow that kind of gift on anyone, even a king.

According to Kalen, some natural scientists thought that bestowments might be stored in the body from birth, rather than gifted as a reward. Blythe certainly didn't understand why she had her gift for staying hidden, when the gods had never been appeased by her lifelong attempts at penance. But if the gods couldn't determine what was in the body, how had they infected Mama with consumption and given Papa pneumonia as their punishments? What did—

"And," the Viper said.

Blythe jerked away from her blasphemous thoughts and back to practical concerns, clicking her knuckles together.

"There are many more peasant riots in the far provinces, where he doesn't visit as often."

Blythe's head swirled. They hadn't even been there a week. What if his charm spread the longer they spent time with him? She would be expected to, at certain certatiae.

And she'd be pretending to like him the whole while. What if the pretending warped itself?

Blythe clicked her knuckles harder, worry knotting her brows together. She could not submit to his entitlement. She couldn't lose herself in this fawning court that disregarded everything she stood for. She could not falter in her loyalty to this mission. To her father. To Kalen.

Gods, Kalen didn't even know.

"We have to tell the others," she said. "So they can try to... I don't know."

"At the end of the day, he's only a man," the Viper said, as pragmatic as always. She straightened from the wall. "Not a god. Whatever influence this is, it is not absolute."

"You're right." Surprisingly, Blythe agreed with the Viper's conclusions more often than not, even if she disagreed with the girl's deadly approach. "There must be something we can do to mitigate."

"What about drills?"

Blythe and the Viper both cast Saidh quizzical looks. He sat on the edge of her bed, one foot resting atop his knee, and papers peeking out of various pockets.

"Like, in the army," he explained, "they make you do all your exercise drills over and over, while imagining the enemy."

"I don't know if we can manage that discreetly," Blythe said. But perhaps he was on the right track.

"No," the Viper agreed, "but negative reinforcement *is* a powerful conditioning tool."

The blood drained from Blythe's face. She might deserve more of the Viper's poison, but could she continue coherently afterward?

"It could even be something simple," she offered, unfolding and refolding her legs in their crisscross position. "Making a list of the reasons we're doing this, or"—she hesitated, but the Viper's unconvinced expression spurred her on—"if the danger is liking him, then the opposite, thinking of reasons we hate him." Blythe didn't believe in hating *anybody*, but she could certainly sum up reasons to dislike or distrust the man. "Recount them to ourselves."

"That could work."

"But if it doesn't?" Saidh asked.

"Then we'll cross that bridge," Blythe said, flattening her hands on her lap. "But right now, we need to let Kalen and Frida know what's going on. In case this charm of the King's is something that leaves a hold."

"I have access to the servants and the kitchen. Leave it to me," the Viper said with a wave of her gloved hand. "We need him working to find this vault, and you're of better use getting information."

That settled it, apparently. In truth, it would be overwhelmingly suspicious to have Blythe marching around the servants' quarters and kitchens. It made sense for her lady-in-waiting to go. But she ached to check on her friends. "Alright then."

Blythe could wait until evening. Only a couple hours remained until sunset, and the dark would help her stay hidden. The palace corridors were mostly lit by large windows, so by nightfall she could glue herself to the shadows.

Waiting wasn't the worst thing. It had been a taxing afternoon, and they rarely left her with downtime these days. Once she was alone, and purely for the sake of the mission, she lay down to rest.

⟫⟫ ⟪⟪

A soft navy covered the sky, brushed with gray clouds. It would be safe to leave soon enough, and Blythe forced herself up from the bed to prepare.

Not that she could do much.

She didn't have a decent servant disguise—yet—and her best bet was to wear Esme's normal attire. With some evening modifications, which Blythe managed to recall from the Viper's training.

The evening gloves rested in a box in the Viper's chambers, around that little fitting podium, and Blythe went in to grab them. The Viper's room was considerably dimmer. The girl had put out her candles before heading off, leaving the space caked with shadow. It offered a soothing embrace.

Even more so when her ears pricked at rustling.

The knob rattled.

Blythe startled, gluing herself to the nook behind one of the large fabric shelves. On the sewing table beside her lay a thick pair of scissors.

She almost reached forward, but refrained from grabbing them. Instead, Blythe listened.

The door clicked open, then shut with a *bam*.

"Shit. That was loud."

Blythe nearly keeled over.

Laughter sprang from her mouth, and she stepped out from behind the shelves. "Kalen?"

"Present," they said.

Blythe rushed over, her eyes accustomed enough to the dark that she could make out their figure fumbling around. She crushed them with a hug, but then pulled back when they let out a soft cry. "Fuck. Sorry."

They put a hand to their ribs, bent with pain.

Blythe's breath left her. "Kalen? What's wrong?"

"Nothing, I'm fine," he insisted. As if she could buy that. Blythe led him across the room, into the relative brightness of her own.

His face was cracked, and bloody, and—and—

She took a delicate hold of their wrist, searching their eyes. "Who did this to you?" Guilt turned in her stomach, because she knew the answer. And it was her own fault that they were here, being brutalized for a probably doomed mission.

Kalen lowered his head. "Don't worry," he said. "The mission isn't compromised."

Blythe blinked. Did they not realize how her heart contorted to see them like this? How her hands trembled as she forced down the ugly rage that wanted to escape? Rage against this place, the Governor, herself—she didn't know.

And she wanted to tell Kalen: *Screw the mission, I'm getting you out of here. We'll go build a new life in Nai'ma or Pule, anywhere they can't find us.*

Pressure built behind her eyes.

She couldn't tell them that. Because even thinking about it, she saw Papa's frail body on that cot and heard her own promise to him.

Was she trading Kalen's life for Papa's? Blythe couldn't afford to contemplate that. They could all make it out of here. They had to all make it out of here.

And Kalen would be miserable running away with her. They'd feel too guilty to leave her if she gave it all up to save them, and they'd spend their days missing out on a nice husband and comfortable lifestyle that he couldn't get as a fugitive cursed by association.

Blythe pressed her forehead to his. "I'm sorry." It was all she could say.

They squeezed her hand, and the two of them sat on the edge of the bed. "I wasn't going to come, but the Viper paid me a visit."

"She told you about the King?"

"Yeah, and I...wanted to make sure you were alright." They cleared their throat, scratching the back of their head. From any distance, their hair mimicked the soft blonde of white sand, but here, up close, highlights glinted as yellow as straw. "The Viper said not to bother checking, but, well, she's not the most trustworthy source. And I mean, I've got a debt to pay, right?"

Blythe's heart sank. She offered a broken smile. "Sure, yeah."

She was, through everything, only a debt in their mind. A burden to be relieved. The past two years between them couldn't have been genuine, not when she was just an obligation. Any fond feelings must have vanished for him with these bruises.

"I didn't see you at the luncheon," she said. She got up from the bed and grabbed a plate from the vanity—she'd piled it high with bread, smoked meat, and dried fruits, saving it for him just in case.

"Oh, I saw you." Kalen took the plate and immediately gnawed a chunk out of the bread. "I thought you were going to implode when that man, Alfons, wouldn't stop trying to talk to you."

Blythe did laugh a little at this. "Was I that obvious? He just wouldn't stop chewing so loudly."

"These royals never seem to stop chewing," Kalen said, shaking their head. He shoved a piece of dried beef into his mouth.

Blythe crisscrossed her legs once more underneath her giant skirts.

"I cleaned up one of their puke, and they asked me to bring them some more tarts!"

This was better. At least, Blythe could pretend they were two bosom friends gossiping. An eternity of foolish chatter with Kalen seemed better than any future with someone else. Maybe she didn't have the right to pretend, but they only had a couple weeks left. She'd offer up her eyes to Deium Erium if he forgave her this.

Blythe turned her head on the pillow to face Kalen curled on their side next to her. The room had darkened too much to see her hand now. She should have left hours ago. How many remained until dawn?

Just five minutes longer.

Really, I shouldn't leave because... Oh, just a few more moments.

But Blythe couldn't lie there forever. She couldn't let the mission—Papa and her friends—suffer for her own comfort. Heaving her heavy body up from the bed, she slinked away without a sound.

Kalen had informed her where the King liked to spend most of his nights, and after a few wrong turns, Blythe situated herself outside the window. It loomed many, many feet above her, but she'd found it, at least.

Only the pale moonlight provided any light over the grounds, but Blythe still wove through bushes and clung to walls. If somebody who happened to have amazing vision as their bestowment walked by, she couldn't imagine an excuse that would work.

Next came the climb. It wouldn't be the first building she'd scaled in the dark. But this damned dress—the petticoats weighed several pounds alone. It might have been better to risk a terrible servant ensemble.

Hells, even sneaking around in her shift might have been better for climbing.

Blythe inhaled sharply. "More working, less complaining," she mumbled to herself. Time ticked on.

It took a while, and two falls on her ass, but Blythe managed to get a groove going. Things moved slowly as she sank an improvised pick into the mortar joints of the bricks, fingers screaming as she worked her way up the façade. But eventually, she reached the ledge of the balcony.

Grabbing onto the bars of the small fence, she kicked her feet in between them to hoist herself up. Falling forward, Blythe tucked into a silent roll.

She flattened herself against the wall beside the window, desperately trying to control her ragged breathing. Not that those inside could probably hear anything, anyway. The booming music and raucous speech hinted that the King was, as she'd hoped, still awake and partying.

"Anton—you dog!"

"More wine, boy!"

"And there were *seven* of these Venekan virgins?"

Blythe pushed wispy hairs out of her face, flattening them behind her ears. Sweat stuck to her skin, but the cool night air offered some relief.

Her muscles tensed. One wrong move...

She peered into the room, willing herself to go unnoticed. It was not unlike the repulsive scene that Kalen had described.

The King held a silver goblet, dancing and drinking with several other men in between overturned couches and tables. With this sight before her, Blythe didn't much need to run through the list of terrible things about him.

Worn musicians played on their violins, lyres, and flutes, and servants on the outskirts held trays with rigid backs. Blythe averted her eyes from the sight of a bottom-naked man over on one couch, roughly pounding himself into a woman. But there weren't much better places to look. Naked bodies adorned the room, draped this way and that, some dancing, used as lap-cozies, or simply unconscious.

How could anyone like a man like this?

And yet, a different type of anxiety took root in her. When Blythe saw handsome men and women, sometimes she couldn't help the feelings of warmth, *desire*, that swept through her. Fantasies of sex for pleasure. Thoughts of a romantic courtship repulsed her, and yet she'd be flooded with physical attraction she couldn't stop or understand.

At night in her chambers here in Fletch, she sometimes caught her eyes drifting to those woodland nymphs in the paintings that decorated her walls. She had more difficulty ridding her imagination of temptations than she should.

How did her body react when her heart couldn't?

That was exactly what the King did, wasn't it? He treated these people heartlessly, using them to satisfy his body. Did that make them the same? Was she just as predatory? Would she be punished for selfish impulses as much as if she'd acted on them?

Blythe clutched onto a white column, trying to get herself together. What might Kalen say?

Probably that there was nothing wrong with wanting some fun. Maybe they would remind her that the King was different because he wasn't treating anyone like a person. He had dozens of sexual servants strewn about the room and would later throw them out like rotten food. That wasn't fun—that was violence.

Frida brought home plenty of girls and had no wicked bone in her body.

Still, Blythe abided by different rules. Deium Erium's favor precluded any sort of selfishness, and especially wouldn't allow pleasures that affronted the gods' standards of chastity. Thinking outside the lines risked acting outside the lines.

She concentrated instead on recounting the list again in her mind.

Hoards wealth. How he looked at young Eleanore. Made this whole competition. Fletch nationalist. Sees women as utterly inferior.

It helped, some. Though it was difficult to reconcile intentionally thinking bad things about someone.

Long minutes passed without anything of note happening inside the room. Blythe almost gave up. Perhaps the King and his men were too besotted to provide any information.

"But I must see *you* at the ball," the King slurred, clapping his cousin Jovan on the back. "Surely you can't be off to Kertiq so soon!"

Blythe's ears pricked. The ball—that was where the King would announce his choice, wasn't it?

"Stay that I would," Jovan replied, taking a sad swig of wine that dribbled down his chin. He set the glass down and grasped the King by the arms. "But you will have all of Fletch to cheer you."

"Bah! Or kill me in a jealous rage!" The King flopped down onto the couch, dragging his cousin along with him. "Though I cannot blame—oh, how the unchosen *will* be devastated."

Interesting.

If the King wasn't just bolstering his own ego, if he believed that an unchosen ally could do him harm... Perhaps that would be a way to divert suspicion from their crew.

Blythe inched closer.

"Then you must do as I've implored, cousin." Jovan turned to the King on the violet couch, tone pleading. "Have *all* of the guards to protect you there. Who knows what those—those shifty Qing are up to? And—and what would any of us do without you?" The man sounded close to tears. But he still managed to down another jigger of something.

"Perhaps you've reason," the King said with an earnest nod. He lay his head back on the couch, staring up at the ornate ceiling where bare-breasted sky nymphs reached to the light of the golden chandelier.

He sighed. "People simply don't understand how hard it is to rule."

What *was* the burden of a King like? Blythe had been stressed with the responsibility of securing food for herself and Papa, then the rest of the building's tenants, and *she'd* certainly dipped into immorality to make it happen.

But she had no time for wandering thoughts. Jovan had offered crucial information.

The King might station all of his guards, or at least most of them, at the ball. Which meant minimal interference or witnesses as they ransacked the vault and escaped. This could be their opening.

If the King remembered this conversation. But his cousin did seem quite persistent. *Who wouldn't want to protect—*

Don't go there.

The longer Blythe spent up here staring at the man, the harder it became to ignore his handsome face, or his odd sweetness with his cousin. His sculpted thighs.

Running on no sleep probably didn't help.

The barest glow of dawn peeked from the horizon. It was high time that Blythe got herself out of here. She'd gotten what she came for.

She inched her way down the wall, jumping once she was a few feet from the ground and landing silently in a crouch. A few gardeners walked about now, but they hadn't spotted her tucked among the shrubbery.

Blythe stuck to the shadows and crept back underneath the vaulted arches leading into the palace. Avoiding the hallways that Saidh had warned against for high traffic, she navigated the way back to her room with minimal confusion.

Nearing the familiar corridors of her chambers, Blythe turned a corner and sucked in a breath.

Wapite.

She started to turn around too late.

"Lady Esme," the—princess?—greeted, stopping with the two men that accompanied her, sounding somewhat taken off-guard. "How unexpected."

"Princess Wapite," Blythe stammered out, throat suddenly dry.

Wapite did very much compose herself like a princess: elegant and intimidating, with that air of confidence that could only come from being pampered and adored. Her umber skin was marked with beautiful tattoos, lines along her chin and circles above her brow.

"Titles are for the Chief and Elders. Just Wapite is fine," she said, the faintest trace of her accent peeking through.

Shit. Should Esme have known that? Sometimes the Ka'lani did come to trade in Jardae. Blythe had worked with some Ka'lani men at the docks in Ostrait before her branding, but titles had hardly been necessary in that sort of labor.

"Apologies, Wapite," Blythe said. "Lovely to pass by you." She tried to start walking again, but Wapite quickly interrupted.

"Strange to see you here, so late at night," she commented. She held her shoulders back, her expression passive.

"I...could say the same of you." Blythe swallowed. What did Wapite care what Esme got up to, anyway?

"Fairly so. I'd merely remark concern for your wellbeing, is all, Your Ladyship."

Blythe's brow furrowed for a second. A threat? No, too direct.

Oh... Because she didn't have any guards or servants with her. Wapite had an entire posse of protectors with her, as propriety dictated.

She just had to channel an ounce of nonchalance. "Thank you," Blythe said and forced a smile. "However, there's no need to wake the castle for a little stretch. My chambers are just around the bend here."

She feigned a yawn. "And I'm afraid I must attend to...some business, before breakfast."

She hardly took a step before Wapite stopped her with a light touch on the arm. Blythe whipped back around, sore from climbing and deeply annoyed by all this prodding.

Wapite let go, looking at her for a brief moment with wide, inquisitive eyes. Almost genuinely confused. It flickered away, and Wapite quickly regained her composure. "You've a tear in your *mantoa*, Lady Esme."

Blythe followed the girl's glance to her puffy ensemble of robes. She swallowed nervously at the jagged gash. Did it reveal her misconduct in some way?

"Best have your lady-in-waiting see to that," Wapite said, before nodding to her guards and turning in the other direction. "Good day to you."

13.

66 Printes, Reg. Marii 6

K alen's eyes shot open in the dark, fresh out of a nightmare. They reached for Blythe's arm but grasped only sheets.

"Blythe?" he mumbled, disoriented. Sitting up, they struggled to adjust their eyes to the dark. But Blythe had gone.

They'd fallen asleep in her bed. That should strike him as more unusual. People like the Viper would certainly remark upon it the wrong way. But finding Blythe had let their muscles relax and lungs take a full breath for the first time since they'd arrived here.

And really, Kalen hadn't meant to fall asleep. But after days of hard labor and barely resting inside a literal cupboard, they didn't think they could have avoided it. Obviously, Blythe knew he wasn't trying to make a move on her—this was no more than she'd done at sea. But Kalen never had any idea how far she relented simply to help him, or whether she felt the same relief, the same flood of calm that privileged him when they were near each other.

She'd gone quickly enough. Had she only entertained his visit to comfort him?

It was his fault they were in the court, and a rendezvous like this could blow their cover. So she would probably resent him for risking coming here, if she'd had the capacity.

They had to play their roles correctly.

Shit. What time is it?

They scrambled onto their knees, searching the window for any trace of dawn. Only the barest shadow of pink loomed on the horizon, but he had to get across the palace before Superior came to gather the servants for the day's work. Before any of the other servants arose and caught him sneaking back.

"Ow!" Stupid dark room.

Kalen paused nearly at the door. The Viper hadn't come in last night before he fell asleep. Maybe she hadn't come in at all.

They crept over to the large archway connecting the chambers. Holding their breath, Kalen listened. Not a sound. Creeping closer, they peered at the bed. Almost too dark to tell, but the blankets lay flat and unruffled.

He wasn't sure why he did it. For protection, maybe. Kalen fumbled over to the small table that still held several scattered vials and tucked two of them into his pocket. Surely, she wouldn't miss a couple.

Had the pile of riches on the table grown even higher?

The Viper had the right idea, here. He had to figure out a way to convince Blythe to skim a bit from the heist, at least stuff their own pockets with valuables.

The doorknob rattled. Kalen's cue.

They dashed out of the room and back into Blythe's, managing not to trip on their way to the door and bursting out of it. Kalen kept a brisk pace as they walked through the hallway, paying little mind to the jolts of pain as they struggled to hold their arm still enough.

If only they'd found some fucking laudanum in the Viper's room.

Frida had taught them to make that pain-relieving concoction, and with the kitchens emptied for the night, he snuck in to down two glasses as the clock ticked.

It would tide them over, at least.

Thank the gods the servants' quarters were dark and still when he crept in. They slithered back into their cupboard and delicately shut the door. A sigh of relief escaped his lips. This was a stroke of rare luck that they refused to blow.

Upon hearing the first servants stir, Kalen feigned a loud yawn and creaked open his placard door. "Morning," they said to Gilles.

The boy looked up at him with a smile. "Morning. Sleep well?"

Kalen watched intently as Gilles made his bed with precision. They followed suit, not ready for a repeat of their beating. "Eh, you? Does this look proper enough?"

"Not bad." Gilles craned his head for a better look. "There." He pointed out a minute wrinkle.

Kalen thanked him, smoothing it out. How could a boy so young—maybe thirteen?—be so put together and competent? A twinge of pity hit Kalen when the answer occurred to him.

Blythe had said they indentured a lot of these servants at the age of five or so, that it ran through peasant families like a chain. Technically, the parents didn't have to sign over their kids, but as indentures themselves, they barely afforded their own living. Let alone the mouths of children to feed.

"Do you miss them? Your parents?" Kalen asked. Then they widened their eyes and cringed. "Sorry! You don't have to answer that. I'll just straighten this out..."

"I see them, sometimes," Gilles said. "Around the palace. A couple days a year we can usually manage to spend together. But yeah. I miss them."

Kalen swallowed. *Why would I bring this up?* "I'm sorry. What are they like?" He shouldn't have asked.

But he didn't know what it was like, either. To have parents worth missing. Parents who would miss them. And there was this fond, shiny look in Gilles's eyes.

"Papa is a man of few words," Gilles said. "But he sneaks me bits of cake on my birthdays. I don't know where he gets them."

The boy locked up his cubby, a real glimmer of youth on his face for the first time. He giggled. "And Mama likes to tickle and make up silly stories. What was your family like, in Jardae?"

Kalen opened his mouth to respond. "They were—"

Superior's entrance cut him off.

Kalen immediately cast his eyes to the ground, and, like Saidh had suggested, bowed deeper than the other servants as they all greeted the man.

Sweat coated Kalen's palms. He dared not move to rub it away.

He needed air. "Please," he gasped.

"You, open your door."

He had to try to stop this fear. Superior was only a man. Kalen could handle this.

He did as instructed. His shoulder and ribs still stabbed him with pain, and his mouth filled with sand as the man grew closer.

"Hmm. Adequate."

"Thank you, sir." Kalen returned to his deep bow, despite the searing pain of ribs tearing themselves apart. He bit the inside of his already-busted lip. The taste of metal filled his mouth. Kalen could not stop his knees from trembling.

Coward.

Flashes of a boot striking them. Over and over.

"You may all begin your prescribed duties for the day." Just like that, Superior left.

A flood of relief drenched Kalen's mind. *Saidh, may the gods bless you a thousand times.* They could have let out a sob from the intense reprieve. He would have to find a way to repay his new...friend.

An idea of how to do that struck them while single-armedly scrubbing a window on one of the top floors of the palace. Maybe he could thank Saidh and get over all his pathetic fears at once. His consistent nightmares about the sea wouldn't stop unless he forced them to.

Through the soapsuds on the glass, Kalen stared at the dock below. They'd all need a way out of that harbor. Not on their Jardaen ship; they didn't want to advertise that it was an Ostraitian mission. And besides, it was hardly a worthy vessel for escaping the Fletch fleet if things got bad. They'd need to scope out getaway ships, find something nondescript and rapid enough to get them to Ostrait in one piece.

It wasn't exactly a gift. But offering to help Saidh with that tonight could be a friendly gesture, right? He'd need a lookout.

They might also have ulterior motives. He hadn't wanted his time with Saidh to end. This could be an opportunity to prove that he could be more than a quivering mess.

To Saidh *and* himself.

❦

Kalen waited until snores bounced around the quarters. Gilles, for one, snored remarkably deeply for someone of his size.

Here goes nothing. Kalen heaved himself out of bed and slunk out of the quarters. Who needed sleep?

Upon reaching Saidh's door, they lifted their fist. Then dropped it. What if someone heard?

Luckily, Kalen had borrowed a couple of Blythe's pins for his hair. Wincing as they pulled one out, they started fiddling with the lock.

He wasn't as good at this as Blythe. Unfortunately, she also had a lot more patience for it.

Kalen grunted in frustration. "I'm never gonna get this."

"Get what?"

Kalen yelped, nearly jumping out of his skin. Saidh had appeared behind him, clutching papers.

"What are you trying to break into my room again for?"

Oh, gods. Now they looked like a stalker. Kalen offered a nervous laugh. They wiped their palms on their breeches. "I thought you'd be asleep. I was coming to get you."

Saidh raised an eyebrow, a questioning look on his face. Then he shrugged, producing a key. "Well, get inside then. I don't feel like getting arrested."

"Can't say I recommend it, either."

Once inside, they laid out their idea.

"It *would* be easier if we could escape directly from the Fletch port," Saidh said. They'd all figured it would have to be a maneuver through another country's land borders first. "But we'd need a distraction."

Kalen leaned against the wall. They grinned, placing a hand on their hip. "That happens to be my area of expertise."

"And you're fine with being at the docks?" The captain sounded skeptical.

"Done with being afraid." Kalen steeled themself. "I want to help."

"Well," Saidh said with a brief pause, "no time like the present."

⤜⤛ ⤛⤜

They strolled through dim corridors, lit by torches leading out of the palace. Kalen did his best to keep an innocuous face as the two of them walked past the brown marble archway, lowering his head as they passed a guard.

So focused on seeming confident, they didn't watch their feet.

He staggered to regain balance after tripping on a cobblestone. "Aw, fuck." Kalen sucked air through his teeth. Pain jolted through their unhealed ribs.

Saidh cast them a glance. "You alright?"

The pair resumed walking immediately, but it was too late. They'd drawn notice. "You there," said the guard.

They tried to keep on, but the man would not be ignored. "I said halt."

"Let me talk," Saidh said quietly, then turned with an irritated expression. "Is there a problem, protigii?"

"What are you doing out here with a palace servant so late? Aren't you from one of the delegations?"

"And who are *you* to question a noble escort's duties?"

"Well, I... It is my job as one of His Majesty's—"

"Then perhaps it is also your job to know that His Majesty, in his infinite wisdom, has seen fit to grant the use of his servant for the evening to retrieve some of Lady Esme's personal effects that were forgotten aboard her ship."

The man bristled.

Saidh rolled his shoulders back. Kalen couldn't help but look up in awe.

"Perhaps that *is* your job, and perhaps you've been lacking. Unless you are ignorant enough to question His Majesty's judgment?"

"No, no!" the guard stammered, eyes wide. "By the gods, and all his grace, my apologies, I—"

Saidh scoffed. He gave the man a dismissive wave. "Just quit holding us up."

And with a gentle shove to Kalen's back, they both moved down the cobblestone path again.

Kalen's body flushed, and their heart jumped into their throat. Once a safe distance away, he let out a breathy laugh. "I have chills, man." That was a greater theatrical performance than they'd ever given, and Kalen considered themself quite the convincing actrix.

Saidh nudged them with his arm. "Experience as a military grunt comes in handy."

The pair rounded a corner, which was thankfully vacant. Ink blanketed the sky, but torches along the path illuminated their faces and the grassy slopes to their sides.

"I can't imagine you were ever a grunt." As their uninjured arm swung while walking, they brushed fingers with Saidh. Kalen jerked his hand behind his back, heat flooding his cheeks.

Saidh didn't comment on the contact. "I was the runt of the pack for a while, believe it or not. Thought they'd find me out in a week."

"Find you out?"

Saidh paused.

Kalen lightly touched Saidh's arm. "My lot are outlaws by nature. But you don't have to tell me if you're part of my lot."

He instantly regretted saying anything. Obviously, Saidh had stopped for some other reason. Gods, he would be offended that Kalen had even suggested such a thing. *Just look at him!*

Surely Saidh would clock them for even thinking they might be anything like Kalen—a frilly byjeka whose chest fluttered at the idea of holding the man's hand by candlelight, who could never fill the role they were supposed to in society, who—

"In Lastrian, our word means 'delinquent creations.'"

Kalen gaped. Saidh resumed walking, and they trailed after.

"Military didn't accept bodies like mine."

Ohhh. Was it bad that Kalen's body flooded with relief? "Thank the gods." Kalen slapped a hand over his mouth. The words had just slipped out again.

"What?"

"No, I just..."

The pair turned again, and Kalen's breath caught in his throat.

The docks lay in front of them, frothy waves splashing against the swaying wood planks. Ships upon ships, but his vision of them already clouded with spinning dots. How could they have forgotten this was where they were going?

"Are you alright?"

"Fine." Kalen's entire body tensed, but they forced a foot forward.

Air. He needed air.

Drowning. He flailed, but the pressure holding him under didn't relent.

Pain exploded in their chest.

"Please, Father," he begged, before his head was pushed into the icy pond again.

Pathetic.

What kind of useless fucking coward couldn't take one step onto a dock? Couldn't leave his stupid fucking room when the clouds grew heavy?

"You don't look alright."

Kalen's jaw clenched, and he forced another foot forward.

Drowning. Water filled their mouth when they screamed.

"I'm *fine.*" The wood sank underneath him. Dampness seeped into his boots.

Air.

He couldn't breathe.

"Kalen—" An arm reached out to him.

Panic gripping his mind, Kalen jerked and pushed away. "I said I'm fucking *fine!*"

His foot slipped.

And then he was falling. He was going to—

Saidh caught them, and Kalen clutched onto him like a lifeline. He was going to drown. He was going to die.

"Please, Father."

"We're gonna get out of here, okay?"

Kalen didn't know how long it took for the real world to come back into proper focus. When it did, he sat on a short-trimmed hill, picking out blades of grass with burning eyes. "Thank you. I'm sorry."

"Why did you suggest the docks?"

Kalen plucked another blade from the ground. "I thought... I should be able to."

"What I said, about not being afraid of things," Saidh said, scratching the back of his head. "It doesn't... It's not a switch to turn."

Kalen sniffled with a faint laugh, wiping at his eyes. "I think I've got that."

"How long do you have before they notice you're gone?"

The servants usually woke just before dawn. It had been around two when Kalen snuck out, but they weren't sure how long their trip and subsequent panic at the docks had lasted. An hour? Two? That would put them at four, and this far into Printes, the sun rose by six. A half-hour walk back, a half-hour to pretend-sleep and get up with the rest.

"I guess I should head back." An utter failure.

And no time to fix it. He couldn't even think of a half-decent joke to break the dreary mood.

Air.

Water filled his lungs—

Gods, he craved a dose of laudanum and to never see that gods-forsaken cupboard-bed again. His heart wouldn't stop pounding.

Saidh got up and offered Kalen a hand. "I wish I could commiserate," he said, mercifully pivoting the subject away from Kalen's episode, "but I just have to take minutes at a conference about saffron capitulations tomorrow."

"Oh, the agony."

"Maybe I'll make a trade deal for Jardae." Saidh shrugged, pausing for consideration. "There are worse spices to go bankrupt for."

"Well, let's not be *hasty*," Kalen said. Their lighthearted exchange beat back the panic. "The people need their turmeric."

⟶⟩⟩⟩ ⟨⟨⟨⟵

"You look chipper," Gilles noted. The boy closed his cupboard door, and Kalen hastily followed suit. Superior's footsteps echoed down the hall, and Kalen scrambled to stand in position. He struggled to push down the waves that crashed in his mind from yet another nightmare. "Not excited for lunch duty today?"

His entire body ached. "Didn't sleep well, is all."

He swallowed when Superior entered the room, already shrinking in on himself.

The man noticed. "You look like shit. Do you think that's any way for a servant of His Majesty to behave?"

Kalen tried to speak, but his throat was too tight for any sound to escape. He couldn't breathe.

"Are you fucking ignoring me, traverae?" The slap shouldn't have been a surprise, but it knocked him flat against the cupboard.

"I..." Kalen barely managed a squeak. Their mouth hung uselessly open.

With the luncheon ahead, the only thing that saved Kalen was that Superior didn't have time to waste. He declared that as punishment, Kalen would be alone scrubbing and restoring some old, abandoned bathrooms that had been assigned to the quarter. In addition to his regular shifts, of course.

The next two days were a terrified, sleep-deprived blur. Kalen served meals, scrubbed anything and everything, waited on spoiled brats, and bowed his head to Superior with shaking knees. He always did something wrong that earned him a bruising.

Only terror stopped him from escaping into several cupfuls of burning wine at night. Even if they weren't caught, Superior would smell the drink the next morning. But Frida's concoctions weren't cutting it anymore; they needed something, *anything* stronger.

One night, when cleaning the kitchens, they came across poppy seeds. Not opium. Just seeds.

But if Kalen could make a tea... Just this once, just to numb them a bit.

When the other servants weren't looking, they tucked the single small bag into their pocket. He hung around at the end of the shift, waiting for everyone to clear out before he turned on the stove.

The water boiled, and he dropped a portion of the seeds in. How much was enough? The bag was small, so they needed to ration it.

Maybe a few more seeds.

Some minutes later, they held a steaming cup. It smelled like release. But for whatever cursed reason, Kalen hesitated.

The vague memory of their half-comatose self on the ship. Frida saying it was lucky they'd weaned him off in time. Guilt for cruel words they couldn't recall. The awful withdrawal and vomiting they were only just getting past.

Everything hurt.

So much.

Kalen emptied the drink and bag of seeds down the sink and sank to the floor, sobbing. He cradled his head on his knees, clutching fistfuls of hair. It wasn't fair. It hurt so much.

They were so tired of being scared.

He'd tried to stop, and look how it had turned out.

Fear alone moved him to his next shift, alone in the bathrooms. As per usual, another servant brought him cleaning supplies, then left to report to Superior that Kalen had shown up.

As his fingers accidentally grazed the water underneath the tank lid of the toilet, bile rose in his throat. *Gods, nobody could do that on purpose. I bet I'm the only one that's lifted this tank lid in half a century.*

Struck by the repulsive reality of it all, it finally dawned on them what it meant that they'd been given cleaning supplies. *Chemical* cleaning supplies.

And now, a hiding spot.

A distraction. Something that made them feel safe.

They could get ahead. Start preparing the bombs they'd need once the heist took off. Make up for all their incompetence.

No one would go rifling through the water inside a vile toilet like this one. It would actually be more stable, too. Certain bombs didn't always mix well with oxygen—they could explode with impact, or with static.

Building the bombs gave him just enough to hold on to. Just enough of a refuge. It staved off the flashes of Father's snarling face, blocked out the freezing terror of Superior towering over him each morning.

The storm in Kalen's mind fell quiet as they worked. They teetered on the edge of new clarity.

Hadn't Saidh said something about fear? That it wasn't about destroying it all at once. And something else, too. Superior was training Kalen like a dog, conditioning his fear and obedience.

If somebody could condition Kalen into becoming this quivering coward, then they could certainly do the reverse. The time had come to start conditioning *himself*.

He started with washing his face in the sink.

It robbed them of breath.

Kalen retreated to making their bombs on the floor, filling pouches and tying their strings.

Several times, he tried again, falling back to his explosives whenever he started to hyperventilate.

Tomorrow night, they would try again. And the night after.

Drop by drop, they'd cure themself.

14.

Late-morning sun shone through the white-curtained bay window as Blythe sat on her bed with Saidh, maps sprawled over the duvet. She shared what she'd heard outside the King's window.

The Viper sat at the wooden desk against the wall, in between the bed and the door. She worked with a hard look on her face, repairing the gash in Blythe's mantoa. Her annoyance, at least, had been tempered by the helpful information.

"I just can't find any trace of this vault," Saidh vented, pulling a silver platter closer and dipping his toast in jam. His eyes scanned the many pages splayed out in front of them. "I've mapped out so many rooms already, I've scoured the libraries... It's not even on the official plan of the castle. I'm going to try tracking some of the guard shifts today. Maybe tomorrow, if the morning meetings don't drag on too late, I'll head into the village. There might be some local lore about it."

"I'll keep trying to find out what I can from the nobles," Blythe said, looking up at him. "There's a young Fletch candidate. She might know something if she grew up here."

"Just careful not to tip her off." Saidh took another bite of toast. Crumbs caught on his round, stubbled chin, and he brushed them off. "These Fletch are paranoid enough already, and the vault might not be common knowledge."

Blythe nodded, reaching for the glass of water on her nightstand. Still so strange drinking it cold, not having to wait for it to boil. "Not just the Fletch. The Ka'lani have been on my ass since we got here, for some reason."

"Has anyone said something?"

Blythe told him about the run-in with Wapite, and the other girl's weird looks at the last luncheon.

He shrugged. "Might be normal nobility pettiness. Jardaens and the Ka'lani are two of the peoples that would most want to be chosen, right?"

"Maybe." She wasn't convinced.

People were already suspicious of Jardae for possibly being a double agent for Ostrait, so if Wapite had determined to find out something fishy about Esme, they had to make sure she didn't.

And that meant Blythe had to be extra convincing at the luncheon today. Not a single incorrect facial expression or misplaced utensil could draw attention.

Saidh left her for a few minutes to get changed.

The Viper had managed to repair the mantoa at her inhuman speed. "Deia Sisu has blessed me in the war against your incompetence," she said, handing Blythe the robe.

"I can't even tell it ripped. You really *are* amazing at this." Blythe threw on the garment hastily. She didn't expect anything in response to her compliment, but that was no excuse to be impolite.

"I know." The Viper turned her back to replace some sewing materials on the shelves, but Blythe heard an almost inaudible mutter. "Thank you."

Blythe blinked. "You're...welcome."

There was a light rap on the door.

"Just hurry up," the girl said. "You can't be late."

⟫⟫⟫ ⟪⟪⟪

Somehow, the afternoon passed without disaster.

Wapite occupied herself in conversation with some of the other candidates, her success evident in the smiles they cast her way. So far, Blythe had only developed acquaintance with Eleanore and an Ashlan noble called Patricio. At least she hadn't made any more enemies today.

They had more pressing matters to deal with when she returned to her chambers.

"Archery?" Blythe exclaimed, throwing her hands up in the air. "We're all screwed. I've only got five days, and I was *terrible* on the ship."

"Well, you're gonna have to make learning," Frida said gruffly. She'd rushed straight from her cooking shift to tell them all, still wrapped in a floury, greasy apron. "The other cooks—it's hard to know how they're saying, the Fletch-loving assholes—but I finally understood." She put a hand to her temple, shaking her head in clear frustration as she switched to low, resentful Ostraitian. "They laughed at me, it's that obvious. Archery is *really* important to these Fletch."

Given the plethora of archers in their sculptures, and the combination of bows and rifles that many guards carried on their person, they *all* should have seen it coming. "It's not your fault, Frida."

But Blythe needed a way to practice. So Saidh led them through a dimly lit passage, narrow enough that only one of them could squeeze through at a time. Lined with cobwebs and with damp cobblestones jutting out of the walls, it was clearly not the main entryway to the armory. Saidh said there were various tunnels from the old palace, and not all of them had been closed off yet. Only the guards were supposed to know about this one, kept around for emergency access, but leave it to Saidh to find every feasible route.

The Viper had finally seen fit to make them some peasant costumes, so they'd all donned simple, dark clothing. Easier to move in, and they'd be dead if caught, anyway.

Blythe tried not to get ahead of herself, planning ways to sneak out and check on Kalen. Saidh had assured her he was keeping afloat, at least. Whatever that meant.

She could only just make out Saidh's figure in front of her, but his sharp intake of breath prevented her from crashing into him when he halted.

That, unfortunately, did not stop Frida from crashing into the Viper, who crashed into Blythe.

"Watch where you're going," the Viper hissed at the woman behind her.

"What's the holdup?" Blythe leaned forward to ask Saidh.

"I can't believe they're making us patrol this ancient hallway," a guard groaned from somewhere around the bend in the passage. "None of those delegates even know it's here."

His partner made a throaty sound of agreement. "Hells," he said, "*I didn't even know it was here until last summer.*"

Their voices weren't that far away. Maybe two minutes.

Killing them or beating them unconscious would lead to too much suspicion from the Fletch. Blythe cast a look at the Viper, hoping for some sort of plan—preferably non-violent.

The Viper shook her head, seeming to read those thoughts.

Blythe took a deep breath, before deciding to do something very stupid.

The cobblestones weren't flush against the wall, and she'd grown used to scaling brick walls to get in and out of mansion windows. This couldn't be too different. She found purchase on the first stone, then the next, barely clinging onto the archway as she climbed higher.

The others would know what to do. Hopefully.

Arms trembling with the effort, she dug her fingers into the cobblestones almost directly overhead of where she'd been, stomach pressed as flat as possible. She took a shaking breath and forced her body to move forward. At the bend, the tops of the guards' heads became visible.

Blythe didn't dare exhale.

She continued past them, praying silently to several gods that they wouldn't notice her. Once a decent length away from the others, her arms threatening to collapse, she did all she could: she loudly dropped down onto her feet.

Immediately, the guards jerked back.

"Did you hear that?"

"Aleid? They send you down, too?"

Both sets of footsteps rapidly turned in Blythe's direction, but the dark saved her. She climbed overhead again before they got close enough to see, teeth clenched together from the strain. The guards mercifully continued in the opposite direction, giving chase to a nonexistent intruder. Hopefully that would give the real intruders some time.

Blythe struggled back down the wall. She scurried back toward her crew, still not risking a sound. The armory doors lay just a few feet ahead, and Blythe worked at a record pace with her lock picks.

Comeoncomeoncomeon.

Click.

Checking in between the cracks of the door, Blythe confirmed the armory was empty before pushing the doors open and hurrying her friends inside.

She closed and locked the door behind them, letting out a sigh of relief. "Alright," she said, turning to the Viper. "What do you think I need?"

Within a few seconds, Blythe held a bow, and a quiver was strapped to her back. The others stocked their arms with arrows, careful not to take too much from any one rack.

They all dashed back the way they came.

After a quick change of clothes, they headed to the forest, where hopefully there wouldn't be any more surprise run-ins with the guards. Saidh soon left to take notes at a conference, abandoning Blythe to the mercy of their resident assassin, who took weapons training very seriously.

Hours later, the Viper groused, "You're still not holding it properly. Why are you all bunched up?" She forcefully adjusted Blythe's arms, bringing them up higher and extending them. "It's supposed to be by your ear, remember?"

There was nothing comfortable about holding a bow. Blythe much preferred to steal away into the shadows, where nobody had to get hurt—including herself. And this bow was huge. It was heavy, and holding it left way too many vulnerable organs in view.

"I remember," she grumbled. Burns made her fingers tender, and aches wore down her shoulders. That fluffy bed in her chambers called to her.

"Not so tight," her teacher reprimanded. Then: "Why'd you move your elbow?" Followed by: "You're thinking too much."

"Then why don't you do this!" Blythe burst out, throwing the equipment down. How easy it must be for the Viper to stand there barking about everything Blythe did wrong when she wasn't the one trying to carry this *entire* heist on her shoulders.

"Believe me"—the Viper gave a dry laugh—"I wish I could." *Because I'd be so much better at it*, she didn't bother saying. Because if the Viper were doing this, the nobles would be too enamored with her to notice if she used the wrong fork, which she wouldn't. And she could probably outdo any of them at the fashions and weapons they prized.

"I'm doing my best," Blythe said softly.

"Well, your best isn't good enough." The Viper's jaw set. Her eyes bore into Blythe's with a menacing intensity.

Blythe deserved the force of it. She had no right to lash out, no right to complain or want a break.

"If you cost me this mission," the Viper informed her, "there will be nothing left of your body to find."

15.

70 Printes, Reg. Marii 6

Kalen had a rare forty-minute break between daily duties and his bathroom shift. He managed to dedicate the first fifteen minutes to a shower in the servants' facilities without blacking out. Granted, ten of those were still spent psyching themself up. And it took another three for their heart to stop thumping afterwards.

But the success surged in Kalen like he'd slain a dragon. And as their stockpile of explosives grew, Kalen latched on to the feeling that maybe they were finally a little useful. A valuable member of the crew, even. One who wouldn't fall defeated at the sight of darkening clouds in the sky.

They spent the remainder of their break ducked into a textile supply cupboard of some kind, hastily sewing up a mysterious injury for the Viper. Who even thanked him. She wasn't so unpleasant when Kalen was being helpful, only focused on the mission to the point that nothing else seemed to occupy her thoughts.

"You're not very chatty," Kalen pointed out. A small stained-glass window in the door provided him with just enough yellowish light to work by.

"Conversation leads to an idle mind." She didn't even flinch when the needle poked into her arm.

"Well, I talk a lot and...hey!" Kalen dipped his eyebrows at the girl's singular giggle. He didn't buy the return of her measured expression. "I've got a needle in your arm, you know."

"Exactly. It's a strange time to pose questions about the weather."

Kalen switched positions to better work the next stitch. Who got cut this deep around their shoulder blade, anyway? They maneuvered awkwardly around the yards of velvet and cotton jutting out from the shelves but managed to find a place for their elbow on a roll of gold cloth.

"Not like you've been coming 'round for tea," he said. "Conversation is how you get to know people."

The girl scoffed. She crossed one leg over the other, as if it was perfectly normal for her to be receiving medical treatment while sat on a pile of hip padding and leaned against crowded shelves.

Kalen shifted on his feet. A drop of blood spilled onto the fabric. "What?" they asked.

"The only point of conversation is to find out a person's weaknesses. And you're not getting that from me."

Kalen let out a long whistle. But pity swelled in their chest. "You know, not all people are looking to gut you."

The Viper stilled. She seemed resolved in her declaration that he'd get no further information. "Perhaps not. But they're all looking for something."

"Some people are just looking to help."

Like Blythe handing him her last match so long ago. They'd once seen the world as just a crowd ready to tear them to pieces, too. And maybe they still did, a little. But not the *whole* world.

"You're naïve."

"You must be lonely."

The Viper bristled. Kalen finished with the stitches and reached for some scrap of cotton to bandage the injury.

"I can't be lonely. I'm such good company." She stood up, grabbing her robe from where it lay draped over the ottoman's arm. "Thanks for the stitches."

Excellent company, indeed.

But still. They'd done something right.

And something about the brief reminder of his past gave him a sense of pride for his—albeit complicated—present. Things were *finally* somewhat, maybe, going Kalen's way. He, at last, hadn't made a mess of things.

⟫⟩ ⟨⟪

Some hours later, Kalen sat cross-legged on the floor of the bathroom—which shone *spotless*. He tied together another pouch, then another.

They'd just re-wet their hair, and it clung to their face.

The tank was almost full. That number of bombs would be more than enough. Mostly explosives, but a couple of smoke bombs in the mix, too.

His shift cleaning had already ended. But they had zoned in, and nothing else existed until they completed this task. The bombs would be set, and they'd have done something genuinely important for the mission.

Though, Kalen likely wouldn't stop making them. There were other toilets.

Their fingers pulled the strings tight on the last bomb for the night.

"Kalen?"

Fumbling to shove the pouches behind his back, Kalen gave an uneasy smile to the young intruder. "Gilles! What—what are you doing here?"

"It's past your shift, I wanted to make sure..." Gilles drifted off, eyes scanning the poorly concealed pouches. And cleaners, and herbs, and a couple rocks.

Kalen really should get them in the water. When they worked alone, the risk seemed fine, but...

"I know what this is."

Kalen swallowed, throat dry. They glanced at the toilet from the corner of their eye. "It's not! I swear," they said, putting their hands open in surrender. "You'll laugh when I explain. Really, it's just—"

"You're working with the Peasant Revolters," Gilles declared, back straight. The child grinned. "I want to help."

The Peasant Revolters? Kalen had heard that tensions were stirring in both Fletch and Ostrait with the laity, due largely to the unpayable debts and food shortages. But he'd assumed that so close to the palace, with the King as he was...

"You want to help?" Kalen repeated slowly. As much as they hated lying to the kid, they couldn't refuse the alibi. Not if it meant the boy would keep quiet.

"Of course I do." Gilles stood taller. He put his chin in the air and gave a brisk nod. "I want to do what I can for my people."

"How did you hear about this?" Kalen asked, one eyebrow raised. Surely a thirteen-year-old wouldn't have deep connections to a political uprising, but it didn't hurt to check.

"Lots of the older servants whisper about it. They never think I'm listening. My dad, too," he added, as if trying to impress.

"That's because it's too dangerous." Kalen put a hand gently on Gilles's shoulder, looking down at his hopeful face. Relying on the kid for some advice was one thing, but they had to draw the line here. "The best way you can help is keeping it a secret."

That hopeful expression immediately gave way to a deep frown. "You think I'm too young."

"Well...yeah." Kalen removed his hand and gave an apologetic shrug. "I'm sorry, kid. It's just too much."

Gilles's round jaw hardened. "I'm not incompetent."

"No, of course you aren't!" Gods, Kalen didn't know how to deal with children. And he couldn't afford to upset this boy.

"Then let me *help*."

"Okay, you want to help?" Kalen glanced over at the pile of bombs. "Then help me get these put away."

Gilles didn't waste a millisecond. They stuffed all the bombs inside the tank within minutes. And the tank was definitely full.

They started to close it when Gilles asked, "Could I take one?"

"What? No! Are you out of your mind?"

Gilles crossed his arms over his chest. "I could use it to help the rebellion. Swoop in next time a servant is being treated badly!"

Kalen shook his head and sat down on the toilet seat. They looked up at the kid. "We can't give things away just yet. And you don't know how to use these. You could get hurt."

Gilles slumped against the brick wall, sighing. "I don't care if I get hurt. I just want to *do* something."

"Hey." Kalen ruffled the kid's hair and earned a tiny laugh. "I care." And the thing was, he wasn't lying. They really couldn't stand the thought of this kid wrapped up in their schemes. It was bad enough he'd landed Blythe and the others in this mess, let alone a child. "And so do your parents."

Gilles sank to the floor. Kalen joined him, sitting with their legs criss-crossed. At least the boy didn't seem angry anymore.

"But they can't protect me. What about when the older boys get rough? Or when a guard or Superior has a bad day?" Gilles's eyes shone, and pity swelled in Kalen's chest. He couldn't protect the child, either. He couldn't even look Superior in the eye.

"A bomb won't protect you," Kalen said.

Gilles didn't look totally convinced, but he also didn't put up a fight.

"But maybe I can get you out of here once the rebellion's plan goes off."

Gilles sniffled, wiping his nose with his sleeve. "I just wish I wasn't always powerless to do things." He bore into Kalen with his round eyes. "You mean it? Could you take my parents, too?"

"I'll do everything I can," Kalen promised.

A moment of silence covered them.

The kid might decide to kick and scream about it, after all.

But Gilles just nodded. "Okay," he said. "I trust you. But you'll see. One day, the Revolters will be lucky to have me."

⇼⇺

Strong rays of sunlight streamed onto Kalen's face from the window above the countertop as he cleaned in the kitchens the next morning.

It could have been bad with Gilles, but they'd managed to fix it on their own. He wouldn't even have to tell the others.

But he desperately needed to know what was going on with the crew. There hadn't been much chance to get word. So they'd wrangled their way onto a shift in Frida's kitchen.

She hadn't acknowledged him yet. Other servants and cooks bustled around the space, so the two of them avoided any suspicious contact.

Instead, Kalen worked his way scrubbing the cupboards, until they reached the one beside Frida, who stirred a pot of sauce.

She kept her back to him. "What is it?" Barely a whisper.

Kalen continued to scrub the light-brown wooden doors, ignoring the rubbing blisters on his hands. A dried tomato stain fixed onto the trim with admirable persistence. "News?"

"Not good," she mumbled.

Kalen watched from the corner of his eye as she extended her body upwards, reaching for a glass jar of some green herb.

Another cook walked nearby. Kalen focused his entire body on scrubbing, ears pricked and waiting for the person to walk away. The seconds passed at a lethargic speed.

Finally, the woman found the bowl she'd rifled around every shelf for.

It took Frida a whole minute to risk speaking again. "Archery. She's hopeless."

Kalen sucked air in through their teeth. These people wanted *Blythe* to use weaponry? The competition was in two days.

He had to go see her.

They couldn't exactly do anything to help—didn't even know whether she'd want them there—but still. They needed to know how she was doing, and the fleeting glances at fancy luncheons and dinners weren't cutting it any longer.

Besides, they'd lasted a full five minutes in the showers last night, and the nightmares had only woken them up once. It was time to tell her about everything they'd been doing.

⤜⤛

Kalen strode down the dim halls after their shift in the kitchen. He kept his head down to avoid the gaze of any passersby but kept a pace almost near running.

Gods, they grinned at the idea of seeing her. They hadn't spent so many days without seeing her since they'd met.

It was just after this corner and—

"Ow! Shit, sorry, I..."

The Viper picked up a fallen dress. "Is there urgent news?" she asked. Underneath the white maquillage, dark circles had formed below her eyes.

"Well, I guess not, but I did start making—"

"Then what are you doing? You can't be seen around here." Her tone was exasperated, and Kalen's stomach sank with anxious guilt.

"I just needed to see Blythe," he said, picking at his thumb. Her door stood just a few feet ahead, and they inched forward. "I heard the archery isn't going well, and—"

"And what? You'll hold her hand about it?" The Viper's lip twitched with obvious irritation. The girl stepped in front of Kalen, blocking their way. "No amount of distractions and coddling is going to help. Maybe instead of putting the cherry on the cake by getting caught in the halls, you could spend your time actually doing something *useful* for once."

Kalen rubbed their arm, looking again at the large white door down the hall.

"She doesn't have an hour to sit and gossip. And neither do you." The Viper didn't relent. The wide frame of her skirts and the sharp cut of her stomacher made her appear both elegant and fatal.

"But, if I could just—"

The Viper's expression flattened, her jaw growing tight. "Let me make this clearer," she said. "If you come anywhere near this wing of the palace, or do anything else to disrupt things, I will have a suicide staged to protect the mission."

"But you need me. I just sewed you up, and the bombs—"

"I haven't spent my time in the palace idle." She flexed her wrist. Was that a dart under her sleeve? "You can be replaced."

16.

72 Printes, Reg. Marii 6

The days had passed too quickly. The competition was tomorrow, and no amount of brutal training had proved effective.

Blythe readied herself for the large pre-competition dinner. A lady-in-waiting was supposed to help with all of this, but aside from the training sessions where Blythe tensed under her scrutinizing gaze, the Viper had been scarce.

"You'll be fine," Saidh reassured as Blythe pulled white gloves over her blistered fingers.

He lay across the vast bed, reading a book about Fletch aqueduct systems. She winced at the sight of her hair in the mirror, but her attempts to fix it only added to the mess.

Blythe gave Saidh an unconvincing smile. "It's just a dinner," she said. But passing for nobility wasn't something she could jeopardize tonight, especially when her failure tomorrow would cast enough suspicion her way.

The door flew open and then shut just as quickly. Heavy bags drooped under the Viper's eyes. Stray hairs had escaped her styling, and her eyes strained red.

Silence enveloped the room.

Whatever progress Blythe had made for neutrality with the girl had eroded through day after day of her failings.

Shoulders drawn back and expression hard, the Viper did the briefest once-over of Blythe. "Sit," she commanded, gesturing to the stool in front of the vanity.

"Hey, don't you think maybe you're being a bit—" Saidh started, but she cut him off without looking up.

She pointed at the door. "Out."

"You can't just treat us like dogs." But he still left.

Blythe sat and tried not to let the pain seep into her expression as the Viper pulled apart her poor excuse for a hairdo.

"Look—" Blythe started, after a few minutes of tense silence.

"No."

The brush yanked Blythe's head back. She winced.

"This is my—our only chance." The brush yanked again, as if to distract from her slip. "I'll break both your wrists in half before I let you screw it up."

Blythe covered her face with her hands, pressure building behind her eyes. "You think I didn't *consider* that? I... Whatever the stakes are for you, I have stakes, too." She dug her nails into her palm. "Injured—'newly crippled,' actually, is how they worded it—candidates are to be sent home in disgrace. No wrists, no heist."

"Then your only choice is to get your head in the game."

With fifteen minutes to spare before the dinner, the Viper stood up to leave.

Blythe couldn't help herself and turned to face the girl. "Once you get your money, what then?" Sure, the vault's contents would go to the Ostraitian elites. But clearly the Viper had plans of her own, judging by that stash of valuables in her chambers.

The girl's expression wavered for the briefest moment. She turned her back and shrugged. "I'll get more."

The door clicked shut behind her.

⤛⤜ ⤙⤚

Candle- and torchlight shone across the long dining hall, leaving an orange tint on the rare parts of the marble walls that weren't covered in red drapery, golden ornamentation, or bright paintings of historic and divine scenes.

Blythe gripped the underside of her seat, digging her nails into the paisley upholstery. She gave a tight smile to Saidh as he pushed in her chair for her. "Thank you, Sir Murad."

"Good luck," he said under his breath.

And then she was on her own.

There was nobody there to give her red peppers to. Holding back a glum expression, she pushed the pieces to the side of her plate.

"And you, Lady Esme?" Paulo, an Ashlan candidate with a lanky frame and mild attitude, asked.

Shit. What had they all been discussing? She'd forgotten to pay attention.

She smiled politely, wiping her mouth with one of the thick serviettes. Archery! It had been archery. The competition tomorrow, most likely. "It will be absolutely splendid to see Fletch's fine archers compete."

"*I'm* excited to compete myself." Wapite grinned, nudging a candidate from Gajeme—a nation that belonged to the Telu Confederacy, along with the Ka'lani.

Unfortunately, Blythe had been seated almost directly across. All the "lesser" candidates were shoved to the part of the table farthest from the King and his inner circle yet again. It had been a struggle to avoid Wapite's suspicious eyes all night.

"As am I," Blythe blurted out. What was the point of that?

"Tell me, do they still do much archery on Jardae?" Paulo asked, taking a bite of steak. "I heard they banned the practice after the war."

Had they? It would make sense. When Ostrait took over, they tried to make their new subjects as Ostraitian as possible. The Fletch national sport might not have lasted.

Wapite chortled.

Blythe glared over at her sharply. Anger burned her ears. "Do you have a problem, prin—Wapite?" Instantly, she regretted the outburst.

Wapite met her eyes with a cutting look, setting down her fork. "Simply remarking on the irony." She glanced over at her friend, who rolled their eyes in accordance.

"And that is...?"

"You've got the grace of a newborn deer, Lady Esme, if the rip in your dress last night was any indication." Wapite raised her chin, jaw tight. She lowered her voice, out of earshot of candidates not directly beside them. "But you *aqowegan* Jardaens roam around shooting with no restraint. They didn't even need to outlaw archery, because there's scarcely anything left to hunt."

Blythe opened her mouth. Then closed it again. Could she really begrudge Wapite being wary of her? If that was true, it sounded fucked.

Even in the city back in Ostrait, hunting small game like rats and rabbits kept a lot of people alive. She understood what it could mean for a people if the game was hunted to oblivion. And the game in Jardae also had pelts that sold for a pretty piece of coin.

Why had the gods allowed Fletch *or* Ostrait to take the island, in the first place? Did Deia Sisu, the goddess of war, only support bloodshed for the sake of it? If gods and kings could indulge in stolen bounties and displace peoples... Why did peasants dying of pneumonia serve penance for much less?

Blythe shifted uncomfortably in her chair.

The Gajeme person laughed to break the tension. "That just means we'll have extra motivation to blow you all away, right?" They raised their glass to clink.

Blythe and several other candidates met it, and she tried to resume a pleasant expression. Behind the twinkle of their eyes as they toasted, the Gajeme candidate shot Wapite a warning look.

"You're right, of course, Noodin," Wapite said. The elegant smile returned to her face, and she took a delicate sip from her glass. "Tomorrow will surely be a day of celebration!"

"But how did you rip your dress, Lady Esme?" Paulo leaned forward, pink flute of alcohol in hand. "It sounds like a scandal."

Luckily, Blythe had prepared an answer for this. Avoiding Wapite's inquisitive stare, she straightened her back. She spoke to Paulo sweetly, digging fingernails into her palms.

"You've caught me," she said, tucking her chin down and making her voice as meek as she could. She couldn't manage to force a blush, though. "I...was nervous about tomorrow. And I wanted to make an offering to Caestore Armei, so I went out to the garden to pray. But the worst bush of thorns snagged my skirts, and I even nearly broke my offering container." She did her best to sound upset at the last bit.

Even the Ashlans knew that letting an offering spill before its burial was a grievous event. Blythe wrapped her pitiable offerings in several layers of rubbery leaves at home, but the Fletch court provided terracotta containers to encase goods in.

"Oh, my deepest sympathies." Paulo touched her hand. Despite her aversion to touching a stranger, she covered his with her own, feigning appreciation. He did seem nice, at least. Not everyone could be terrible here, and she had to remember that. *Even the King is just a man.*

Blythe turned her head and found Wapite's eyebrows strangely still furrowed.

She should say something else. Or Wapite would only keep pressing, and she couldn't keep up with all these lies. "But it *was* so strange seeing you out so late, Wapite."

The Viper had advised putting other nobles on the defensive whenever possible. Guilt simmered in Blythe like always, but the girl only bristled briefly before waving her off with a laugh.

"You know we have all sorts of rituals," Wapite said airily. "I have to walk a mile before I lie down for the night."

Blythe thought she caught the widening of Noodin's eyes in surprise, but they agreed all the same. Maybe she'd imagined things.

At least the conversation shifted to more idle matters.

"What will you wear as you compete?" a Barcan candidate asked, not sounding very interested himself.

"Oh, isn't the mousse lovely?" said Ivanna, a Valsav candidate, barely containing a yawn.

"I wonder how many targets we'll have," mused Paulo, but even his eyes drifted in longing down the table. To the King and the real conversation.

And something about being relegated so far away *did* sting. Everyone seated near the King glowed with laughter. What were they saying? Would Blythe struggle less to stop fidgeting if she immersed herself in a better conversation?

At least the dinner was almost over.

The partying afterwards wasn't mandatory. In fact, the ladies were yet again encouraged to cool their temperaments with mint baths, and it was doubtful the King would notice her absence, based on how the dinner had been going.

Even across the ridiculously long table, though, Blythe would be astonished if he didn't notice Wapite. Blythe herself lingered in looking at the girl. But it was wise to analyze her as closely as possible to determine the threat she posed.

And to prove this was a real threat, she needed to see what in ten hells Wapite was up to. Or how much she suspected Blythe, even if those weird exchanges with Noodin meant nothing.

The bells rang to signal the end of dinner.

Chatting with a few other Telu Confederacy candidates, Wapite rose from her seat. Around one in the morning already. Those who had given up on a chance to make an impression on the King headed for the doors.

Wapite met her delegation escort by the doors and leaned to whisper something to the man. He nodded and opened the door for her.

Blythe had to follow them. She strode toward them, weaving in between the crowds of people with quick smiles and excuses.

But then in front of her stood King Marius's circle, and she failed to escape his gaze.

Now she had to stop and do the whole curtsy thing, because she hadn't spoken to him tonight yet, and it was some royal custom. Deepening her curtsy, Blythe repressed a scowl. "Good evening, Your Royal Majesty, and praise to the gods for your grace."

Her eyes flitted up once permissible. Wapite had gone.

"Evening, Lady Esme," he said pleasantly.

He knew her fake name? Blythe looked down at the tawny floors, unwelcome warmth creeping to her cheeks. *Stop being flattered! He would kill a child and laugh!* Though maybe she exaggerated unfairly. He couldn't really be *that* cruel.

Blythe fumbled for the right response. "Thank you for the feast and your company, Your Majesty."

"And to you, dear girl!" The King pulled her by a gloved hand into the circle of chattering nobles. He winked at her and lowered his voice. "I wish I'd spotted you sooner."

Blythe flushed, a smile splitting her features despite herself. She needed to get out of here.

He's the reason he didn't spot you. He chose the seating. It was dangerous to spend too much time with the man.

Creeped on Eleanore.

Thinks poor people are inferior.

Hoards...

Blythe kept trying to run over the list in her head. But the conversation kept at such a fast pace, and she couldn't afford errors or distraction in her responses.

And she couldn't just leave. The King had invited her *individually* into his chatting circle—she wouldn't recover from snubbing him like that.

As the King started to tell stories about his hunting exploits, a hilarious encounter with a Dunsik monarch, and even some of the tales that usually would have turned her stomach, Blythe hung on every word.

⟫⟫ ⟪⟪

As the hours passed, Blythe kept refusing drink after drink from the servants. Finally, another candidate told her to loosen up a little, and she caught the King's eye. She didn't want to disappoint him or spoil the fun.

She feigned a grin, desperate to remember that list of his wrongdoings, but the music boomed, and so much dancing and jesting flurried around her. Blythe downed a large gulp of fizzing alcohol. It was sweet on her lips, and the King winked at her again.

"Atta girl," he said, his voice a jovial rumble. He snatched her waist, and warmth spread through her body. "I do hope you'll stick around for the next dinner," he murmured into her ear.

His frame pressed against hers. It was a changing-partners dance that she didn't quite know, but Marius took the lead.

"I hope so too," she mumbled. Her heart skipped in her chest.

The King spun her around, and she giggled, mind swirling with an unsettling giddiness. She downed the next drink she was handed.

This wasn't her. Blythe didn't usually drink. But hadn't she often wished to have a chance at being someone else?

Marius's chest rested against hers, their feet moving in rhythm. He tilted her chin with his fingers, and she beamed up at him. His crystalline eyes were mesmerizing.

But just like that, the tempo shifted, and he handed her off to another partner.

"Milady."

"Your Grace," she replied, but her eyes drifted over to the King. Her heart sank, urging her to be in his arms again. Jealousy flared inside her at the woman now flattening herself against him with no shame. Blythe wanted to rip her hair out.

Is this what fancying someone feels like?

Mind buzzing with drink and legs moving along to the music until the violins paused, Blythe almost didn't hear the servant approaching her with hors d'oeuvres.

"Milady," said a voice she should have recognized.

Kalen appeared in front of her, dressed in black and white, holding a silver platter of pastries. Barely faded bruises still blossomed around their cheek and eye.

A lump formed in her throat, cutting through the false merriment. *This is what men like the King do.*

"Thank you," she said, taking a roll. She glanced pointedly at the door, hoping they'd understand her.

"You're most welcome, milady," he said. But she caught their discreet nod.

Kalen headed off toward the shining alabaster doors, and she cleared her throat. She had to do this before things got foggy again. "I'm afraid I must take my leave," she said, tone apologetic, with a deep curtsy.

"So soon, Lady Esme?" her dancing partner asked.

Thank the gods the King occupied himself with someone else. Had Blythe really wanted to *hurt* that woman a moment ago? "Well, I'll need my rest for the competition tomorrow," she said. She cringed inwardly. "We maidens are too fragile as it is."

The words made her want to vomit but satisfied the man. "Until then," he said, kissing her gloved knuckles. His lips looked wet. Fortunate that she had gloves on.

Leaving as quickly as possible, Blythe shot out of the doors.

Kalen waited there, and she pulled them behind a lofty marble statue. "Thank you. Seriously."

Her head still spun, and she struggled to catch her breath. A wave of revulsion crept over her now, thinking about how the King had gripped her body against his own. "Gods, I might be sick."

The drink gurgled in her stomach, threatening to spill out of her mouth. "This charm bestowment is not to be triflil...trife... Fuck, trifled. It's not to be trifled with."

Kalen's eyes were wide with concern, and they handed her another pastry. "It'll help. With the drink."

Blythe forced the food into her mouth, and then grabbed another. "How are you holding up?" she asked, mouth full. These pastries made her nose wrinkle with distaste, but that buzzing in her mind had to vanish as quickly as possible. Her head *had* to be on straight.

"Me? Fine, better, actually. But are you going to be okay?" They put a hand on her arm. "Sorry if I did anything suspicious, but I just couldn't let you carry on all...not yourself."

Blythe swallowed, wiping the crumbs off her skirts. "I'm so glad you snapped me out of it." Her smile wavered, and anxiety knotted her chest. She leaned her back against the oak wall, trying to breathe. "How am I going to do this if I already lost so easily?"

Kalen shook his head. "It's not just you." They sat down on part of the statue, leaning on their elbows. "There's something too compelling about him. It's just *enthralling* being nearby, and I've barely interacted with him, thank the gods."

"I think I might keep a pin in my pocket. Prick my finger whenever I think something nice." But was that an acceptable thing to do? Wasn't thinking nice things what she always strived to do? Though, at the least she could use it to shock herself from slipping away. And Deium Erium would be pleased with the pain of it.

Kalen shrugged and bit down into an éclair. "Wouldn't be a bad idea, honestly."

Blythe put another decadent pastry into her mouth. It sank like a rock.

"There's a servant whose parents were personally sent to execution by the King. And he *still* loves the man."

"Really?" Blythe sighed. How could they fight against something like that? She'd never encountered a bestowment that dangerous. Her own had been among the most distinctive of those she'd encountered at home. Most developed gifts as simple as perfectly threading each needle or not bruising from bar fights.

"Not all of them, though. There seems to be a revolution in the works..."

The doors opened, and both of them held their breath. A drunk man and very drunk woman stumbled out, hands climbing all over each other. The pair made their way down one of the corridors, and Blythe didn't speak until the footsteps faded.

"You can't be caught here with me." She had to force out the words. But the door could swing open again at any moment. All she wanted was for the two of them to stay huddled behind this sculpture and talk for the rest of the night. Not that there was much of it left.

Kalen hesitated. Then his shoulders deflated. "I really shouldn't let them notice I'm gone. But I had so much to tell you—"

Blythe wrapped them in a hug. She kept it light, remembering their injured ribs. "Stay safe for me."

⤜⤜⋙ ⋘⤛⤛

Bleary and ready to collapse onto the bed, Blythe ripped her shoes off, throwing them to the floor. For once, she was glad she presented as a delicate lady. The men wore heeled shoes to show their endurance and increase their imposing height. Blythe's feet already blistered, so she couldn't imagine putting up with that.

"At least it's not 'til afternoon," she mumbled, tugging at her skirts. Her fingers fumbled with the stupid strings at the back of her stays. Gods, the pressured garment was great to wear, but did it have to be impossible to remove oneself?

How petty she'd become already, groaning about such trivial things. Did Papa even have warm clothes right now? Were they feeding him enough?

Clang!

Blythe's muscles tensed. The noise had come from the Viper's chambers. It wouldn't be Kalen sneaking in again, would it? They'd get in serious trouble if they were found out.

Blythe slinked into the chandelier-lit room, clinging to the shadows. Of course she couldn't just go to bed. Why would anything be easy?

The Viper sat at her desk. She had one of her robes laid out on its surface, and a pile of stolen coins, jewels, and small treasures beside her.

Peering closer, Blythe kept herself focused on evading perception.

What was she doing?

Then it hit Blythe: the girl was sewing valuables into the hems and pockets of the dress.

But this couldn't be for the Governor. Not when they'd have a whole heist full of Fletch gold to appease him. The Viper wanted this for herself. Like Blythe had suspected.

But what *for*? She could have been making plenty of money if she took hit-woman jobs for anyone besides the Governor.

Maybe it was the lingering drink, wired irritation from the exhausting night, or some sort of weird hope that she could turn the girl to their side, but Blythe made a decision. She cleared her throat. "You're up late, Viper." Then, taking the risk, "What's all this for, really?"

The girl's eyes flicked immediately to where Blythe gently stepped into plain sight, arms flexing for a brief second.

The Viper gave a resigned sort of shrug. She put down the needlework. "Well, I'm not going to leave empty-handed if you screw this up."

If Blythe lost the competition too badly, the Fletch wouldn't necessarily assume they were spies. But they could send her home in disgrace, which meant no chance to pull off their heist at the final announcements.

"And what of the Governor?"

The girl gave a bitter laugh. "That's always the question, isn't it?"

The Viper's hair had grown unkempt, and without the makeup she wore in the day, the deep bags underneath her eyes were pronounced.

Tentatively, Blythe edged onto the ottoman across from her. Pity twisted around in her. "What do you need this money for, Viper?"

Blythe half-thought the assassin might just knock her out to avoid answering any questions. But it seemed she'd been caught in an unusual moment. "Because I'm vain and like shiny things," she bit out.

Blythe probably should have left. After all, it was her fault this archery thing wasn't panning out, and the Viper had made her disdain clear.

She began to edge off of the seat.

"I pay my debts."

Blythe blinked, stunned at the admission.

The Viper gestured broadly at the pile of valuables and the stuffed dress. "This should be enough to appease him. Then I can do as I like."

As she sank back onto the ottoman, a lump formed in Blythe's throat. The Viper was too smart to get into debt with the Governor, and even if she had... Surely doing hits of all kinds would be a quicker method to pay him back? Why work exclusively for a man who hung debt over your head when you had the easy means to kill him?

There was only one situation that forced enormous, ever-accumulating debt and employment. "Are you... Did your parents *indenture* you to him?"

The Viper's hands briefly squeezed against the lush fabric of her skirts before unclenching. She pushed the fabrics off of her lap and turned to Blythe, jaw stiff. "I hardly phrase it so crassly. And you'd do well to keep it to yourself." The girl stood, back tense.

"But I don't understand." Blythe trailed after the Viper as she strode across the room, nearly tripping over a pile of thread spools. "Someone like you, I'm surprised you haven't just..." Blythe tried not to feel that a murder like that would be righteous.

The Viper spun around, hands braced on the white frame of the powder-room door. Her carefully polished nails dug into the wood. "Of course you wouldn't," she spat. "People like you aren't used to paying what they owe. *I* go about the world honestly. And the Governor has fed me, clothed me, taught me, taken me under his wing when no others would blink at the orphan girl without a good trust." The Viper's eyes widened. Her ears turned red, and her lip furled—as if she blamed Blythe for the words she'd let spill.

But Blythe's chest only tightened. Voice soft, she asked, "But who told you that those things were a debt to be paid?"

The Viper's brows dipped. "Everything runs on coin."

"Kindness shouldn't," Blythe countered. She reached out, the wavering offer of a smile on her face. Maybe the girl wasn't as callous as she was conditioned. Maybe, like Kalen, she'd grown up with a price attached to every bit of praise, sympathy, help.

The Viper's face flickered. Her hands slid from the door frame, eyes trained on Blythe's outstretched hand.

Then her shoulders straightened, and a look of disgust wrinkled her porcelain features. "Kindness is a fairytale."

The door slammed in Blythe's face.

But that small confession had watered the growing empathy in Blythe's bleeding heart. The Viper was a real girl, not an evil, ruthless assassin that cackled while torturing people. A real girl whom the Governor had taken as maybe a young child, convinced the world was devoid of humanity, and now used for all kinds of dirty work.

Would Blythe think twice about killing people if she thought the world only offered men like the Governor?

She hated her uncertainty.

"I will try tomorrow," Blythe said. At the foot of the door, she left a few gems she'd originally pocketed in the hopes of bartering with the girl to make a less-cumbersome mantoa. Maybe, even if tomorrow marked this mission a failure, the Viper would still have enough to break free from whatever the Governor's hold was.

Blythe turned away, feet squishing against the rosy carpet. Just to the right stood the adjoining door to her own chambers, and she clasped the golden handle.

"Maybe you won't do so badly."

She might have imagined the peace offering, but she decided to take it. "Thanks."

If the Viper was capable of that small kindness, she must be capable of more, with time. Would they *have* any time to coax it from her?

17.

73 Printes, Reg. Marii 6

Three loud bangs reverberated throughout the room. Blythe startled awake with a yelp, knocking over a jar of ink. "Shit, shit," she muttered, shaking her hands in a frantic search for a cloth to lap up the ink spilling across the desk.

"Who is it?" Blythe called in her best Esme voice. She pressed a tea towel into the mess. Ink bled onto her palms as she righted the jar, but she resisted the urge to wipe it onto her shift.

Eyes still bleary with sleep, but hands too inked to rub them, Blythe threw the stained cloth into the wastebasket.

What time is it? She hadn't meant to fall asleep reading. She'd just wanted to go over some archery technique diagrams before... The competition was today.

"It's Frida! I've got food."

Food. Okay. That meant it wasn't too late if there was time to eat. The smell of seared bacon drifted through the door. Blythe quickly washed her hands and rushed over to let her friend in. As Esme, she'd been able to request that her own cook bring her meals, which gave them more time together.

Breakfast time *indeed*. "Gods, Frida." Her eyes bulged as the woman carted in the copious trays of steaming food, a wide grin stretching across her face. "Is lunch being hosted in my room today?"

"You need to make strength!"

Blythe allowed herself to be led over to the bed to sit. It was the only surface large enough to contain all of these plates and bowls.

"You must have had to bribe the whole kitchen to make all this."

Frida crossed her arms. The sunlight from the high window cast over her short black hair and kissed the white ruffles of her Ashlan clothing as she took her seat on the bed. "I do *not* outsource my cooking."

The feast stretched in front of Blythe, crowding her head with uncertainty. A plate was piled with steaming bread that made her stomach growl and bright-red raspberries that could have been straight out of a painting.

What's the right thing here, Papa? It seemed wrong to eat all of this while others starved elsewhere, but just as wrong not to eat if not being strong for the mission endangered others. It seemed right that she go hungry to offset the expensive fabrics that adorned her body while others shivered in the cold. But also wrong to hurt Frida's feelings, because she'd spent her time cooking all of this.

According to Papa, the right choice always existed. But in this confusing place, discerning it proved harder and harder. What would she become if she couldn't figure it out? What sorts of punishments awaited her already?

Knowing she would *have* to eat at the luncheon later, Blythe decided that the best she could do was take a few small bites. Frida's feelings would be spared some, and the rest could be for others. She still had those plainclothes, or rather the Viper did. Maybe she could find a way to see Kalen, to bring them something...

"Blyyyythe? Have the spirits taking you, niné?" Frida waved a hand in front of her face, and she startled back to reality.

"Do you think they feed the servants here well?" she asked, toying with the edge of a pillow by her side.

Frida shrugged. "We hand them the leftovers from the day. There's usually being a lot."

"...but?"

Her friend grimaced, folding her legs to the side. She hesitated before quietly continuing in Ostraitian. "But I'm not sure how much goes to the superiors, and what goes to the rest. Or what just goes out to the pigs."

Blythe nodded, swallowing. She took a sip of water.

"...said he was running something similar in Lastray. But dancing with this girl, it was..."

Blythe shook her head, snapping back into the conversation. "Sorry?"

"You should come," Frida suggested. She'd been talking about some underground tavern.

"I can't afford to get distracted," Blythe said, "especially right now. But it sounds fun."

Truthfully, it sounded loud and overwhelming. After being in the court, Blythe had surely experienced enough parties for the rest of her life.

"It's the only place I can actually understand anything," Frida said in a huff of Ostraitian. She picked up a roll, though her shoulders sagged. Gray circles lay underneath her eyes. She'd chewed her nails down to almost nothing.

She had said something about the Ashlan cooks constantly speaking Fletch to kiss up on behalf of their delegations. Blythe should have pressed more then, but she and Frida didn't do that. Still...

"We exist out of here, soon," Blythe attempted in the little Ashlan she knew. "But not dead. Soon...but to be much alive and happy. Thanking you for...doing friendship."

A laugh escaped Frida, and she shook her head. "Your Ashlan is... Thanks. I feel a bit better about my Fletch."

Years ago, the two of them had huddled close as they laid brick after brick, fingers numb inside frozen mittens.

"Do you hear about snowman who falls in love with his mittens?" Frida had asked through chattering teeth and a thick Ashlan accent.

Blythe had looked up from where she'd been applying mortar with shaking hands, a ghost of a smile cracking her chapped lips. "No, what happened?"

"Well, of course. Is glove at first sight."

Blythe's lips tugged upward at the memory. "I meant it," she said. "Promise."

"Do you *also* promise to help me eat these pastries?" Frida asked, switching back to quiet Ostraitian, her tone teasing. "Or is Fletch jam not up to your 'refined Jardaen tastes' now?"

"Well, if you insist—"

A tart collided with her cheek, dusting her with finely ground sugar. It fell onto the plate in her lap, and Frida snickered around her own golden, icing-dusted pastry. "I *do* insist."

"I guess the Viper won't have to worry about powdering my nose," Blythe said, rubbing at her face with a still-stunned chuckle. She leaned back and took a crunching bite of the dessert, letting the sugar melt on her tongue.

"It's a snack with many benefits," Frida said, stretching her legs out.

Blythe leaned a head on her friend's shoulder. Silence created a peaceful lull. If she forgot about everything else, it almost wouldn't have been so bad to stay here.

Was that the niggling voice that wanted her to be close to the King, or was it the plush, royal bed in her chambers tempting her to selfishness?

Maybe she could buy Papa a soft bed to lie on. He always tried to hide his aches. Maybe if the three of them—although Saidh might also be amenable—managed to liberate some of the heist money for themselves...

But they'd have to do it so the Governor didn't find out quickly enough to harm her papa. And so the Viper didn't find out and kill them all.

It was possible.

She shouldn't even be considering it.

They just had to figure out how. And then maybe it wouldn't be so bad, living the comfortable life that Papa always dreamed for them. A little pond by their large house in a new country could be enough. She would put to rest at last this nagging yearning to stand on a ship with the wind rushing against her cheeks.

But stealing was wrong, even from the Fletch.

And yet, maybe living a normal life would make her more normal. Wouldn't Papa be thrilled if she finally found a man she could tolerate marrying? Although the thought of giving him grandchildren produced severe nausea, that was thinking much too far ahead.

Selfish theft had gotten her into this mess. The gods would only amplify their wrath.

But wasn't it worse if it was all for nothing?

It didn't matter. Whatever the future held, *today's* survival mattered most. And succeeding in this competition was the first step.

The door flew open. "Come, hurry up." The Viper kicked the door closed, arms full of Blythe's sports habit, a standard design for all the candidates to wear in this competition.

Tiny Fletch irises dotted the burgundy fabric, the only decor in this surprisingly minimal piece. Probably to honor the god of bows, Armei, who apparently valued a measured focus on the hunt alone. Only a minor deity in Ostrait, but the Fletch paid a lot of lip service to him.

If they worshiped differently here, how could Blythe know the Ostraitian way was correct? She and Papa didn't even follow that, exactly. Deium Erium was a footnote to most. Papa knew he could help alleviate their curse, and she always trusted Papa's truth, but...*how* did he know?

These were questions for another time. The certatia offered her enough uncertainty today.

"See you after the show," Blythe whispered to Frida. Her friend squeezed her hand before shooing her to trail after the Viper.

An hour of prodding Blythe didn't understand followed. The garment fit just *fine*. It didn't fall off of her, and it didn't hike up to her shins. But the Viper almost entered a trance when she worked. Even gentle with her commands to raise this arm or lower that one. It seemed almost cruel to ruin it, especially when the girl *had* been awake just as many nights practicing alongside Blythe, who wasn't the easiest student.

Blythe would make it up to her today, though. She'd muster up some scraps of skill and perform mediocrely. Maybe then the Viper would lose some of her resentment, and Blythe could attempt to make some sort of bond with the girl. An opening existed somewhere. She had a duty, now. To show the Viper compassion.

Noon struck just as the habit and cosmetics reached the Viper's standards. Saidh rapped against the door, and the pair went to meet him.

"Milady," he said with a formal nod. He extended his arm, and she looped it around her own.

Blythe offered the Viper a small, awkward smile. It felt odd not to say some sort of goodbye, but odder still to say anything.

The girl gave a flicker of a nod.

Blythe turned with Saidh, ready to face the bustle of chatter a few corridors ahead.

"Good luck." Blythe angled her body around again as the girl stepped back. The Viper wrinkled her nose and stared at her fingernails in a quite obvious way. "Seems like you'll need it, anyway."

⟫⟫⟫ ⟪⟪⟪

Their steps clacked along the marble floors, growing closer and closer to the loud buzz within the equipment area.

"I have a note for you." Saidh pulled a crinkled piece of paper from his coat pocket, leaning down. "It's from Kalen."

Blythe snatched it up in an instant, desperate for news, any news, that Kalen could give her. *Are they well? Did they find something out? Are they getting enough to eat?*

She stared down at the scrap of paper. Not the lengthy letter she'd hoped for, but it surprised a laugh out of her.

In a messy scrawl unlike Kalen's usual calligraphy, with ink half-blotting over the last letter:

IF YOU'RE NERVOUS, IMAGINE EVERYONE IN THEIR UNDERTHINGS.

A bell tolled as they reached the equipment room, and Blythe stuffed the note into her pocket before the curious noble eyes landed on her. Anxiety already tightened her chest.

"Not the worst advice," Saidh whispered. He opened his mouth like he might say more, but closed it again.

"Lady Esme!" A man in a similar habit to her own, save for it being in velveteen purple rather than red, beckoned her over. "Right this way, if you please, Your Ladyship."

Gods, this was happening. She actually had to do this.

If only Kalen had been able to say more. Though she counted herself lucky he'd gotten her word at all, with the situation he was in—that *she'd* put them in. That she had to get them out of.

Saidh nudged her with his arm.

Blythe shook her head to snap out of it, allowing herself to be led toward the purple-clad man. They walked along a polished swirl of white-and-gray marble, which met an expanse of gleaming silver walls. Only paintings adorned the walls, picturing valiant huntsmen and knights sweeping to victory. Four statues of Armei framed the two doorways. Nobles swarmed the place like an infestation, following their own men in purple to racks of glistening golden weapons.

Blythe's man stopped in front of a rack with three other candidates present. "You may choose the bow that suits you best, Lady Esme." He took off before she could thank him.

Saidh stood silently at her side, chin straight as a military man's would be. Blythe watched as the three others scrutinized the bows, taking ample time in their decision.

It didn't make sense. All the bows were the same: ceremonial, regulation.

"Delightful day, isn't it, Lady Esme?" said the Hassaen candidate, a stout young woman with white-blond hair and freckles dotting every part of her daisy-white face.

"Quite so, Lady Anna," she agreed, smiling. That was the pleasant thing to do.

The other two nobles kept their gazes trained on the glimmering weapons, fingers trailing down each one. They were from the small nations of Calad and Irisia.

"Is there a magical bow hidden somewhere?" Blythe joked with Anna. What could all of this fuss be about?

Anna raised an eyebrow. "Of course there is. Don't be daft."

Blythe blinked. "What?" Had she missed something big in her studies? Did they actually believe in magic like that here?

Anna rolled her eyes and hefted a bow off the rack. She passed it to Blythe, whose arms sank with the sudden weight.

Heavy. Heav*ier*. If she'd been training with the regulation bow from the armory, then what was *this*? Mouth agape, she looked at the woman for an explanation.

Anna just shrugged, taking the bow back off of her. She brushed a stray lock of snowy hair back into place. "Look around you," she said plainly, clearly bored that Blythe couldn't keep up. "Are you really surprised? You must be younger than you look." Anna walked away, leaving Blythe on her own.

Saidh couldn't do anything—they weren't supposed to confer once in here. But he discreetly flicked his eyes to the other end of the room.

The big players crowded the upper end of the room, far away from her. A pattern revealed itself. All of the key allies—the high Fletch nobles, the Lastrian candidates, the really wealthy prince from Qing, the most stunning woman from mid-sized nation Pythia—they all jostled playfully with each other, bows already strapped to their backs.

The closer the racks got to Blythe's, the less impressive the candidates. They got either less strategically valuable, less outlandishly attractive, or both. Blythe was toward the back of the room, crowded in with tiny nations that nobody cared about and a couple of low-tier Fletch nobles with average faces.

At the rack across from hers, the Telu Confederacy delegates grouped together. Even Wapite stood there, despite her relentless perfection, though the bow looked weightless in her hands.

If the King hasn't noticed her, what hope is there he'll want you? Blythe averted her eyes.

The Caladi candidate sighed, finally resigning herself to the bow at the bottom of the rack.

The King had proclaimed that everyone would have a chance to win his hand. But only certain types of people were *supposed* to. So he'd use rigged competitions like this to carefully weed out the undesirable marriages, while maintaining deniability that he interfered.

If Blythe used this bow, she was out. She would be sent home in disgrace, and the Governor would kill Papa.

Even with a standard bow, she hadn't stood a competitive chance. But now? There would be no hoping enough candidates performed worse than her. Twenty-three were to be sent home today. A third of those remaining. She could not survive that.

Hefting up one of the weighted bows, she didn't even know if she could make it out to the arena.

The high-rankers made their way to the antechambers that connected to the stadium. The purple men occupied themselves with escorting them to the right rooms.

Almost all the way across the room. A rack—unattended.

Act like you belong and you will, echoed the Viper's advice.

Summoning all of her strengths for escaping notice, Blythe rolled her shoulders back and strode over to the weapon racks. Casually, not even letting her eyes drift down for fear of suspicion, she tucked her bow onto the rack and took another. Everyone busied themselves, too anxious to notice her.

Keeping her face as measured as possible, she strode back over to her area.

"Lady Esme?"

Fuck. Fuck. Fuck. *Fuck*. "Yes?" she choked out. She faced the purple-clothed man, who held an arm out to her. Was he asking for her to give him the bow?

"I'll walk you to your station, Your Ladyship." The man tilted his head at her. "If you're quite alright?"

Blythe forced a smile, smoothing her skirts. An enormous sigh of relief threatened to escape her. "Yes, thank you."

She'd gotten away with it. She could also get away with her archery performance. Couldn't she?

⟶⟩⟩⟩ ⟨⟨⟨⟵

Blythe fidgeted in her station, seated on a smooth, marble bench with no back support, boxed in dark wooden walls with two other candidates and no idea what lurked ahead.

"I'll just be glad to have it over with," the Irisian beside her, Viscount Finn, said with a shrug. The tassels on his shoulders bounced. "My country is just fine without Fletch purse."

"Then why come?" Again, Blythe earned herself two looks that said they couldn't believe her naiveté.

"Do they teach ladies nothing in Jardae?" Anna scoffed, and Blythe's cheeks burned. But she'd have to play into it, or else risk suspicion.

"What need have we for dry politics?" Blythe waved the girl off, aiming for a superior tone. She choked down her disgust at saying such things. "I know we need His Royal Majesty, and I am willing to die for the honor of his hand. Is that not enough for a lady to know?"

"No, it is not," Anna said curtly, crossing her burly arms. Blythe liked her. "A lady plays the role of a wife *and* a diplomat. And any diplomat knows you can't refuse an invitation from the Fletch King."

Blythe pretended to be hurt by this, jutting out her lip a little. Maybe she oversold it, but nothing seemed too extravagant with these people. "Well, I don't see why anyone would want to refuse. It's just ungrateful." Gods, even *she* hated Esme sometimes.

"Yes," Finn replied dryly, scanning out the tiny, frosted window of the door. "I'm sure your poor little delegation of four had *no* trouble scraping together the funds to come here. And you were even exempt from the gift-giving!"

"That's not true," she pointed out. "We did bring a gift. He was called...Kalen, I believe." Talking about him like that stung her mouth.

"Well, some of us had to let go of a servant *and* fifty of their best white horses."

Why was Blythe even participating in this fake argument? She really didn't even care about the outcome. Had the court already made her catty and combative?

"I just...I really want the King to be worth it, you know?" she said, changing her tone and throwing in a little sniffle. She dabbed her eyes with a handkerchief for good measure, and cast her eyes toward the door. "The journey was rough. We lost so much. I apologize for having lashed out, Viscount, it's just... I can't think we came here for anything short of awe."

Anna nodded, and Finn reached across the woman to pat Blythe's hand. "I understand, dear," he said.

"And he *is* rather lovely," Anna added. "Have you seen him play the lyre?"

"Oh, and those stories he tells!"

Blythe smiled, turning back to the pair. These nobles didn't actually seem so bad.

"Have you had the chance to meet him, dear?"

"Not properly," Blythe said, the dismay in her voice almost authentic. That one dance had been cut short too soon. "And I'll admit, I'm terrified of being a nervous wreck when I do."

Finn laughed, winking at her. "I spilled wine all over my shirt," he said. "*Completely* by accident, I assure you."

"I heard someone threw themselves off a horse," Anna said with a chortle. She leaned back against the wooden wall. "Just so he would help them up! He did, of course, such a gentleman."

Blythe laughed along with the pair of them.

"I can't say I blame them. The sight of that man on horseback?" Finn let out a low whistle. "Enough to drive anyone mad."

"You should avoid looking at any paintings then," Blythe teased. The walls were thick with triumphant pictures of King Marius. Not that she'd been looking.

"And whyever would I do such a thing? Might as well enjoy a bit of madness before I return home to Irisian stability."

The bell tolled.

Any trace of Blythe's smile vanished. A tight knot formed in her stomach. The hairs stood up on the back of her neck. *Run. I need to run.*

But where could she possibly go?

The door—which was the entire wall, really—swung open. Light struck Blythe's eyes, and she squinted, a roar of cheers pounding into her head. A rush of fresh air tickled her face.

An enormous stadium appeared before her eyes. A coliseum, the pristine relic of Fletch antiquity. She sat level with the circular area on the ground, trailing her awestruck gaze up, up, and up at the brilliant limestone arches that only stopped at the clouds. A screaming crowd of nobles, merchants, and aristocrats in their brightest attire encircled her, waving their Fletch flags and banners to shape a sea of red. Triumphant music blasted from every direction, and the smell of hot, buttery pretzels permeated the air.

Blythe's pulse beat in her ears. *Please. Please let me disappear.*

She was an ant, waiting for a boot to crush her into the soil. Smaller than she had been shrinking into herself as a child, the first time her bestowment had granted her unremarkability.

Something startled the crowd into silence. Their cheers vanished so quickly, the space vibrated with the echo of their loss. Blythe followed their eyes, hands clenching fistfuls of her skirts.

And there he was: King Marius. High above the crowd on a terrace that overlooked the stadium, marked by rich ruby fabrics and a glimmering golden crown atop his head. That heart-stopping grin lit up his features as he waved regally, greeting the desperate crowd. Nobody could tear their eyes away, and Blythe was no exception, despite herself. High above them all, the striking picture of complete jubilation, he did not seem to be merely a man. A caress of reverence swept through her, fighting against every thought in her mind.

I do not kneel for idols. And I will not kneel for this man. Blythe grasped at threads of defiance. She forced her head down, squeezing her eyes shut. She'd forgotten the pin in her other gown. *Remember the list.*

"My people! Are you ready for the festivities to begin?"

The noise of the crowd pierced Blythe's ears, and she jerked her head up. Had to clap. Had to play along. She had to play her part.

Finn let out a loud whistle. She'd forgotten the other two sat beside her. They didn't seem to notice her any more than she did them. As she screamed and cheered with the crowd, Blythe's nerves built up into anticipation, excitement, exhilaration.

"King Marius! King Marius! King Marius!" the crowd chanted, whipping their flags into a frenzy. Someone held a sweeping banner painted with his likeness. "King Marius! King Marius!"

Anna and Finn chanted along wildly. And what else was Blythe to do but join? Anything else would seem suspicious. An intoxicated fire soared through her veins.

Members of the crowd sobbed with joy. "King Marius! King Marius! King Marius!"

Then someone shouted, "Caestore Marius Optore!" *Divine Marius the Greatest*, an allusion to the traditional Fletch epithet for Deia Sisu—Caestia Martia Optia—with whom he shared a name. They deified him, claimed his lineage to her.

A moment of silence stunned the crowd.

They roared back, "Caestore Marius Optore! Caestore Marius Optore!"

The urge swelled within Blythe. She ground her teeth together to keep her mouth shut. The words pushed like a cluster of physical letters, trying to force their way out of her mouth. What was wrong with her? How could all of these people be wrong? Wasn't it cruel of her not to give the King the honor he deserved?

No. She dug her nails into the skin of her arm. *I will not be eroded.*

A charming politician, mob mentality. The list—she had to repeat the list. Confetti burst from two sides of the stadium, fluttering down into a rainbow. The sun shone on King Marius, the wind sweeping back his hair.

No, she would not look at him. She bit the side of her cheek until she tasted blood.

Head swirling, she only now noticed the targets that stood in the arena. An array of six, with three basic targets at the front, each with giant white circles and smaller red circles shrinking until the center point. Then, scattered around, were three others: a gleaming white stag toward the back, a golden apple suspended in the air at the other end of the arena—the only section without the clamor of guests—and a red dot that spun on a rotating barrel, appearing once every few seconds before it vanished.

"It is my pleasure," King Marius's voice boomed, at once a commanding rumble and soothing hymn, "to announce our first candidate to take the stage! Let us welcome my dear friend, His Royal Highness, Sultan Imperial Prince, Behcet of the Shuruq Province, Son of the Lastrian Empire!"

Behcet jogged out of his station with a wide grin, waving to the King and then broadly to the crowd. His archery habit, designed the same as her own, shone with a golden decoration at all the hems. He flexed his large biceps for an adoring public, taking his bow with complete ease as he reached the shooting podium. This was the sort of candidate who was supposed to win.

Each candidate was given six arrows. The crowd soared from their seats as Behcet effortlessly hit every single target. Goosebumps dotted Blythe's arms.

"The honor of welcoming Her Ladyship, the lovely and chaste Duchesse Celeste Lavigne, Daughter of His Lordship, the late Duke Henri of the House Lavigne!"

She moved like a dancer. She pierced through five targets with ease and gave a deep curtsy below the King.

One by one the candidates dazzled the audience, golden bows slicing through the air.

Slowly, their shots grew clumsier, their titles less resplendent. Fear clawed at Blythe's mind, begging her to denounce herself and get the execution over with. She could not go up there. How had she deluded herself that this could turn out okay?

Papa was going to die. Kalen was going to die. Frida. Saidh. All dead when she exposed herself in that arena.

"Her Ladyship Eleanore Toussaint, Daughter of His Lordship, Baron François Toussaint!"

The petite girl waved meekly at the audience, struggling slightly to aim her bow. She missed her first shot, and the second. But she managed to hit two targets dead center, more than her predecessor had, and the audience gave a polite round of applause. Members of the crowd cooed as she gave a deep, humble curtsy, and then made her exit.

There were too many others to keep track. A few missed the targets completely, and the crowd jeered at a wisp of a girl who couldn't even lift her bow to aim. They cackled at the Coldosan man who shot his own foot.

They cheered less now for the honor of candidates, but rather for their humiliation. Blythe imagined all of those eyes trained on her, crinkling with taunting laughter. Bile rose up her throat.

Anna went up and, sturdy as a rock, she managed to hit four targets.

"Congratulations, dear!" Finn clapped her on the back upon her return, and Blythe forced a smile.

It wouldn't be long now. They would call her. And she would have to walk up there and...and...

"Wapite, of the Telu Confederacy, representing the Ka'lani Nation," the King announced, and Blythe snapped to attention.

The girl walked up to the podium with straight shoulders, an unyielding expression on her oval face. A thin band in all colors rested around her forehead, large circles of emerald green adorned her ears, and white strands of fabric cascaded from the ends of her braided hair. Where most of the candidates by now trembled at their turn, her confidence did not waver.

She lifted the bow with ease.

Blythe tilted her head. Was that strength, or had they both had the same idea?

Wapite aimed. First, she hit the center of the three main targets, prompting remarks of surprise from the crowd. She hit the deer and the rolling barrel. Anna murmured something about Telu bloodlines. Wapite missed the apple, her arrow clattering against the stone wall behind it.

Shocked at the first near-perfect performance in at least an hour, the crowd whistled and shouted. Many cheered her on, though some cursed that all of the Telu peoples had those *talents*. But there had been many successful archers at the beginning, and bows couldn't be *all* of their bestowments.

Wapite seemed to shoot with plain skill. Precision, more than a hunter would need. *Had Wapite trained for this?* But no, she couldn't have—the entire competition had only been announced just before Blythe's arrest.

But the bow.

They'd been in the same area of the racks. And Blythe's had been nearly too heavy to hold. Wapite was a little bigger than she was, sure, but not hard and muscle-bulging like Anna. The girl's build was softer. And if Wapite was also desperate enough to risk getting a better bow...

She'd do whatever she could to get one more person out of the running. Especially if she could snuff out a fraud like Esme.

"That's you, isn't it?" Anna nudged Blythe's arm, nodding to the arena. "Good luck!"

Fuck. She hadn't even heard her name called.

Arms shaking, Blythe pushed herself up off of the seat. She stumbled forward, half-tripping onto the marble shooting podium. Struggling for a steady breath, she took in the overwhelming sight of the towering, thunderous stadium of people, and the looming targets too far from her.

A freezing fear gripped her.

She had to grab the bow. She had to shoot.

Her legs wobbled.

"Fucking shoot already!"

"What in ten hells is she waiting for?"

Blythe swallowed. Fingers trembling, she grabbed her bow. She remembered just barely to exaggerate the weight. Maybe they would pity her a little.

Loading an arrow, her entire body tensed. She made the mistake of looking up to King Marius. His eyes met hers, expectant, waiting. A question lingered there: *Do you dare dishonor me by refusing?*

And she couldn't.

She drew the arrow back.

If she didn't take this shot, Papa died. Kalen died. She pictured herself sobbing over their bodies. She'd condemned them both for her own cowardice. Her own ineptitude.

If you cost me this mission, there will be nothing left of your body to find. The Viper's threat echoed in her mind.

Blythe winced as she let the arrow fly.

It landed about five feet away from the target. She sagged with the faux-weight of the bow. Pressure built behind her eyes.

She didn't have to be the best, however. She didn't have to beat Wapite or Anna. She wasn't actually trying to win the King's hand. She only had to perform less terribly than a third of the people here.

It shouldn't be impossible.

Only the first third hit more than four targets on average. Many of the rest had only hit one, if she ascribed a generous average. She just had to do better than that. Hit one.

Blythe drew the bow again, letting out a ragged breath.

She adjusted her shooting stance, lining her feet up how the Viper had tried to drill into her. "Please," she whispered to no one.

And missed.

The knot in her stomach tightened. *Concentrate*, the Viper in her mind hissed. *You'll never hit anything if you don't clear your mind. The target is all that exists.*

Blythe closed her left eye, narrowing her field of sight. *The target is all that exists.* She let the arrow fly.

By the gods' fucking grace! Her arrow embedded itself into the wood within the middle ring of the white target.

It wasn't a center hit. But that was okay. She still had two shots. If she could land those on any part of the target, or hit even one of them at center... That might be enough mediocrity to remain here. She lifted the bow again.

The arrow landed half a foot behind the target.

Her heart plummeted. Only one shot left. And even if she hit the center, that would only put her slightly above the lowest third of candidates who had shot so far. Her only hope, and a frail one at that.

Blythe drew the arrow back, her thumb grazing her lips.

Concentrate. Concentrate. Concentrate. It repeated like a mantra in her head, but how could she let go? This was her last arrow. The one thing that determined whether Papa was dead. Whether Kalen and she and Frida were dead.

Please, Deium Erium. I beg of you.

Impatient stomps from the crowd mocked her.

With no choice, she let the arrow fly.

18.

73 Printes, Reg. Marii 6

B lythe's arrow cut through the air, skimming the side of the wooden target before it clattered to the ground.

Hot tears pooled in her eyes as she returned to her seat.

Anna hugged the side of her shoulder. "Cheer up, Your Ladyship. That was a splendid effort."

She could barely hear the words. Not over the vision of her father, hanging limp and colorless from a noose, a mob with bared teeth throwing tomatoes at his carcass. They ripped the wedding band off his finger to melt it down, careless of the flesh that peeled with it.

Saidh was saying something as he escorted her away from the stadium, but his voice was warbled nonsense against the sharp ringing of her ears. His arm guided her forward through each turn.

Then she was at the doorway of her chambers, and the Viper stood in front of her. "You have twenty-four hours." The assassin left without another word.

Frida hugged her, and Blythe returned it tightly. It might be one of the last she got. And the gods could wait to punish her for indulging; they'd have infinite hells to torment her with when she died.

Behind Frida, a mop of yellow curls offered a wavering smile. Frida and Saidh stepped out, giving the two of them space.

Tears soaked Blythe's face as she crushed Kalen in an embrace. They held her back just as tightly, and she couldn't bring herself to let go.

"I'm sorry." Her throat squeezed. But maybe—if the King just sent them home, if she got on her knees for the Viper and begged... "It's my fault. Only I should be killed. Maybe—"

Kalen pulled back, looking at her with shining eyes. "It's mine," he choked out. "You saved my stupid life, and I got you into the mess of bigger robberies because I wanted to be the one helping *you* for once, because... I shouldn't have been so reckless. I shouldn't have sentenced us to—to *this*."

Blythe shook her head, stunned. How could Kalen think they were to blame for any of this?

"But if this is it? If this is all we have," Kalen said, clutching both her hands, "I can't do this thing where I pretend you're helping me pay off a debt, when all I want is to live our life without excusing it, I—"

"You...were pretending?" Shock rippled through her. If their time together was all *real*, if he'd never been trying to fulfill some obligation or gain anything by being at her side, risking his life, if there had never actually been an *ends* to the means of caring about her...

He could have run this entire time.

But if their heart had doomed them to her fate out of some measure of actual love? It was so much *worse*.

Every moment of selfish joy she'd let herself live by sucking them into her curse. All of the treacherous love in her own heart that she'd failed to repress in time to protect them from it. And now she'd deceived them so much into loving her that they didn't even resent it. They would die here, and they held her hands with tearing eyes and red cheeks, all the same.

This *was* her fault.

And she couldn't bear letting Kalen suffer it. Not when there was a way out. She only had to be horrible enough to choose it.

Awe swelled within her at the sight of their wide eyes. Not the kind that consumed her and made her small, but the kind that lifted her to hubris, made her feel that the moral rules of man could not govern her. It didn't matter what penance she had to pay, or if the hole of sins grew too deep to ever dig herself out of, or how much good she owed Deium Erium—she would *not* allow Kalen to succumb to consequences meant for her.

"We both know that," they were saying, "but I'm tired of the conditions and caveats, I just want you to know that—"

"I have a plan," she interrupted, pulling them up with her. Her jaw set with resolve. "I'm going to keep us in the running. But I need your help."

Their eyebrows briefly furrowed, then lifted. "What do you need me to do?"

Blythe strode to the Viper's room with Kalen close behind. "I forgot to tell you one rule about servants."

She tore through a chest, taking various garments into her arms. The servant clothes would do well for this.

"What's that?"

"They love to gossip."

Next, she needed the vials. She dug through cubby after cubby. This one was it, wasn't it? The one the Viper had used to knock her out. She was almost entirely certain.

"I need you to spread rumors," Blythe said. Asking for any kind of help was abhorrent enough, but given the task ahead, it raked talons through her chest. That couldn't matter right now. Still, she tried to rearrange the cubbies, to leave little trace of her intrusion. If it didn't work, best not to upset the Viper further. A quick untimely death was still better than a slow one.

Kalen worked to tidy too, tucking away the loose garments. They tilted their head, waiting for her to continue.

"I don't think I'm dead last," she explained in a rush, mind swirling. Her idea was outlandish, but not more ridiculous than being here in the first place. "If I can just nudge a few people out of the running, I might be secure enough to stay."

"Still don't see where I come in?"

Blythe presented them with the little vial. "I'm going to sneak these into a couple candidates' wines. Hopefully, it knocks them out. Frida can help me carry them into...suggestive positions." It was one of the key rules that candidates could not sleep with one another while they were guests here. They had to save their purity and show their respect for the King.

"And you need me to make sure the servants find them," Kalen said slowly.

Blythe nodded.

They beamed, cupping her face excitedly. "You're a genius!" He looked like he was working up to say something more, but she cut him off.

"We have to hurry. It has to be before dinner, so everyone is sober enough to notice their absence."

"Where should I get the servants to find them?"

"The gardens." Blythe considered a moment. "By the King's favorite rose bushes. I heard someone say they remind him of his late mother."

Can you really be so cruel to Marius? a voice within her nagged. Kalen's mischievous smile stretched across tear-stained cheeks. Yes, she absolutely could.

⁕⁕⁕

Blythe chose three indiscreet noblemen as her targets. She would not allow them to compromise any of the women, whose prospects and reputations would remain ruined their whole lives. She slinked one by one into their chambers, her vial in hand.

How much should she use?

The Viper hadn't needed a lot, just the tip of her darts. But was there a difference between injection and ingestion?

Blythe settled for two drops in each of the unattended goblets. It wasn't difficult. Every candidate was meant to rest until dinner, and so they were alone. All she had to do was wait for the turn of their heads, and she vanished back into the shadows before they noticed.

It took immediate effect.

Having left each of them unconscious, with no clue how long it would last, she rushed to meet Frida in the kitchens. Saidh had said she'd be alone in the saucier station for a few hours today.

She took it more in stride than expected. "Where?" she asked.

"This way."

One of the tunnels Saidh had shown them led to the gardens, where they built the perfect scene of a covert threesome gone awry. The gardens sprawled so vast, some of the greenery so dense, that lovers could plausibly think it a good hideout. But it was public enough that the servants would not be at risk when admitting they'd been walking past.

One by one, they dragged the men through the tunnels and next to the rose bushes, on full alert for footsteps. Then they went back for the decorations.

Blythe's moral compass stuttered, but she couldn't afford to be squeamish. This, or death.

She and Frida strategically positioned the bodies. Gods, she could hardly bear to look. These men hadn't asked for this. But she'd picked these three in part due to the sinister "conquests" each had bragged about. Perhaps the two of them delivered some sort of retribution?

She hated that it would be more effective if she undressed them. She unbuttoned coats and discarded shoes, and the nausea rising in her demanded that it be sufficient. It was already wrong, how they were draped across each other, how...

Focus.

This, or death. This, or losing everyone.

They decorated the scene with wine bottles, strawberries, and a small canister of black powder for good measure. If the poison was too strong, it would look as if they'd been snorting opium. In reality, it was some harmless spice that looked awfully similar. They rubbed the container with vinegar to mimic the smell.

Gods, what if the poison *was* too strong?

"They'll just feel woozy," Frida assured her, with a pat on the arm. "And it'll only be a slap on the wrist. They're from powerful families."

It was somewhat comforting.

Blythe looked warily at the decorations. "You're sure it's not too much?"

Frida shrugged. "With these people? Nothing seems to be enough."

Footsteps sounded around the corner.

Blythe yanked Frida's arm, ducking the two of them behind a large bush. They knelt in the dirt, ears pricked.

One appalled shriek.

"Francette, come over here, quick!"

Things were in motion now. The sky dimmed already. How much time did she have before dinner?

She and Frida scrambled away from the scene, taking the long way back around to the tunnels. Frida lifted the grate, and Blythe dropped down inside. With no time to waste, she thanked Frida before sprinting her way back down the network, getting as close to her chambers as possible before slowing.

Blythe threw on her clothes as quickly as she could without help, fumbling with the pins on her stomacher. The Viper might have given up, but Blythe clung to the hope that *her* efforts would be enough. Unable to properly style her hair, she affixed a scratchy wig to her head.

She was just a lady headed to dinner.

A lady who planned to compete awhile longer.

19.

I t didn't take much to spread the rumors.

In the corridors of one of the target candidates' chambers, Kalen waited until another servant turned the corner, duster and rag in hand.

He strode along as if he'd just come from cleaning the room, muttering, "I can't believe the disloyalty."

The passing boy gave him a curious look, slowing his pace.

Kalen looked up, as if surprised they'd spoken aloud. "Oh, sorry, I— It's just an upset, you know?"

"What is?" The boy had stopped now, head tilted with vague interest. A servant did well to know what they walked into. Not all of these nobles acted kindly to the staff.

Kalen pretended to look torn, casting a fleeting glance to the candidate's chambers. "I'm sure it's just because I'm getting used to things here," they said, putting their predisposition for rambling to good use for once. "But it seems horrible that we're all supposed to keep it quiet, I mean doesn't His Majesty deserve better? To serve the likes of them, when he's been such a gracious host... Oh, but even if the whole staff

knows, they'd have our tongues out before believing us over such esteemed delegates, and... Really, I'm sorry to bother you. I should go."

Kalen made as if to start walking again.

The boy grabbed him by the wrist. "The candidates? But what have
they done against him?"

They restrained a smile. "Oh, you didn't hear?"

Easy enough to convince the boy of a well-known secret affair between
the candidates, and easier still to slip in that they were going to desecrate
the King's beloved gardens tonight before dinner. The horror of it all!

"Oh, but don't say anything. Really, it wouldn't do any good."

"By the gods, you have my word."

Naturally, every servant in the palace knew about this "secret affair"
within the hour.

"Of course I *knew*," said servant boy Boswell to servant boy Milos.
Towels wrapped at the waist, the pair walked past Kalen as he scrubbed
soap into his hair. "But did you see how big the two of them were? They
said they'd put my skin inside out if I told!"

"What, you couldn't take 'em?"

"I could take *you*, so shut up." The two boys jostled amicably, their
scuffle a dim noise underneath the run of water that soaked Kalen's hair.

They hadn't cringed at the cool rain of the showers in some time. For
the first time, he'd become used to having freshly cleaned hair. He closed
his eyes to savor the vivifying droplets that ran over his face.

The memories still lurked there, taking turns to bubble to the surface.
But in their mind's eye, their own middle finger stuck up in front of the
recollection of their father's shouting face.

Now, stepping inside this shower made them almost...free.

If they could do this—find pleasure in their father's tools of childhood torment? Gods, maybe he was more than he always thought. Not just an incompetent coward. Not a failure of a man.

No, if they could be sitting here—smiling to themself!—underneath a trickle of water? They could do anything. And they weren't *failing* to be a man, they were saying Fuck You to everything their father had tried to beat them into being.

"But I heard they found opium with them."

Kalen's water ran out as another gaggle of servants shuffled into the bathroom.

"And one of them was wearing the old Queen's wig..."

Kalen wrapped a white towel around their waist, pride surging in their heart. He'd actually helped to pull this off for Blythe, and the rumors only grew more entertaining as the night went on.

Apparently, the King had already left dinner quite abruptly.

"Surely not!"

"I'm telling you! He was dressed up as His Majesty's mother the Queen, doing *you know what* in her gardens!"

"And a lot of it, too, by the sounds of it," chimed in a third. "They were still out cold when His Majesty's investigators arrived."

"One of them still had a fake cock up his—"

"No!"

"I'm telling you! Gods, and they could have had His Majesty's real one. What were they possibly thinking?"

Kalen walked past, and one of the group's members gave them a nod of acknowledgement. *Huh.* Usually, other servants either ignored or bullied him. He nodded back.

The boy leaned over and whispered something to his friends as Kalen continued on back to the quarters. Excitement stirred in Kalen's chest. They wanted to do *more*.

And it seemed the perfect time to make things up to Saidh. Last time at the harbor, he'd been too afraid. They hadn't gotten a chance to find a suitable ship. But now that the palace was almost scoped, their crew would do well to plan the exit strategy.

And it was more than that. Kalen was ready.

Today, the shadow looming over him shrank farther than ever. Those droplets from the shower felt like renewal. Like a chance to finally fight instead of turning tail and running away.

The last nightmare they'd had, they had been swept out to sea like usual. But this time, instead of drowning, he'd started to swim. It must have been a sign.

Kalen knocked on Saidh's door quietly. Not two seconds later, he was pulled inside, the door shut and locked.

"Do you have news?"

Kalen proposed the plan to scope out the docks again. Piles of maps and drawings littered Saidh's desk and floor, all vault-related, to be sure. "Come on," they said. "It seems like you could use the air."

Saidh hesitated, glancing at a pile of books a few feet away. "There are a couple ships I've been keeping my eye on, but really, I don't need company."

Of course, Saidh wouldn't want them to come along after last time. Why would he even think otherwise? Their shoulders sank.

But he wouldn't give up so easily. "Nonsense." Kalen attempted to pull their shoulders back, but their grin remained sheepish. "Everyone needs a lookout."

"I don't think it's such a good idea. After last time?"

Kalen flushed. "I hoped... I mean, I *know*. This time is different. And I want to make it up to you."

"I didn't ask for you to help last time either," Saidh pointed out, brow raised.

Kalen rubbed his arm nervously. "I can't swim." The words stuck like glue in his throat, but he forced them out anyway. "I need someone to teach me."

Truly, they hadn't meant for this to be a quid-pro-quo situation. He'd only wanted to make up for the stitches and being so weird the last time they went out to the docks. But how else were they supposed to fully face the water, if they still feared drowning whenever they were near it?

Kalen's dream had been telling him something.

Blythe could teach them. But she clearly had enough going on right now, and maybe it would be good to accomplish something without her.

They still reeled at the realization that she'd believed their pretense of paying a debt this whole time, and they had no idea what to make of her reaction. Had she been appalled? Certainly, she hadn't been *glad* that they'd spent the past two years with her for no reason but for the sake of loving her?

If she hadn't been playing along, did that mean she'd been perfectly alright with parting ways after they robbed the Governor? Maybe if Kalen could face the waves, then he could face her. Maybe he could be brave enough to ask and receive an answer, even worthy enough for her to love them back instead of discarding them as a sin.

"I don't mean to be rude. But you nearly passed out just seeing the water." Saidh crossed his arms, and Kalen's hope started to drift.

"What's the harm in another try? I can help this time. I promise."

Saidh grumbled something Kalen couldn't hear. Then, "Why can't you swim?"

Kalen took a step back.

They tried to laugh it off. "Ah, you know. Fell down a well as a kid."

Saidh hummed. He straightened up, looking Kalen up and down. "You're serious, aren't you?"

"Yes." Though, not about the well. It had been a pond, and they'd been pushed.

Saidh slung a coat over his shoulders. "Alright, let's do it, then."

⁙

The docks swayed underneath Kalen's feet, cool water soaking through his thin shoes. Butterflies flapped their wings in his belly, but they didn't churn his breakfast into nausea this time. The waves crashed lightly against the wood, almost black in the dark, and a salty mist cleared their nose.

"I wanted to scope this one first," Saidh murmured. A large ship towered over them, red-and-gold flags flapping in the wind. From one of the farther Fletch provinces, perhaps.

They'd seen the crest on one of the delegates, and the name rested on the tip of their tongue. "You want to run away from the Fletch in a Fletch ship?"

"They're the fastest." Saidh shrugged, climbing the steps aboard. He kept a wary eye on Kalen, but they surprised themself by following suit with only a slight tremble.

The nightmares clawed their way up. But the bees vibrating in Kalen's chest, telling him to give up and run away, were the same that had stopped him going near water at all. He'd gotten past them with the sink and then the showers, and they had to keep pushing forward.

"Only way to outrun a Fletch ship is with another one," Saidh continued, once satisfied that Kalen wouldn't keel over. "Or one from Ostrait, but that's unlikely, given the circumstances."

"Please, father." His head forced down again, again.

Water rushed into his mouth, lungs screaming for air.

Kalen rested his hand on the wooden lip, looking down at the sloshing water. With a sharp breath, he stepped fully onto the ship, a swell of pride drowning out the buzzing fear. "How come, then?" he asked.

They crept through the main deck. Kalen paid attention to the docks below, while Saidh did some sort of analysis of the ship's condition.

"It's the steam power." Saidh took on a different tone whenever he started explaining something about boats or history or politics. Like an excited kid sharing a discovery.

Kalen didn't really care about steam power, but as Saidh talked about it, they kind of smiled to themself. *Holy shit! I'm on a boat and not having a bad time!*

That only made Kalen smile wider, though they tried to temper it so they wouldn't be grinning like an idiot. *I'm on a boat, I'm sober, I'm with a cute man, and I'm hardly even panicked.*

"The Ostraitians invented it, actually, burning coal instead of relying on wind to make the ships go faster. For ages they had the only coal mines, too, which is how their navy got so formidable." Saidh paused to examine some diagrams at the wheel, which Kalen couldn't understand for the life of him.

Waves splashed underneath them. Kalen flinched, but only for a half-moment.

A half-moment. They could *so* live with a half-moment.

Saidh continued without missing a beat. "But eventually the Qing found some coal reserves. Didn't have much use for them, though, being continental, so the Fletch secured a trade monopoly with them. Cost them a pretty piece of coin, so there aren't as many ships, and of course there are the Ashlan pirates that hijack them sometimes. But anyway." Saidh cleared his throat, as if he'd realized how long he'd been rambling on. "None of the other delegations have steam power. So a Fletch ship would be best."

Kalen kept their eyes trained on the ground below. A scuffle sounded, from around the bend, but they couldn't see anything out of the ordinary.

"I'm gonna check out the cabins," Saidh said, already bounding across the ship. He turned to look back over his shoulder. "But whistle if you see anything."

Kalen gave him a mock salute, regret pinging in their chest as he vanished behind a cabin door.

Alone, the air turned eerie. The stars twinkling above didn't seem nearly enough to light up the sky, and the low moan of bullfrogs could have been howling sea demons. Gooseflesh dotted Kalen's arms, but he willed it to vanish. He could handle being alone for a few minutes if he could handle being here in the first place. And honestly, what was the worst that would—

"You don't *understand*! We were *drugged*! My father *will* hear about this, and—"

Kalen whipped his head in the direction of the voices, scrambling to the very edge of the ship for a better look.

"Do you know how much it's costing your father to make this go away?" the delegation escort hissed, yanking along the strapping noble candidate. A handful of Fletch guards marched behind, all of them headed...

"Securing that bridewealth was your only job. You'll be lucky to marry a baroness now."

Oh, no.

"But I didn't do it! I only ever touched the servants, and it's not like they count. You *have* to investigate this!"

Kalen remembered where the crest was from now. The Fletch candidate, one of the ones that Blythe had framed. This was his ship.

Kalen whistled sharply.

"You'd better pray they don't investigate your opium use."

"But I didn't take any! Not since we've been in the capital!"

Saidh hadn't emerged.

The footsteps grew closer, their looming figures only a few ships away. Kalen ducked below the lip, fear simmering. Crawling along the deck, he scurried into the cabin area, shutting the door behind himself before standing up. Heart pounding, they scanned the room for Saidh.

The dining hall sprawled much larger than that of the small ship they'd arrived on, with high oak walls covered in red-and-gold bannisters and delicately carved chairs and tables. Three other doors led to other cabins. Gods, how would they even find Saidh in time?

Kalen let out another sharp whistle.

The floorboards outside the cabin creaked, voices growing louder.

"Could we not at least stay to make our case?"

"What more leniency do you expect from His Majesty? At the very least, you can show him the respect of groveling out of sight."

The knob of the cabin door rattled. Kalen sucked in a breath and sprinted for the door across the room, flattening themselves against it on the other side.

"*Shh.*" Saidh put a finger to his lips, crouched behind a floral chaise a few feet away.

Kalen crept forward, ducking beside him. Their mind reeled. They had to get out of here before the delegation left the docks. "Do you know which door leads back outside?" he whispered to Saidh, whose stout frame was only half-hidden by the chaise.

Perhaps they could creep back down the stairs and onto the docks again, like nothing happened. But he had no idea how to navigate this ship, and heat already wafted into the room, the smell of burning coal vague but undeniable.

Saidh looked torn. Perhaps he didn't know the layout so well as Kalen assumed, but with a bestowment for navigation, surely...?

Kalen breathed a sigh of relief when finally Saidh nodded. "Follow me."

They weaved through several rooms in silence, accompanied only by the sounds of their breathing and the clicking metal of the starting engine. The voices had faded away, and a loud whistle shook Kalen's eardrums.

They entered a small chamber made of cheaper wood and filled almost entirely with barrels and sacks of flour. Saidh shut the door behind them, slumping against the door with a guilt-ridden expression, running a hand over his face.

There was no other door.

Kalen's body went rigid. "Saidh?"

The resignation in his companion's slumped shoulders, the room so very far across the ship and nondescript enough to go undetected in. This wasn't just a wrong turn.

Another loud whistle pierced the air. Sweat stuck to Kalen's neck. The ship rumbled to life beneath their feet.

"Look, it's for the best, okay?" Saidh said, not moving from his position against the door.

Panic gripped Kalen, his pulse thumping in his ears.

"We might not have another shot to get out of this, and who knows if the King won't still kick Blythe out? Every second here is time wasted, is a risk. I'm sorry."

Kalen bristled. They eyed the door, stepping toward Saidh with hands flat in surrender. "We have to stay. Saidh, we *have* to get out of here. Now."

Saidh shook his head, meeting Kalen's eyes with some mix of apology and resolve. "I was going to go alone, but you insisted and—"

"And *what*?" Heat rose to Kalen's cheeks. His muscles tensed. Saidh was larger, stronger, but they could not back down from this. Blythe needed them. And he needed her. "You thought you'd kidnap me? Were you planning to ditch us this whole time?"

Saidh flinched. Kalen tried to shove his way past, but that was futile.

"It's not like that!" He pushed Kalen back, but in a gentle sort of way. It only infuriated them more. "I thought it could be worth it, the money. But every day I'm gone is a risk, and if I die out here, they're all screwed! Blythe might have skirted by this time, but how in nine hells are we supposed to make it until the end of the competition? I could at least get you somewhere safe."

"Every day you're gone from what? Some shitty smuggling business in Ostrait?" Kalen scoffed, hardly believing his ears. And trying to throw in that bullshit about wanting them safe? They'd be safe with Blythe by their side.

"I'm not just a smuggler!" The confession blanketed the air between them.

Another loud whistle, and the ship rumbled. Heat sweltered against Kalen's skin. "Please." Their voice softened with desperation. "We have to get out of here."

Saidh's shoulders fell, and he opened the door. "Follow me. There isn't much time."

It didn't take the pair long to hit the open air of the deck. The ground swayed beneath their feet, the smell of smoke thick in the air. Kalen's hands crashed forward onto the lip. The ship had jerked forward. Saidh panted beside him as dark waves crashed against the hull with intimidating force.

"I can't do this," Saidh whispered. "I can't leave them behind."

"What did you mean?" Kalen grabbed Saidh's wrist as the man turned to walk away. "You're not just a smuggler."

Another loud whistle. And another.

"I don't only smuggle rye and opium."

The deck shook with such force, Kalen could scarcely remember to breathe. They had to jump. They had to jump down *there*.

Maybe he wasn't ready after all.

"I smuggle people."

"*What?*"

"People like you. And me," Saidh explained, taking his wrist gently away from Kalen's grasp. He looked to the looming water, then back to the cabins. "I get them to safety. My sister and I, we run these hideouts. And when I was caught in the military, I started using the trade to pay for them. Without the money I earn... I can't leave them with nothing if we die out here."

Kalen's heart squeezed.

Saidh wasn't simply a selfish coward. He had people to protect.

But so did Kalen.

The ship lurched forward. They both gripped onto the lip again, and Kalen's eyes widened in horror as the hull disengaged from the dock.

Time was up.

"I'm sorry," they said.

Saidh turned his head just as Kalen shoved forward, sending him over the ship with a startled yelp.

There was a large splash drowned out by the roaring of the ship.

Kalen couldn't allow themself time to think. They threw themself into the frothing ocean below.

⤜⤛⤚ ⤙⤘

Kalen gasped for air, thrashing his arms against the water. He kicked his legs, gripped with terror as the first mouthful of saltwater shocked his lungs.

Pushed down into the icy pond. Bubbles escaping his mouth with a scream.

An arm snaked around his waist, holding him above the surface.

"You weren't kidding." Saidh grunted, stroking backwards for the both of them. He dragged them both to the shallows, then dumped Kalen onto his knees, pulling himself to the shore, body limp with exhaustion.

"Thank you." Kalen's breath came raggedly, and gooseflesh chilled their skin. He turned himself over to sit on his behind, watching the ship grow in distance as water fell against his chest, swishing around their exposed knees.

He forced air through his lungs. In and out. In and out.

Eventually, it became a natural rhythm again.

A grin split their face.

They were *in the water.*

Kalen sat in the water up to his tits, and he'd almost drowned, but he'd still tried to swim, and his blood pumped with a mix of fear and pride, and the part of him screaming that he had to get out immediately was so much quieter than it had ever been.

"I fucking did it!" they screamed, fists in the air. The chill of the waves rolled over him like freedom. The memory of their father's face surfaced, childhood horrors clawing their way to the top, but they just stuck up their middle fingers to the sky. "Fuck you, old man!"

Saidh dove forward, slapping a hand over Kalen's mouth. "Do you *want* us to get caught out here?"

Kalen almost didn't care.

Saidh slowly removed his hand. He sat back with Kalen in the water. "I could kill you for that," he said.

Emboldened, Kalen splashed him with a laugh. "But you won't."

"No, apparently not," Saidh grumbled, looking regretfully at the retreating vessel. "I could find another ship."

But then Kalen and the others would have no exit from the court. They'd be questioned for their missing delegation escort.

"I respect what you did," Saidh continued, arms folded over his chest. He shook his head. "But you have no idea what it cost me."

Kalen hesitated. "Wouldn't it cost more to walk away from a chance like this?"

"A suicide mission that they might decide not to pay me for?"

"Well, what if we took our own payment?" This was a risk, and he hadn't even broached the matter of convincing Blythe yet, but what was the alternative? Plus, they'd taken a risk jumping into the water, and look at them—they'd nearly grown used to the cool ocean around their body. Exhilaration coursed through him.

"A double con?"

Kalen nodded. "Something like that. We'll skim a little, without the Viper knowing. You could share in the profit, all those Fletch jewels to trade. But only if you stay."

Saidh leaned back on his elbows, face tilted to the starry sky. "Still doesn't solve the fundamental problem. We're almost certainly going to fail."

A small smile quirked Kalen's lips. "Well, with that attitude, we will. And like you said, you could always decide to leave if it goes south."

Saidh considered. "And Blythe and Frida would agree to this?"

"Yes." *Eventually.* "At least stay to hear the King's announcement. I'm certain we'll have survived this competition, and then we can really try to prepare for the next."

Saidh held out his hand.

Kalen shook it. "Market concluded." They paused. "I knew you were secretly a softie."

Saidh turned away, the embarrassment in his expression visible even in the dim light. "I'm not."

"I'd say your secret is safe with me, but I'd rather not start a friendship off with lies." Kalen beamed, nudging the man with his shoulder. "Now, how about that swimming lesson you promised?"

"You've *got* to be kidding."

"Are you not a man of your word?" Kalen teased, raising an eyebrow.

Saidh gave a long, somewhat dramatic sigh. He sat up and put a hand on Kalen's back. "Okay, lean back. I'll show you how to float."

Butterflies fluttered again in their stomach, but mostly the good kind. "Like this?"

"Next your legs... Yeah, now you've got it."

They could do this. They *were* doing this. What else could they do?

20.

73 Printes, Reg. Marii 6

It happened hours into the dinner. The King had been in the middle of telling another enthralling story. Blythe had nearly forgotten what she'd done, the many hours of his presence proving alarmingly mesmerizing.

"Your Majesty." A man leaned to whisper something in the King's ear.

Marius stiffened, clenching the fists that rested on the table. "You're quite sure?"

The royal face relaxed back into a serene smile, and he got up from the table. He clinked a glass as if everyone wasn't already paying attention to him. "It has been a pleasure dining with you all, but I'm afraid I must retire." Dismayed expressions answered him, and he gave an apologetic nod. "A leader never rests."

There was a tangible loss when he left the room.

Blythe tried not to feel it. It was good he was gone, wasn't it? *He beats servants and ogles barely bloomed girls, and you have work to do.*

The nobles already frenzied with gossip.

"Why do you think he left?"

"What if the Princess is ill?"

"Did he not like the food? I'll have a word with those ingrate Ashlans."

"Hey, watch your mouth! It was probably your obnoxious chewing that drove him off."

"I wish we could follow him."

"Well, do you want to know what I heard from my head servant?"

"No! In his *mother's roses*?"

Blythe had no trouble slipping away. Nobody was going to remark on her absence. And at that moment, the King and his important officials would not be meeting in the strategy room—nor would the servants be bothering with tidying it.

Indeed, the halls were empty. Blythe slipped a hairpin from her wig and made quick work of the lock.

It was a less ornate room, with dark-red walls lined with wooden shelves packed thick with dusty books and rolled papers. In the center of the room lay a gold-and-brown table with small soldier figures and flags on it, the map of Barcana sprawled underneath. But her attention fixed behind the table on a beautifully carved oak desk, littered with maps.

Blythe rushed to it, sifting through the piles as quickly as her fingers would move. War map. War map. Economic district. War map. Floor plan, but just for the stadium. War map. It would have been absurd to think he'd have the right map lying on his desk, but the papers rolled on the shelves were so caked with dust, they must have been older than the vault itself.

In fact, none of these shelves looked like they'd been touched recently. And this desk had only legs, no drawers. So where had the King stored all of these papers on his desk, if he hadn't grabbed them from the archives lining the walls? Surely he didn't keep them piled here at all times.

Then she saw it.

A bit of paper, no larger than her pinky, stuck out where the desk met its legs.

She ran her fingers underneath the lip of the desk until she found the miniscule latch, so easy to miss. Scooping the contents of the desk as carefully as she could onto the floor, Blythe popped up the desk top to reveal a cache of documents. There it was, resting right on top.

She pulled the map out, flattening the desk top to get a proper look. Not much of it made sense to her. She could see the rough location of the vault in the southwest wing of the palace, but which one of these symbols was the entrance? How would she know what floor it was on? This was Saidh's area of expertise.

Blythe snatched a bottle of ink and a pen up from the ground. She did a frantic scan, desperate for a piece of blank paper.

Screw it. She'd inscribe the map on her skin if she had to.

Blythe dipped the pen in ink, just about to do the first stroke, but the hairs stood up on the back of her neck.

"Isn't it unladylike to steal?"

Blythe nearly jumped out of her skin, whipping around to face the enemy. The pen clattered to the floor as Wapite's footsteps grew closer.

Blythe swallowed. Her back pressed against the desk, heart hammering as she struggled to conjure some explanation. "This isn't what it looks like."

"Go on, then." Wapite crossed her arms, raising a brow.

Would she buy that I was looking for a privy? Blythe scrambled for any excuse. Her thoughts ran to the gossip from dinner.

"Okay, I give in," she said, sinking her shoulders. She cast what she hoped was a sad, bashful look at the drawers. "I...I hoped to find out what disquieted His Majesty, King Marius at dinner tonight. I know my performance today was lacking, so I wanted... Perhaps if I comforted him..." A damn good lie if Blythe said so herself.

Wapite's eyes narrowed. Her lip twitched with irritation. "Like with everything you say, somehow my mind fills with doubt."

Shock struck her as Wapite stepped closer, forcing Blythe to look up in order to meet her gaze filled with challenge. *What does she know?*

"I assure you." Blythe straightened her shoulders, mustering up a tone of righteous defense. "Helping His Majesty is all I want."

"Liar." Wapite leaned an arm on the desk, her soft cotton sleeve brushing over Blythe's hand as she peered over her shoulder, taking the map into consideration. Wapite tipped the jar of ink, spilling it across the parchment.

Blythe's body went cold.

"You're not even from Jardae. But don't worry." Wapite stood up straight. Her tone was measured, laced with a threatening undercurrent, yet not hateful or even unkind. "I won't send you to the ropes. As long as you're on your way home by the next certatia, and the King is unharmed, there will be no need."

Blythe's breath caught in her throat.

"Understood?"

But something flickered to life in her mind, dots that didn't connect. Why in six hells wouldn't Wapite turn her in now? If she knew Blythe was a liar, if she was trying to ruthlessly get into the King's good graces, then why? Why give Blythe weeks longer to gather information, to scheme?

Unless Wapite couldn't turn her in.

A sudden confidence surged within Blythe. She stepped closer in defiance, so close their chests nearly pressed against each other. "You're bluffing." Meeting Wapite's earth-brown eyes, she let out a dry, disbelieving laugh. "I should have asked earlier. What are *you* doing in these chambers?"

A heated tension blanketed the air between them. Neither would back down from their stare.

Adrenaline coursed through Blythe's body, and she pressed forward, forcing Wapite to stumble back.

The girl caught herself quickly. She held her ground with a set jaw and closed fists. "I'm *not* in these chambers," Wapite finally said. "And neither are you. Agreed?"

Blythe hesitated.

Alternatives were in short supply.

She took Wapite's outstretched hand. "We will not speak of this." They shook on it.

Despite the temporary truce, Blythe's mind reeled. Wapite had some scheme of her own.

And she sounded willing to go to any lengths to succeed. *But then why protect the King?*

Unfortunately, Blythe would have to deal with this mystery on her own. Finding this map had been her way of making up for her nearly fatal incompetence in the tournament. She couldn't burden the others with yet another problem she'd created.

What was she worth here, if she simultaneously failed in playing her noble role and succumbed to it? She'd bought time with her appalling actions in the gardens, and with calling Wapite's bluff. But time for what? To further burden everyone with her inadequacies? To lose all sense of virtue in this court?

She alone had to correct the Wapite situation. As well as her own deteriorating behavior.

Despite the alluring release of biting back. She had to make things right.

All she could manage tonight, however, was collapsing on her bed.

⋙ ⋘

Esme sat across Marius's lap, dress puffed up around her and legs hanging over the arm of the throne. He whispered something delicate in her ear, and she leaned in with an aristocratic giggle.

Rows and rows of gleaming golden tables stretched before them, happy nobles clinking their bubbly drinks and stuffing themselves with chocolate strawberries. They'd been eating for hours and hours, but the servants couldn't refill the plates quickly enough.

His mouth was on her neck, leaving red imprints of the royal crest wherever lips met skin. She wore them proudly, barking at the servant fanning her to wave faster if he knew what was good for him.

"Don't you remember me?" Their face transformed into a familiar one, but only a distant memory told her it was Kalen.

"Pray that I don't." Her fist clenched around her skirts, stiff fingers made of iron, creaking as they closed.

A deep chuckle rumbled Marius's chest, and the nobles across the room chortled between bites of delicacies.

Three man-sized wheels, with those impure candidates found in the gardens. They were all strung up naked, bodies splayed out like starfish and rightful mortification plain on their faces. Served them right for trying to compete with her.

A satisfied smile crept onto her lips, watching her nobles play. Some poked and prodded, some spun them 'round and 'round, and some launched food to see which target they could hit. The fingers gripping her waist told her she'd made the perfect choice.

Suddenly, jail cells were in the dining hall. The starving prisoners looked on at the feast, peasants amassing likewise at the windows to drool.

"Blythe! Blythe!" one of the prisoners called out, and she jerked her head in his direction.

"Couldn't you spare me some bread?" Papa asked, a frail shadow of a man barely holding himself upright on the steel bars of the cell. A cough struck his slight frame, doubling him over.

The chandeliers went out. The skies outside darkened.

Marius's hand drifted up to her neck, squeezing around it hard enough to bruise.

"Please, myn caeure."

A laugh erupted from her, a wicked thing that turned easily into a snarl. "It's just a means to an end, Papa."

Blythe peeled open her eyes, nausea turning in her stomach and goose-bumps coating her skin.

Early sun shone down on her from the window. She threw off the covers, and then the dirty shift that clung to her body.

"Just a dream," she murmured to herself.

Putting on layer after layer of luxury fabrics didn't much help. But even silently stewing in anticipation of the King's announcement tonight, the Viper insisted on keeping up appearances again, now that they weren't utterly done for.

"You think this might be your last day in the glorious Fletch palace," the girl reminded her, powdering her face with white. "And that means you try to leave a lasting impression. Soak up how beautiful the palace is and hope that just maybe, His Majesty will see you in the gardens looking too lovely to send home."

The Viper had regained some civility after Blythe had explained what she'd done to skew the odds in her favor for the competition and described the map she'd found. It almost seemed things were even now between them—or would be, after the King's announcement solidified things.

"That's actually smart," the Viper had said begrudgingly. The compliment didn't sit right with either of them.

Now, when she spoke to Blythe, her measured tone masked something that didn't sound quite like irritation.

"Will I need to speak with anyone?" Blythe asked absently. *A means to an end.*

The Viper set down the powder brush, her expression in the mirror pensive. "No, I don't think so." She nodded, as if to agree with herself. "No, you're too distraught from your"—she passed a brush through Blythe's hair, yanking rather harder than necessary—"irredeemable performance in archery. You're too jealous of the other candidates. Close your eyes."

Blythe complied, not bothering to peer at which color would be dusting her eyelids.

"Okay, open." The Viper shook her head. She touched it up and added some stuff on Blythe's cheeks.

The silence that enveloped their walk through the corridors might have been awkward, except that Blythe wasn't keen to talk, anyway.

A soft breeze grazed her cheeks, the dewy smell of the air stirring something in her. Maybe it was good to be out of those stuffy walls, away from all the outrageous gold and silver dotting every corner. At the sight of the forest, a sort of hope emerged in Blythe. A tree was a tree, here or at home. Maybe she could be the same, a force of nature that couldn't be uprooted to sway to these rhythms of noble life.

If there are no kind people, then you have given up on yourself. Papa loved that adage. Blythe trailed her fingers along the violet petals of a flower bush.

Some decent nobles existed in the palace; they weren't all brutes. Even the worst of them surely had good somewhere, and Papa would likely affirm her duty to try and nurture that when she could. Misguided and overindulgent, perhaps they were, but she didn't have to let that infect her, she could—

"Morning, Lady Esme," Anna said pleasantly, giving her a curtsy.

Blythe drew herself back to the world enough to give the proper reply. "How d'you do today?"

"Lovely, thanks. The cooks are preparing a divine breakfast." Anna smiled, at Blythe and the Viper both, inclining her head just slightly. "Will I see you there, Your Ladyship?"

"I'm sure it will be a fantastic occasion, but I must disappoint," Blythe said, giving the woman an apologetic smile even though she was sure Anna was only trying to be nice by including her, assuming it might be her last chance. "I'm going to fast until the next dinner, in gratitude should I be allowed to stay."

The Viper's eyebrows rose, but she didn't object. Anna bid them farewell, and good luck, and Blythe returned the favor.

"A fast? Putting on that sort of show could work out..."

Blythe didn't reply. She hadn't intended a show. She simply couldn't bear to eat right now, and perhaps wouldn't be able to bear it until she got home.

Everything was too complicated here. She hadn't thought past her plans last night, and who knew what would unfold as a result? But then, the consequences would have been worse if she hadn't acted. Did that make it right, wrong, or something else entirely?

She just wanted life to be simple again. To know what was good and suffer it for the peace of mind.

A fast would be good. Keep her grounded in herself. Hunger was much more familiar than the strangely bloated feeling that crept up on her after some of these meals. Maybe hunger would help her close her eyes without seeing Papa's sunken cheeks.

They'd strayed off the carefully carved stone paths now, wandering across the trimmed green slopes where supplies for games, picnicking, and painting dotted the little landscape. As they walked past one section dipped with mud, a group of boys laughed and jeered, kicking around a ball. Blythe let the Viper guide them both toward some better-kept grass. But when she looked back, the ball wasn't round.

It was a tiny, wrinkly blotch of pink and brown.

Her face contorted in disgust. Did these noble children have nothing better to do than kick around the carcass of some poor piglet? Where was their respect?

Then the most awful thing twisted knots into her stomach. After a kick several feet forward on the grass, the tiny creature staggered to its feet. The children ran after it as it desperately and dazedly tried to limp away.

Something uncontrollable overtook Blythe, and her body propelled her forward.

"Lady Esme?"

She wasn't going to be fast enough.

She gained on the closest of the children and yanked him backwards by the shirt, propelling herself forward in a senseless sprint. Just as she reached the piglet, she slipped and fell flat onto her stomach. Blythe clawed herself forward in the mud, nails digging into the earth.

She wrapped the small creature in her arms, shielding it as another boot hit where it had been standing just a moment ago. She pulled herself onto her knees, holding the whimpering piglet close to her chest.

Another pink-and-brown thing lay half-buried in the mud beside her, this one undeniably dead.

Burning tears streamed from her eyes. Blythe's legs trembled as she stood.

"What in the hells, lady?" decried one of the boys, and the rest shouted at her for ruining their fun.

"What the fuck is *wrong* with you people?" she screamed at them. "Is your immeasurable wealth not enough for you? Must you also paint blood onto your hands? None of you even know what it is to suffer. How *dare* you inflict it onto a creature without defense?"

The boys did not waver from her bloodshot stare. The lead boy met her eyes with square shoulders and a set jaw. "We are men of the Fletch court, and we can do as we please. Now, return our pig before we have you executed."

Blythe stepped forward, loathing seeping from her voice. "You are not men. You are cruel, thoughtless little boys that think you're entitled to others' lives because of the silver spoons you've been sucking on since birth."

Just as quickly as it had arisen, the red cleared from her vision. Her throat tightened so she could scarcely breathe.

Gods. What had she done? How could she—

She'd never spoken to anyone like that. Was this how she avoided corruption? By shaking with rage and saying horrible things to children and, and...

"Guards!"

Panic gripped Blythe. *The pig*. She quickly passed the creature into the Viper's arms while the boys occupied themselves waving the guards over. Her heart seized. The assassin was just as likely to condemn the animal. But if nothing else, Blythe needed to try.

"What—" the Viper started.

Blythe cut her off, speaking in a low, desperate voice. "Please," she begged. "Please protect it for me. I...I'll pay you back somehow, but please. Just take it away."

The Viper did not answer with a promise, but she slinked underneath an arch of the palace and into the shadows.

Blythe blinked and could no longer see her. Her shoulders sank with despair. The girl would surely take it to the kitchens, and Blythe had been callous and vindictive and terrible for nothing. How could she have spoken with such hatred? How could she throw away their entire mission?

A pair of guards approached. "What seems to be the problem?"

"She stole our pig!" The rest of the group clamored to complain to the guards, ordering them to execute the horrible lady who had destroyed their game.

All Blythe could do was stand there and let the shameful tears fall. But she'd had to go after the creature, hadn't she? What kind of world was this where boys played at cruelty for their leisure?

And now she would be killed, their mission ruined because she dared to notice.

No—because she'd stooped so low as to bite back at them. Because she'd matched their cruelty with her own.

"She doesn't have a pig," one of the guards commented, and Blythe sniffed.

Maybe the Viper wouldn't kill the piglet, and even so, maybe Blythe could at least save herself and her crew from this.

And Papa. But could he really embrace her again?

"What?" The boys exclaimed in mixtures of anger and disbelief, demanding to know where she'd put it. One asked her if she'd stuffed it in her pockets, which in hindsight, might have been a better idea.

Blythe could only lie. That was all she was good for these days.

She turned to the guards, tears still in her eyes and mud all over her dress. "I don't have any pig," she sobbed to the guards, drawing away from the boys. "I was, I was just walking along and they... They attacked me. Oh, they were saying the most awful things, and look now, they've ruined my best dress! Please, you have to help me, sirs, I've— I'm quite frightened."

The guards turned more sympathetic, now that they had a potential damsel in distress.

Blythe didn't deserve any sympathy. In fact, when she saw Wapite, she somewhat hoped the girl would forget their truce and out her then and there.

"Boys, is this true?" a guard asked, and the boys protested. Lots of "my father will hear about this" and "arrest her you, imbeciles!"

But for some reason, at the perfect moment to lay bare her suspicions, Wapite instead walked away as if she had seen nothing.

And the guards, annoyed with the boys' insults and compelled by Blythe's pathetic figure, decidedly turned to her with pats and comforting words.

"They were just being boys, Lady Esme," one of the guards assured. "But don't worry, I'm sure we can have your dress repaired."

"You think so?" she asked, the reply numb and unconvincing, even to her own ears. "I'd be ever so grateful."

"Of course, Your Ladyship," said the other. They walked her into the palace, and she let them lead the way. She was disoriented enough from the ordeal not to know the way back to her room.

They stopped at her chambers.

"You're not hurt, are you?" one asked at the door, peering closely at her face. "We were just thinking whether you might need a doctor, Your Ladyship."

"Oh, I think I'll be alright," she said with a nod, not fully paying attention. She really wanted to get back into her room, to find some way to sort out her mess of confusing thoughts, and to cry in fucking solitude.

"Do you have anyone to watch over you, Your Ladyship?" the second guard asked, peeking into the chambers from where he stood and furrowing his brows. "Or do you need someone to wait with you? You could have a concussion."

The first guard's hand drifted to the small of her back.

She froze. *This can't be happening.*

"Please, Your Ladyship," he said, with wide eyes and a honeyed voice. "Is there *anything* else you need?"

"My guardian is just next door," she blurted, chest constricting. "And my lady-in-waiting is inside." She swallowed around the lump in her throat, forcing a polite smile to the surface. "Thank you for your concern, protigii. But I'll be quite alright."

"Of course, Your Ladyship," said the first guard, though his face briefly fell. He stepped out of the doorway, and the pair of them bowed to her. "We're happy to assist with *whatever* you might require. But I can see you need your rest."

"Good day, Your Ladyship."

"Good day." She closed her door immediately and sank into the shadows of the nearest corner, collapsing in a heap between the chaise and the wall.

What *was* that?

Her reeling mind convulsed with admonishments. *Consequence or coincidence?* She locked her arms around her knees, unable to stifle hiccupping sobs.

Something wet touched her hand.

A squeal reached her ears. Eyes blurred from burning tears, Blythe lifted her head to see a small, pink snout nudging her.

Shocked out of her delirium, Blythe wiped her eyes before lifting the wriggling piglet into her arms. That meant... She scratched behind its ears. But where was the Viper?

Blythe stumbled through to the adjacent chambers, still cradling the piglet in her arms. She jolted at the state of the room. Smashed bottles of poisons leeched onto the floors, everything thrown from the shelves. An ottoman lay overturned, and that shining dress the Viper had been working on so diligently for herself was shredded and slashed, scissors impaling the mannequin.

It took Blythe a few moments to register the small, disheveled figure slumped on the ground in the far corner of the room. Stripped to a shift and eyes strained red, the assassin raised her head.

"Viper?" Blythe asked tentatively, too nervous to take a step forward.

"Arabella." Chin held high with a sort of quivering resentment, she added, "I've never met anyone like you. And I wish I hadn't."

21.

74 Printes, Reg. Marii 6

When Superior interrogated Kalen this morning, he kept his shoulders back and calmly opened the door to reveal a perfectly made bed. His hands barely trembled when the man loomed over him with a snarl.

Other servants took to gathering around them and asking about the affair with the disgraced candidates, and they happily made up all sorts of fun details. Gilles shouldn't have listened in on such an adult conversation, but then, he lived in an adult situation. The boy's laughter was music to Kalen's ears.

Still, as they served breakfast and lunch, Kalen grew concerned. Blythe wasn't present at either.

They made their way to the kitchens and huddled beside Frida in an empty storage cupboard to talk.

"Blythe *yelled*? At *children*?"

A bite of bread went down dry in his throat, and he set the rest on the shelf beside him. Gods, they needed to see her and make sure she was alright.

"She did get some new informations about the vault," Frida added, hastily shifting to reassurance. She gathered some jars into a little basket, the smell of dried thyme and rosemary permeating the air.

"Are you to serving the announcement tonight? She'll *have* to be going there." Frida huffed out a sigh, hoisting the basket onto her hip. "I wish I could find myself there."

"I'm not, but maybe there's a way." Kalen smiled encouragingly, following behind as Frida walked out of the cupboard. Nobody paid them any mind, shuffling around in a frenzy to get ready for the King's announcement dinner. "It won't be too much longer."

"It's nice at least I can help out with the underground staff bar while we're here." She hefted the basket onto the stove as Kalen pretended to busy himself with sweeping the floors. "Did you want to come seeing it tonight? Celebrate once the announcement is over?"

"I'd like nothing more," Kalen said, then continued reluctantly, "but I don't think I can handle it right now." They swept dust into a careful pile as Frida busied herself with sprinkling a multitude of spices into a pot. "You were right," they said. "About the laudanum. It affected me more than I thought."

She wrapped Kalen in a hug, and he melted into it.

"I'd give it to you again," Frida admitted, "if it meant you'd survive."

This was an offer. There would have to be a voyage back to Ostrait, after all. Kalen shook their head. "I don't think I'll need it this time. I actually think I'm going to be okay." They pulled away from the hug and offered her a tentative smile. "Will you stay? In Ostrait, when we get back? Open that shop like you said?"

Frida hesitated.

"You always say you miss the water," Kalen said. Ale could be made on a ship. Frida could travel with Saidh on his smuggling journeys, if she wanted, and if she wasn't put off hands-on crime after this.

"I was a good boatswain." She stirred the pot with a large wooden spoon. "Before it got ruined. This could be my way back to that life, to honor my memories."

Frida had worked on an Ashlan ship her entire life before Ostrait, working her way up from the lowest ranks. She spoke of the job, the water, with nothing but fondness. But she clammed up at any mention of the people. And she wouldn't tell them why she lit a candle each night. They knew better than to prod by now.

A guilty look passed over her face. "But I'd stay close enough. You wouldn't be without having a roommate."

"A miserable roommate wouldn't do," Kalen assured. "I'll miss you, but I'll find my way. You do what you need to be happy."

Frida's lip quivered, and she looked pointedly away. "Stop being sweet. I'm gonna cry in the tomato sauce."

Kalen laughed. "A little extra salt never hurt."

"Please, kid? I'll owe you like a million favors."

Gilles hesitated, scratching the back of his head. "But I really wanted to see His Majesty. And are you sure this is even allowed?"

"The bathroom is so clean you wouldn't even have to work," Kalen tempted, knowing how scarcely any servant found rest. He'd been putting off mentioning that the bathroom was suitable, and somehow nobody cared enough to check as long as he seemed busy and unhappy.

"And"—Kalen dropped their voice—"it's for the *cause*."

Bringing up the Peasants' Revolt drew Gilles in, and while a bit of regret for the lie did simmer in Kalen's conscience, it worked.

"You'll tell me all about it, right?"

Kalen ruffled the kid's hair. "Of course! And the next time I'm assigned at a King's event, you can go. I promise."

"Pinky swear?" Gilles asked, then flushed, turning his head away.

Kalen held up his pinky. "Pinky swear."

⤜⤜⤜ ⤛⤛⤛

Kalen scuttled into the dining hall with the other servants, platter of appetizers in hand. The candidates were already seated by the time his quarter arrived, and he scanned the immense hall for any sight of Blythe.

It didn't take long to spot her. She sat at the usual end of the table, with the lesser kingdoms, though she didn't chat as the others did. She nursed a glass of water and seemed to be in her own world of thoughts, as she sometimes was. Understandable, given the anticipation of the King's decision.

Her hair wasn't as tightly kept as the Viper usually did it. And the maquillage, even from this distance, presented a lot less prominently than expected for such an important evening, especially for someone hoping the King would grant her grace.

Clink clink.

The entire room fell silent.

The King stood at the head of the table with a raised glass, and Kalen cursed themself for unconsciously mimicking the heartwarming smile that stretched across His Majesty's face.

"Cheers to all of my exquisite guests!" His voice spread like butter, melting appreciation onto even the most stone-faced of nobles and spurring applause. "And as we all detest a long to-do, I shall not keep you waiting any longer. Let me welcome the valiant candidates that I'll have the pleasure of getting to know better."

Kalen held their platter in a death grip, ears locked onto the King's every word. Noble name after noble name, the list went on for an eternity.

"And finally," King Marius dragged out, letting the audience simmer. Kalen forgot to breathe.

"How could we let go of our beloved court jester? I look forward to more entertainment from Lady Esme, of House Albreit!"

A shaky sigh of relief escaped Kalen's lips.

The delegation escorts clustered on the other side of the room, which now filled with laughter and further clapping. Kalen's eyes met Saidh's, and he caught the slightest of nods. *He's going to stay.*

But Blythe had hardly reacted at all. Her polite smile didn't reach her eyes as other nobles presumably teased or congratulated her.

"I can't believe he kept such a mess around, can you?" Another servant passed by Kalen. Of course, they were meant to start making their rounds now.

They laughed awkwardly. "No, so strange."

They cringed in embarrassment for Blythe, but that couldn't negate the rush of relief. They hadn't failed, not yet, and they could still make it out of this alive, together.

Because whatever their future looked like after this, they were strong enough to tell Blythe they wanted her in it. Whatever that meant for them, they had hope they could figure it out now. They had a chance.

And I'm gonna make that chance as big as possible. The other servants wanted gossip? They would deliver.

Kalen worked through the night, taking orders from barking nobles. All the while he eavesdropped, invisible to them as a mere servant. They gushed with fellow servants about how lovely His Majesty was, how annoying such-and-such noble's requests were, and what they thought the next competition would be, all the while sprinkling in careful tidbits of gossip about the other candidates.

It was kind of fun spinning the stories, and his quarter loved him for it.

The night was coming to a close when they finally caught Blythe relatively alone. "Would you care for a pastry, milady?"

"I would," she said, slowly lifting one from the plate. Her eyes met his in a silent exchange. "I'll probably have more tonight." *I can't say anything now, but I need to see you again later.*

"Of course, milady," he said, delicate with the words he chose. "We'll be serving until two." *I can sneak out to see you sometime after that.*

Kalen didn't waste time heading back to the quarters after the shift's end. All the announcement dinner's servants eagerly climbed into their cupboards, and Gilles headed back in from the shift in the bathroom.

"Kalen!" The boy hurried over as soon as he caught sight of them, and they paused beside their open cupboard door. Gilles dropped his voice. "How was it?"

True to his word, Kalen recounted every detail he could think of—at least those that wouldn't compromise their mission. They also thanked

Gilles profusely for switching shifts with them and pulled a pastry from their pocket. "Here, I grabbed this for you."

Gilles's eyes widened as his small hands closed around the confection. He inhaled deeply, but then looked back at Kalen, worrying his lip. "They won't notice it's missing, right?"

"Of course not," Kalen assured. Jam soon spotted the corners of the kid's mouth, warming their heart. "And even if they did, surely His Majesty is generous." Nobody wanted to think the King wasn't generous, so this appeased Gilles's anxieties.

"Oh, what did he look like? What did he say? Will you tell me again?"

Taking pity, Kalen indulged the boy by gushing over the King for a few minutes. It was an alarmingly effortless thing to do, and they had to jerk themself out of admiration.

Gilles yawned.

"Alright, we can talk more tomorrow," Kalen said, patting the boy on the back. "Come now, try and sleep."

Gilles frowned but climbed into his cupboard all the same.

Almost an hour later, the quarters were filled with snores, and Kalen slid out of his placard.

Blythe opened her door before they could even knock, pulling them inside by the arm. "The Viper's out for the night," she said, locking the door. Her hazel eyes bore into Kalen. "We have so much to talk about."

22.

"Wh-what?" Blythe barely stammered out a response. She let the wriggling piglet jump to the floor.

"What am I even supposed to do now?" The Vi—Arabella?—wiped a hand across her eyes, smearing the makeup further. She barked out a bitter laugh and stood from her heap on the floor, jabbing an accusatory finger in Blythe's direction. "You just had to show up and ruin everything. You—you made my whole life— And I'm just supposed to carry on?"

Blythe's heart raced as she struggled to make sense of the situation. "Arabella?" she asked slowly, frozen where she stood. "I don't understand. I'm sorry about the pig, I'm sure we can—"

The girl carried on as if Blythe had never spoken, a wild, desperate look in her eyes. "Life wasn't good, but it at least made *sense*! People are terrible, all they do is use you, and so what does killing a few of them matter? It gives you a roof over your head, doesn't it? And aren't you doing the world a favor by getting rid of the next piece of scum?"

Arabella didn't acknowledge the tears pooling in her eyes, and Blythe didn't dare. She wanted to reach out, despite herself. Calm the girl down, offer some comfort. But silence seemed the only safe option.

"And then you show up, and you're so sickeningly *nice* to everyone," Arabella spat.

Blythe's mind reeled with confusion, unable to sift through the complicated layers of emotion that laced Arabella's words.

"And I think, okay, whatever, she's a con artist, and this is her next con. Even when you were... How you acted with me, despite what I'm here for, I figure: it makes sense. She's saving her own skin, right? But"—the girl's voice thickened—"I can't explain the pig." Arabella looked down, shaking her head. "That creature had nothing to offer you."

She met Blythe's eyes for the first time, searching for an answer as if her life depended on it. Her shoulders deflated. "You did it simply because you actually cared about the *stupid* animal. Risked the whole mission, your life. And it can't even thank you."

"Of course it couldn't thank me," Blythe couldn't help but say, shifting her feet on the carpet. "I just...couldn't watch it be hurt."

Something started to click together. The girl was angry because...she thought Blythe was a good person? Blythe constantly chastised her own wickedness, but she'd been kind enough to prompt some sort of *change* in a girl trained to kill?

Pity stabbed at her chest. How bad was Arabella's life that she didn't know people could be kind? Had the Governor really convinced her that love, compassion, didn't exist? That they were just performed to some end?

"Tell me you're the exception," Arabella pleaded, her arms wrapped tightly around herself.

But Blythe couldn't lie to her. "I'm not."

"I have to go," Arabella burst, pushing past Blythe and yanking a fallen scarf from the ground to wrap around her disheveled hair. She aggressively wiped at her face with a towel and made for the door. "I'll be back."

"Wait, but—"

The door slammed closed.

Hours later, having bribed a footman to take the piglet and set it free, Blythe recounted all of this to Kalen, who listened with perked ears and eyes like dinner plates. "I can't believe you broke our assassin."

"I *didn't*—"

"Nice work!"

Blythe's head turned around and around. Arabella was in an unpredictable state, more so than usual, which couldn't possibly be good. This was no place for her to have an existential crisis, and Blythe felt an odd sense of accomplishment mixed with guilt for spurring it.

"It's good though, right?" She crisscrossed her legs atop the high bed. "Like, she seemed upset, but... Isn't it good that she might understand not all people are vile and worth dismembering?"

"I'd certainly be happy if she thought I wasn't worth dismembering." Kalen shifted to sit on their knees. The words were comforting, though he sat farther away than usual.

"She still isn't back," Blythe thought aloud, hugging a pillow against her stomach. It was almost four in the morning. Was Arabella alright? And what if she didn't come back in time for the luncheon? People had only ignored her absence last night due to the commotion. "Maybe I should try to—"

"Oh no, nonono." Kalen firmly shook their head. "Remember that time you tried to feed an injured coyote?"

Blythe flushed. "It wasn't full-grown. And I was just supposed to leave it? Cold and hungry?" She had a large bite scar on her left thigh, but that was beside the point.

Arabella might be cruel at times, but she'd had to be. A life without Papa to tuck her in, or Kalen to squeeze her hand, or a shop owner that gave her scraps to make soup—it was too hard to imagine. How could the Governor have forced Arabella to live without that?

"Just promise you'll be careful?" Kalen asked, and Blythe reluctantly nodded. Still, their expression withdrew into something more serious. "I wanted to tell you..."

"About you and Saidh?" Blythe forced herself to tease, prodding him with her elbow. A lump formed in her throat, but she had no choice. Kalen *should* withdraw from her, and even if she couldn't manage to tear herself away from him yet, she at least couldn't sabotage their chance at finding someone to actually make them happy. She'd seen the looks between them and Saidh.

It was selfish that it hurt.

Why did Blythe not want the best for him? Kalen deserved all the happiness in the world. She'd gotten them into this mess, so the least she could do was shove down her longing and not burden them with guilt.

"What?"

She forced a smile. She'd gotten quite good at that here. "It's pretty obvious with all the eyes you make at each other."

"*He's* making eyes at me?"

"Of course he is, you're fantastic," she said. "You weren't going to tell me you were together? Because I'm completely happy for you. You should go for it!"

Kalen's expression flickered, and their shoulders sank.

Did they feel guilty, because they knew she was going to die alone? She had to try and convince them otherwise, for their own good.

"Oh, no, that wasn't..." Kalen sighed. "But thanks. I think we're definitely getting friendlier."

"That's promising." She offered a playful wiggle of her eyebrows. Kalen always did that when they read something salacious. She scooted back a bit, shifting her legs. "What was your news, then?"

They grinned. "I can swim."

"*What?*" Blythe clapped her hands together, this time in genuine excitement. "That's amazing! I mean, how?"

"Saidh taught me, actually, in the harbor. I've been working up to it."

Blythe's heart plummeted, and she cursed herself for it. *Why didn't he ask me to teach him?*

But by the gods. Kalen had learned to *swim*—almost impossible to imagine for the person who would spiral into panic at the mere sound of a wave. It couldn't have been easy for them.

"I'm so proud of you." Blythe hugged him close, pride bursting in her chest. This was no small feat.

Kalen turned bright red. "Thanks," they murmured, casting their eyes down.

A door shut some chambers over, in Arabella's area.

Kalen swallowed, and Blythe nodded to her own door. "Best spare yourself."

They were gone before Arabella entered the room, on the surface perfectly composed but with red, strained eyes. She held out a dress, this one a sporting habit, and gestured toward her chambers. "Come, you're shooting today. We'll have to get you properly fitted."

Blythe walked cautiously after her. "Arabella? Don't you want to talk about what happened last—"

"I don't know what you're referring to."

And that was that.

As much as Blythe wanted to prod, she resisted. Arabella would talk when she was ready. The girl wasted no time getting to work on the fitting, though her movements weren't as precise as usual. Blythe said nothing when she had to re-measure or re-stitch a few times.

When Blythe finally stepped off the podium, she ran her hands over the white floral fabric of the sporting habit. Breeches, at last, though still puffed around by skirts she didn't feel at home in. "Thank you. You know, I'm actually looking forward to today."

It took Arabella a moment to respond, occupied with replacing needles in the sewing kit. "Oh, that's new," she said vaguely.

"Lucky you taught me on the ship." Blythe offered a small smile as they walked through to her own chambers.

After they'd taken the Jardaen ship, there had been enough guns to spare. Arabella had insisted Blythe learn to shoot. She'd only agreed reluctantly, given her failures in combat and archery training, but Arabella had proved an effective teacher in this regard.

"There's two things you have control over in life," she'd said, oddly pleasant as she'd aimed the rifle into the distance. "Your body and your gun."

Something relaxed in her whenever they'd fired off shots on deck. But now, the mention of shooting sparked a torn look on her powdered face. "You were...competent."

Sitting at the vanity, Blythe couldn't smile as Arabella spread gloss onto her lips. At least the maquillage was quite minimal today, only basics needed for a sporting event.

Still the compliment marked a peculiar change in the girl that made her beam inside. Maybe—if she could be there for the assassin, offer compassion to a girl who had never seen it before—maybe Blythe could make up for the corruption of this court. For dragging her friends into this, for setting up those candidates in the garden, for being unkind to Wapite and those boys.

They might be done for now, but Blythe would seize this potential for change in Arabella.

~~>>>> <<<<~~

A canopy of trees framed the cobblestone walkway that led into a well-kept meadow, with resplendent tables of food and golden chairs for each candidate. Blythe was going into this meal with a mission.

She couldn't worry the others with her mistake, but Wapite's presence hung in the air as a threat, which Blythe had to deal with. She had to wheedle out more information by getting close to Wapite. And maybe Wapite would grow to like her and wouldn't have the heart to send them all to the ropes.

When the meal finished, everyone stood around the field chatting as the attendants assigned partners. Every third person was matched. Blythe positioned herself two people away from Wapite, ignoring the questioning glances from other candidates as she wormed her way into their conversation.

"Lady Esme, you'll be partnered with Princess Wapite," said one of the attendants.

Wapite scowled. "Not a princess."

"Apologies, Your, er... Apologies."

Blythe smiled at her, slinging the rifle over her shoulder. "Guess we'll have to work together."

"Guess so," she muttered, and they walked off a few feet to their shooting circle.

"You can shoot first," Blythe offered.

Wapite's lips dipped into a frown, and she hesitated before taking hold of her gun. She aimed at the sky, but the rifle didn't rest on her shoulder as it should. Blythe threw a dinner plate in the air, but Wapite's bullet didn't even come close.

Wapite's muscles tensed, and she shifted on her feet. Was she *bad* at something? "Your shot," she said quickly, and Blythe took aim.

The plate shattered in the air. "Must have been a lucky shot," Blythe said.

"I'm perfectly fine at this," Wapite snapped, "these rifles are just— Never mind."

Blythe gave her a moment to recompose, which didn't take long, and then tossed the next plate in the air.

Another hard miss. Some nobles in the next circle sniggered.

Wapite's jaw tightened, and she picked at her fingernails. This afforded Blythe her opportunity, though really, she would have offered anyway. "Can I...give you some advice?"

Wapite didn't say anything for a moment. It sounded almost painful when she said, "Yes."

"Great! So, you see what I'm doing with my shoulder here?" Blythe launched into an explanation, echoing Arabella as she used her own gun to demonstrate. "If you don't have it snug enough, it'll ruin your shot. A lot of people mess that part up."

"This is ridiculous. Why are we hunting plates anyway?"

"Do they not have guns where you live?" Blythe asked, not trying to be rude. It would explain why she wasn't a good shot yet, and the girl seemed desperate for the benefit of the doubt when it came to mistakes.

"Of course we have guns. I just find them useless." Wapite huffed, half-heartedly throwing the next plate for Blythe.

Pride surged in her when it fell to the ground in pieces. Finally, she was doing something right in front of these nobles. "Aren't they better for hunting?"

Wapite shrugged. "Depends who you ask."

Blythe would take an ambivalent response over her usual hostility.

"How are you ladies getting along?"

It was him.

The King wasn't usually present at the luncheons, but he appeared before them like a savior, a rippling vermillion mantle draped at his back. Blythe's breath caught.

Wapite's entire demeanor changed as he guided her arms. "Better now," she said, adjusting her stance to match his. Yet she only smiled when he looked, and Blythe caught a discomfited frown as his hands wandered lower on her waist.

Unwanted jealousy heated Blythe's cheeks. *Why didn't I think of acting like I couldn't shoot?*

She stabbed her hand against the needle in her pocket. Biting down on her lip, she thought of the list. This was not a good man.

And something about Wapite's posture when he left showed the other girl knew it, too.

Perhaps her mysterious plan was to kill him. But that wouldn't make all that much sense. She'd wanted him unharmed, and the Ka'lani already warred with Ostrait, not faring super well from what Blythe had been able to gather. It would have made more sense for Wapite to actually try and marry the man.

And she did seem to be trying. She wore immaculate Fletch clothing and spoke like a Fletch native. This was the first break in her flawless facade.

So why didn't she like him? It took a lot of effort not to.

"How are things going on the home front?" Blythe asked nonchalantly as they continued to shoot.

"I'm sure you've heard." Wapite huffed at another missed plate, making an obvious effort to keep her expression pleasant. She turned her head and spoke lowly, "Whatever this ploy is, do us both a favor and give it up."

"Can't I just be nice to a fellow competitor?" Blythe mumbled, readying her rifle for the next shot. But the bells clanged, signaling the luncheon had ended.

Just in time, too. They'd run out of plates. As she exited with the rest of the prospective royal brides, the King lingered in merry conversation with Wapite. *That should be me.*

Shoulders sagging, Blythe walked with Saidh back to her chambers, where the others waited. Another mint bath prescribed to the ladies afforded her cover. They'd agreed to meet so they could work out how to get the rest of the information about the vault. She'd hoped to have some new insight regarding Wapite, but without it, finding the vault only grew more urgent.

"You're sure you didn't see any entrance markers?" Saidh lifted a scrap of parchment to show her the symbols again.

Blythe sighed, leaning her back against the chair in front of the vanity. "I don't know. She— I had to get out before the King saw me."

Saidh, Kalen, and Frida had all made themselves comfortable on the edge of her bed, tucking into a tray of pork tarts and profiteroles. Arabella sat hesitantly in the corner of the room, perched on a pink chaise. Nobody seemed to know how to act around her now, and she didn't exactly give them hints.

"Well, we know the general area," Saidh said, running a hand through fluffy black hair. "But we can't very well snoop without drawing suspicion. And I expect it's hidden well, a secret door or something."

The map was ruined. She couldn't even try to go back for it.

"Shame we can't just poison all the guards," Kalen said, and Blythe shot them an incredulous look. "What? I was just *saying*."

"It wouldn't be a bad idea if they weren't already suspicious," Saidh noted.

A wave of relief passed through Blythe. They couldn't hurt all of those people. And it would be her fault—she'd been so close to finding the location, and she'd failed.

"They eat a lot of meat here," Frida added, leaning back on her arms. Her short hair still stuck to her forehead from the sweat of the kitchens. "Food poisoning isn't being uncommon."

Blythe winced. Except she had no ideas of her own. They didn't have time for her to sneak into every room in the palace, hoping to stumble across relevant maps again.

"Do you have anything that works with food?" Kalen asked, and everyone's eyes turned to the girl sitting silently in the shadowed part of the room.

Arabella shifted in her seat, a wary look on her face. "I might. It would induce a couple hours of vomiting."

"Surely we can't put people through that?" Blythe asked, but the others ignored her.

"All that cooking for nothing?" Frida groaned, crossing her arms over her chest. "Better be worth it."

"I don't think it would take more than two hours," Saidh said. He nodded as if to himself, looking more sure. "It's not a huge area. We could split up, search each corridor."

Blythe stood from the vanity, taking a shuddering breath. "Well, it seems settled." She clicked her knuckles together and glanced at the door. "I just need to clear my head a bit."

Though her last walk hadn't gone splendidly, this time the fresh air was what she needed. Lilacs scented the air, Papa's favorite. She conjured his face in her mind over and over, to convince herself this plan was the only option.

It wasn't her choice, not really. But did that absolve her?

If she'd just gotten it right when she had the maps. If, if, *if*.

But she couldn't send Papa to the gallows. The guards would recover, but if she refused to go along with this, Papa wouldn't.

⇝⇝⇜⇜

A light breeze wafted through the air, sunlight streaming down on the guests and warming Blythe's face. She sat at her usual end of the long white table, an empty silver plate in front of her. Servants brought out enormous trays of food.

Blythe swallowed when the glazed lambs debuted, the expansive platter covering a good meter at the center of the table.

This had been the easiest way. The guards would share in the feast, eating after the candidates had finished. All of these people would fall ill, and Blythe would feign the same to evade suspicion.

Legally, guards could not abstain from meat. It would be said they "sabotaged their strength." But hopefully some of the candidates weren't fond of this particular delicacy. Though serving spoons dug into the feast, and plate after plate filled up.

"Doesn't it look lovely?" Eleanore asked, seated beside her. She inhaled deeply, cutting into the flesh with her knife.

Gut rot made of guilt bubbled in Blythe's stomach. To her, everything smelled rancid.

Gods, she couldn't do it. She couldn't go through with letting *all* these people— This wasn't just corrupt guards or abusive kings. *Eleanore is just a child, for Deium Erium's sake!* But she'd already scooped two slices onto her plate, and everybody else reached in to help themselves.

Panic gripping her, Blythe shoveled her own cut of lamb into her mouth. She took a second slice, a third, a fourth. Ignoring jibes about her need to gain weight and the starvation in Jardae, she forced the mealy bites down her throat.

The more she ate, the less they did. The more she ate, the more penance paid.

She could do one more slice, couldn't she?

Bile rose in her throat, and she pushed it down. She leaned forward in her stays to ease the pressure on her bloating stomach.

"Wow, you must really like lamb," Eleanore said, not rudely but definitely with an air of concern.

Blythe managed a smile, wiping at her mouth with a serviette. "Oh, it's my favorite. But there's no sheep in Jardae."

"I don't blame you, then! This is the sort of thing I can hardly get enough of, either, and we have it all the time."

After today, Blythe would never touch lamb again.

23.

K alen knew it was time when they mopped up the first pool of vomit. They'd been cleaning the dining area for hours in preparation for the upcoming pre-certatia dinner. The third certatia had come much quicker than they'd anticipated, but this could be a good thing. It hardly seemed likely the dinner would take place, and hopefully some of the candidates would be sick enough to miss the certatia itself.

With everyone retching, slipping away offered minimal challenge. Kalen found Arabella, Frida, and Saidh already clustered in the hall they most suspected for the vault. They were all the way on the south side of the palace, near a bunch of unimportant storage facilities and extra kitchens. A good place to hide the treasury, actually.

Kalen leaned his hand against the beige brick, taking in the immense arches above them and the cobblestones beneath their feet. He didn't think he'd ever be properly used to the grandiosity of this place, though the rancid stenches currently permeating the air did take away some of the wonder.

"Has Blythe already gone?" She was meant to take advantage of their limited window. While they all searched for an opening to the vault, she would be back in the King's strategy room, scaling the rafters this time. The King and his men would likely be discussing what to do about the upcoming competition, and she'd be there to overhear potential details.

But they'd planned to meet first, and it wasn't like her to be late.

"I'm here." There was a tightness to her voice as she turned the corner, posture drawn inward and body tensed. She wore the same raggedy servant clothes as Kalen now, hair messily pinned back and face tinged green. Her smile was obviously forced as she joined the group. "Are we ready?"

Concern gripped them. She looked ready only to pass out.

"Gods, you didn't. Did you?" Kalen stepped closer, but she turned away before they could look at her face too closely.

"I'm fine," she choked out.

Frida's eyes grew wide as the same realization hit her. "You weren't supposed to eat it!" Their friend rushed over, forcing a hand to Blythe's forehead even as she cringed back. "How much did you having? Did they force you? Does your liver to feel okay?"

"I... It was suspicious not to eat."

Kalen turned to Arabella. "You've got to have an antidote or something, right?"

But the girl only shook her head. "I never really needed it in my line of work." She straightened her shoulders, gripping Blythe by the arms. "But we have limited time. You've got to get to the rafters."

"Okay, I'll—" Blythe jerked away and doubled over, vomiting on the floor.

Kalen's heart clenched. No way in fifteen hells could they send her to spy like this. Not even the guards looked so frail. All life had drained from her face.

Saidh cleared his throat, back against one of the walls. "Does she really look up to spying?"

Arabella huffed. She pulled on the sleeves of her rosy jacket, looking at Blythe with something like disdain. "It's not my fault that her bleeding heart is always ruining everything. She did this to herself."

Blythe winced, and Kalen positioned themself in front of her. Fear twisted in their chest. The Viper was sent to kill them all if they were disobedient. But he would not stand by while she put Blythe through that.

This whole plan had been their idea. "She's not going."

"Kalen, really, I—" She doubled over again, putting a hand over her mouth.

"What are you meaning, it was her own fault?" Frida asked, arms crossed over her chest. "She was trying not to give us away."

"Right," Arabella said, rolling her eyes. "I'm sure five slices of lamb were necessary for that, then?"

Kalen turned to Blythe incredulously. "Why would you do that?"

"Five slices?" Frida swallowed, and she peered nervously over her shoulder. "That... One slice was enough for a grown man, I..."

"Because that's all sentimentality gets you." Arabella glared at Kalen, menace dripping from her voice. "We don't have the luxury of playing nurse."

Kalen ground their teeth together. Normally they would have cowered, mind racing with the knives and darts she probably held on her person. But he was tired of being intimidated and threatened, and after all he'd overcome? They weren't putting up with this.

He turned to meet Blythe's eyes and lightly took hold of her hand. "Please. Will you let Frida take you back to your chambers?"

With a sigh of resignation, she nodded.

"What do you think you're doing?" Arabella demanded, hands curled into fists at the sides of her skirts. "Don't you get that we're all dead anyway if she fails the next competition?"

Kalen stepped forward, tilting his chin up to meet her gaze. Their heart pounded, flushing their skin with anger. "Then I guess we fucking die."

Frida had taken the cue, half-carrying Blythe through the halls.

Saidh, who had remained quiet for most of the encounter, now stood up from his place on the wall, putting his hands up in front of him. "Whoa, look, I agree she's in no condition for this," he said, looking at Kalen with a regretful expression. "But I didn't agree to just die here. Arabella is right about one thing. We can't let this opportunity go to waste, and the clock is ticking."

"Fine," Kalen bit out, a snarl on his lips. "*I'll* climb the rafters. It can't be that hard."

Silence hovered among the three of them, only the sounds of retching guards in the distance as ambiance. The torches had dimmed, with nobody bothering to relight them, and the immense walls imposed higher than ever.

"You want to risk your life? Go ahead," Arabella finally said. "But when they catch you, say you're with that Peasants' Revolt."

Turned out, it *was* that hard.

Even once they'd snuck past the guards—hunched over buckets and groaning—they had no idea how Blythe could manage to climb all the way up to the rafters.

There weren't exactly ladders lying around, and the reliefs that decorated the walls were hardly deep enough to find purchase with his feet, which he figured out the hard way. The marble columns reached higher than they could properly see, taunting them with their smooth, gleaming surfaces. Kalen failed several times trying to shimmy up.

They couldn't try to climb the tapestries. If they tore, he'd undoubtedly be found out.

A large clock ticked above the crackling fireplace, and Kalen's breath hitched with the realization that they'd already wasted all the time they had. The King conferred with his guards every night at 8:00, and the servants would be here any moment to prepare for serving His Majesty. They arrived twenty minutes early so their Superior could affix red cloth around their eyes. To avoid possible information leaks, some servants were rendered mute by way of a certain "elixir" that burned their throats, and they were never taught to read or write, obviously. One of the boys in Kalen's quarter—they didn't know his name, of course, because he couldn't speak—was one of those.

Staring at the red tapestries that hung in every corner of the room, their ample fabric ribboning from the sky to the floor, an idea struck Kalen.

Tearing the tapestries to the floor risked too much. But surely a tiny swatch wouldn't be noticed? *Only one way to find out.*

His father had said that sewing materials would never prove useful, but as he cut precisely along the folds of a tapestry to make a blindfold that looked just as neat as the ones he'd seen on palace servants, Kalen disagreed wholeheartedly.

And that wasn't all the giant tapestries were good for, either. They gave Kalen the perfect hiding place when he heard the shuffling feet and one loud man's voice ushering the servants into the room.

Their pulse thumped in their ears. They expended every effort to take small, silent breaths.

The Superior—not Kalen's, but dressed in similarly enviable ruffles and embroidery—spent an eternity examining each servant's blindfolds and retying them quite tighter than necessary when he deemed them unfit. The servants stood more still than the divine statues affixed at the back of the room, heads bowed.

Eventually the man was satisfied with his efforts, and he asked them the same question asked of Kalen's quarter before shifts. "And whose lungs do you breathe for?"

The servants knelt down on one knee, swiping two fingers across their foreheads in salute to the King. Kalen caught themself doing the same and shook their head, lowering their arm.

As the Superior made his exit, Kalen discreetly slid into the back row.

"But Your Majesty, with all due respect—"

A tall guard with several bands of honor around his arm strode in, the King following languidly behind him. Kalen hastily attached the blindfold around their eyes.

"Wouldn't all due respect mean doing as I say, Lucien?" He spoke as if he'd rather be doing anything else.

Kalen squinted through the red filter of their blindfold to find the King. He could make out little, but it seemed the King wore his coat open, and his hair fell lazily over his shoulders instead of being drawn back or tightly curled.

"Of course, Your Majesty." Kalen imagined Lucien was wringing his hands about now.

There was a creak across the room as the King rested against the edge of the large oak desk, sighing. "Then why don't you let this business go, hmm? You're paranoid, my friend."

"Sire, it is my duty." A red-tinted Lucien squared his shoulders, but his voice still wavered.

Kalen didn't blame him. King Marius radiated a god-like aura difficult to contend with.

"With the strange state of your desk last week—"

"I told you, I sometimes like to drink in here. I probably just forgot."

"And now all of my—your men incapacitated? It can't be a coincidence."

The King groaned, holding his hand out. "Drink." Within seconds, something that might have been a goblet appeared in it, and the sound of a long sip affirmed this. The servants had fallen so silent, Kalen had half-forgotten them.

"They sicken themselves at least once a month on meat," the King said.

Kalen's knees ached from being on the floor, but they'd grown used to it after all the cleaning shifts. At least the King wasn't suspicious.

"If you're going to interrogate anyone, maybe ask the cooks if they bother to clean their knives, ein?"

"But Your Majesty—"

"Lucien, I'm telling you. Even if these were assassins, I'm still alive, aren't I? So are all the guards. So they're incompetent, at that."

Kalen bristled a little. He almost wanted to explain that they hadn't intended to kill anyone in the first place, so actually they were completely competent, but this seemed like bad timing.

"But, the Eunics advised—"

Something darkened in the room. The King raised his voice, slamming down the goblet as he stood. "The *Eunics*? Those traverae have no respect for my authority." He almost spat the words, menace dripping from his rumbling voice. "And I'm starting to think you don't, either."

Kalen strained their eyes as Lucien bowed deeply.

"Please, forgive me, Your Majesty." His words came close to a stammer. "I've spoken out of turn. Of course, nobody would dare to harm you."

"There!" The King's demeanor immediately changed again, and he slapped Lucien on the back with a thud. "Now we can be on to more pleasant matters!"

Kalen leaned forward. This was it. What could the King be more excited about than the certatia tomorrow?

"Oh, yes," said Lucien.

Please be something decent.

"And how are the arrangements coming?" the King inquired, taking another sip of the goblet as he sat atop the desk.

"They should arrive in a few hours," Lucien said. "Your men have protected the shipment most valiantly."

What shipment? Gods, Kalen hoped they wouldn't make Blythe fight tigers or another horrible creature in that coliseum. Apparently the Fletch still did that for fun, sometimes.

"Good," the King said, making a pleased sound at the back of his throat. A lovely sound, but Kalen tensed in anticipation of the King's next words. Whatever he revealed about the certatia would make or break their mission.

"I'll tell Albert to have the cooks prepare an iced-cream dessert, and perhaps some other confections?" Lucien asked.

Kalen's shoulders dropped.

"And keep the Eunic noses out of the cost, would you?"

"Of course, Your Majesty."

Vanilla. They were talking about an order of vanilla for the King's dessert, not the competition.

Kalen withheld a groan of frustration. Without so much as a hint about the certatia, they'd all be doomed tomorrow.

⤜⟩⟩⟩⟩ ⟨⟨⟨⟨⤛

Kalen closed Blythe's door behind him softly, and Frida greeted them with a whisper in Ostraitian. "She's out cold, but the fever is down, at least."

His shoulders sagged with relief. They shouldn't have taken the detour with so little time before the quarters' curfew check-in, but they had to know she was alright.

Sure enough, she half-lay on the sprawling bed, propped up by pillows, with a cloth on her forehead. The room smelled no worse than the halls, but no better, either.

"I just don't understand it," Kalen said, brows furrowing. She *knew* it was poison. She *knew* the plan. And she did all this to, what? Prove something to herself?

"Me either, the night has been..." Frida cleared her throat. Her eyes were puffed, wet with tears Kalen had never seen her shed in all their time together. Her teeth bit down the edge of a shaking lip as her gaze landed on Blythe. "It was scary for a minute."

A flame of irritation lit in Kalen. They stayed here for her. And she kept trying to throw her life away to...

He didn't even know, really. Because she couldn't handle feeling guilty about something? Normally they admired her compassion more than anything, but why did she care more about preserving the feelings of Fletch elites and squealing pigs than she did their mission? Than she did *him*?

Kalen had done so much just to survive this place.

But they weren't even allowed to be mad, because look at how frail she was. "Did she let you give any medicine, at least?" they asked.

Frida sniffed, gesturing over to a night table piled with herbs and mugs. "Eventually. But honestly, she was delirious. Went on about Esme keeping her dad in a cage?"

Frida wasn't one to panic. But her chewed nails and glassy eyes betrayed an alarm Kalen didn't know how to address. Once, they'd been stranded under the awning of an abandoned building, less than a hundred feet from the tavern but immobilized by a sudden downpour. Frida found them, and instead of asking for details, she...

Kalen wrapped both of his arms around her, squeezing tight. "I've got you, man."

She took a shuddering inhale, leaning her head on top of his. Tears fell onto her skirts, turning spots of orange to brown. "Thanks."

They sat for a minute before she shifted away with an awkward laugh, swiping a sleeve across her eyes. "At least we got the job done."

"Are you talking about the vault?" It might have been their first concern under different circumstances.

Frida's face lit up in a grin. "We found it."

Kalen returned the expression, a disbelieving laugh escaping them. "Here's to a successful robbery." They lifted an imaginary glass in the air, and Frida "clinked" it with her own.

A chime echoed from elsewhere in the palace.

Unease crept back into them. Blythe hadn't stirred at all, her face ashen and head lolled to the side. "You'll watch over her tonight?"

Kalen feared leaving, like the bed might swallow her whole while he was gone. But the clock ticked on, and they couldn't risk missing check-in.

"Won't leave her side," Frida assured.

And Kalen believed her. "I'll see you soon."

It wouldn't be soon enough.

Kalen scrambled back through the halls, painfully aware of the late hour. At the entrance to the quarters, Superior waited. His large figure shrouded in the darkness of the archway, his glower screeched Kalen to a halt.

Father stood in the doorway, arms crossed over his broad chest. Kalen blanched when he saw him, the hairs standing up on his neck.

It was past curfew. He'd hoped to sneak in through the back.

"Superior, sir." Kalen wouldn't let themself tremble. They were past this.

"Did I send you out?"

"No, sir."

"Do I look like a fucking idiot, boy?" his father snarled, grabbing him by the cuff of his shirt.

He squeezed his watering eyes shut. "No, sir."

"Does it honor His Majesty to disobey my orders and go out gallivanting?"

Kalen swallowed. "No, sir." He wanted to push Superior away from him, to scream or run in the opposite direction. Things he never would have dared to *think* in front of his father.

But he couldn't do any of those, because the mission mattered more than feeling safe.

Superior towered over him, and despite himself, Kalen shrank inward. The man pulled him closer by his shirt, knuckles white and face contorted in disgust. "You ungrateful traverae. I don't care if you were a delegation gift. The next toe you step out of line, I will personally tie the rope around your neck."

Tears welled in Kalen's eyes, and his legs shook.

"Understood?"

He barely stuttered out a response.

Superior let him fall to the ground. "You're lucky that I have use for your disloyal ass."

This is for the mission, Kalen reminded himself as Superior dragged him through the halls. The stash of bombs hidden away in the bathroom wasn't meaningless. They could do this. And after the mission, if he just lasted a little longer, if he kept his head down for now, then he wouldn't have to make himself small anymore.

They'd survive long enough to become someone braver.

With an hour until dawn, the certatia setup was complete, and they were finally dismissed. It took them almost forty minutes to trudge back to the quarters, their whole body threatening to go limp with each movement. His heart pounded inside his skull, skin burning and clothes soaked with sweat.

Kalen hadn't craved the laudanum this much in a while. He hadn't been spared the rod.

He passed by the showers, hugging his arms closer to himself. A vague flicker of torchlight illuminated the quarters enough that he found his bed. Undoing the latch, they creaked the door open.

"Kalen?" A small, bleary voice peeked out of the next cupboard, and a messy tuft of brown hair emerged.

"Go back to sleep, kid," they mumbled.

"I heard everything with Superior, are you okay?" The boy's round face filled with worry. He chewed on his lip, and Kalen sighed.

"I will be, it's alright."

The kid threw his feet over the side of the cupboard, looking down at Kalen and his bruised face with scrunched brows. "I don't understand. If you're with *them*, can't they do anything?"

Kalen grunted, trying to push themself up into their own placard, but their arms gave out. "It's not that simple."

Gilles offered them an arm, and they managed to hoist themself up with his help. Kalen sat with his feet over the edge too, looking over at the kid with tired eyes.

"I don't see why not." Gilles folded his arms and crossed his legs, a dash of defiance creeping into his hushed voice. "What's the point in a Peasants' Revolt if they can't help peasants?"

What could they say? "They are helping, just in the bigger picture," he finally managed. They winced as they shifted slightly, gashes on their back grazing their shirt. Was the bigger picture going to save this kid?

Kalen's bigger picture was a lot closer than the actual Peasants' Revolt, surely. He could get the kid out of here with them.

"I don't want a painting." Gilles sniffed, and Kalen yearned to wrap the boy in a hug. "I just, I want a way to protect us."

"My mission for them is ending soon, and I promise," Kalen swore, meeting the boy's eyes solemnly, "we'll be safe after that, okay?"

Gilles shrugged. "Everyone always says things will be better when I'm older, or when this or that happens." He pushed himself farther into the cupboard, so that Kalen only saw the shadow of his arm pulling a blanket on. "I'd rather be safe now."

24.

B lythe woke with a splitting headache. Her stomach was hollow, like she hadn't eaten a scrap of food in months. Her throat burned raw, and chills still shook her body underneath the covers.

She groaned at the sunlight streaming in, dread settling in her chest like concrete. Would they discover anyone had died? Last night, gasping for air between fits of vomit, she thought she might. *Why did they have to suggest this?*

Blythe tried to push down the resentment. The others had found the vault, which meant she had a chance now to save Papa and the rest of them. After that, she wouldn't have to swallow down the terrible things she had to do here. She could do good.

Snores reached her ears from across the room. She forced her eyes open. Frida lay collapsed in a chair, out cold. Blythe's heart panged. This kind of care was undeserved, but she wouldn't have made it through the night without it.

Now Frida was exhausted, and it was her fault. Had Arabella been right? Did Blythe's bleeding heart do more harm than good?

It wasn't long before Frida woke to return to the kitchens, not saying all that much when she left. Blythe sat with Arabella pulling her hair into some shape.

"Your friend didn't come through." Arabella was especially tense this morning, despite the good news about the vault.

"About what?" Blythe's mind clouded with fog, and she'd been sitting half-absent as the girl worked on fitting her. She hadn't even noticed the extra pomp added to the day's outfit, more than usual for a luncheon.

"The *certatia*."

Oh. Nausea rippled anew through Blythe's stomach.

"He didn't return with a single piece of information."

There was a sharp pull on Blythe's hair. In the mirror, she almost detected a hint of panic in Arabella's eyes. The panic in her own was definitely real. She couldn't believe that she'd forgotten it entirely.

"I'm sure it will be fine," she lied.

Arabella focused on pinning an assortment of feathers on top of Blythe's head, teeth gritted together. "Unless it's a stray dog you can't feed."

"What does that mean?"

Arabella put her handful of pins down on the vanity. She let out a dry laugh. "Gods forbid you make a couple nobles sick so the rest of us can survive, right?" The girl shook her head, looking away from the mirror. "I can dress you perfectly for the part, but the production still suffers when you choke on the lines."

"We didn't have to make them sick," Blythe found herself protesting. Had there been another option she'd failed to think of? Or were the others right, after all? But in what world could poisoning everyone be a good choice? Quietly, she asked, "Aren't you tired of hurting people?"

"I can't *afford* to be."

Silence permeated the air. Arabella started working again, applying white layers of makeup to Blythe's face and neck.

"You know you don't have to go back to him," Blythe said eventually, trying to be soft. "Even if we fail." Blythe's Papa didn't have the option of running away, but Arabella did. She could take all those jewels she'd stashed and never look back. Why hadn't she done so already?

Arabella paused with the makeup brush in hand. "Yes," she said, "I do."

"Why?"

She tipped her chin up. "Haven't you ever wanted to make someone proud?"

⟫⟫⟫ ⟪⟪⟪

The candidates all waited for their turns outside of the certatian room. They sat along the walls of the anteroom in marble chairs decorated with family crests. Massive chandeliers lit the space in an orange hue, giving an eerie tint to the many portraits on the walls. A trio of violinists played on an indoor balcony above them, fast-paced music that made Blythe's heart race with anticipation.

Wapite sat several chairs over, but their eyes met once. Her eyebrows dipped down, mouth a thin line. The threats she'd made in the strategy room weren't idle. Maybe she couldn't snitch on Blythe for the maps, but there were other ways to get rid of her if she didn't get sent home after this competition.

Throwing the event was not an option, however. Bile rose in her throat again at the mere thought of doing poorly.

Perhaps Wapite herself would fail and be sent home, leaving nothing to worry about. Extremely unlikely. Still, there wasn't too long before the final announcements by the King. If Blythe could evade assassination and execution until then, she would soon escape Fletch.

In the meantime, she needed to know what in six hells this certatia had planned for her.

A man appeared in the doorway, sounding a trumpet. Everyone snapped to attention as he called the first name off the list. The strapping candidate made his way to the entrance, and Blythe sat on the edge of her seat, desperately hoping for a glimpse at what lay ahead. The man only closed the door behind the both of them.

Ten minutes passed before the sounds of cheering reached Blythe's ears, drums beating in a frenzy beyond the closed door.

The man emerged again and called the next name. Twenty-one minutes.

The name after that. Thirteen minutes.

Blythe tried not to fidget as the time dragged on, but found herself bouncing her leg and clicking her knuckles anyway. Maybe the real competition was seeing how long they could sit there.

Gods, what if it was some sort of fight to the death? The ancient Fletch had liked gladiatorial sports, and would that explain the staggered times? They could be how long each person lasted.

She didn't think she'd last two minutes with a tiger.

Name after name was called, and, like with archery, there was a definite difference between the higher- and lower-ranking nobles. The wealthier or better connected, the less time they took.

So, not a fight. Blythe exhaled a sigh of relief.

But now she had no clue what it could be. Finishing fast wasn't something men usually boasted about, but this lot sure cheered hard.

Forty-three minutes.

Eighty-seven minutes.

Thirty-five minutes. Eleanore wasn't in the top seven of times.

Sixty minutes.

The room was much emptier now. Only five of them remained once Wapite got called. She took twenty-four minutes.

"Lady Esme, of House Albret." The words finally came, and her legs wobbled as she made her way to the entrance.

She stepped forward, taking in the brightly dressed crowd seated tightly along the left side of the room, with King Marius and other esteemed nobility on splendid thrones in the front row. Candidates sat all along the second row, some jovial and some sulky. Blythe received a lackluster clap.

The stranger scene lay to the right. Four black walls and a flat roof, with a wooden door facing her. A stiff-backed man guided her toward the structure.

"Wait, but what's the goal?" she asked in a panicked whisper.

They approached the room, and he opened the door to reveal something almost like a study. "You must leave," he said plainly and nudged her inside.

Her eyes widened as he took out a pocket watch. "What do you—"

"Your time begins now." And he shut the door, leaving her to examine the false room in front of her.

Cryptic note on the mirror, oddly positioned bookshelves, an old letter written in archaic Fletch. Locks scattered all over the room, and a lockbox by the exit door. *This must be some kind of puzzle.*

Inne hwat year did Cornelius Deshu marre his love sow trew?

That was the incomprehensible note on the mirror. A heart-shaped box rested underneath it, glittering with rubies. Across the room, a strange clock had fourteen numbers instead of the usual twelve, and the hands were on hooks beneath it.

Perhaps if Blythe had known the answer to whatever question it asked, she would have tried to position the hands according to the right year. But she did not.

And all of the other clues seemed to draw on obscure references bathed in scholarship.

Three minutes had passed, probably.

That was when it dawned on her, and she could have slapped herself upside the head. *It's a locked door.*

All the man had said she needed to do was leave.

Blythe took one of many pins out of her hair and got to work. Shocked gasps greeted her when she emerged. The man stammered out her time: four-and-a-half minutes.

Elation coursed through her, and a real grin stretched across her face.

Some of the crowd cheered, though some of the candidates bellowed with flushed, outraged faces.

The King regarded her with a curious tilt of his head, offering a congratulatory clap. This silenced the angry members of the crowd. As the quirk of a smile appeared on his alluring lips, Blythe pricked herself with the needle in her pocket.

Pride still simmered below the surface, warming her chest.

The sound of drums filled the rose-scented air, as the trumpet man guided her to a seat in the second row. She found it hard to remember to breathe while the King's eyes followed her, and she averted her gaze from him when the next candidate appeared.

Seventy-nine minutes. The final three didn't fare any better. Blythe had outdone every single competitor.

⁕⁕⁕

Arabella and Saidh escorted Blythe to the celebration hall, where the top candidates mingled over hors d'oeuvres and drinks in the gleaming gold-plated room, paying little mind to the acrobats dancing high above. With her two allies soon occupied in conversation with other delegates, she had to fend for herself.

People stopped her ceaselessly.

"How did you crack the mirror puzzle so quickly?"

"It took me ten minutes, and I've read the book it's from!"

"Did you have Fletch tutors?"

"Who designed that dress? I'd love to have one made for myself."

Maybe she should have waited a few more minutes before unlocking the door.

A cacophony of music ensured that she missed a lot of what they were saying anyway, with countless distracting bodies dancing or weaving between social circles in the room. She accidentally answered someone that her favorite food was daisies.

"I tried to be civil," Wapite muttered. Blythe barely even caught sight of her as she strode past, greeting another noble like the exchange hadn't happened.

Blythe smoothed out her skirts, doing her best to humor the next noble trying to speak with her. How could any of them possibly be enjoying this?

"That's quite the spectacle you made."

Nobles around her immediately bowed and curtsied, and she looked up, startled to see the King standing in front of her. She stumbled into her own curtsy, remembering to keep her eyes down. Her hands tensed around her skirts. "Good evening, Your Majesty."

"You know, we were all beginning to question Jardae's commitment," he said, "but you've certainly impressed me tonight."

She pricked her hand. "Thank you, Your Majesty."

He whisked her into a dance. The candidates, the delegates, the ladies-in-waiting, the servants—even the curtains had eyes on them.

"I hope you'll forgive me for not noticing you sooner, Lady Esme," the King said as he spun her around. Her mind worked to remember the dance moves as they happened, at least serving as some kind of distraction from the heat of his body so close to hers. The rush of his hands on her waist. Part of her wanted to urge him to grab tighter.

"I am honored, Your Majesty," she said, "that one such as yourself would notice me at all." And it did seem a wonder he'd taken an interest.

Blythe couldn't say she looked plain in all this makeup, but she'd never thought of herself as beautiful. Though maybe he thought her handsome, which sent a jolt of euphoria through her.

She bit the inside of her lip.

"Come," he said, taking her free hand with an outstanding gentleness. "It's a bit loud here for conversation, don't you think?"

It wasn't as if she could disagree. He led her to a more secluded part of the room, separated by a dividing wall, where only one silent servant stood inside. Navy chaises and a round silver table filled the small space, the lights dimmed and the music softer, to the relief of her senses. A starry night's sky was painted on the ceiling.

Blythe pricked her hand again as he seated them beside each other. She should have been more worried. In no other circumstance would she have followed a man where others couldn't see her, and she tried to encourage the fears that should have been plaguing her mind.

Don't forget how he struck Kalen. How he looked at Eleanore. This man is violent. Entitled. And those things never combine well.

But wasn't she being harsh?

The pain in her hand only dulled as he flashed her a disarming smile. "You look lovely tonight, Lady Esme."

"Thank you, Your Majesty. As do you."

"Please," he said, lifting her chin up with two fingers to meet his inviting gaze, "call me Marius."

Her breath caught at the sight of him up close. His square jaw with a perfectly kept trace of stubble, full-bowed lips, and piercing blue eyes all warmed more than her cheeks. "Anything you wish, Your—Marius."

She pricked her hand twice. This sort of familiarity was dangerous. Couldn't they go back to titles?

"You must need refreshments after such an eventful day," he said, waving over the servant. The boy had blended in so well that she'd forgotten his presence, but he soon placed a bubbly drink in her hand. And she'd already seen that you couldn't refuse a drink from the King. Anxiety twisted in her chest, and she took a small sip.

The King laughed. "You don't have to worry, the courtiers aren't here to judge." He leaned forward with a devilish grin, as if they were schoolchildren conspiring against the teacher. "We can drink plenty."

Blythe laughed along and pointedly took a larger swig of the drink. Her brain already buzzed with a sort of foreign lightness.

Kalen. Eleanore. The Peasants.

"Perhaps we should..." Blythe fumbled for a reason to return to the safety of the crowd. Her mouth didn't want to form the words. "I hate to deprive the other nobles of your presence."

"Nonsense!" Marius leaned back in his chaise, clinking his goblet to her glass. They each took a drink. "They get enough of me already. And I'm sure they were assaulting you with chatter."

He was right on that last part, actually. She had been hoping for the noise and questions to stop and grant her a moment's peace. "If you insist."

"I do." He had the servant refill her glass.

Her mind swirled, and something slipped from her grasp as she edged forward in her seat, letting their knees touch.

"Do you enjoy my company, Esme?" He gazed down at her lips, and she squeezed her thighs together. His voice drew her closer with its low rhythm. "I've often wondered, with how little I've seen of you at dinners and parties."

She should get out of here, some tiny voice prodded. Kalen, hadn't He—he hurt Kalen?

He looked hurt, and her heart clenched. Marius nudged her drink in her hand, and she smiled gratefully before taking a sip. "Of course I do, Your—Marius." Her words were a bit clunkier now, the room out of focus except for him. "I'm just a bit shy."

"You know, I used to be a bit shy, too," he admitted, nodding with a deep understanding. "Hiding away from court gatherings behind my mother's skirts."

Blythe stared, transfixed. "Surely you were never shy."

"Sometimes I still get shy. With gorgeous men and women, especially." Marius winked at her.

She blushed as he traced a thumb over her hand.

"There just isn't room to show it, unfortunately. Everyone expects so much from a king, only wanting the performance and not the man. I suppose... It can be lonely."

"Well, you don't have to perform for me," she found herself saying, this sudden vulnerability taking her off guard. It wouldn't be right for her to leave now, would it? If he felt so alone and was opening up to her?

She'd helped Arabella, hadn't she? Wasn't helping others the only saving grace Blythe had here?

"You know, it's strange, but I believe you," he said. "You're different than the rest."

Something about it didn't seem exactly right, but her brain was too light with the sensation of his hand sliding to rest on her knee.

"But if I'm troubling you..."

"No, not at all," she assured. Alarm bells rang as His-—as Marius's—hand moved up her thigh, but she couldn't move away now. It wouldn't be fair to him. Didn't he deserve comfort like everybody else? It was only friendly, anyway.

"It's important to have company, *proper* company, isn't it?"

"Oh, of course." Her words came out slurred, but when he handed her another drink, she took it. Couldn't disappoint.

He looked at her with such adoration, and every time He spoke, well, she tried not to squirm for the growing heat between her legs.

Another drink, and purple spots dotted her vision. She giggled but couldn't immediately recall what for.

When he nudged her chin up again, his eyes bore into hers, and he became the only thing that existed. She felt carved out, hollowed, the void filled with thoughts of devotion, as if all that could fill the shell of her was His praise.

"Do you want to make me happy?"

"More than anything."

"Tell me you want me," He breathed, lips tickling her skin.

And Esme did as He asked.

Everything began to blur. Hot lips on her neck, sweet murmurs in her ear, deft hands working their way underneath her skirts.

Her head spun, and the room drifted far away. Pulled onto His lap, teeth biting into her neck, no longer gentle. A sharp tug on her hair. A whimper, a laugh.

"Wait—"

His body looming over her. A tongue sliding into her mouth.

The King slumped on top of her, a dead weight as His eyes rolled back. A blurry figure had entered the room.

"Wha..." Blythe tried to make sense of the swirling black dots that floated around her eyes.

The servant lay crumpled on the floor. Someone lifted the weight off of her, and there was a thud.

"Grab my arm. He won't be asleep long." The voice wasn't friendly. She had red hair.

Blythe took her arm. "...Ara?"

"Shut up. Try to walk straight."

But why do I have to leave Marius?

Blythe shivered on the cold tile of the bathroom floor. The contents of her stomach had long since emptied, and the sobs had given way to quiet, shuddering breaths.

This was the third time she'd bathed, and she sat there wrapped in a damp towel.

Why did I let him? Why did I drink that? Why did I...

A light rap at the door. "Can I, ehm...come in now?" Arabella asked.

"Okay."

She opened the door hesitantly, holding out a pile of beige. "Here. I think... Here."

Blythe took the bundle with numb fingers, and Arabella immediately turned toward the door again. "I'll be just outside."

It was the plain clothes Blythe preferred to wear. She managed to pull them on, hanging the towel over the side of the tub. She drew her hair back into a tie, trying to suppress the revulsion that still clawed like rot inside her.

The worst part was that it was her fault. If she hadn't been afraid to be rude, if she had been willing to hurt his feelings, she could have gotten out before it...

If Arabella hadn't been there...

When Blythe emerged from the bathroom, Arabella sat on the opposite side of the hall. Blythe sat across from her, and neither spoke for a moment.

"Thank you," she said eventually.

"There are some freedoms that can't be taken."

"Then..." Blythe swallowed, clutching her right arm to hold herself together. She couldn't do this alone. "Will you help me? I need one of your poisons."

Arabella's eyes widened. "What? You know I can't let you do that."

"I'm not going to kill myself." Blythe stared down at her lap, trying to make sense of everything. *Hate only makes you lose yourself*, Papa often said. But maybe he was wrong.

She'd lost herself in her failure to hate the King, and now she would have to face him again at the final dance. A simple prick of a needle wasn't enough. She needed to condition every fiber of her being, erode every nagging impulse that didn't fester with loathing for the man.

She needed to burn out every whisper that continued to tell her she'd overreacted, that persuaded her to give him the benefit of the doubt.

"I need the one the Governor had you use on us." It was for the mission. It would make her stronger.

But surprisingly, Arabella hesitated. "I don't know," she said, a conflicted look passing over her face. Something almost like concern wavered her tone. "It's intense. I'm not sure it's a good idea. Maybe I could get one of your friends and—"

"It's what I need. Please." Blythe vividly remembered the excruciating fire that tore through her veins. She exhaled shakily. "My mind has to belong to me."

25.

78 Printes, Reg. Marii 6

After an entire day of dropping poison on her own tongue, Blythe admitted something she never had before. *It's not fair.*

She shouldn't have to torture herself to keep her mind intact. She didn't deserve this kind of pain. It wasn't fair that she only ever tried to be good, and look where it kept getting her.

And as she stared at his portrait, writhing as claws scraped underneath her skin, she *hated*. She hated him for making her hate. For the guilt she felt when she imagined him dying, choking on his own fucking alcohol. She hated him for the bruises on her neck and her thighs, and for the nagging in her head that she really ought to forgive and move on.

The droplets fermented hatred, but each dose also enlarged his image in front of her, cloaked with golden malice.

"I do love a challenge," the ghost of him sneered, twisting a knife into her abdomen. It wasn't the poison burning her skin anymore, it was his hands. Squeezing, squeezing the life out of her.

"Scream louder, you know I like it."

When she closed her eyes, he loomed over her, a taunting smile on his face. "You don't want to hurt my feelings, do you?"

Blythe cowered, curled in on herself, desperately trying to keep her eyes open as they swirled with black and purple. It burned, burned, burned.

When the dose faded, the image of him did not.

She remained there, trembling, salty tears streaming down her face, her body searing with aches.

And she couldn't do it anymore. Her mind was no more her own when drenched in fear like this. She had Arabella send for her friends.

With her head in Kalen's lap, Blythe let herself take comfort in their fingers running through her hair. She didn't begrudge Frida offering her a hot tea, and took it gratefully. They didn't ask questions but told her they would keep her safe.

With a blanket over her shoulders, she stopped trembling. "I can't go back out there," she said.

"You don't have to," Frida replied, and Blythe believed her when she said she'd handle it.

"Please don't leave," she asked.

With the candles still lit and Kalen next to her that night, Blythe only woke once from the nightmares.

Frida remained almost constant. She brought a bowl of chicken soup that first afternoon, carrying it over to where Blythe had hidden half underneath the covers since waking.

Blythe hesitated before taking it. "Thank you. For being here."

At that moment, Frida looked so much older, and so much sadder, than Blythe had ever noticed. "Of course, niné."

The bowl warmed Blythe's hands, and Frida took a seat on the edge of the bed with her own plate of fried rice. Her eyes were red, strained.

"You don't call anyone else *kid*."

"She used to scrunch her nose up when trying not to laugh, like you do." Frida sighed, set her plate atop the nightstand, and turned to Blythe with a quiver in her fond smile. "My Catalina."

A lump formed in Blythe's throat. She set the soup to the side, reaching across the bed to take her friend's hand with a gentle squeeze. "What happened, Frida? Before you came to Ostrait?"

She cast her eyes down to her lap, silent for a few seconds. "The captain wouldn't dock, and we'd run out of lime and orange rations. I found a scrap of potato peel, but I didn't watch her careful enough, and Catalina, she gave it to one of the younger kids. I couldn't do enough for her, and I held her, but she just...faded." Frida swiped her free hand across each of her wet cheeks, and Blythe moved closer to hug her by the arm, her own throat tightening.

"She was my sister," Frida said, swallowing, "but she was also my little girl. And I couldn't help her."

"Frida, I'm so—"

"You scared me, a lot, with the lamb. I saw how thin your face was, and..."

Pressure built behind Blythe's eyes, and the two of them wrapped each other in a tight embrace, sobs hiccupping from each of them. "I'm sorry. I..." She had been stupid. All this time. "I didn't know that I hurt you by hurting me."

What was the point in obsessing over the good when it couldn't do right by the people she loved? Suffering penance when it did wrong by not just herself, but others, too? "I won't put you through that again. I promise."

"I'm just glad you finally let me be here for you."

Blythe nodded, pulling away with a sniffle. "Will you tell me about her?"

"Someday. When I'm ready, when we're both...in better shape than this," Frida said, with a tiny laugh and thick voice.

Blythe leaned into her arm, resting her eyes. "I'd like that."

➤➤➤ ⫷⫷⫷

Eventually Blythe worked up the courage to leave her chambers. She couldn't stay in there, not if they intended to pull off an entire heist, which still had barely any plan aside from "sneak in when the guards are occupied and escape on a ship."

The last certatia, the dance, hung over her like a noose.

She had to face him somehow, or else there would be too much suspicion, and the guards would be alert. Neither of her friends, or even Arabella, said it aloud, but the knowledge lingered in the air.

Too much to think about right now. But she at least had to go outside. There was another problem she might actually be able to handle.

She'd told Kalen about Wapite, about the threats and strange behavior. To her surprise, their eyes had lit up with recognition.

"Wait, the Ka'lani candidate? With the green earrings?"

"Yeah, why?" Blythe straightened. "Have you heard something?"

"Germaine, he always complains about how much horse-feed the Ka'lani use," Kalen said, nodding along to their own words. "Apparently, they go riding every night, but I figured it's a spiritual thing."

Could it have been a matter of faith? Blythe didn't know enough to rule it out, and she hardly wanted to interfere with that sort of thing. But the circumstances rather demanded it.

Kalen agreed that it couldn't hurt to look and offered to go himself.

Blythe shook her head, squeezing their hand. "I need to come, I think." This problem remained her responsibility. And the chambers had become stifling. Perhaps they only reminded her of her pain.

Besides, a growing part of her said that *she* wasn't the one who should be hurting. *She* wasn't the one who should be trapped, hiding away like she'd always done.

They let Arabella know they were going for a walk.

"Take this." She pressed a small knife into Blythe's palm. Returning to her effort to repair a torn dress, Arabella pretended not to hear the confused "thank you" that followed.

Blythe pocketed the weapon. Quite a change that the girl seemed to be making a strange effort at...something, but Blythe would never *really* be able to hurt someone with it.

"That was odd, right?" Kalen whispered as they left the chambers.

"I don't know, she's been..." Blythe drifted off as they reached the threshold. She inhaled sharply before stepping over it.

"Are you alright?"

She nodded, though her hands shook at her sides. "I have to do this." For Papa. For Kalen and Frida. For herself, maybe.

The two of them kept to the shadows but didn't outright hide. They passed well enough as a pair of servants, and with Blythe's bestowment discouraging perception, Wapite shouldn't recognize her in passing. As they'd anticipated, she walked with two other girls, holding a horse's lead.

Blythe barely breathed in her effort to overhear their conversation. She'd gathered a rough understanding of the Ka'lani language working at the docks years ago, and she did her best to piece together what they were saying.

"I'm eager to be done with this," Wapite said, and Blythe caught something else about liars. "I miss home."

"Then why...find it ourselves," the taller of her friends said. Her tone was exasperated, like they'd had this conversation before. "Get out of here."

The hooves of Wapite's horse clacked against the cobblestones, and she petted it on the mane.

Kalen looked to Blythe for an explanation, but she couldn't keep up fast enough to translate. She only put a finger on her lips, at which they frowned.

"Nobody would blame you, Wapite...original plan?" the shorter friend asked, and Blythe edged forward slightly.

Judging by Wapite's quick, huffy response, she disagreed.

The entire beginning of it was lost to Blythe, but she was relatively sure of the last bit. "...here to stop the war, not start another."

"It wouldn't be...could you just..."

"Who says the *Eunics*," the taller girl said, the Fletch word for "Eunic" sprinkled in there, "won't just back out? These...not trusting."

What did the Eunics have to do with anything? They were a council made up of cult representatives, and the only group that could sometimes overrule the King's decisions. Specifically, they tried to curb his spending, from what Blythe had studied. Was Wapite working with them to try and win the competition?

"The *Eunics* already helped with the puzzle. And they *need* me." Wapite and her friends had reached the gate, now just a few feet from Blythe and Kalen, who retreated further behind the shrubbery. She mounted her horse. "I don't need to trust them."

"Please," the short girl reached for Wapite's hand, ignoring the horse's whinny. Wapite met her with a pained expression. "You could be killed."

"I know," Wapite said, voice faint. She squeezed the girl's hand, turning her gaze away and smoothing the horse's mane. "But it's almost over. I have to...for us."

They exchanged tender words that Blythe didn't understand.

The two girls turned away as the horse started a quiet pace toward the woods. This presented a new problem: it was one thing to feign gardening, but two servants would certainly be remarked upon in the middle of the woods. And Kalen wasn't used to being subtle.

"Maybe we should just give it up for now," he whispered as the two of them peered out at the forest. Anxiety twisted in Blythe's chest with each second they wasted. "We can wait her out. There's only a few days left until the announcement."

But Blythe couldn't live with another threat looming over her head. And she needed to know what all of that conversation had meant.

If the King chose Wapite—which, from Arabella's reports, seemed ever more likely—then their mutually assured destruction would disintegrate. Wapite could fashion any accusation against Blythe, and her protests would only seem like the last-ditch efforts of a spy to harm the queen.

Blythe needed something on Wapite before the certatia. Something that the court could substantiate, ideally without her public involvement.

And it definitely seemed like there was dirt to find.

"Remember our system," she said. They'd devised it back home. Kalen had to leave if she wasn't back within two hours. One long whistle: needs help. Two whistles: held up, but okay. Three whistles: mission completed, returning.

"Wait." Kalen's eyes swam with fear, and that did something to her heart. "What if she's armed?"

"Hey, hiding is the one thing I'm good at," she said, nudging them with a small smile. Surely, without the flamboyant court gowns, her bestowment would be back in shape and Wapite would never know she was there.

"Please, could you..." Kalen began to reach out, but their arms retreated in hesitation. They'd been more careful about initiating physical contact since what happened with the King. "Just please protect yourself. No matter what."

Blythe always did a poor job of hiding her own fear, so she swept forward and grasped Kalen in a tight embrace. "I'll be okay."

But she knew what they were really asking her to do. What she hadn't done, with the King. *Protect yourself, even if it means hurting someone.*

Still, there was a reason she'd lied to Arabella about their plans.

⤜⤜⤜ ⤛⤛⤛

It took Blythe a little while to catch up, but luckily Wapite kept to a relatively mild pace. It made sense, if this was rather routine.

Soon, the sounds of hooves crunching against leaves reached her. Blythe slinked between the trees, at home in the shadows that the court had deprived her of. She trekked just behind Wapite for about twenty minutes, when the horse slowed and something in the air shifted.

Blythe didn't even register what was happening until she was slammed onto her back, a blade at her throat. The wind left her lungs, and Wapite's knees pinned her arms to the ground.

"Who *are* you?" Wapite breathed heavily from the jump, but her grip didn't ease as Blythe strained against it.

Panic flared in Blythe's chest, and she flailed with an aggression she didn't know she possessed. One long whistle.

The knife drew blood, and she stilled.

"I asked who you are." Wapite spoke through gritted teeth. "And if the answer that comes out of your mouth is a lie, I will know."

Blythe tried to gather herself amidst the black spots that dotted her vision and the ragged breaths that shook her body.

Wapite had seen her.

Recognized her.

"My name is Blythe," she wheezed. The pressure let up only slightly.

Wapite huffed. "Well, you're making it hard not to kill you, Blythe. Why couldn't you just go home? I know you aren't here by choice."

Wapite's bestowment must have been something to do with seeing past lies, many of which Blythe had been telling about her desire to be there and compete for the King. "I'm just as dead if I leave," she admitted.

"Then I *am* sorry." Wapite looked at her earnestly, a solemn resolve in her voice. "But there's so many more lives than yours at stake. I can't let you get in the way of this. I promise, I'll make it quick." She brought her arm up with the knife—

A terrible flash.

Light. Smoke.

Blythe jerked away from Wapite, scrambling backward in the confusion. She coughed, but grasped onto new hope as Kalen stumbled toward her through the trees.

Wapite got to her feet, blade in hand. But her own chest heaved from the smoke. Blythe and Kalen had drawn up face coverings, well accustomed.

The horse had fled. They could probably outrun her.

But where would that leave them? She surely wouldn't hesitate to kill them at the palace now, and it would be easy to say they attacked her.

Blythe hadn't run away empty-handed, however. She palmed a piece of paper into Kalen's hand, mind swirling too much to make out the words in the dim light.

"By the gods," they said.

The three of them stood in a strange sort of stalemate, and Blythe didn't so much as blink away from Wapite's movements. "What?"

Wapite seemed to spot the paper and made a hasty dash forward. Her knife sliced through the air, and Blythe cried out as it embedded within her leg. She fell against a tree.

Kalen's feet were swept out from underneath them in an instant, but he shouted out before the girl could produce another weapon. "We can make a deal!"

Tears welled in Blythe's eyes, pain searing in her thigh. But she looked over at Wapite with desperation, trying to scrape her way over to them. "Please, let him talk."

"The—the paper," Kalen stammered out, holding up the crumpled letter.

"What about it?" Wapite asked warily.

"You made a deal with the Eunics, right? The King announces you as his choice, and the Fletch army provides support against the Ostraki invasion back home, yeah?" Kalen panted for breath.

Blythe ground her teeth together as fire spread throughout her leg.

"But in a little while, the King happens to die, and you become regent to his young nephew. The Eunics can basically control the government, make lots of money from your people's trade, and you get to save everyone."

And only she could pull it off. The King would enthrall any other candidate well past the capacity for treason. Even the Eunics had to sequester themselves in a castle miles from the main palace to avoid his influence. They needed her bestowment for seeing past deception.

"So?" Wapite tightened her grip around an arrow. "You can read. Are you just stalling?"

"No! No, I..." Kalen swallowed.

Blythe continued inching toward him. It couldn't end like this.

Her head throbbed, and her mind grew foggier. Kalen said a deal. If Wapite needed the Fletch army to save her people... It came together in Blythe's head now, too.

"The Eunics can't be sure of your loyalty, can they?" Kalen asked, opening their palm. A pouch rolled from it, and Blythe was close enough now to discreetly snatch it up. "That's why you have to keep meeting. They don't trust a lesser kingdom on the throne."

"Get back from him, *now*." Blythe held up the pouch in her fist. Her voice commanded, though her arm trembled. Sweat coated the back of her neck.

Wapite registered the bomb. She hesitated, clearly debating whether to call Blythe's bluff. "You won't throw it," she said. "I know you better than you think."

"I will."

Wapite's eyes widened, and she retreated back a few feet.

Kalen dusted themself off and knelt beside Blythe, who lowered her arm.

"What sort of deal are you offering, exactly?" Wapite pressed, warily keeping her eyes trained on Blythe's hand.

Blythe smiled, though it was likely more of a grimace. "Won't the Eunics be sure of your loyalty when you risk your life trying to stop Ostraitian spies?"

Wapite's brow furrowed. Then her expression cleared with understanding.

"And they'd surely be a lot keener to take on a war against Ostrait," Kalen added. "Fill the empty coffers, restore some pride."

A tense silence enveloped them as they waited for Wapite to speak.

Finally, she took a strip of cloth from inside her jacket, offering it down to Blythe. "We'll need to get that fixed up. It seems we have a long discussion ahead of us."

It was a long, painful night as they talked and Kalen sewed up her thigh.

"What will you do," Blythe asked at some point, halfway through her stitches, "once you've got the throne?"

Wapite raised an eyebrow, poking at the fire they'd made with a stick. It crackled, the warm orange glow bringing a sense of casual peace to their conversation, as if weapons hadn't been drawn in the same place an hour ago. "Well, I don't intend to *keep* it."

Kalen paused his work to give her an incredulous look. "You'll just give it up?"

"I'll get military support for the Confederacy. Arrange deals with the Eunics. But after that? I'm doing this to lead *my* people, not the Fletch. They won't stand a foreign queen for long, anyway."

Blythe turned to their ally with a newfound respect. "Your people are lucky to have you."

Wapite sighed, resting the stick on the ground. She leaned back on her elbows and gazed up at the stars. "I really hope to prove you right."

And she actually might.

As their plans brewed, hope took root that they would all make it out of this alive. It seemed more possible than it had since they'd left Ostrait.

They just had to be fast enough.

26.

81 Printes, Reg. Marii 6

B *lythe was willing to explode someone for me.*

That thought kept running through Kalen's head as they made the slow trek in the dark woods, returning to the palace.

Wapite had agreed to provide her horse after coaxing it back, and Blythe slumped forward with her forehead against his shoulder. She'd barely managed not to pass out while they made their plans, but it had been inevitable once they were both a safe distance away.

Kalen hadn't thought she...

But this.

Blythe had never even punched someone before. And she'd been willing to kill for him.

The horse whinnied as they reached the outskirts of the palace grounds, and Kalen hurried to quiet the beast. "Shh, there's a boy," they murmured, patting its mane.

It took a few tries to wake her, but eventually Blythe stirred, lifting her head. "We're here?"

Kalen struggled to get them both down. He was hardly accustomed to riding on his own, let alone with an injured passenger. Blythe cursed at the impact her body made, nearly crumpling on the ground.

It ached to leave her behind, but they had to get back to the quarters and face whatever punishment Superior had in store for his tardiness. They couldn't risk not showing up and exposing them all as spies before the plan was in motion.

But as they approached the quarters' entrance, Superior didn't loom in the doorway. A wave of relief cascaded over Kalen's shoulders.

Then they heard it. Sobbing, a young cry that echoed from the abandoned bathroom Kalen had so often scrubbed.

"Gods help me," he muttered, and dashed in the direction of the cries.

A familiar voice. "Please, I promise. He had nothing to do with any of it."

Gilles.

Kalen ran as fast as their legs would carry them.

"You fucking Revolters are pathetic. I'm giving you a chance here."

There was a horrific silence.

Kalen reached the room just as Superior wiped off his blade, the child's body tied to a chair where he stared up at nothing, round cheeks drained of color and neck coated in blood. The toilet lid's cover was shattered on the floor, bombs splayed out around it.

The man turned to him with a wicked sneer. "Just as I thought."

Kalen's eyes burned as he struggled to tear his eyes away from his friend's lifeless body. "*I want a way to protect us,*" Gilles had sniffled. He'd covered for Kalen until the last. Kalen had sworn they would both be safe.

Superior stepped forward deliberately.

Vision a blur as Superior grasped his shirt, spitting out slurs, Kalen saw his father standing in front of him.

"This is what ungrateful traitors get, you fuck."

Father smashed his head against the toilet seat.

Pain exploded in their skull. Kalen's head was forced into the water. *His lungs screamed for air. Strong hands held him under.*

"I think I'll send you to the cells, traverae," the man snarled.

Water filled his mouth as he screamed and flailed, terror clouding his mind.

"They have fun with traitors."

But a rage that had been simmering in their heart unleashed. They would *not* allow the fight to leave their body this time.

No, Father. He gritted his teeth, struggling against the weight that pinned him down. *You betrayed me.*

Their hand closed around something hard on the floor of the pond.

Kalen cracked it against the man's temple. "*You* are the failure."

Flushed with hot anger, Kalen pushed the man back. He cried out with a hand on his head. They moved quickly, scooping up a pouch and launching it.

Kalen scrambled across the room as it hit Superior square in the chest, catching fire on impact. The man screamed as the flame spread, desperately trying to put it out.

His shrieks were a delightful melody, and he squawked around, helpless to stop the bubbling of his own flesh. "Help me! You—"

Kalen cut his commands off with a harsh shove. Glass shattered.

The screams grew more distant, until they stopped with a loud thud.

Kalen's father finally died by their hands. In a rush of victory, he transformed in Kalen's memory into a man shriveled by his own cruelty, small and petty.

Still, their pulse beat in their ears and their chest heaved as they struggled to keep their eyes away from Gilles.

He hadn't wanted to wait.

Kalen fell into a heap on the tile floor, sobs running like tremors through his body.

But they would lose a lot more if they stayed there. A man had just screamed bloody murder in the dead of night, and while that might not draw attention from the lot so accustomed to punishing servants corporally, the bodies and explosives surely would. They could not allow this man to destroy another life, certainly not the lives he cared about.

Kalen had never hidden a body before. So they closed up the bathroom and found someone who had.

"The gardeners are out at dawn," she said and whisked her cloak off of the rack. "We better get moving."

She offered no reprimand, though Kalen's explanation wasn't the most coherent. He led her to the grounds outside of the window, where the smell of singed hair overwhelmed their senses. Superior splayed out like a rag doll, and Kalen could dimly make out the dark pool of blood underneath him.

"It would have been easier if you'd just pushed him," Arabella commented with an air of dismay, head tilted with consideration. She peeled off her white gloves and tucked them into her pockets. "Nobody burns themselves before a suicide."

"What are we going to do?" he forced himself to ask, startled by her calm. Their hands shook by their side.

"Well," she said, "it only needs to last a day. Yes, I think the harbor would do fine."

Neither of them were very large, but Arabella was a good deal stronger than she appeared in all that finery. Kalen grabbed the arms and she the legs. She only paused to knock two guards out cold.

They made their way across the docks, all of it a blur as they lowered themselves into the water and tied the man to the underside of the boards.

They came up soaking wet and wrung out their clothes on the deck. Arabella threw several layers back on. Kalen hadn't thought to remove any.

"Thank you." He looked down, afraid to ask what he needed to. But they would not allow their fear to dishonor the child again. "The boy, we can't—" His voice cracked. Kalen took a shaky breath. "He had parents, good ones. He deserves to...to be with them."

It was completely impractical. Dawn crept closer, and hiding Gilles's body here would be the natural solution. But he couldn't. They'd failed to protect the boy, but they could reunite him with his parents. They would give him burial rites instead of finding his body bloated and decayed.

Arabella surprised them once again. "It would be unjust to deny him freedom in death."

Many worshippers of the gods believed that without the proper death ceremony, the blessing of ashes and the payment for passage into the next world, a soul would remain in servitude in one of the infinite hells that sprawled across the afterlife, feeding the great beasts with their discontent.

Kalen believed enough that it troubled him. "You'll...you'll help me?"

"Come, let's get him to my chambers before day breaks." She was already walking away. "I have what we'll need."

Somehow, they made it without being seen. Kalen didn't really remember carrying him, but then Gilles lay on Arabella's bed, hands folded over his chest. The tears began again as he struggled to recognize this as the same boy who'd been laughing just a day ago.

"You should go, I'll take care of it." There was something almost akin to sympathy in Arabella's voice. Then she added, "I can't afford for you to slow me down. This is a risky detour as it is."

"But he..." Kalen's thoughts muddled. They had to make sure... They couldn't just leave him there.

"Stay in Blythe's room if you want." It wasn't like there would be anybody checking in on them tonight. "I'll get you when we have to move him."

He stumbled blearily into Blythe's chambers, where she sat awake in the candlelight, picking at the new bandages wrapped around her leg. She jolted alert, immediately struggling forward with an obvious wince. "Kalen? Are you hurt?"

"I'm not hurt," he said numbly, sitting on the edge of her bed.

She held them while they wept, cradling their head as the words tumbled from their mouth and the horror constricted their throat. "It's my fault, it's all my fault."

"It's *not*." They'd never heard such authority in her voice, and it sliced through the fog in their mind. "It's *theirs*, and we're making them pay for it."

"Tomorrow," he murmured.

"That's right, tomorrow."

But something couldn't wait until yet another tomorrow. It couldn't wait until the life might be sucked from him and he died before having the courage.

They pressed their forehead to hers. Eyes closed, they spoke softly. "Blythe, you never let me finish before, but I need to say it. I don't love you in a charitable way, or temporarily, or conditionally. I do because when I'm with you, the world is warm and I can breathe, and because you talk to the plants and give them names when you think I can't hear you, and because you stick your tongue out a little when you're working on puzzles, and because... You see me, *really* see me, and you've never turned away. And whatever you feel, please just don't taint the most beautiful part of my life by discarding it as sin."

"I'm done caring that it might be. I always failed when it came to you, anyway." Blythe pulled back and clutched their hands decisively in hers. "I think I might owe you my life, because I'm sure I was dead when we met. And I don't care anymore if loving you is selfish. Because if I don't, I'll die again anyway, and I want us to live. Really live. The gods can fuck right off if they want to take that away."

An overwhelming relief struck Kalen, clouding the tragedy of the day and shielding him temporarily from the downpour outside this room. "I guess we have to live then," they said.

Blythe clicked her knuckles together, shoulders held back with nervous resolve. "I also don't want the important parts of our life to change." She swallowed. "If we aren't partners in crime anymore, I still want us to be partners."

"What?"

"I don't know if our lives will end tomorrow, or next week, or in twenty years. But I'd like to spend them together. Not my life and your life, I want it to be *ours*, something we make together. If you want. I don't know how, or if I even make sense, but...I had to say so. I don't want to be on the fringe of your life with someone else."

Kalen wrapped her in a sudden hug, and she let out a startled noise. "I thought I was only being foolish." Water pricked their eyes again. "Of course I want that. Look, we'll never be blood, or wear wedding bands, but all the same...I want us to be family. When I think of family, I see your face."

She tucked her head into the crook of their shoulder. "Family. You mean that?"

They sniffled. "I do."

They'd never had a family before, but they would fight through infinite hells for this one.

⤜⤜⤜ ⤛⤛⤛

Their comforting confessions and new plans for the future were soon cut short when Arabella appeared in the door as a reminder of what had to be done. Kalen would have to face Gilles's parents and tell them their son was dead, because of him.

"Wait," Blythe said.

Kalen took a step back in confusion as she rushed over to one of Esme's dresses, tearing at the gems that lined the neck of the gown.

But when she pressed the rubies into their palm, they understood. "Half for his payment, half so they can run," she said.

They nodded, closing their fist around the stones.

Arabella had arranged for them to meet the parents in a meadow, on the outskirts of the palace grounds. She'd turned her shelf into a makeshift coffin, and the boy lay as if he merely slept, a good scarf around his neck and flowers in his hands. His head rested on a small pillow, and blush gave some false life to his cheeks.

"You did this?" Kalen asked.

"We have to get moving," she said.

With a sheet covering the coffin, they made their way through the tunnels. It was lighter than it looked, Kalen's heart ached to realize.

The parents waited, eyes red and puffed, crying out when they saw the small box that held their child. Arabella delicately removed the sheet, and their wails pierced the cold, misty air.

Both fell to their knees, poured over the coffin as if they hoped there would be room in it for them, too. "My baby, my baby. Please, somebody wake him."

"I don't understand. What's happened to him?"

Kalen's throat swelled too thick to form words. He bit his lip to stop the tears from spilling again.

Arabella answered calmly, "The man who killed him is dead. He will not receive burial rites, but your child can."

Kalen extended a shaking hand, offering them the rubies.

"He'll be free to reach the next life," Arabella said, and when neither of the two reached out, she took the rubies from Kalen's hand and put them in the mother's. "And you can be free in this one. I suggest moving south."

"I'm sorry," Kalen said. "Really, I am."

Arabella left for some errand, saying she would be along shortly.

"He was only a little boy," Gilles's father said.

Kalen couldn't form an answer. The parents turned away from him, clutching each other, desolate as they faced the coffin.

All he could give them was privacy.

⇛⇛⇛ ⇚⇚⇚

Kalen was the first to arrive back in Blythe's room. Each of them nursed a piece of buttered bread, sitting cross-legged on the lavish bed with not a word spoken between them. A stray beam of sunlight fell over Blythe's face, which had looked rather pensive since he had arrived.

She finished eating and wiped a hand across her mouth. "I've been thinking," she said, her tone so casual, he almost thought he misheard what followed. "We should rob this place blind."

"What?"

"Could strip my chambers of valuables, for a start," she continued. "There's certainly enough to fill even these huge pockets."

"And...we would keep this profit?" Kalen leaned forward with a raised brow and restrained excitement.

Blythe met his eyes and gave him a resolved nod. "Yes. I think we've earned it."

There was no hiding their pride. He hadn't even remembered to ask her.

Frida and Saidh arrived just in time to fill them in. The four of them clustered on the bed for a rundown of their plans, but their voices fell silent when Arabella entered the room.

Was it really necessary, though? They technically wouldn't even be going against their deal with the Governor. She would only have to keep quiet about their additional loot, rather than hand it over to the Governor as a bonus.

"Is everyone updated on the plan?" she asked.

A guilty look crossed Blythe's face, and she met Kalen's eyes with a question in hers. They nodded.

"Not quite," she said.

Saidh's eyes widened with alarm, and he shifted uncomfortably on the bed, averting his eyes from the assassin.

"Well, let's get on with it then." Arabella gestured to the papers splayed across the bed. Her gaze shifted between Frida and Saidh. "Do you know where your positions are?"

"There's a part of the plan we haven't told *you*," Kalen interrupted, his breath catching as she took the smallest of steps backwards.

"I see." She ran her hands delicately over her silver taffeta skirts, her doll-like face not betraying her thoughts. "So you plan to skim a profit."

Blythe swallowed. "Yes. As do you."

A loathsome eternity passed as the room stilled with tension.

"I figured as much," Arabella replied coolly. "And I suppose what he doesn't know won't hurt any of us."

27.

82 Printes, Reg. Marii 6

E vening came, as it was doomed to.

Still, nothing could prepare Blythe as she walked with her arm looped through Arabella's, feigning smiles, in a dress with skirts nearly as wide as she was tall.

She tried to imagine a nice cottage in the country for her, Papa, and Kalen. There would be a pond where she and Papa could fish, and Kalen could spend his time creating beautiful things for himself and experimenting with new dyes that would stain their white cupboards.

It's only a dance, she repeated to herself like her life depended on it.

He wouldn't even bother with her. The entire court would be at this dance, and with the rumors he'd circulated about her... Clearly, he'd had his fun, and he would move on to shinier things. Like his budding courtship with Wapite.

Blythe's legs trembled underneath her dress, but she forced her chin up as they walked into the bustling ballroom.

"Lady Esme," greeted one of the courtiers. "Please, right this way."

The entire space glimmered with gold, from the steep arches high above them to the shining chandeliers and tiles. An orchestra across the room played smooth melodies to which the dancers matched their rhythms, with some notable flaws. Arabella had slipped something to each of the other candidates except Wapite, to disorient their muscles. It was almost a sure thing the King would choose Wapite, with the Eunics' support a compelling influence even for a would-be god-king. But the fear lingered that he would rebel in favor of a wealthier or handsomer Lastrian or Fletch candidate, so ruining their chances with poor footwork seemed a worthwhile precaution.

It wasn't long before Blythe was asked to dance. Everyone was eager to find out why she'd been missing, to prod for details on her mysterious illness.

"My doctors say it must have been the burgun fever," she replied. Arabella had encouraged her to act as if she wanted the attention, because apparently faux sympathy afforded some sort of currency among the nobles. She did her best. "Yes, it was so isolating! And to think, I missed precious time in this wonderful palace."

"Oh dear" and "I never!" and "My gods, that sounds so frightening!" were common responses.

Ironic that, as they praised her miraculous recovery, she currently only stood straight thanks to several medicines Frida had provided. She almost couldn't feel her injured leg, it was tied so tight. But it was the best they could do to disguise the wound.

Luckily, she hadn't been a great dancer to begin with.

The time ticked by.

Eleanore and her new fiancé, the young Prince Manuel, came to wish Blythe well. They would be off to Ashlos after this and appeared sweet on each other.

Not quite eight o'clock. Almost time for the announcement.

Blythe just had to last a little longer, and—

She froze when his voice reached her ears. The hairs stood up on the back of her neck.

A sharp tug on her wrist spun her around to face his taunting grin. "It's good to see you again, Esme. Let's take this dance."

Her heart raced with terror and disgust. She stumbled back. "I don't want to dance."

Marius's eyebrows dipped, and he swept her against him with a firm hand at her back. He lowered his voice. "I don't think I fucking asked."

Revulsion crawled over her skin as he forced his fingers through hers, jerking her into the steps of the dance.

His hand squeezed her thigh and his weight trapped her underneath him as he bit and bruised her neck.

His lips grazed her ear. "I won't be ignored."

His wet tongue forced into her mouth.

Something shifted, and Blythe was only partially in her body. This was happening to someone else. "Apologies, Your Majesty," she said, though it rang hollow. "I would never intend to ignore you."

"I suppose you'll have to make it up to me sometime," he mused, hand straying further down her back.

"Yes, I suppose I will."

"These powerful experiences can be intimidating for womenfolk, frail as you are." He crushed their bodies closer together, and she thought about reaching into the soil of her garden back home. Brown earth underneath her nails, doodlebugs ambling away as she placed a seedling.

"Mmm, is that so?"

"Indeed."

Her body shuddered as his fingers grazed her neck, pushing her hair back. She imagined it was the wind moving her hair, a thick mist of ocean air cooling her face and sails flapping behind her.

"But you'll grow used to it. All of the courtesans do."

The loud thundering of the clock mercifully struck them apart.

Lips pressed against her hand.

The King walked away, and her scrunched, tense shoulders suddenly fell back down. Her breath returned to her lungs as she dazedly stumbled forward with the remaining candidates taking their seats.

The King stood in front of his grand throne. "Let us applaud all of the stunning candidates that have honored us thus far!"

A round of claps. Blythe forced her own hands to move together with them.

"But I'm afraid only one can be the royal bride." The crowd was silent, hanging on to his every word.

Blythe clenched her jaw, unable to maintain the pleasant smile that should decorate her face.

Drums beat rapidly, torches around the room sparking aflame.

The King took a sparkling crown off the podium next to him and strode torturously slowly over to the seven candidates seated to the side.

Anxiety twisted in Blythe's chest. *What if he doesn't pick her?*

Wapite's hands lay primly folded in her lap, though her eyes also widened with anticipation.

"It is my honor to choose," the King drawled, gaze drifting in a final sweep over the candidates, "my new queen, Wapite Mariae of House Calette, future mother to the Fletch throne!"

A tide of relief crashed through Blythe. The crowd roared with violent celebration, streamers popping from canons on the balconies and a triumphant chorus of trumpets sounding from the orchestra. Candidates clapped begrudgingly, some red in the face with disdain.

The King gently took Wapite's hand in his own, pulling her from her seat to kneel down before him.

"Do you accept your duty as Queen, wife, and future mother to the heir?"

"Yes, Your Majesty," she replied.

He set the crown on her head, and she stood with him. The King drew her into a kiss, and a few members of the crowd swooned. Blythe averted her eyes.

Things were in motion now.

As one noble after the other slithered forward to congratulate the King and Wapite and inquire about wedding plans, Blythe took her cue to slip away.

28.

82 Printes, Reg. Marii 6

There was a thin wall behind the throne, with a small door that servants used to bring the King his requests as quickly as possible. Guards walked by the adjoining hall approximately every seven-and-a-half minutes.

Kalen knelt in that small space, assembling an enormous array of red explosive sticks. A lit fuse would blow the King and half the courtroom sky-high.

Blythe ducked in from the opening in the hallway. She struggled to get fully into the space with her large skirts, leaving the wider wooden door ajar in the corridor.

They greeted each other in hushed whispers until her eyes landed on the pile of explosives. "What in five hells are you doing?" she asked, voice rising with alarm.

"Blythe, I can explain—"

"You promised!" Her arms flew to her sides in outrage. She was practically shouting now. "We agreed on *smoke* bombs."

Kalen let the irritation creep into their own voice, gesturing to the explosives. "*This* is our only chance, and you know it. All smoke is going to do is piss them off! Do you know how much I've gone through for this to work?"

Footsteps echoed faintly on the other side of the hallway.

"And that gives you the right to, what? Murder the entire court?" The disgust in her voice almost hurt. She started forward, but her feet scuffled as they shoved her back. "We agreed not to *hurt* anyone!"

"Gods, could you drop your fucking moral code for two seconds?" Kalen spat out, not holding back the venom from his words. "We'll *all* be hurt if you can't stop living in some fairy tale."

The footsteps sped up. "Hey! You there!"

"Well, a fairy tale is better than fucking terrorism!"

Guards yanked Blythe back by her hair, and she let out a startled yelp as they took hold of her. In seconds, a harsh grip on his arm dragged Kalen into the hallway.

The guards' eyes widened as they took in the pile of explosives.

"Are you happy now?" Kalen hissed, lashing out but unable to break free from the man's hold. "We all get to die, but don't worry! Blythe didn't do *anything* wrong."

"We've found the Ostraki spies!"

"Do not resist, Lady Esme."

The guards bellowed for backup, and the floor soon rumbled with more footsteps.

"Fuck you, Kalen," she seethed, even as they were wrenched further apart.

Three men marched Kalen thrashing down several winding hallways, then shoved him into a separate cell with busted cheeks and lips.

Their body slammed against the hard concrete.

"Limp-cocked traverae." A burly man spat at their face, delivering a swift kick to their ribs before slamming the door shut.

Thank the gods. They actually bought it.

29.

82 Printes, Reg. Marii 6

T he guards took their time searching Blythe for weapons. When they discovered her injury, one of them dug his thumb deep into the wound until it bled fresh.

They left her in a shift and stays, ripping each pin from her hair.

She spat out blood with a smile on her face. Wedding music boomed from the other end of the palace. With a threat to the King, the Eunics would encourage him to be prudent and solidify his marriage immediately.

Hours passed, and she ignored the guards jeering about how they'd have to put in a request for her before she hung. She focused on retying her bandages, pulling her tousled hair back from her face, and gathering her strength.

Eventually, a tall, heavily bearded guard came to her cell. He leaned forward with a sneer. "The King has decided that your last meals will be delivered within the hour."

Blythe made a show of pleading for the man to change the King's mind, throwing Kalen under for persuading her against the Fletch, and begging for her life. But this was good: she hadn't been sure whether the crime was so great that they would refuse the last meals altogether.

But if the Fletch liked anything, it was boasting. "We're so rich that even enemy spies get fed a decadent last meal."

In reality, someone usually laced them with painful poisons, according to Arabella. Made the last moments before hanging even worse, stripping prisoners of their dignity.

Blythe barely refrained from beaming when Frida entered the cell block, trays in hand.

She delivered the last meals to Kalen, Saidh, and Arabella out of view, and then she marched to Blythe's cell with a plate. "Last meal for Esme, traitor to the crown, to be executed tonight."

"Careful," one of the guards said, jabbing his partner in jest, "that one's spicy."

Frida nodded with professional caution before sliding the tray through the tiny slot at the bottom of Blythe's cell.

Blythe furled her lip in mock disgust. "I don't want anything from you people."

One of the guards scoffed. "Then fucking starve."

Frida turned her back and began to walk away.

"I'd rather starve than be the King's lap dog," Blythe said, standing close to the bars with her arms crossed over her chest. She tilted her head. "Does he give you nice belly rubs?"

"What the *fuck* did you just say to me?" Both of the men stomped forward, jaws and fists clenched so hard, they turned white.

And both of them collapsed when Frida smashed them over their heads with thick wooden serving trays.

"Nice one!" Saidh whooped, and Frida grinned. Blythe shoved her fist through the meat pie on the tray in her cell, cleaning her lockpick off on her shift before making quick work of the door.

Frida had no time to waste getting back to the kitchens. It would cause alarm if a cook never returned from serving several dangerous prisoners, and they might find the tied-up chef she'd swapped places with. Besides, who else was going to smuggle hallucinogens into the King's wedding feast? They wouldn't get all the guards, but it would disrupt the palace enough to even out the odds a little, at least.

Not a perfectly *good* thing of Blythe to participate in. But nobody would die from hallucinating, and this was a matter of survival. And maybe her survival was worth sacrificing a bit of goodness when she had to.

Maybe she was done with Deium Erium and all his fucking rules.

Blythe burst out of her cell, and soon the others were free. She hugged Kalen a little too tightly, and they wheezed.

Arabella cleared her throat. "If we could get moving?"

Blythe couldn't help but hug her, too.

She accepted, if stiffly, then nodded to the passed-out guards. "They won't stay that way."

That much was true. The four of them hauled the men into cells and disguised Kalen and Saidh in their uniforms. Blythe took Kalen's breeches and chemise—she could hardly be taken seriously as a threat in her underthings—but Arabella remained in the stays and shift.

"These cells are stifling, anyway," she said, head high and shoulders back, without a trace of insecurity. Cuffs were linked around her wrists, and the key to those cuffs slipped in her pocket. Kalen, Saidh, and Arabella took off in their direction.

Blythe had her own things to take care of, at the other end of the palace. And then they could finally escape this wretched place.

⤙⤚

Blythe slinked through the rafters until she reached the new Queen's chambers.

She dropped down without a sound, and Wapite greeted her with a raised brow. Blythe nodded, and Wapite outstretched a key to her.

The Eunics used to keep control of the key to the vault. But the aspiring god-king couldn't have himself patronized by them holding that much economic power over his head, so he had in recent years commanded control of the key himself. The Eunics were none too pleased about this matter, from Wapite's reports, and it was one of the first things they'd hoped she would restore to them.

In a roundabout way, she would deliver.

What better proof that the King shouldn't have had the key in custody than if he lost it to an Ostraitian thief?

And there the King was. Across the room, hands tied behind him against a thick column, sitting on the floor with a busted lip and no glamour of amicability.

It had been part of the plan. He would come to Wapite's chambers for consummation, and she would take the key that never left his person. Except...

"You... You didn't kill him."

Wapite shrugged in her ruby-adorned wedding gown. "The Eunics will take care of it shortly." They would come to bless the consummation and find him tied up. "It should be enough to convince them. They think he's got valuable information, so they might settle for exiling him if he cooperates."

Blythe swallowed. They wanted to keep him *alive*?

Wapite might not understand how intense the King's pull was, and perhaps the Eunics didn't either, so used to secluding themselves from him. But Blythe did. Letting the King live meant letting him walk free.

"Could you give me a minute?" Blythe asked, blocking out his taunts in her mind as the pair of them reached the door.

Wapite glanced anxiously at the clock. "We aren't exactly swimming in time."

"I just need a minute." For what, she wasn't sure. But she had to face him properly.

"I'll wait in the anteroom." Wapite took a decisive step out the door. "But if you aren't out in ten minutes, you'll have to get another hostage."

She closed the door behind her, leaving Blythe reeling.

What was she *doing*?

"Couldn't resist another moment alone, I see," the King goaded, shining his teeth at her in a vindictive grin. He knew he'd get off with the Eunics. He knew it would only take some charm and sweet talk before he was on top of the world again.

She should leave.

"You're going to rot," she said. But neither of them believed it.

And somehow her feet were moving, and she was right in front of him. The face that laughed over her in her mind, the hands that took and took and took.

"Then what are you doing here?" He raised a mocking eyebrow.

She jammed her knee into his stomach, her knife at his throat.

"Would you really murder me?" he asked quietly, eyes wide and hurt.

Fuck her heart for clenching. "Yes." Her voice wavered, but she tried to hold the blade steady.

"In cold blood?"

She hesitated.

That was all he needed.

He tore free from the ropes, tackling her to the ground.

Help! But her voice failed her as he pried the knife from her fingers and it clattered unceremoniously to the floor.

His bulk trapped her underneath him, forearm crushing down on her throat. "You seriously thought it would work, you fucking bitch?" He laughed, eyes gleaming with something that sent a deadly panic surging through her body.

All that torturing herself. It hadn't protected her, or anybody.

As her lungs screamed for air, Blythe bucked up her knee. He cringed back in pain, and she lunged forward, cornering him against the wall.

But he was stronger. Pain seared her flesh where Marius gripped her arms, and hot pressure built behind her eyes.

"Nowhere to go now." The King flashed her that same terrible grin, dropping his head down closer to her ear. "But don't worry. You might even like what comes next."

Something wild unleashed within her. A beast made of nothing but wrath violently tore free of its chains.

Blythe sank her teeth into his shoulder. She bit down like an animal, his screams piercing her ears as she pulled back and spat out a chunk of flesh.

Snatching her blade back from the ground, she slashed it across his throat.

Marius choked and sputtered, blood spilling from his neck and mouth. "Please. Help," he wheezed.

She snarled. "You don't *deserve* it."

He went limp under her legs.

Wapite burst into the room as Blythe stood, wiping the blood from her mouth and chin. "The Eunics are co— *What?*"

"Come on, they won't see us this way," Blythe said, and the two of them ran for their exit. Pain throbbed in her leg with every step, but they had to make it.

"But the, *aije*... What have you done?"

Blythe's breath shuddered, and she pushed one foot in front of the other. She'd been so determined not to let this court make her cruel.

Letting him live would have been the cruelest thing imaginable.

30.

82 Printes, Rega. Wapitae 1

Kalen and Saidh strode through the corridors side by side with Arabella in front of them, her head bowed. They intercepted the pair of guards who were on their way to take over for the vault shift, a large metal key dangling at the red-headed man's belt. Saidh spoke confidently, greeting the men with the sort of shoulder-bumping and arm-locking typical of male camaraderie.

Kalen just hoped their uniform wasn't too obviously loose.

"Hey, Eric and Lyam, right?" Saidh asked, then nodded over to the painting that hid the vault entrance. "We're meant to take over your shift today."

The red-headed man, who looked like a Lyam, punched Saidh in the bicep as if they were longtime friends. "Aw, what did you do to get banished down here?"

Nobody liked guarding the vault because of how it was set up: a pair of guards were locked inside to protect the vault from all angles, complaining afterward to their comrades about the stuffiness and boredom of enduring six hours in there.

Saidh groaned, crossing his arms. "Nothing Gabriel hasn't gotten away with a million times."

Kalen made an effort to nod along in commiseration.

"What's with the girl?" The other guard, a gruff man who had more eyebrows than Kalen had ever seen on one person, pointed at Arabella.

"That's the other thing," Saidh said and shoved her forward. She let out a startlingly pathetic whimper that Kalen could have believed. "Big man thinks she's harmless enough for the pleasure houses, if you could bring her along."

The men might have taken a closer look and realized she matched the description of a certain Ostraitian spy. But they simply exchanged grins. After all, they'd just been spared from a shift and told to visit the pleasure houses.

"Sure thing," the guard they'd decided was Lyam said, taking rough hold of her chains.

Kalen's mind stirred with anticipation as they made their way to the painting.

The guard who had to be Eric took the giant thing down like it weighed nothing, placing it at their feet. "Say," he said, eyeing Kalen curiously.

Kalen's heart pounded.

"You're a bit scrawny, aren't you?" Lyam asked. "How old are you?"

Pushing back their shoulders, Kalen feigned what righteous indignation they could. "Father thought the military would toughen me some. You can speak to him if you've got a problem—"

Eric scoffed, waving him off. "They send so many flowery rich boys these days. Whatever, I guess you can stand still in a room well enough. But honestly, the military used to *mean* something."

Lyam put the exterior key in and knocked four times on the otherwise inconspicuous brick. The door only operated if the key on the outside and the key on the inside were both in the right positions, to prevent possible infiltration or corruption. Only the King had a key that could open it outright.

A click sounded from the other side, and the vault slowly creaked open to reveal two exhausted men.

"By Lox, it's about time," one sighed, wiping the sweat from his forehead.

There was a ritual pat down of the men. Couldn't have them stealing anything—gods no, that would be terrible. They placed the interior key in Kalen's palm, stepping down onto the floor.

Saidh and Kalen heaved their ways up, and Eric pushed the heavy wall closed. They could only glimpse as all four guards started off toward the pleasure houses with Arabella in tow, laughing and pulling at her hair. They had no idea that soon they'd be unconscious and tied up in storage rooms somewhere.

Kalen let out a long sigh of relief as the door clicked shut. "Gods, we've actually done it," they said, taking in the room with wide eyes. They weren't even standing on a floor. At least a foot of gold coins glimmered under their feet, and the pile only got higher and higher further back into the vault. In the center stood a tall marble podium. Atop it sat the Crown Jewel, a ruby the size of Kalen's fist encased in silver claws.

"Not yet." Saidh gestured to the pile and started filling his coat. "Come on, we've got gold to steal!"

A smile twitched Kalen's lips. They took the first coin in their hands, turning it over in wonder. This was so absurd, and it was actually working!

Maybe mischievous Lox *was* on their side for once.

They each stuffed their pockets, their boots, and even underneath their hats with loot, waiting for Blythe and Wapite to come and free them.

Had it been too long?

The heat stifled in here.

"I'm sure they're fine," Saidh said. The two of them lay back against the still-immense pile of gold as they waited. "The time probably just seems to be slower because we're stuck."

Stuck. Gods, they were. "What if they never come and we die because the air runs out?" Kalen shook their head. "Sorry. Not constructive."

Saidh shrugged, flipping a coin with his thumb. "Honestly? I was thinking the same thing." *Clink,* the coin fell back down.

Kalen crossed one leg over the other, blowing out a puff of air. "D'you think I'll count as a virgin sacrifice, then? Shame. The gods don't deserve me."

"I'd offer to fix that," Saidh said, then wrinkled his straight nose, "but, gross."

"Wow," Kalen scoffed. They turned a coin over in their hands, not looking back at the man who'd insulted them quite excellently. "I mean, that's harsh."

Saidh shifted upwards a bit, reaching an arm out in surprise. "Oh, I didn't mean you specifically. Just sex in general. Sorry."

Kalen sat up a little, tilting their head. At any rate, it was a relief to know they weren't utterly repulsive.

"What's it called?" Their friend thought aloud, a frown etched on his face. "I think in Ostraitian the word is *blauhjarta* for chaste women."

Understanding dawned on Kalen. They crossed one leg over the other. "There isn't really a word for men," he supplied, "but I know what you mean."

"Ah," Saidh said.

An awkward pause followed.

"Well, I'd still take you to dinner. Sometime." A flush crept over Kalen's cheeks, and they looked away.

He and Blythe had agreed in advance that neither of them minded for Kalen to engage in some casual courting, or for her to explore with physical partners if she ever felt ready. Their partnership took priority but didn't have to limit other relationships they enjoyed.

"That could be fun," Saidh said mildly.

Before Kalen could savor the swirl of relief and anticipation, something rattled at the door.

Both of them shot up, and Saidh had a rifle at the ready. Kalen technically also had one, but they didn't bother pretending they could use it.

"You can set that down," Wapite said and tossed each of them a burlap sack. "Sorry for the...delay."

They hoisted Wapite into the vault, and she and Saidh immediately got to work filling the bags. Kalen extended his arm down to Blythe, heart lurching when he saw her face and shirt soaked with red. "Are you—"

"It's not my blood," Blythe breathed, letting him pull her up.

With the door open and visible like that, they didn't have time to discuss. Still, Kalen had a feeling about whose blood it was. *Good.*

Soon, they descended with treasure-filled bags strapped to their backs, the crown jewel included. Wasting no more time, they dashed through the tunnels.

Five turns later, they almost crashed into Frida, her arms full of two barrels.

"Ri, what is that?" Kalen panted, and she tilted one so they could see.

"Supplies."

Blythe shook her head. "You're the best at hand-to-hand. We need your hands free to buy us time."

"I know some ports where we can stock up, anyway," Saidh said, and Frida set down the barrels. Wapite handed her the sack she'd been carrying; it wouldn't do for her to look that compliant as a hostage.

"Your other friend *will* be there, won't she?" Wapite asked.

"Friend" didn't quite apply to Arabella, but she did seem the punctual sort. "We can only hope."

31.

82 Printes, Rega. Wapitae 1

Blythe held Wapite by the waist, the tip of a blade against her neck. They were out of the tunnels now, exiting the large archways of the palace to step onto the winding gray path that led to the docks.

Two rows of guards waited.

"Help me, please!" Wapite called out in terror, and Blythe managed a convincing bark at her to shut her mouth.

"Rifles down, or the Queen dies," Blythe announced, letting her icy glare linger over each of the guards. She pressed the knife a little closer, and Wapite feigned a yelp for emphasis.

The men hesitated, lowering but not casting aside their weapons.

"Your King is already dead, but your new Queen may live if you let us pass," she said.

"That's it," Saidh added, "kick them into the water."

Slowly, the guards complied. Some of them had glazed, unfocused eyes, the hallucinogens taking effect. Water splashed as rifles fell into the ocean, sounding like hope.

One of the men put his hands out. "There's no point to this," he said. "If you let the Queen go now, we'll make your deaths quick."

Frida snorted from beside her. "Some bargain."

But from inside the palace, horns blared. Footsteps thundered behind them, and the hairs stood up on the back of Blythe's neck. This wasn't part of the plan. She thought they'd have more time.

"Into the water! All of you!" She started forward, and her allies followed, but the guards didn't move. "Do you want her to die?"

Where was Arabella?

"Please," Wapite cried, but the men only exchanged looks.

Blythe raised the knife higher, but it was clear on their faces: they were calling her bluff. They knew this was her only leverage.

Footsteps. Shouting. Too close. They had to get out of here.

She caught Kalen's eye. It was enough for them to get the message.

A burst of heat and light shook the docks. Men screamed and dove into the water. Boards swayed underneath Blythe's feet, and she let go of Wapite as the air turned foggy and black.

A few men remained across the burned gap in the docks, stumbling for balance. One of the ships' sails caught aflame.

Saidh jumped across the gap first, then Frida, both with fists at the ready. Wapite went next, detaining a guard with false pleas for protection. Behind Blythe, vague shadows of the reinforcements sprinted from the palace archway, firing shots without clear aim.

Blythe jumped, pulling Kalen with her and only narrowly dodging a burly fist. A second ship caught aflame. *Where the fuck is Arabella?*

She lashed out with her knife as someone grasped Kalen by the shirt. Her eyes stung and watered.

"Go!" Saidh shouted, discarding a body into the water. A tiny opening appeared in the brawl. They were running out of time, and they needed the ship ready to take off. In all this smoke, her bestowment could ensure she went unnoticed.

A bullet whizzed past, searing her ear.

Arabella should have been here by now.

Blythe ran through the haze, gritting her teeth through the pain in her leg and skirting by the men quickly enough that they did not see her. She ascended the nearest Fletch ship in no time.

Her mistake was looking back.

32.

82 Printes, Rega. Wapitae 1

K alen launched his last explosive. It caught one guard in the leg, catching fire before being kicked harmlessly into the ocean.

Saidh grunted beside them, swinging punches with only one arm, feet teetering on the edge of the docks. Arms restrained Frida, and Kalen was kicked to the ground, a boot crunching against his head. Rifles cocked.

Kalen winced, squeezing their eyes shut.

Thud.

Thud. Splash. Thud.

Thud. Splash.

The pressure vanished from Kalen's head, and he cautiously peeled open his eyes.

"Holy fuck," Saidh panted.

Guards fell like dominos. Their bodies crumpled on the dock and bobbed on the waves.

Kalen lifted their eyes up to the stepped roof of the palace, where Arabella perched in a flowing white dress, dart-blower in hand, picking off the few stragglers that had tried to duck for cover.

She stood, examining the scene but not lowering her weapon, and a terrible dread clutched at Kalen's stomach. *She's going to kill us all.*

Why wouldn't she take all of the profit and glory for herself?

Wapite collapsed a few feet ahead, her head smacking against the dock, confirming his fears.

They had just ducked behind the corpse of a large guard, when she scaled back down the building, weapon sheathed at her back.

The horn of a ship blared.

Arabella was with them in an instant, and Kalen scrambled to their feet beside Saidh, who helped Frida up.

"You had us worried there," Frida said, her breath ragged. Blood blossomed on her shoulder. Saidh wobbled, favoring one leg. Intense pain radiated in Kalen's abdomen.

"I made it, didn't I?" Arabella huffed.

The ship rumbled, the horn blaring again.

Blythe crashed down the steps, desperately waving them over. "Come on! I don't know how to un-start this thing yet!"

It was slowly rocking away from the docks.

She barreled toward the lot of them, ushering Saidh forward first. Arabella and Frida leapt onto the steps next, but the gap grew larger between the ship and the water. Kalen's legs screamed at them.

The scorching heat of flaming ships was overwhelming, the fire surging higher and higher between those vessels still docked.

Blythe's arm wrapped around them, and they staggered forward together.

"What about Wapite?" he yelled over the roar of the fire.

New guards spilled from the palace, but their shouts were drowned out.

"They'll get her," Blythe screamed back. They were almost there, almost. "Too suspicious for her to be awake."

The gap extended at least two meters wide now.

"We're going to have to swim!" Blythe shouted.

Without thinking, Kalen dove into the water, his partner close behind. Every stroke tore at their abdomen, the waves pushing them back further than they could kick.

"Grab on!" They didn't know who shouted it, but a round of floating cork appeared just ahead. Blythe had hold of her own and grasped Kalen's hand, helping to pull him the last stretch.

Their arms wrapped around it. And he was being pulled. Up, up, up.

Arms welcomed them onto the deck, hoisting them to their feet. The ship lurched as it picked up speed.

Ears ringing, Kalen watched with a vengeful grin as a blur of guards scampered down the docks. He teetered forward, steadied by the wooden lip and throwing two middle fingers in the air. "Fuck all of you!"

Saidh laughed from the wheel, and Frida did a victory dance of her own. Even Arabella had cracked a smile.

Rifles sounded in the growing distance, but bullets never reached their new ship.

"I can't believe we got away with that," Blythe said. Droplets of water rolled down from her hair and onto her flushed face.

"It really is—"

The world went dark.

33.

Aknas 82, fra Hjemi bur. 53

"You scared me for a second," Blythe said, handing them a glass of water and sitting beside their legs on the bed. They'd slept through half the night, but chandeliers provided ample lighting.

Kalen looked around dazedly, a question on his face.

"Arabella sewed you up as good as possible," Blythe explained, "but we didn't want to give you anything for the pain."

It was lucky they hadn't bled out. But the bullet had gone straight through, which apparently was a good thing. They slowly sat up, inching over to join her at the edge of the bed.

"I didn't dream all this, did I?"

Blythe shook her head and assured them that they'd really done it. She had to assure herself, too. "The others are asleep, but everyone is safe and patched up."

Kalen's mouth dipped down. They lowered their eyes. "Not everyone."

That poor little boy, Gilles.

Blythe's heart swelled. "No, not everyone."

Kalen took a small sip of water before resting the glass beside them on the cedar nightstand, shoulders deflated. They cradled their wounded abdomen and leaned their head against her arm. "But we made it. We're together."

She leaned her head atop his, gazing out the metal porthole at the deep-blue waves rolling against the ship. A breath of salty air filled her lungs. "We're going home."

Blood still crusted underneath her fingernails.

Kalen covered her hands with his, pressing their foreheads together as he spoke firmly. "You had to. Don't you *dare* start thinking that man's life was worth more than yours. It wasn't. Not to me."

The King had needed to die. And as far as penance went... Should she really resist seeking atonement? But she *hadn't* sought it yet. And they were on this ship, sailing away with Fletch gold. If the gods still existed, they must have approved.

Blythe sought assurance in their gray-blue eyes. "Do you think he'll be happy to see me?"

Kalen nodded. "If your papa cares about anything more than the gods, it's you."

"I just can't wait to show him that things can—that they *have* to be—different."

A fresh start waited for them at home, and she was going to make the most of it.

⤜⤛⤚

Each day they sailed farther from the Fletch palace, Blythe's anticipation grew. Nightmares woke her several nights, but they woke Kalen, too, so the two of them would stay up together, talking or reading, and fall back asleep with the chandelier of their cabin still lit.

With the hope that this mountain of misery would finally detach from her and Papa's backs, something light and content sprouted in Blythe. It grew clearer that she'd guilted herself about the only things that made life worth living. The ceaseless penance had added to her turmoil more than any divine consequences could. Now that she'd done the unimaginable and the world was far from crashing down on her... She would live. A healthy, happy life. And she would make sure Papa did, too.

"What are we all going to do with the money once we go back for it?" Kalen asked one day as four of them sat playing cards.

Blythe placed a Five Singing Doves on the table, drawing another card from the deck while Frida took her turn. "We could buy land."

"I'd like to get that cow, when we do," Kalen mused. They frowned at their hand and folded their cards.

Saidh took his time deciding before placing down a Seven Goblets. Not bad, but Blythe was already in the lead by two rounds.

"Just one," Kalen continued. "Those fluffy ones with the fringe, you know? And we can make a lake for you and Louis to fish."

Blythe beamed. She didn't think she'd ever let Papa go once she wrapped him up in a hug. Whatever challenges they might have to work out, she wouldn't let him out of her sight for a while.

"What about you, Frida?" she asked. "Are you and Saidh still planning on that smuggling ship?"

Frida nodded, tossing Saidh a grin as she beat his card. "Yeah, that's the plan. But we'll dock plenty in Ostrait; you're not getting rid of me that easy."

The door creaked open, and Arabella hesitantly walked through to the wooden pantry next to the counter. "I didn't mean to interrupt," she said, her eyes lingering on their table filled with cards. "I just needed some cinnamon."

"There's an extra seat," Frida said, gesturing beside herself on the flat bench.

Blythe gave Arabella a reassuring nod and smiled when the girl took the offer, clicking the pantry closed and perching herself on the edge of the bench.

"Well, I suppose there's nothing else to do."

"I'll deal you in," Saidh said, a bit reluctantly, and passed her six cards face down. "It's Squire's Bid, do you know the rules?"

"Of course."

The game continued, looping Arabella in for her turn. She seemed to have a terrible hand. Her face remained perfectly neutral when Frida slapped down another high-ranking card. Blythe didn't tempt fate by pointing out that her friend had pulled the card from her boot.

Kalen worked on a tower of some glass jars. "We were just talking about what to do with the money," they said to Arabella.

"What will you do?" Frida asked, ripping a bite out of some dried mango.

That reminded Blythe to eat, and she took an intentional mouthful of the mashed potatoes on her plate. It was so strange, eating this often and this casually even though nothing forced her like it had at court. But she'd been getting better at it.

Arabella stared at her cards, brow dipped down. "I...I'm not actually certain."

"Oh, I wasn't trying to prod," Frida said.

The girl played a half-decent card, taking a slice of dried orange from the platter at the center of the table. She didn't meet anyone's eyes for a moment, then drifted her gaze past all of them, a hint of a smile on an otherwise uncertain expression. "Maybe I'll look for a fresh start, outside of Ostrait. But for now...could somebody actually explain the rules of this game?"

⤜⤛

They reached Ostrait in another eight days.

Blythe bounced on her toes as they slowed the ship in preparation to dock. Two considerable trunks of gold and jewels rested on deck, and Arabella kept the Crown Jewel on her person for safekeeping. This was their ticket out. To more than Blythe had been born into.

She could almost see him.

The Governor waited on the shore with a line of his men and coaches, ready to snatch up the gold as soon as they landed.

Storm clouds swelled behind them in the gray sky. A light breeze kissed her cheeks as she linked arms with Kalen and Frida at the bow, jostling only slightly as Saidh steered them expertly into the docking channel.

The moment they anchored, Blythe made for the stairs.

Her path was blocked by two men in uniform.

"It's all there, just let me see him." She tried to shove her way past, but they formed a solid wall, pushing on deck. More guards followed behind.

"What the fuck is this?" Frida asked as the five of them were quickly surrounded by a force of a dozen men with guns raised. The Governor waltzed onto the deck with a smug smile, thanking his men.

Cold washed over Blythe. "We had a deal," she ground out, glaring up at the Governor. "We got you your *gjelda*. Tell your men to put down their guns. Where is my father?"

A look of astonishment passed over his pale face before a deep laugh erupted from him. "Your *father*?" He patted her cheek. A gut-wrenching chuckle followed. "You naïve byjeka, he was dead before you were out of the harbor."

The air left her lungs.

No.

She'd misheard.

A misunderstanding.

"Where is my papa?" she repeated.

The Governor turned away from her in boredom. "Did the mission go as planned, my dear Viper?"

Arabella stood still as a statuette. She'd known. She'd known all the while that Papa was— She *known*.

That was why she'd agreed to help them. Because she knew that it didn't matter, that the Governor was going to kill them anyway and she'd get what she wanted. And she *knew*.

Arabella—the Viper—didn't answer right away. But she bowed her head and then spoke softly. "Some minor hiccups, sir, but all the necessary funds accounted for."

"We had a deal!" Kalen cried out, but only Blythe met their eyes, her own full of tears and confusion.

This couldn't— No, it wasn't right. It wasn't fair. It *couldn't*.

Blythe watched from somewhere outside herself as the Viper produced the Crown Jewel. She handed it to the Governor, and he turned it over in his palms with a satisfied smile. He smoothed her hair and thanked her.

"The Fletch are declaring war sooner than we'd hoped," she said, "but I think these criminals can still prove useful. They have information, and a connection with the new regent."

"The King is *dead*?" The Governor made an excited noise from the back of his throat and clapped his gloved hands together. "Oh, well, this *is* interesting. And who is regent?"

"His new Ka'lani Queen, sir."

"Good news, indeed! The Fletch won't stand a chance with some foreign byjeka on the throne. Very well, we'll transfer them all to the capital for interrogation. Our Royal Majesty said he would prefer to oversee the execution at the palace, anyway."

A dart pricked Blythe's neck.

⟫⟫⟫ ⟪⟪⟪

Thump.

Thump.

Thump.

Blythe's head smacked against the floor of the carriage as it moved.

Papa took hold of the ropes, and she giggled, kicking her feet on the wooden swing.

"You ready?" he asked.

"Yes! Yes!" She shouted with glee as he swept underneath the swing, and she soared above him and the grass.

"Oh, I got your feets!" he teased, pinching at her toes the next time she swung forward.

"Again, Papa! Again!"

Thump.

Thump.

Thump.

Thump.

She didn't bother trying to move. It hurt, but it didn't. She wasn't even too sure she existed anymore.

"Where are you going?" he asked as she headed out the door, a sash of criminal tools across her chest. His words were something of a wheeze. "It's safe, isn't it?"

"Of course, Papa," she said, giving him a hug so that she could hide her face. "I'll be back in a few hours. Don't worry."

She and Kalen just needed this last heist. Light one more fire, and Papa wouldn't have to worry about her ducking out at night anymore.

Why had she been so doe-eyed? Had she really been foolish enough to think the Governor would honor his word?

All this time, the Viper had been toying with her. Taunting her.

And Blythe had been so desperate to be *kind* enough, *good* enough, that she'd let it happen.

"Papa, you needed that food! You're not well."

He gave her a chapped smile, eyes softened. "Myn caeure, I cannot eat if others are starving."

He'd starved his whole life, and yet Deium Erium had not shown a scrap of mercy.

Thump. Thud.

Horses whinnied. They weren't moving anymore.

Time passed, years or minutes.

"Which story do you want to hear tonight?" he asked, but he already knew. *"Alright,* The Grasshopper and the Mountain *it is. Once, there was a teeny, tiny little grasshopper..."*

The carriage door opened and light shone in, piercing her eyes. The Viper's face greeted her. Head cloaked in a brown hood, she held out a steaming roll of bread. "I brought you something to eat."

Blythe's eyes pricked. There was a nail a few feet in front of her on the floor. The head of it was dented, the body twisted and speckled with orange rust.

"I'll just, ehm, I'll set it here, okay? You should—"

"I don't want anything from you." Blythe's voice rang hollow. It might not even have been her speaking.

The Governor's Viper shut the door, leaving Blythe alone in her mobile prison.

34.

I t had been about a day and a half, from what Kalen could estimate. Another two days, and they would be in the capital, Caudebek.

Tears stained their face and blood their hands, but they couldn't back down. Not this time.

Gilles had not died for nothing. Louis had not died for nothing.

Kalen had been chewing on the ropes that bound his hands for hours. Their jaw ached, but the fibers were wearing down, slowly. Just two more minutes. Another two, he could do it.

It came loose eventually, and they got to work on their feet. Kalen could move now, at least.

But that didn't make him any less trapped. What would Blythe do?

The carriage stuttered to a halt.

"What's that?" the driver called, and somebody shouted back something about making camp for the night. This would be Kalen's chance to free themselves and their friends. But how? They had nothing.

Except the guards had made a mistake. It was smart of them to use rope instead of cuffs, knowing that Blythe could pick locks and that she would have taught some of them the trick. But he'd gotten free. And the door to the wooden prison holding Kalen only had a standard lock found on most carriages.

"You can use a lot of things to pick a lock," Blythe had explained once, trying to teach them. "A hairpin, a chicken bone, a nail."

He'd never had much success with it, but now would be the time to try if ever there was one.

They carved their fingers bloody but managed to wrench a single nail from the floor.

The carriage door flew open.

Kalen startled back, but then directed a burning glare at her face. "Come to finish the job?" he spat.

Everything they'd surrendered. All so she could bow and get a pat on the head from the Governor. A pat on the head and back to her gilded cage.

And she'd killed them all for it.

"I thought you should eat," she said, voice strangely hushed, and extended a roll of bread. Her body was covered in a brown wool cloak, and she set the roll down as he stared at her.

"How fucking could you?" they asked, rage boiling underneath their skin. They'd all *trusted* her, despite everything, and her betrayal cut into him. "You really are just his heartless murderess."

"I didn't—"

"Viper?" The Governor's voice bellowed from a ways away.

Her face briefly dropped, pale and stricken with a sort of fear familiar to Kalen. "It's for the best."

The carriage door shut. Light footsteps fled the scene.

But the reason the Governor had called became apparent quickly. A rising tension of voices rumbled outside. Not guards, not nobles. The voices of desperate women and men.

"Bread over gold!" many of them chanted.

"Your *guards* have enough to eat!"

There could have been hundreds gathered outside the carriages, but Kalen had only the tiny cracks of light in the wood, not big enough to peer through.

"Viper," the Governor's voice rang out, calm as ever. "Please, do the honors."

"Bread over gold! Bread over gold!"

The unmistakable thud of bodies. Screams that tore through the air as the crowd tried to scatter.

Kalen let the nail fall to the floor, pressing his palms into his eyes.

The shrieking sound of futility bombarded him. If a mob couldn't survive the Governor, what hope did he have?

35.

Brunis 6, fra Hjemi bur. 53

T he carriage stopped yet again. Each time, there were angry voices outside. Each time, those voices stopped abruptly.

Blythe lay there just as she had been. Then a folded piece of paper fell through one of the cracks in the wooden boards. She took it gingerly in her hands, sitting up to squint at the words.

"Ar-chive of Testi...monials," she mumbled. She half thought to just leave it there. What could it matter, now? But her eyes landed on the name printed below.

LOUIS CARON: FINAL WORDS

A lump solidified in her throat. There was no discarding the document now.

Between the dim light and trying not to soak the paper with fresh tears, it took her a little while to make sense of the letters. But Papa's last words were not long.

"I plead to the gods, if You are at all benevolent, that You take my blood as payment to watch over my daughter, and that she may live a happy life, so long as she is guided by compassion and decency. All the gods to you, myn caeure."

Blythe let out a scream of frustration, smashing her tied fists against the carriage wall. "How did all that compassion help us, Papa?" Her throat grew raw with her demands. "What decency did they give you? What happiness, Papa? What fucking happiness is left?"

When she finally slumped back, her hands were mangled, sobs racking her body.

The carriage jolted to another stop. Her head smashed against the wall, already throbbing with pain.

More shouts outside. "Bread or the King's head!"

Just like before, they quickly fell silent.

Light streamed in as the door opened. "Blythe—"

"*Fuck* you."

She held another fucking loaf of bread. As if the other wasn't sitting stale in the corner. "I thought that reading them would..." The Viper swallowed and set the bread down. "It's better on the inside than it looks."

"One day he'll discard you like you're nothing," Blythe snarled, fists clenched around the rope that held her back. Her drenched face burned. "I hope you're left for the *fucking* flies. I hope there are seventy hells waiting."

The Viper stepped back, some illusion of hurt in her eyes. "I didn't know. I promise, they're only unconscious, I—"

"You're a fucking liar." Rage consumed every fiber of her, the only thing that now pumped her heart and filled her lungs. "I'll kill you in a *second* if I get out of here."

The Viper only nodded and wiped her cheek. "I understand."

After the door clicked shut, another round of sobs tore through Blythe's body. She clenched the bread, digging her nails into it as she squeezed.

Bread? Fucking *bread*? Was it some kind of joke?

But as her fingers sank in, something cold and hard shocked them.

It's better on the inside.

Blythe hastily ripped apart the loaf. Her vision still swirled, but there was no mistaking the two items that lay in front of her.

A hairpin. And the small knife Arabella had given her in the palace, after Marius.

It didn't make sense. Why would—? Unless—

Doesn't matter.

Blythe cut herself free from the ropes and crawled to the door. She tucked the document into her shirt and the knife into her breeches, taking the hairpin carefully in her hand.

She tumbled out of the carriage, folding herself into the shadows behind it.

Kalen.

Frida.

It wasn't too late for them.

She found all three of their carriages, freeing them one by one. Less able to hide than she was, they couldn't waste time fleeing into the woods. They begged her to come, but she had a job to do. She would meet up with them a quarter mile away.

There was nobody left to disappoint. So what did it even matter?

⁕

Blythe burst through the opening of the Viper's tent with a single focus, her teeth ground together, her knife at the ready.

The Viper was waiting.

But she remained still. On her knees, hands folded in her lap, and head bowed.

Blythe pressed the blade to her neck, though her arm trembled. "You know why I'm here."

"I do," she replied quietly. She looked up at Blythe with a startling, unmistakable sincerity. "And I am ready."

Blythe tightened her grip on the knife. But she couldn't force her hand to move. *Why* couldn't she force her hand to move? "You knew he was dead," she accused. Her chest tightened. "You lured us here. It was all a lie."

"I didn't know." Arabella closed her eyes, body braced. "I thought the Governor was many things, but I knew him as an honest man. I was wrong. My life was wrong, and I will pay the price of that. The price of freedom."

Blythe wavered. Could this show of sincerity be real?

Just do it! She was letting herself be duped. Again. But what did Arabella have to gain by saying this? Not the Governor's appreciation.

"It's alright," Arabella said. But her breath hitched. "I'm ready."

Maybe she hadn't lied. She was a scared girl who told a powerful man what he wanted to hear to save her own skin. Like she'd been doing all her life. Maybe he'd kept her in the dark just as much.

Arabella wasn't the villain here. No blade flashed in her hands, no blasphemous words ripped from her mouth.

This compassionate change in the assassin was the only sliver of good Blythe had preserved in her weeks-long tirade of irreverence, and she'd come ready to slaughter it. To soak herself in another person's blood.

Good or bad, all Blythe could do now was run.

36.

K̲alen barely hid themself behind the trees, desperate for a line of sight. There she was, sprinting from a tent, hidden by the line of carriages that separated them from the guards' campfire.

They crushed her against them, water pouring from their eyes. "You're okay, we're okay," they blubbered, not willing to release her for fear she'd dash away again.

Blythe was just as much a mess, only barely coherent. "She didn't know, and I almost killed her, but she didn't know, and I think she helped us escape and I almost killed her and she saved them all."

Saidh's and Frida's eyes widened with shock.

Kalen cradled Blythe's head against their shoulder, trying to make sense of it. "Where is she?" he asked. "She's alive? Blythe, she's alive?"

"The tent," Blythe mumbled. She pulled back and smeared a hand across her watering eyes. "The tent. I... It's my fault. I told her she should die. It's—"

"Wait," Frida said, and they followed where she pointed. "That's her, isn't it? Over there."

It *was* her. And she walked to the Governor at an alarming speed. His mouth moved as he exclaimed something in surprise. What was in her hand?

She plunged a dagger into his chest.

Men screamed out in horror, and guards wrenched her arms behind her back. She sank to her knees, eyes on the ground as they trained rifles on her.

Something urged Kalen forward.

They wouldn't shoot her yet. The Ostraitians were very particular about recording last words, especially if someone was unarmed.

"Third carriage, fourth row," Saidh told him, and Blythe moved to follow.

Kalen shook their head. "I let you go. It's my turn."

They understood the enormity of what Arabella had just done. The Governor was more than her boss. Arabella had attacked something close to her father, killed him as her only escape.

Kalen couldn't let her die, not when he'd been her before. *She deserves to become more.*

She had a chance now. They were going to make sure she got it.

Kalen ran for the carriage, slamming his body into the door until it gave way. In it were all their personal effects, including three pouches.

"And I beg the clemency of Deia Sisu." Arabella's delicate voice grew louder as they crept closer, looking for the right opportunity. "In the hopes that this last battle has served some penance—"

Finally, she lifted her eyes.

They gestured for her to get down, and, thank the gods, she understood. He launched the bombs at the campfire a few feet away. The resulting explosion knocked him off his feet.

Black smoke filled the air, the guards a blur of panic and mixed orders. Eventually, the two of them met on the way to the forest, gasping for breath as the tree line cloaked them.

Arabella doubled over, coughing. "Why?" she asked.

"We all need a chance."

She turned to Blythe, as they all did now, waiting for an answer.

"You didn't choose any of this." Blythe let out a shuddering breath before clutching the girl in her arms. "I'm sorry. We'll get you safe."

Arabella held her back with one arm, eyes pinched shut as she grasped tightly onto Blythe's coat.

Was safety something anyone could promise, ever? Kalen wasn't sure anymore.

Maybe it wasn't a destination. But could they find it by looking out for each other?

37.

Brunis 6, fra Hjemi bur. 53

"And you're sure these farmers will take us in?" Kalen asked as the group of them made their way north through the woods. Saidh had said there was a farm a few hours' walk away, where they could lay low and lick their wounds. "I used them as a safe house a while back, a sort of go-between. If they're alive, they'll take us in."

It was their best hope. None of them looked to be in great shape, and Blythe had said scarcely a word since they began walking. They needed warm beds and some supplies so he could stitch everyone up.

Their arm throbbed something terrible, and they didn't even know when they'd hurt it again. The sun dimmed, and mosquitoes flocked to them all, nipping at their skin with no sign of letting up.

Blythe walked beside him with a hollow look in her eyes. Her hair fell unrestrained, wisps moving across her face with the breeze.

A secondhand pit of grief formed in Kalen's stomach. They were at a complete loss for what to say, and it wasn't like they could ask her. Even Frida came up short, just pausing to offer Blythe water every so often.

It would be stupid to ask if his partner was alright. Clearly not. None of them were, but Blythe... He had no idea what it meant to lose a life so entwined with his own. Feeling how far away she drifted right now ached enough.

The only real loss he knew was Gilles. A child he hadn't known even a month, and whom he desperately tried to keep from his thoughts.

Kalen slapped another mosquito off his neck.

"I'm on the edge of covering myself in mud to stop them," Frida said, and Saidh groaned in agreement.

Arabella remained equally as silent as Blythe, hanging to the back of them all and not letting her red-strained eyes meet anyone else's.

"Should only be another couple hours," Saidh said, scratching aggressively at his hand.

Blythe was covered in red dots but not reacting to them. They had to say something. Maybe, like him, what she needed was a distraction.

"Do you remember what those plants were?" he asked, though, truthfully, he remembered clearly. They were some of the first she taught him to spot when they began foraging together. "The ones that stop the itching?"

Blythe turned her head and, after a second, nodded vaguely. She stopped walking to pull some leaves up from around the base of a tree, then put the bunch in their hand.

"Thanks," they said and did their best to offer a reassuring smile.

She nodded again and let them take her hand, before continuing on as she had before. What were they supposed to do, when they couldn't even reach her? Still, they shouldn't try to make her speak if she couldn't right now.

Kalen passed out some leaves to Frida and Saidh, who talked amongst themselves about their joint smuggling plans. He hesitated before offering some to Arabella.

She blinked before slowly extending her hand to take two. Her torso bent inward. "Thanks."

Hours later, and not a moment too soon, the trees broke. They revealed an expanse of green beans, squash, and other sprouted vegetables, muted by dusk but a beacon all the same. To the end of the large field stood a brown-and-yellow house with an inviting wooden porch and windows glowing with lamplight.

Kalen squeezed Blythe's hand, but she didn't squeeze back.

"Come on," Saidh said, gesturing for them all to follow. "I think the path was just up here."

We made it. Though a longer path to recovery surely stretched out in front of them, the worst was over. Wasn't it?

⤜⤜ ⤛⤛

"Saidh, is that really you? Well, we'd just about assumed the worst!" An older fellow with round cheeks, tawny skin that browned at the bridge of his nose, and brows thicker than his eyes opened the door not a second after Saidh had rapped on it, yanking him forward into a handshake and clapping him on the back.

Saidh flushed, trying to explain their situation succinctly.

"Can't deny that, looking at the state of yous. But gods, boy! What was it like, this Fletch palace? You know, our Germaine delivered a shipment to them for, what was it now, maize? I think it was, oh, must be a decade ago now, and *he* said—"

"Who's that at this hour, Dion?"

A stern-looking woman appeared behind him in the doorway, gray-brown hair pulled taut and a deep crease on her forehead. Her eyes widened at the sight of them. She gave Dion a sharp look. "Would you keep chatting until they bleed out on our porch? Lovely to see you, Saidh, dear. Let them inside, you bonehead." She walked away, muttering, "And I'm sure he's misplaced the sewing kit again."

"Oh, you know Marienne," the man brushed off, ushering them inside but not ceasing to ask questions of Saidh. He didn't seem at all surprised by the lot of them and just made straight for a quaint little kitchen.

Kalen still held Blythe's hand as they took seats in simple wooden chairs. He thanked Marienne as she passed each of them a steaming cup of tea.

Blythe nodded but stared blankly at the mug rather than drinking.

"Husband's not much for words, then?" Marienne asked, and it took Frida coughing across the table for Kalen to realize the woman spoke to them. Before attempting an explanation even occurred to them, she moved on with a sigh. "Ah, well you're lucky. Mine's a man of too many words."

She left the five of them at the table to tend to the over-boiling soup on her stove while Dion rummaged around in some other room, looking for the medical supplies.

Kalen took stock of their mangled states. Even red welts and bits of leaves aside, they all looked like creatures that had crawled out from a deep hell. He supposed they had, in a sense. Blythe's hands were raw and bloodied, and brown-purple bruises blossomed all around her face, a large gash split open just under her eye. Frida's shirt was stained with new blood from the bullet wound he'd stitched up after Fletch, her nose bent at an unnatural angle. Saidh rested a leg on an empty chair, ice piled on top of his knee, and red crusted his hairline. Arabella hid her broken arm, discreetly cradling it, but she couldn't hide the black eye or the lip she'd clearly chewed to oblivion.

Kalen's own arm throbbed with a hot pain they weren't sure would ever go away, and breathing too deeply prompted an agony that spotted his vision. Their nails were a gross mix of purple and rust-brown, fingers too sensitive to pick up the mug of tea that they could have actually really used.

Still, when Dion returned with needles, thread, and beige scraps of linen, looking rather green at the prospect of stitching them all, Kalen took it into his sore hands.

"Mr. Lorenson," Saidh said, looking up at the man as he set two bowls of soup on the table, then turned to take another two from Marienne. "Really, I hate to barge in so late, and I think we're all a bit out of sorts anyway. If you and Mrs. Lorenson wanted to head up to bed, it would be no trouble, and I can fill you in come morning, if that's alright?"

Relief flooded Kalen when the two of them headed upstairs. He was not equipped for pleasantries and a bit more wary of these strangers than was probably called for, given they'd taken the scraggly group of them in without an ounce of hesitation.

He and Saidh stitched up Frida first, as she'd lost a lot of blood already and didn't make a whole lot of sense when she spoke. She swore at them and said something in Ashlan that might have been a curse on his nether regions, but she lay still while they worked, except to flex her fists open and closed.

Arabella eventually dropped the act and allowed her arm to be set, but then she snuck an emerald of unknown origin into Saidh's shirt pocket.

Kalen and Saidh exchanged medical help with each other. When Blythe's turn came around for the gash on her cheek, they turned to find she'd gone. The winding stairs creaked, and Kalen followed after her, coming to one of the three tiny rooms Marienne had made up for them.

"Blythe?" They peered inside to find her lying on her side, socks still on and wool waistcoat still buttoned.

"Marienne said this room is ours," she told him, slowly turning onto her back so he could see her face. Her gash shone with fresh blood, and that eye squinted half-shut.

Kalen sat on the other side of the bed and took the sewing kit out of his pocket. "Would you let me sew you up now?"

"Okay."

"Are you?" they asked softly. "Going to be?"

38.

Brunis 6, fra Hjemi bur. 53

Blythe saw it whether she closed her eyes or opened them. That same fearful vision that had driven her in the court, pushing her to do those awful things.

Papa's limp, bruised body hanging from a thick noose, stripped of color and bloated with death. His eyes stared unseeing, but they still accused her. Or maybe they pitied her. It was more like him to take her foolish betrayal kindly.

Had she really thought her self-indulgence wouldn't be punished? That she could kill a man, wear his blood on her shirt, and the gods would not take from her as they always had? That she could ignore the demand for penance, just because she couldn't bear the weight of it, while creating a list of sins so long that they punished Papa on her behalf? Papa, who did nothing but suffer with a smile to protect her from the same fate.

As she drew him now with a stub of charcoal on a piece of parchment that had been a list of some kind, no happiness would reach his expression, no matter how she tried to adjust his eyes or mouth or shading. But she had to complete it. She had to bury him before it was too late.

Kalen lay out cold on the bed behind her, passed out before she'd given up hope of sleeping and taken to working at this little desk. The door hung open—he needed it that way to sleep, now—and she left the room without a single sound.

There was no shortage of shovels on a farm, and soon she dug in the nearby forest, piling scoop after scoop of dirt onto a worn piece of canvas.

Her shirt was drenched in sweat, arms numb but still moving. How many feet was that? Five or six?

A light glow started to appear in the sky.

Blythe placed the picture down in the grave and collected whatever she could that might serve as an offering. Berries, the tiny metal buttons on her clothing, sugary sap on the bark of the trees, bright purple flowers that stung her hands. A slice into her palm and the blood that dripped from it.

Pathetic.

As if some scraps would compensate for all her rage and violence and defiance.

Standing in the pit, a jolt of terror struck her. What if Papa was only the beginning?

The gods weren't mild in their wrath. If this proved they were real, if it proved they would never stop taking from her as punishment, if she'd committed such irredeemable hubris against them... What would they take next, if they weren't appeased?

What if Kalen didn't wake up?

Panic rose like bile up her throat.

They couldn't take him too. She had to do something, offer enough to ensure there wasn't even a chance they could die for her recklessness.

Kalen was the most beautiful person, and they deserved to be happy and live, and she...

Maybe she knew what she had to offer. The only thing she never had. Kalen didn't want to live without her, but maybe they had to.

Why else had she piled all the dirt on the canvas in the first place?

The edges hung over the side of the grave, enough for her to reach. If she pulled hard enough, all the dirt would crash on top of her so quickly, she likely wouldn't have time to change her mind.

Blythe lay down in the grave beside the picture of Papa. Why was she hesitating? All she wanted was to see him again, and maybe this sacrifice would be enough. It would be so easy.

A cool droplet of water landed on her face.

She'd never feel rain on her skin again. Nor the gentle mist or howling winds of the sea, or the rubbery leaves of a plant under her thumb, or the intensely sweet melt of chocolate on her tongue.

Kalen's squeaking, hysterical laughter. Frida loudly belting lewd songs to the beat of her bongo drum—Frida, to whom she'd made a promise.

She'd only just started to let herself feel alive, and she *wanted* it.

Even as the sobs hiccupped her body, Blythe couldn't force her hands to pull down the canvas. She wanted she wanted she wanted.

She wanted *more* than this.

She'd walked around half-dead for so much of her life, giving and self-chastising and trying to be enough. Papa had done the same, and all that remained of him was this picture, about to be soaked with rain or covered by dirt.

Hadn't the gods gotten enough of her?

How could she offer them a life when she'd scarcely ever had one? When her life had only begun the moment she decided the gods weren't worth it?

Blythe dragged herself to her feet. She clambered up from the grave, retching into the dewy grass.

Wiping a hand across her mouth, she took strangled breaths in and out. Burning tears consumed her vision.

"I'm sorry, Papa." She pulled with all her might until the dirt fell into the pit below. "But I need to live."

⇝⇜

The floor creaked as Blythe slipped back into the room. Kalen jerked, but their expression quickly relaxed. They sat up, cross-legged and immensely bed-headed, with a subtle tilt of their head.

"I had to bury him." Blythe had mostly been washed off by the downpour of rain on her way back to the house. She'd left her mud-soaked shoes outside and pulled her hair securely back from her face. Her clothes were still more than damp, but she could only manage to be concerned with so much.

Kalen's eyebrows lifted with brief surprise, but he nodded solemnly. "What's that?" he asked as Blythe stepped further into the room.

She'd half-concealed the little blue book behind her back, unsure still whether she should be anything but bereaved. Was there space for something other than grief?

"They have a small bookshelf downstairs." Blythe shuffled to sit beside Kalen, passing him the book. The cover was blank, just plain felt. "I don't know what it's about, but... We could read together."

Kalen opened it immediately, turning to her with a warm, relieved smile. "I've been absolutely *deprived* of literature."

That smile swaddled her with comfort and assured her she wanted to be here more than anything.

39.

Brunis 7, fra Hjemi bur. 53

Kalen woke up first. Even exhausted from yesterday, he couldn't shake the court habit of rising early. He used to sleep until noon if he could.

Blythe sat up amidst his rustling, nose tilted up in the air. "I smell eggs." It must have been a good sign, if food was on her mind.

They didn't know the exact details of last night, but all that mattered was that she'd gotten the closure she needed. Her eyes were clear, voice no longer flat with fatigue.

And sure enough, she proved right about the eggs.

When the two of them drifted into the kitchen, Marienne, Dion, and Frida were all drinking tea at the table, with bowls of eggs, bread rolls, fruits, and cheese spread out along the counters behind them. They paused their chat to say good morning, and Kalen didn't waste time before arranging themself a plate. Blythe trailed close behind.

"I don't suppose either of you got up to some midnight chores?" Marienne inquired, sipping her tea.

Kalen and Blythe exchanged perplexed looks, taking their seats at the round table.

"No?" Blythe replied, shifting her chair forward with a squeak.

The counters glistened, the floor tiles shone, and... Were those curtains there yesterday? They were a lovely rose pink. "I think I have an idea of who," they said.

"Who what?" Saidh bounded down the stairs and turned into the kitchen, wrapped in a thick green wool shirt about two sizes too large.

"You might need a hem there," Dion said.

Saidh laughed. He turned to the man. "Thanks again for hanging my stuff to dry."

"Wait," Frida said. She wiped some jam from the corner of her mouth. "But that leaves the... Why would Arabella do that?"

"Oh hey, it's *really* clean in here," Saidh remarked.

Kalen shrugged and took a bite of their bread roll. They should ask Marienne and Dion if they could borrow some flour before they left—it was flammable enough to help out in a pinch, and they harbored no delusions that their days of landing in pinches were over.

"Have you seen the girl?" Marienne asked. She adjusted the long navy sleeves of her dress, gaze moving around the table. "She was right somber yesterday."

"She's been through a lot," Blythe supplied. Sunlight poured in from the window, illuminating her face. Now stitched and cleaned, the gash on her cheek was puffed and pink rather than oozing red. The swelling around her eye was almost down to nothing. "And if I had to guess, I don't think she understands 'free lodging.'"

Kalen hadn't understood, either, when they'd met and she told him he had somewhere safe to go.

Dion blinked at Blythe's statement. Evidently, Saidh still hadn't given the couple a full account of everything.

Marienne considered. "Well, she should eat, at least. Before everything goes cold."

Frida inched up from her seat, but Kalen interrupted. "I can get her." Frida meant well, but she'd been renewed with a cheerful, abundant-bear-hugs type of spirit since they'd finally arrived at safety. That might be even more overwhelming than the prospect of free lodging.

Besides, a sense of responsibility had taken root in him, though he didn't quite know what to do with it. Arabella needed someone to rely on, to look out for her and understand her. They could be that sort of person now.

There was no answer when Kalen rapped on the girl's door. A damp breeze hit Kalen's face from the gaping window in the hall, droplets of water cascading down from the pitched roof and onto the inclined pane of glass.

They peered out from the opening, craning their head up and allowing a trickle of water to smack him on the forehead. There she was: perched, darts loaded, and staring out into the forest ahead.

"What in nine hells are you doing?"

Arabella startled. "I'm guarding the house."

"We're in the middle of nowhere."

"I, ehm." She looked away from him, apparently coming up short for once.

"Look, there aren't strings attached to us staying here. It's only for another day, probably, and they don't mind."

She said nothing.

Neck already aching from the awkward angle, Kalen continued, "If you're so desperate to do something, Blythe and I were going to offer the 'farm chores' sort of help, not, you know, 'poison any suspicious foxes' help."

Her face betrayed a mixture of affront and nerves, the latter still a bit unsettling to see.

It was scary, leaving behind the only life you'd ever known. Even *if* that life was terrible. And maybe she thought they all still hated her.

Maybe they had some right to, but he and Blythe agreed the girl needed a chance. And maybe a moral philosophy text or two. Frida already looked at her like a sopping wet kitten rather than an assassin. And Saidh was a businessman, really; he could get over a bit of blackmail.

Arabella crawled back through the window, with some difficulty due to her injured arm, bound in a sling. Still, she didn't take the hand Kalen offered. "Who's in charge?" she asked, head held high. "The chatty one? Or the lady?"

Kalen sighed. "Nobody's..." They shook their head at her unconvinced expression. *Never mind.* "The lady."

Small steps. She would get there eventually.

⟫⟫ ⟪⟪

An hour later, Kalen and Blythe harvested tomatoes alongside Dion. Frida had volunteered herself and Arabella to help with the cows.

Frida had shown marked enthusiasm about the prospect, claiming, "Nothing relaxes the mind like caring for bovines!"

Arabella had done a poor job of masking her uncertainty. "Oh. I've definitely seen cows," she'd said with pursed lips. "Not to worry. I can handle myself."

Saidh had borrowed a horse to travel to the docks and secure them a discreet ship.

"What do you want to do?" Kalen asked Blythe, dropping a handful of tomatoes into his basket. "When we get the money?"

Small pieces of sunlight broke through the clouds and glistened in the puddles of water all around the farm, heat sticking the humidity to their skin. Summer didn't last long here, but once it arrived, it sweltered. The air would soon become thick enough that they might as well have been in hot springs.

"I guess we can't stay in Ostrait anymore. Maybe Pule, like we talked about once? Or I heard Nai'ma has beaches made of gemstones. Apparently in Barcana, there are these creatures that look like sharks, except you can swim with them." Blythe paused, letting out a contemplative breath. "I don't know. I never really thought I'd be able to go anywhere. But there were so many interesting places I heard about in Fletch."

"I always wanted to see Qing, but I didn't think I'd get on a boat in this lifetime."

"Irisia is lovely this time of year," Dion chimed in from behind several green stalks. "We send a lot of our visitors over that way. And you know, you haven't lived until you've tried a good reindeer sauté. Pair that with a nice wine? *Mmm.*"

A chicken pecked at Kalen's feet, and they bent to scratch its neck. "I definitely want us to finally have our chickens. Maybe that cow..."

"I miss *our* garden. What if we found some way to remake it? We could add lilacs."

"We could." Their possibilities stretched infinitely now. And with Blythe at their side, they'd happily greet whatever future lay ahead.

Saidh returned the next afternoon, a ship secured. He'd managed to get a carriage, too, and returned the borrowed horse to Marienne and Dion.

"Now, you'd better not make yourself a stranger," Marienne said, lips a thin line as she stared Saidh down.

"Ah, no, ma'am."

"You stay safe out there, son." Dion wrangled him into a hug, and Kalen laughed at Saidh's flustered expression.

Saidh, ever a mature gentleman, did not raise his middle finger. Once he managed to escape Dion's grasp and long-winded goodbye, he took the driver's seat of the carriage. The rest of them were sealed inside—which did not bring back pleasant memories—in order to avoid notice. The Governor's men would still be out looking, so Saidh had disguised himself as a Lastrian merchant in the hopes they could evade too much suspicion. They only had to get close to the harbor, where it would be easiest to blend in amongst the bustling crowds.

The benches of the carriage stretched across either side of the interior, with just enough room that their knees didn't all touch when they decided to play cards. Frida cheated, as per usual, but Blythe won, also as per usual. Arabella had folded a few turns early out of "boredom," but the wrinkle in her brow told another story.

The three of them continued with a new hand, and Arabella took out a book to occupy herself with.

"Ri. I *saw* you put that in your sleeve," Kalen complained. They might not have much hope of winning, but they would certainly like to achieve second place one of these times. "If you're going to cheat, can you at least do me the courtesy of being *good* at it?"

Though Kalen could do much worse than losing at a friendly game of cards. They counted themself lucky. Safety was just within reach.

40.

Brunis 8, fra Hjemi bur. 53

"Stop those criminals!"

With the Governor's men on high alert, they hadn't been able to avoid detection.

"Get out of our way! All of you!"

But even injured and outnumbered, the five of them had made it to the harbor by the scruff of their necks—saved by both their combined skill sets and the large crowds.

Blythe scrambled up the ship's steps, and Frida hoisted her up by the arms.

"You were right," Kalen said as the ship rumbled forward. He cast a glance to the guards still shouting down at the docks, trying to get another ship in time to catch up with them. Little did they know, Saidh had worked in that harbor long enough to accrue some favors. "We *really* need to find somewhere else to live."

"Well, shit," Frida said, looking around with a laugh. "This ship is more than large."

Blythe spun to her friend. Was she jesting? It clenched her heart that she might never see Frida again if they went separate ways. She knew Kalen felt the same, but neither of them had wanted to intrude on their friends' plans.

Still, they all worked so well to keep each other safe. Wouldn't it be a shame to part ways now?

"Do you mean that?" Kalen asked, glancing between Frida and Saidh.

Saidh nodded, his arms resting on the wheel a few feet away. Waves swayed the ship as they gained speed. "We could certainly use your skills if we're going to make the most of this smuggling business," he said.

Frida beamed, scooping Kalen and Blythe into a hug. "Yeah! Kalen, you can help us with medical stuff and fending off Ashlan pirates. And Blythe will have a much easier time sneaking to pick people up. Plus, the two of you know how to grow things, and fresh food can be way too scarce at sea for my liking."

"We discussed a little before we arrived in Ostrait," Saidh explained. He kept one hand on the wheel and consulted a map with the other. "But we didn't want to pressure you. You could have a much less eventful life in Irisia or Calad."

Blythe and Kalen had already decided, so she didn't mind answering for the both of them. "We're in."

A seafaring life could have everything they wanted. To stay together, to have their bit of peace with a garden and some smaller animals, and to have their bit of adventure, too. If she was going to choose life, she was going to *live* it.

Besides, Blythe couldn't completely give up helping people. Outcasts, people like themselves. She could help for the joy of it now, rather than fear of divine displeasure.

Frida turned to Arabella next. "Speaking of the Ashlan pirates," she said, mustering up an imitation of a professional tone, though another smile clearly tried to break free, "we could use your help, too. That, and you made pretty convincing disguises for us in Fletch. We could use some of those as well."

Arabella's brows rose, and she straightened her back. "Well, I suppose there will be some money to be made." She turned to Saidh, slipping a hand into her pocket, tone hesitant. "You'd also agree to this?"

"Why not? You're skilled, and it's not like you can turn me in to the Haelguards now. As long as you don't endanger our clients, we're good. Alright?"

She nodded but averted her shining eyes. "Yes, I accept the terms."

"I guess we're a proper crew now," Blythe said.

Excitement surged through her. The salty mist cooled her skin, and a wide-open expanse of blue possibility stretched before her. Her partner and her friends surrounded her, their expressions filled with hope. There was no way to know what this future would look like, but it belonged to the five of them.

"Well, we need a name," Frida chimed in.

Kalen rested a finger on their chin. "And a flag."

"And our own ship," Saidh added. "This is just a rental."

"What would we be called?" Kalen mused, leaning their arms back on the lip of the ship. Blythe leaned back with them, less concerned about names and more mesmerized by the drifting white clouds and the swaying underneath her feet.

"We'll have to have a dull merchant name when we reach port," Frida said with a brief frown. "But we can always have a secret, better name."

"What about *Unsinkable*?" Blythe offered, but even she wasn't quite feeling it.

"*The Bloodthirsty Dragon*?" Frida suggested. "I wouldn't mess with a bloodthirsty dragon."

Arabella tilted her head. "*Plague Assistance Medics* would probably keep people away."

"Or draw the plague-ridden people *in*," Frida said.

Kalen snorted at his own stroke of inspiration, barely able to get the words out. "What about...*Full Mast*?"

Frida snickered along, nudging his shoulder in appreciation.

Saidh cleared his throat. "What about *The Natural Outlaws*?"

Something brief passed between him and Kalen. "I like that," they said, and Blythe agreed.

Frida and Arabella each hummed with thoughtful approval.

Blythe leaned her head on Kalen's shoulder, watching the gulls fly overhead. Her breaths came slow and easy, and she allowed her eyelids to fall shut.

Whatever they called it, this was *Home* to her.

GLOSSARY

aije: an expression of shock or surprise. Origin: Ka'lan.

Aknas, -um: the calendar season of spring, roughly March through May. Origin: Ostrait.

Armei: the god of bows and hunting, most prominent in Fletch. Origin: Fletch.

Brunis, -um: the calendar season of summer, roughly June through July. Origin: Ostrait.

bellae (sg. and pl.): prepubescent noble girls, who customarily receive oratory and singing lessons and often join a royal choir for a year or two once their skills have developed. Origin: Fletch.

bestowment, -s: a special skill an individual may possess, which is unique to them and can range from the arguably mundane to more notable abilities. There is no test to determine a bestowment, and as such, they are based on individual perceptions and claims. Many believe these are gifts given by the gods. Origin: Ostrait.

blauhjarta, -am: a term most often used to describe chaste women, especially those who emulate the ideals of courtly romances. Best translated as "soft-hearted." Origin: Ostrait.

byjeka, -am: a slur against women and feminine men, implying pathetic weakness of both the mind and body. Best translated as "little bitch(es)." Origin: Ostrait.

Caestia, -iae: the title "Divine," given to female gods. Origin: Fletch.

Caestore, -orii: the title "Divine," given to male gods. Origin: Fletch

certatia, -ae: a special competitive event, particularly used to describe royally funded sporting festivities. Origin: Fletch.

debtors' brown: markets are forbidden from selling colorful dyes to those in debt, and debtors may be arrested if caught in luxury colors or fabrics. As such, brown clothing has become a visual marker of debt. Origin: Ostrait.

Deia, -am: the title, "Radiant," given to female gods. Origin: Ostrait.

Deium, -es: the title, "Radiant," given to male gods. Origin: Ostrait.

Erium: an obscure Ostraitian god of charity, who grants divine amnesty to those who do the penance of a moral, ascetic life. This god has gained some following among the severely impoverished but is not popularly worshiped. Origin: Ostrait.

Eunic Council: a council of cult representatives in Fletch, who extend individual authorities over divine cults and may collectively veto some of the King's decisions, particularly with regards to financial matters. Origin: Fletch.

fra Hjemi bur: used to date years since the birth of the King. Origin: Ostrait.

gjelda, -am: a bounty of currency or gold. Best translated as "loot." Origin: Ostrait.

Haelguard, -s: guards that enforce city laws, punishments, and debt collections. Origin: Ostrait.

Haunis, -um: the calendar harvest season, roughly August through October. Origin: Ostrait.

healing-debt, -s: debt accumulated from medical care and/or medical leave from an employer, paid to the government and other related parties with steep interest. Those who fail to pay their healing-debt may be jailed, indentured, or sent to work at the mines. Many landlords do not rent to those with healing-debt. Origin: Ostrait.

Lox: a trickster deity common to both Ostrait and Fletch, also responsible for luck. Origin: unknown.

Martia: the Fletch goddess of war, especially leadership in battle. Origin: Fletch.

myn caeure: a term of endearment. Best translated as "my heart." Origin: Jardae.

niné, -si: kid. Origin: Ashlos.

Optore: masculine epithet meaning "the Greatest." Origin: Fletch.

Optia: feminine epithet meaning "the Greatest." Origin: Fletch.

protigi, -ii: a term of address for royal guards in the Fletch palace. Origin: Fletch.

Printes, -iares: the calendar season of spring, roughly March through May. Origin: Fletch.

Reg. Marii: used to date years in the Reign of King Marius. Origin: Fletch.

Rega. Wapitae: used to date years in the Reign of Regent Queen Wapite. Origin: Fletch.

Sisu: the Ostraitian goddess of war, presiding over both physical and figurative battles. Origin: Ostrait.

Sofnas, -um: the calendar unfruitful season, encompassing late fall and winter, roughly November through February. Origin: Ostrait.

talent, -s: the Fletch term for bestowment. Origin: Fletch.

traverae (sg. and pl.): a slur used against feminine men, implying emasculation and/or a weak, disloyal character. Origin: Fletch.

DEAR READER,

Thank you so much for picking up this book. It means the world to me that I get to share this story with you.

I really hope you enjoyed reading. If you did, please consider leaving a short review somewhere or recommending this book to a friend. I can't tell you how much I'd appreciate it.

If you have any thoughts, reactions, or questions about the book, I'd love to hear them. Feel free to email me at smpearceauthor@gmail.com, I promise I write back.

ABOUT THE AUTHOR

S.M. Pearce is a dark fantasy and dystopian author, whose professional career began back in 2018 after her first published work, *Outliers*.

S.M. lives in Ontario, where she studies history and classical civilization at the University of Toronto. When S.M. isn't reading or writing, she enjoys over-analysing episodes of Doctor Who, learning new languages, and small-scale farming in her backyard.

Milton Keynes UK
Ingram Content Group UK Ltd.
UKHW010711140823
426838UK00001B/106